## "I'm glad we met, in spite of the strange circumstances."

"I'm glad, too." Maybe from the moment he'd first seen her in that video, he'd known he'd seek her out. Something in her called to him.

She tilted her head up and rose on her toes to bring her face closer to his in silent invitation—an invitation he wouldn't refuse. He'd been wanting to kiss her, hesitant only because of the tenuousness of their relationship. Her lips warmed beneath his, as soft and sensuous as he'd imagined they would be. He deepened the kiss.

A flash of light distracted him, and reluctantly he lifted his head to look around. He saw nothing but the array of news vans and reporters across the street, though he couldn't shake the sense that something had happened that he should have paid attention to.

# COLORADO CRIME SCENE

## BY
## CINDI MYERS

First Published in Great Britain 2016
By Mills & Boon, an imprint of HarperCollins*Publishers*
1 London Bridge Street, London, SE1 9GF

© 2016 Cynthia Myers

ISBN: 978-0-263-91908-0

46-0616

Our policy is to use papers that are natural, renewable and recyclable products and made from wood grown in sustainable forests. The logging and manufacturing processes conform to the legal environmental regulations of the country of origin.

Printed and bound in Spain
by CPI, Barcelona

**Cindi Myers** is an author of more than fifty novels. When she's not crafting new romance plots, she enjoys skiing, gardening, cooking, crafting and daydreaming. A lover of small-town life, she lives with her husband and two spoiled dogs in the Colorado mountains.

For Vicki L.

# Chapter One

Luke Renfro never forgot a face. The blessing and the curse of this peculiar talent defined his days and haunted his nights. The faces of people he knew well and those he had merely passed on the street crowded his mind.

He sorted through this portrait gallery of strangers and friends as he studied the people who hurried past him on a warm, sunny morning on Denver's 16th Street Mall, searching for anyone familiar, while at the very back of his mind whispered the question that plagued him most: What if he'd overlooked the one person he most needed to find?

He shoved aside that familiar anxiety and reviewed the details of his assignment today: young Caucasian male, probably early to midtwenties, slight, athletic build, five-eight or five-nine. He'd been clean shaven in the surveillance photos Scotland Yard had forwarded from London, his brown hair cropped very short. But even if he'd grown out his beard or dyed his hair, Luke would recognize him. It was what he did. It was why the FBI had recruited him and others like him, copying an idea implemented by the Brits—to assemble a group of "super-recognizers" to look for known criminals and stop crime before it happened.

Also on the list of people he hoped to spot was a fortysomething man with a swarthy complexion and iron-gray curls, and a stocky Asian man with a shaved head and a scar beside one eye. If he spotted any of these people, he was to bring them into headquarters for questioning.

He crossed the street and strolled past a row of restaurants starting to fill up with the early lunch crowd. A strong breeze made the banners strung overhead pop and snap. Welcome, Racers! declared one. Colorado Cycling Challenge! proclaimed another. The man Luke was searching for wouldn't miss the race, though Luke hoped to find him before he ever had a chance to attend.

A flash of honey-blond hair in his peripheral vision sent a jolt of recognition through him, a physical shock, like finding something important he hadn't even realized he'd lost. He whirled around in time to see the woman step onto one of the shuttle buses that ran up and down the length of the pedestrian mall. Heart pounding, he took off down the sidewalk after the bus, ignoring the annoyed looks from the hipster couple he jostled in his haste.

He hadn't expected to see her here today, though logically he shouldn't have been surprised. She'd been in some of those Scotland Yard videos also, and the image of her heart-shaped face framed by a stylish short haircut, her wide hazel eyes staring into the camera from beneath a fringe of honey-colored bangs, had stayed with him, standing out from the sea of anonymous faces filed away in his memory.

She stepped off the shuttle four blocks down, in front

of a chain drugstore, the breeze blowing her swept-aside bangs into her eyes. She stopped and brushed the stray locks off her face, allowing him time to take in her skinny jeans, athletic shoes, pale green tank top, and a scarf of mingled blue and green knotted at her throat. Then she started walking again, long, confident strides covering ground quickly. Staying back half a block, he followed her as she headed to a boutique hotel and entered the lobby. Luke hurried to catch up, weaving his way through a family unloading luggage at the front door and two men consulting a street map just inside the entrance.

Soft classical music filled the lobby, which was decorated in Victorian red velvet and gold brocade. Luke scanned the crowd of tourists and businessmen, but the woman wasn't among them. A check of the elevators showed both were stopped on upper floors. Had she opted for the stairs, or passed through to the hotel bar? He hesitated. Did he enter the bar and search for her, or return to the mall and his original quarry?

"Excuse me."

He turned and stared into the angry eyes of the woman he'd been following. Hazel eyes of mingled green and gold, fringed with gold lashes. Eyes that had disturbed his dreams, though in those fantasies, they'd been considerably friendlier than they were right now. "Who are you, and why are you following me?" she demanded.

"I don't know what you're talking about." Bluffing was as important a skill for an agent as it was for a poker player.

"I'm not stupid. I saw you following me." She folded her arms under her breasts; he wondered if she was

aware how that emphasized her cleavage. If he pointed
this out, she'd no doubt add "sexist pig" to whatever
other unflattering descriptions she'd ascribed to him.
"I want to know why."

She was calling his bluff. Time to fold. But that
would mean leaving and walking away, and he hadn't
gone to all this trouble to do that. Maybe a better answer
was to show her his cards—or at least some of them. He
reached into his jacket and pulled out the folder with his
credentials. "Special Agent Luke Renfro. FBI."

Her eyes widened, and some of the color left her
cheeks. "What is this about?" The words came out as
a whisper, and all her bravado vanished. In fact, she
looked ready to faint, her breath coming in quick, shallow pants.

Her reaction—more fear and guilt than an innocent
citizen ought to exhibit—had all his instincts sounding
alarms, his senses on high alert. He touched her arm
lightly, though he was prepared to hang on if she made
a run for it. "Why don't we go into the bar and talk?"
He nodded toward the hotel bar, which at this time of
day was almost deserted.

"All right." She allowed him to usher her into the
bar, to a red leatherette booth. The lighting was subdued, the music almost inaudible. Luke sat across from
the blonde, and the waitress, who'd been seated at one
end of the bar, hurried over to them. "I'll have a glass
of iced tea," Luke told her. He looked to the woman
across from him. "Would you like something stronger?"

"Just water." She pushed her hair back out of her eyes
and settled her hands flat on the table in front of her. Her
nails were short, polished a deep blue. She wore silver
earrings that glinted in the bar light when she turned

her head to look at him. Her hair, thick and shiny and sexy, curled around her ears and the nape of her neck.

It bothered him that this woman had stuck in his head when so many others didn't. Maybe that's why he'd followed her, to see if up close he could identify the reason he'd become so fixated on her. But maybe it wasn't simple attraction at work here. Maybe his cop instincts recognized some guilt in her he couldn't yet put into words. He didn't want to think of her as a suspect, but he had to if he was going to do his job correctly.

"Why is the FBI following me?" she asked, reminding him they were alone again.

"First, tell me your name, since you already know mine."

She hesitated, then said, "Morgan Westfield."

The name itself didn't set off any alarm bells. Though his photographic memory for faces didn't carry over to names or facts and figures, he'd learned the names of key suspects in his current investigation—at least, the names they knew. A series of terrorist bombings had rocked the cycling world in the past two years, with bombs killing and injuring racers and spectators alike at key races around the world. The Bureau hoped that by sending members of the team they'd code-named Search Team Seven to Denver they could prevent another attack. Was Morgan somehow involved and Luke hadn't realized it?

"You were following me and you don't know my name?" she asked. "I don't understand."

"You were at the Tour de France last month," he said. "And the Tour of Britain before that." But not at the Paris-Roubaix the year before. Or maybe she'd managed to stay out of range of the security cameras for that event.

"You've been following me all this time?" Her voice rose, and anger returned the color to her cheeks.

He hadn't been following her, but maybe fate or instinct or blind luck had led him to her. The waitress brought their drinks and glanced at them curiously. "Will there be anything else?"

"No, thank you." He handed her a ten. "Keep the change."

She stuffed the bill into her apron and retreated to the bar once more. Morgan leaned over the table toward him. "Why is the FBI following me?" she demanded again, tension straining her face.

"I'm not following you," he said. "I'm actually looking for someone else. But I remembered you and was curious."

"You remembered me?" She sat back, frowning. "But we've never met."

"No. But I've studied surveillance videos of both races." And many others. "I remembered seeing your face."

"That's crazy," she said. She didn't seem as nervous now, but more annoyed, as she had been when she'd first challenged him in the lobby. "There were thousands of people at those races. Hundreds of thousands. Why would you remember me?"

"It's what I do. It's my job, actually. I'm paid to remember faces, and to recognize them when I see them again."

She took a long drink of water, her eyes never leaving his. "I'm not sure that explanation makes sense."

"You know how some people have photographic memories, right?"

"You mean they can read a phone book or encyclopedia and remember everything on the pages? I thought that was just something in movies."

"No, it's a real phenomenon. My brother is like that. Once he reads something, it's committed to memory." A familiar ache squeezed his chest at the mention of his twin brother. He'd give anything to know where Mark was now. To be assured he was safe.

"But it's different for you?" Morgan prompted.

He nodded. "With me, it works a little differently. I never forget a face. Not if I've spent even a few seconds focusing on it."

"I thought they had computers that could do that—scan video for familiar faces and stuff."

"Facial-recognition software can't compete with the human brain," he said. "After riots in London in 2011, Scotland Yard's team of super-recognizers identified 1200 suspects from video surveillance. Computer software identified only one person."

"So I shouldn't be flattered that you remembered me—it's just something you do."

"Some faces are more pleasant to remember than others." He smiled, but she continued to regard him with suspicion.

Fine. He needed to be more suspicious of her, as well. "What were you doing at the races?" he asked.

"I'm a writer. I was covering the races for *Road Bike Magazine*."

"So you work for the magazine?"

"No, I'm a freelancer. I write for a lot of different publications, though my specialty is bicycle racing."

"Are you in Denver to cover the Colorado Cycling Challenge?"

"What if I am?"

And what if she was here to do more than write about the races? "I'm here for the race, too," he said. "We'll probably see each other again."

"I never saw you at those other races."

"I wasn't there." Before she could ask the obvious question, he said, "I saw you on surveillance video."

She closed her eyes. Maybe she was counting to ten before she went off on him. When she opened them again, her voice was calm but chilly. "Why don't we stop this game of twenty questions right now and you give me some straight answers. What is this about? Why were you looking at surveillance videos of me? Why were you following me just now?"

"You want the truth?"

"Of course I want the truth."

"I wasn't looking for you on those videos, but you stuck in my head. I remember a lot of people, but most of them don't make any strong impression on me. But you did. I wanted to meet you and try to figure out why." That was the truth in its simplest form. Basic attraction leads to impulsive action. His bosses would not approve.

"Seriously?" She stared at him.

He nodded. "You said you wanted the truth, and that's it."

"I can't decide if that's the worst pickup line I ever heard, or the best." Some of the tension went out of her and she sat back, studying him.

"You have to give me points for originality," he said.

This coaxed the beginnings of a smile from her. She had full lips, highlighted with a pink gloss. He wondered what it would feel like kissing those lips, then he pushed the thought away.

"So how does this memory thing of yours work?" she asked. "Do you just automatically remember everyone you've ever seen?"

"I have to focus on them for a few seconds, but yes, after that I'll recognize them again." As a small child, he thought everyone related to the world that way. Once he'd learned a face, he never forgot it. He remembered not only that he'd seen a person before, but where and what they'd been doing. Most of the time, it wasn't a particularly useful talent, not like Mark's memory for facts and written information. That talent had allowed him to breeze through school. He'd earned his PhD in physics before his twenty-fifth birthday, while Luke had been only an average student.

Then the FBI had come calling and he'd found his niche, the one place where his particular skill could make a difference.

Two men entered the bar, dressed casually in jeans and T-shirts, engrossed in conversation. He'd seen the older one earlier on the street, buying coffee from a food cart. The other one was the wrong race for any of his suspects, though he filed the man's face away for future reference, as was his habit.

"You're doing it now, aren't you?" Morgan asked. "Memorizing people."

"It's my job," he repeated.

"Is that why you're here—to memorize people at the bike race?"

"Let's just say I'm here for work, and leave it at that."

But he knew before he said the words that she wasn't the type to leave it. "You're looking for someone, aren't you? Someone else you saw on those surveillance videos." She went very still; he wondered if she was holding her breath, waiting for his answer.

"I really can't talk about my assignment with a civilian. It's confidential." Maybe he'd already said too much.

"But I'm free to make an educated guess. And since you are a federal agent, I'd guess that you're here because of the terrorist who's been targeting bike races."

"Let's just say that after the bombings in Paris and London, there's a big law enforcement presence at this race." But only one small group was there with his assignment—to look for people who had been present when the other bombings occurred and bring them in for questioning. Only a handful of people had shown up at both the races where bombs had detonated, all of them men. Which didn't mean others weren't involved. That Morgan wasn't involved.

"There was serious discussion about canceling this race," she said. "The organization was just getting back on its feet after the doping scandals of several years ago, and now some nut job is setting off bombs at some of the biggest races." She leaned toward him again, her voice low. "That's why you're here, isn't it? You're looking for the bomber. Do you know who he is?"

Was she asking the question as a journalist or out of idle curiosity—or because she had a more personal interest in the answer? "I can't say."

"Of course, you know who he is. You said before you were here searching for someone who wasn't me. You're looking for the bomber." She stared into his eyes, as if she could see into his head and decipher the image of the bomber there. "Why can't you tell me who it is? I attend a lot of these races. Maybe I can help you find him."

"Or maybe he's a friend of yours and you'll run right to him and tell him the FBI is looking for him."

She gasped. "You don't really think that, do you?"

"I don't know. I don't know anything about you but what you've told me."

She tried to look wounded, but mostly she looked afraid. Because he'd hit too close to the truth? "Why does it matter so much to you?" he asked.

She stood, bumping the table and sending water from her glass sloshing onto the surface. "I have to go," she said.

"What did I say to upset you?" He stood, but she had already brushed past him, hurrying out of the bar and into the lobby.

He started after her but stopped in the door of the bar. What would he do when he caught up to her? Clearly, she was done talking to him. And he had no reason to keep her, only a gnawing uneasiness that something wasn't right.

Moving cautiously, keeping objects and other people between himself and Morgan, he followed her across the lobby. She stopped in front of the elevators and pulled out her phone, punching in a number. The anxiety on her face increased as she listened for a few seconds, then ended the call. She hadn't said anything, and he had the impression whoever she'd been trying to reach hadn't answered.

Had she been calling the bomber to warn him? His stomach knotted with a mixture of anger and disappointment. He didn't want her to be guilty, but he couldn't discard all the evidence that told him something wasn't right.

The elevator doors slid open and she stepped inside. He moved from behind the pillar that had shielded him and her eyes met his. Beautiful eyes, filled with an aching sadness. The sense of loss hit him like a punch. He recognized that grief because he'd felt it himself. Who had she lost, and what had he done to cause her such fresh pain?

## Chapter Two

Morgan choked back a sob as the elevator doors slid
closed. She squeezed her eyes shut and hugged her arms
tightly across her body, forcing the emotions back into
the box she usually kept so tightly shut. By the time
the elevator opened on the twelfth floor she felt more
in control. She checked the hallway for signs of Agent
Renfro. She wouldn't have put it past the man to run up
twelve flights of stairs to catch her outside her room.
But the carpeted hallway, which smelled of old cigarette
smoke overlaid with the vanilla potpourri that stood in
bowls on tables by the elevators, was empty.

Safely in her room, she pulled out her phone again
and hit the button to redial Scott's number. She pressed
the phone to her ear, listening to the mechanical buzz,
then the click to his voice mail. His familiar voice, terse
but cheerful, said, "Leave a message," then came the
disconnect. The mailbox had been full for months, and
he never answered her calls. But she never gave up hope
that one day he would pick up. And sometimes she
called just to hear his voice. Three cryptic words that
helped her believe he was safe and all right, somewhere.

She sank onto the edge of the bed and stared at the
still life of a bowl of fruit on the opposite wall, the col-

ors blurring as she kept her unblinking eyes fixed on it. If only she could dull her emotions as easily. At first she'd been annoyed—and yes, a little intrigued—that the good-looking guy in the suit was following her. She was sure she'd never seen him before, but, unlike Agent Renfro, she didn't have a good memory for faces. When he'd flashed his FBI credentials, she'd been afraid she might faint right there.

She'd been terrified he'd approached her because of Scott. He was in some kind of trouble—big trouble, if the feds were involved. She'd almost said as much but had swallowed the words. Why give the agent a name if he didn't have it? Worse, why put Scott on his radar if she was mistaken and he was looking for someone else?

She'd let herself be a little flattered when Luke Renfro told her he remembered her and was interested in knowing her better. Clean shaven, with thick dark hair cut short and deep blue eyes, he was the kind of man who would make any woman look twice. Relief had filled her at the thought of innocent flirtation. The FBI agent was good-looking, and when she allowed herself to relax and feel it, she could admit to a certain sizzle in the air between them.

He was interesting, too, with his unusual talent for remembering people. It was like knowing someone who could do complicated math in his head, or someone who remembered the phone numbers of everyone he knew.

Except Luke's talent had a more sinister side. His talk of the bombings hadn't made her feel any easier. When he'd all but admitted he was looking for the bomber, she'd wondered again why he'd approached her. Maybe the line about wanting to meet her was just an excuse. Maybe he'd only been pretending not to know her name in order to see what she'd say. He could have stopped her because he knew about her connection to Scott and he wanted to see if she knew anything more.

As much as she told herself Scott would never do something so horrible, how could she really know? The man she loved wasn't the man he had been lately. He might be capable of anything, even something as terrible as this.

"Scott, where are you?" she whispered. "What have you gotten yourself into?"

LUKE RETURNED TO his surveillance of the mall, alert for any sign of Morgan, as well as his suspects. Was she mixed up in the bombings somehow, or was she just an unneeded distraction from the more important work he had to do?

Dusk descended like a gray curtain as he made his way to his hotel, down the mall from the one where Morgan was staying. Once in his room, he shed his jacket and tie, and telephoned his supervisor to give his report. "No sign of any of our suspects," he said. "But a lot of familiar racers, support people and fans are converging on the city. Maybe I'll have better luck at the kickoff banquet tomorrow night."

"Steadman thinks he saw one of our guys at the airport yesterday afternoon, but he lost him in the crowd." Special Agent in Charge Ted Blessing had the smooth bass voice of a television preacher, and the no-nonsense demeanor of a man who was comfortable with wielding authority. "If Steadman is right, we've got to stop this guy before he makes his move."

"If Travis says he saw the guy, he saw him," Luke said. Though he had no doubt Blessing would go to the mat to support his team, the Special Agent in Charge had never bothered to hide his skepticism about the whole super-recognizer phenomena. "And if he's here, we'll find him."

"Unless he gets past us again. He's avoided detection so far. Which is one reason our analysts think he can't be acting alone."

"I thought they'd decided that he was a lone wolf. Has some group claimed responsibility for the other attacks?"

"No. But other intelligence has come in that points to a terrorist cell with links to each of the bombing locations. We've got people trying to track down a connection to Colorado right now. Plus, we finally have results from the tests on the explosives he used in the London bombing. Scotland Yard believes the bomber used military-grade C-4. Not impossible for a civilian to obtain, but not something you'd pick up at the local hardware store, either."

"Maybe some of the other suspects on our list are involved."

"Maybe. Anything else of interest I should know about?"

The image of Morgan's frightened face flashed into his mind, but he pushed it away. "Nothing yet," he said. He wasn't ready to offer her up for the Bureau's scrutiny. Not until he'd had time to try to discover her secret himself.

They said goodbye and ended the call and he retrieved his tablet from the room safe and booted it up. Time to do a little research into Morgan Westfield.

The knot in his stomach loosened a little as he read through the search engine results on her name. She'd been telling the truth about being a writer. Every hit featured one of her articles, mostly about cycling. He read through her recap of the Tour of Britain, caught up in her depiction of the excitement and tension of a sport he hadn't thought much about before being assigned to his case. The Bureau had briefed him and his fellow agents on the basics—how races are organized into stages, which could combine circuit races, cross-country treks and individual time trials. He understood the concept of racing teams that worked together to support one or more favorite riders, and had read about the dedication of the men for whom professional racing was their life.

But those facts hadn't breathed life into the events the way Morgan did in her article. Reading her words, he felt the struggle of the racers to meet the demands of the challenging course, the devotion of the fans who followed the peloton from stage to stage and the resources that went into putting on an event that was popular around the world.

He hesitated over the keys, then typed in another name, one he tried to refrain from searching but always came back to, month after month: Mark Renfro. The familiar links scrolled down the screen: an article Mark had written about the destructive potential of so-called dirty bombs, a piece for a scholarly journal on nuclear fission, a profile of him when he won a prestigious award from the University of Colorado, where he taught and conducted his research.

Farther down the page were articles about his disappearance almost a year before: Top Nuclear Physicist Missing. Professor Mark Renfro Missing, Feared Dead.

Luke read through that article, though he'd long ago memorized the text.

Mark Renfro, professor of nuclear physics at the University of Colorado in Boulder, has been reported missing after failing to return from a hiking trip in Colorado's remote Weminuche Wilderness area. Professor Renfro set out alone to hike to the top of Wilson Peak on Monday, and has not been seen since a pair of hikers reported passing him on the trail at about noon that day. Renfro was an experienced hiker who had reportedly been struggling with depression since the death of his wife in a car accident six months earlier. One colleague at the university, who wished to remain anonymous, stated he feared Renfro had arranged the hike with the intention of committing suicide.

Luke exited the screen, familiar anger rising up inside him. Mark had not committed suicide. Yes, he'd been devastated by Christy's death in the accident, but he would never have left their four-year-old daughter, Mindy, alone. Something had happened to keep him from coming back to the girl. Luke was certain his brother was still alive, and he would give anything to bring him back.

He'd driven Mark to the trailhead that day and arranged to meet him back there in two days. Luke's work schedule had prevented him from accompanying his brother on the hike, but Mark had taken these solo treks before. "I get some of my best ideas out there with no one else around," he'd said. Far from being depressed, he'd been in good spirits that morning. In the early hours, the sky showing the first faint hint of light, only one other car had been at the trailhead. Luke had scarcely glanced at the two dark figures inside. He wasn't working, and he didn't need to clutter his mind with more strangers' faces.

But what if he had taken the time to memorize those men? Were they the key to finding his brother and he'd missed his chance? He closed his eyes and tried again to picture the scene, but his mind came up blank. All he saw was Mark's face, smiling, eager to set out. Not the face of a man who was walking to his death.

THE NEXT MORNING, aided by a sleeping pill and a half hour of yoga, Morgan was feeling calmer. She headed down to the hotel's free breakfast buffet, her mind on her plans for the day. In addition to writing several articles for *Road Bike Magazine*, she'd been hired to blog about each day's race stage for the popular *Cycling Pro* website. Today she had an interview with an Italian rider who was one of the top contenders to win the race, then a Skype meeting with one of the UCI officials to get his views on the race. The Union Cycliste Internationale oversaw every aspect of sanctioned modern bicycle road races. In the wake of the bombings that had rocked other races, they had a lot riding on the success of this Colorado event.

Thoughts of the bombings brought her back to Agent Luke Renfro. He obviously knew more about the attacks than he was telling her. Maybe she needed to find him and pump him for more information. He'd said he was going to be around for the race. Maybe she'd spot him tonight, at the banquet to kick off the race festivities, before the racers headed out to the starting point in Aspen tomorrow. Under the guise of making small talk, she could question him, and maybe get a better feel for whether or not he was as dangerous to her peace of mind as he'd felt last night.

She found a table at the back of the breakfast room and was slathering strawberry jam onto a piece of wheat toast when Luke Renfro pulled out the chair across from her and sat down.

Her initial pleasure at seeing him again quickly gave way to nervousness. Her heart fluttered and she had to set aside the knife before she dropped it. "What are you doing here?" she asked, avoiding meeting his gaze.

He was dressed more casually today, in a blue pin-striped oxford shirt open at the collar, the sleeves rolled up to reveal tanned forearms lightly dusted with brown hair. He smelled of shaving cream—a clean, masculine scent that made her stomach flutter in rhythm with her racing heart.

"I had some more questions for you." He unfolded a napkin across his lap, then picked up the mug of coffee he'd brought with him.

"You won't tell me anything, so why should I share anything with you?"

"After I got back to the hotel last night, I went online and read some of your work. You're very good. I'm curious why you're a freelancer, and not on staff with one of the top cycling publications."

She told herself it wasn't creepy that he'd looked her up online. Everyone did it these days, whether they were checking out potential job applicants or prospective dates. So why did it make her so nervous that this particular man had been checking out her background? "Those staff jobs aren't necessarily easy to come by," she said. She sipped her coffee, her hands steady enough to drink it without spilling. "Anyway, I prefer the flexibility of freelancing."

"I didn't mean to upset you yesterday," he said. "What, exactly, did I say that made you so afraid?"

"I wasn't afraid." Her voice squeaked on the last word and she looked away.

"You may be an excellent writer, but you're a lousy liar."

When she dared to look at him again he was smiling. His lack of hostility soothed her a little, and in that moment she made a decision. She pulled out her phone and thumbed to the picture library. She turned the screen toward him. "Is this the man you're looking for?" Her voice quavered, and her heart pounded painfully, drowning out the clatter of cutlery and chatter of the diners around them.

She'd taken the photograph of Scott almost a year ago, on a hike in the Texas hill country, near their home in Austin. He stood with his slender frame leaning against a bent pine tree, a breeze blowing his blond hair across his face. He'd refused to smile for the camera or even to look directly at her. At the time, she'd thought he was merely being stubborn and moody; now she recognized the first signs that he wasn't himself, that what he always referred to as "his demons" were getting the best of him.

"Who is this?" Agent Renfro asked, his expression giving away nothing.

"First, tell me if he's your bombing suspect." Even saying the words made her feel a little faint, but better to know the truth than to keep wondering.

"No."

Relief flooded her, leaving her weak and shaky. She

set aside the phone and sagged back against the chair. "Thank God," she whispered, not even caring that he saw her so undone.

"But I've seen him before," he said, his smile gone, his voice serious.

"Where?" she demanded. "When?" *Was he all right? Was he safe? Was he in trouble?*

"First, tell me who he is. And who he is to you."

"He's my brother. My older brother. Scott."

Something—surprise?—flickered in Luke's eyes. Followed by sympathy. He definitely didn't look as threatening. "He was in London," he said. "At the Tour of Britain."

"Oh." She put her fingers to her lips, too late to hold back the cry. To think that she'd been so close to him but hadn't seen him.

"You're looking for him, aren't you?" Luke's voice was gentle, his blue eyes full of understanding. "That's why you freelance—so you can travel around and look for him."

"Yes." She swallowed, reining in her emotions. "He disappeared ten months ago. But before that, he was a bicycle racer. A really good one. He was part of the US Olympic team in London. Then the trouble started."

"What kind of trouble?"

"He began disappearing. He claimed to hear voices— his devils, he called them. He tried to hurt himself. Doctors diagnosed schizophrenia. They put him on medication and he began to get better. But he had to give up racing. He continued to follow the races and found work as a photographer."

"When I saw him on the surveillance videos, he had a camera."

She closed her eyes, summoning an image of her brother with his camera. In the memory, he was taking pictures of her, laughing and joking around. This was the memory she wanted to keep, not the one of the troubled young man who had left their family so bereft and confused.

She opened her eyes again and found Luke watching her, calm and patient, waiting for more. "We thought everything would be all right," she said. "The medication had side effects—he gained weight, he couldn't sleep—but we thought he had accepted that. That he was building a new life for himself. And then one day he just...vanished."

"No signs of foul play?"

She shook her head. "Later, when we put all the pieces together, I realized there were warning signs— things we ignored because we wanted so desperately for things to be all right. He was unhappy. He stopped socializing with friends. And then we learned he'd stopped seeing his doctors. He didn't refill his medication. He lied to us and told us everything was fine, but we should have known better. We should have seen the signs..."

His hand covered hers, warm and strong, pulling her out of the mire of guilt she'd almost allowed herself to slip back into. "Beating yourself up won't bring him back," he said.

She nodded and gently pulled out of his grasp, though reluctantly. He was so calm and steady, not freaking out at the mention of mental illness and not pulling away from her. She didn't normally associate law enforcement officers with such empathy. The police who had responded when they'd filed a missing persons report on Scott had been coldly suspicious and unhelpful. They didn't have time to waste searching for a twenty-six-year-old who'd decided to drop out of society; especially a twenty-six-year-old who was crazy.

"I'm going to ask you a question that's going to be hard for you to hear," Luke said. "But I want you to answer honestly."

She nodded. Hadn't she already asked a million hard questions of her own over the months since Scott had left?

"Do you think it's possible that your brother has had anything to do with the bombings at bike races?"

"No!"

"But when we spoke yesterday—when I said I was looking for the bomber—that's what you were afraid of, wasn't it? That's why you showed me his picture this morning?"

Reluctantly, she nodded. "I thought you might believe it of him, but I don't believe it," she said. "Scott was never violent toward anyone else. Even when he was at his worst, he only tried to hurt himself, not others."

"Mental illness can make people do things they wouldn't otherwise do," he said. "He may have a grudge against professional cycling since he's no longer able to participate in a sport he loved."

"But you only saw him at the one race, right? He wasn't at the Paris Roubaix, where the first bomb exploded?"

"He wasn't in any of the videos I saw." He didn't add that it was possible her brother had avoided the surveillance cameras; she was grateful for that.

"I don't think he would be comfortable in a place where he didn't speak the language," she said. "Unfamiliar situations upset him, but he knew London from his racing days. He always liked it there."

"Do you think your brother is here, in Denver?" he asked.

She nodded. "He trained in Colorado for the Olympics and he loved it here. For a while, he even talked about moving here. He has friends competing in the race, so that's one more reason for him to be here."

"What will you do if you find him?"

"I think if I could just talk to him, I could convince him to come home with me. There are other medications he can try, ones without as many side effects. I can help him get better if he'll only give me a chance."

"Do you think he'll listen to you?"

"I hope so. We've always been close. Our mother died when I was seven and Scott was nine. My dad worked a lot, so it was just the two of us a lot of the time. I could always talk to him when no one else could."

"I'll keep an eye out for him, and if I see him, I'll let you know."

"I'd really appreciate it." It was probably the kind of offer anyone would make, but coming from him, it carried more weight. He was going to be looking closely at everyone associated with the race, and since he never forgot a face...

"If you see him, call me at this number." She pulled a pen and notepad from her purse and scribbled her number, then slid the paper across to him.

He studied the number, then folded the paper and tucked it into his pocket. "I guess that's one way to get a pretty woman's phone number," he said.

His teasing tone surprised a laugh from her. She sipped more coffee and pretended to contemplate her now-cold breakfast, though she was really watching him through the screen of her lashes. A man who could make her laugh despite her sadness was remarkable, indeed. "I hope you'll be in touch," she murmured. And not just because of her brother.

# Chapter Three

"See anybody familiar?"

"By this time, everyone here is familiar."

"You know what I mean."

"Then, no. I don't see anyone we're looking for." Luke stood with his friend and fellow Search Team member, Special Agent Travis Steadman, outside the hotel ballroom where the banquet to kick off the Colorado Cycling Challenge was set to begin in fifteen minutes. A crush of well-dressed men and women filled the hall, the slender athletes mingling with more robust race fans, national media and a good number of security personnel, both plainclothes and in uniform.

Scanning the crowd, Luke quickly identified racers, racing fans, hotel personnel and people he'd passed on the street since his arrival in Denver. But the crowd contained none of the suspects the team had identified from surveillance videos. "What about you?" he asked Travis. "Have you seen any of our suspects?"

The tall, laconic Texan frowned. "Not since I spotted Boy Scout in the airport yesterday. I can't believe I let him slip away." The team members had nicknamed the suspect Boy Scout for his slight build and clean-cut good looks.

"He's been either very good or very lucky so far, but he won't get away this time," Luke said. "Not with the team here, actively looking for him."

Travis nodded. "Everything points to him being here. A friend of mine with the Denver Police said they've heard a lot of rumblings that something big is going to go down at the race."

"Then why not stop the race?" Luke asked. "Why risk lives?"

"The UCI won't do it," Travis said. "When nothing bad happened at the Tour de France this summer, they persuaded themselves they were in the clear. Never mind the intelligence we've received to the contrary."

"Obviously, the feds are overreacting, as usual." Luke repeated the complaint they heard too often in the news.

"The UCI are determined to prove they can run a safe race here in the States," Travis said.

"You can bet it will come back on us if they don't." Luke shoved his hands in his trouser pockets and jingled his change, eyes still sweeping over the crowd. "What if we're wrong and none of our suspects is the bomber?" he asked. "What if it's one of the racers? Or a racing official?"

"The Bureau has other people looking at them," Travis said. "We're focused on the outliers, the people who don't have a logical reason to be at every race where there's been a bomb."

"The people who we were lucky enough to capture on video," Luke said. "I worry about the ones who slip past, unnoticed." He'd let down his guard one time and failed to notice the men who might have the answers to what had happened to his brother. If Luke had been more vigilant, maybe Mark would be home right now with his daughter, instead of "missing, feared dead," as the notation in the police file of his case indicated.

"Our man is here, I know it," Travis said. "Focus on what we can do, not what we can't."

Good advice, though Luke found it hard to implement. He continued to scan the crowd, then stilled as he recognized a familiar blonde head.

"What do you see?" Travis asked. He leaned closer, following Luke's gaze, then nudged him in the side. "The woman in the blue dress? Definitely a knockout."

Morgan had traded her jeans and tank top for a form-fitting evening gown of a shimmery, iridescent blue silk. She carried a cocktail in one hand, a small silver evening bag in the other and turned her head from side to side, as if searching for someone.

"She looks familiar," Travis said. "Someone from our videos?"

"She's a journalist, writes for racing magazines," Luke said. At that moment, Morgan turned in his direction and their eyes met. The now-familiar jolt of connection went through him, and he started toward her.

"Hey, Luke. I was hoping I'd see you here." She touched his arm. "What a crush, huh?"

"Yeah, a lot of people." But he wasn't looking at any of them anymore, only her.

"See anyone, uh, interesting?" Her eyes filled in the question behind the question—had he seen her brother?

He shook his head, but before he could say more, Travis inserted himself between them. "Since Luke's not going to introduce me, I'll have to do it myself," he said. "I'm Travis Steadman."

"Hello, Mr. Steadman." She shook his hand. "Are you with the FBI, too?"

He grinned. "How did you know?"

"You have that look about you."

"What kind of look?" Luke asked.

"Very official."

"It's an unfortunate side effect of our training," Travis said.

"Are you two headed to Aspen for the first stage of the race tomorrow?" she asked.

Was she making conversation or asking for another reason? Luke hedged his answer. "I'm not sure. What about you? Do you follow the racers around the state?"

She shook her head. "I wish I could, but it's not in my budget. As the racers get closer, I'll make a few day trips, maybe get in a few interviews with the top athletes. But most of the time I can stay in Denver and follow the race on television. At the end of the week, I'll be in a good position to report on the final stage of the race and the results."

Luke liked this answer. Unless his superiors changed their minds, the plan was for him and a few others to stay in Denver all week, as well, while the rest of the team followed the racers. Previously, the bomber had waited until the last day of the races to make his move, when the biggest crowd and the most media coverage were in place. But there was no guarantee he'd stick to that pattern. Meanwhile, maybe Luke and Morgan would have the chance to get to know each other better.

The crowd began to move toward the ballroom doors. "I guess it's time to go in," Travis said.

"May I?" Luke offered Morgan his arm. "That is, if you haven't already arranged to sit with someone else."

"No, um, that would be nice." She laid her hand on his arm, a touch as light as a butterfly, yet he felt it all the way up to his chest. He was definitely in trouble, but he wasn't sure he wanted to get out of it. At least not yet.

By the time they made it inside, most of the tables near the front were already full. Travis steered them toward an empty table at the back, near the kitchen. "Not most people's idea of choice seating," he said, "but it works better for our purposes."

"I get it," she said, as she took the chair Luke held for her. "It's a good place to watch the rest of the crowd."

"She's a fast learner." Travis took the chair on one side of her, while Luke sat on the other side. "How did you two meet?" Travis asked.

"Um..." She glanced at Luke.

"I recognized her from the surveillance video and started following her," Luke admitted. "She caught me and demanded to know what I was doing."

"She caught you?" Travis grinned. "Didn't we teach you better than that?"

"Ladies and gentlemen, please welcome our mayor." The introduction saved Luke from having to come up with a reply. As they ate their salads, a parade of local dignitaries made speeches praising the athletes, the sponsors, the spectators—pretty much everyone, up to and including the sanitation workers.

"Notice how no one's mentioning the bombings," Travis said.

"I'm sure it's in the back of everyone's mind," Morgan said. "No sense putting more of a damper on the evening by bringing it up."

"Where were you when the bombs went off in London and Paris?" Luke asked.

"You were at those races, too?" Travis was immediately more alert, focused on her. Luke sent him a quelling look.

Morgan didn't appear to notice the exchange. "I was stuck on a shuttle in Paris," she said. "Furious because I was missing the arrival of the winners at the finish line. By the time I got there, the ambulances were carrying away the injured. I realized how lucky I'd been."

"And in London?" Travis asked.

"I was at the finish line, interviewing the leading American racer. We'd moved into the doorway of a building across the street to get out of the sun." Her eyes met Luke's, beautiful and troubled. "The explosion was so loud. It stunned us. We stared at each other and for the longest moment we didn't hear anything else. Then someone screamed, and we knew it had happened again."

He took her hand under the table and squeezed it. "I'm glad you were okay."

"I knew the two racers who died that day," she said. "I had interviewed both of them for an article before the race. They were nice guys, funny and easy to talk to." She shook her head. "I don't understand why anyone would do something like that. Why resort to violence for the sake of violence?"

"Terrorists act to induce fear, and to draw attention to themselves," Travis said.

"But why bicycle races?" she asked.

"It's an international sport," Luke said. "It's popular and draws big crowds. Or maybe this person has a grudge against the sport or the athletes."

"A former racer," she murmured, and he knew she was thinking of her brother.

"It could be anyone." He squeezed her hand. "First we find them, then we worry about their motives."

An army of servers arrived to clear the tables and deliver the entrées—some kind of chicken over rice, in a maroon-colored sauce. Luke leaned over and whispered to Morgan. "Any idea what this is?"

"Not a clue."

Luke ate without tasting the food, one eye on the crowd, the rest of his attention focused on the woman beside him. She was definitely more relaxed now, though with an underlying sadness he understood. Which didn't mean she wasn't involved with the bombings, he reminded himself. But his instincts told him no. She was exactly what she appeared to be: a journalist covering the races, and a sister looking for her missing brother. The two of them had more in common than she knew.

A commotion near the front of the room drew his attention. At the table directly in front of the podium, people were standing. "Someone call an ambulance!" a man shouted.

Luke and Travis rose as one, shoving back their chairs. "What's going on?" Morgan asked, her fork paused, halfway to her mouth.

"We're going to find out," Luke said. He pushed his way toward the front table, Travis on his heels. "Security," he said, flashing his badge when a man tried to block his way.

"What happened?" Travis asked when they reached the table.

"The president has had some kind of attack." The thin-faced man spoke with a French accent.

"I fear he is dead," an older woman in a black evening gown said.

"The ambulance is on its way," the first man said.

Union Cycliste Internationale President Alec Demetrie was a familiar figure to Luke, and to anyone in the professional cycling world. But the inert, ashen-faced man slumped in his chair was almost unrecognizable. Luke felt for a pulse but couldn't find even a flutter. He met Travis's gaze and shook his head.

"What happened?" Luke asked the woman, who he recalled was the president's wife.

She took a deep breath, visibly pulling herself together. "He had a few bites of the entrée and complained of it tasting off. I told him he should send it back to the kitchen, but by then he was already unwell. I tried to get the attention of one of the waiters, then Alec slumped in his chair and…and…" She stared at her husband, unable to say more.

"Paramedics, let us through!"

Luke stepped back to allow two uniformed EMTs to reach the president. He motioned for Travis to follow him some distance away from the table and was surprised when Morgan joined them. "Is he dead?" she asked, keeping her voice low.

Luke nodded. "What do you think?" he asked Travis.

"Maybe he had a heart attack," Travis said. "But I think we'd better make sure someone takes that plate as evidence."

"I overheard what the woman said about the food tasting odd," Morgan said. "Do you think someone poisoned him?"

"I think I'd like to check out the kitchen," Luke said.

"I'll question the waitstaff." Travis nodded toward

the dozen or so black-clad servers who stood along the back wall.

Morgan turned to Luke. "I'm coming with you," she said.

"I'd rather you didn't." He didn't like to involve civilians in his work. And if there really was a poisoner in the kitchen, the situation could be dangerous.

"You can't stop me," she said, then slipped her arm in his. "Besides, you're less likely to arouse suspicion in the culprit if you look like a diner interested in complimenting the chef, instead of an FBI agent snooping around."

"I never worry about looking suspicious." But he covered her hand with his own to keep it in place on his arm.

"Right. Because you're an FBI agent and whatever you do is right."

"I didn't say that."

"You didn't have to. I think the attitude comes with the badge."

"You don't look too upset about it."

A sly smile curved her lips. "I like a man with a little attitude."

At the kitchen door, they had to push their way through a crowd of workers who had gathered to view the excitement in the dining room. "What's going on?" asked a man in a white chef's toque and apron.

"One of the diners became ill," Luke said. He scanned the crowd of workers, searching for a familiar face.

Not all the workers had left their duties to gawk at the door. A dishwasher stood with his back to them, rinsing dishes, seemingly oblivious to the commotion.

Another worker carried a trash bin to the back door. As he reached the door, the dishwasher moved to open it for him.

Faster than he could articulate the information, Luke's brain processed the data his eyes transmitted: young male, early to midtwenties, slight, athletic build, five-eight or five-nine, clean shaven, short brown hair. "You there, by the door," he called.

The man dropped the trash can and reached behind him. Time slowed as Luke drew his weapon from the holster beneath his jacket. Light glinted off the barrel of the gun the suspect they'd dubbed Boy Scout pulled from his waistband. Morgan screamed, then launched herself toward Luke as shots rang out.

They fell together, Luke propelled backward, crashing against a counter, Morgan sagging against him. Adrenaline flooded his system and he struggled to right himself, gripping his weapon in one hand, pulling Morgan up beside him with the other. "Are you all right?" he demanded, forcing himself to look for the wound he was sure was there.

"I'm sorry." She looked up at him, tears streaking her face. "I had to stop you."

"Are you all right?" he asked again. No blood stained her gown, but he knew the man at the door had been aiming right at them.

"I'm fine." She struggled to pull away from him, but he held her firmly. "I couldn't let you shoot him."

The shooter had missed. Luke glanced toward the back door. Both the men who had been there were gone, the door standing open, the trash can on its side.

He gently set Morgan aside and raced to the door. The alley outside was empty, with no sign of the two men, and no apparent place for them to hide. He pulled out his phone and called his boss. "We've got a shooter on the loose," he said as soon as Blessing answered. "Two men took off on foot from the kitchen of the hotel." He gave a brief description of each man. "I'll be in touch after I've finished assessing the situation here."

He holstered his weapon and returned to the kitchen. Around him, the voices of the others in the room rose, full of questions and protests. He ignored them and found Morgan, standing where he had left her, shoulders hunched, expression stunned. He slipped his arm around her and guided her to a quiet corner. "Who did you think I was shooting at?" he asked.

"The dishwasher. I know you think he's guilty, but he's not. He would never…"

"Shh." He put two fingers to her lips. "I was aiming for the other man. The one by the trash can. Didn't you see the gun in his hand?"

Confusion clouded her eyes. "A gun? I wasn't looking at him. I was watching the dishwasher. He was…"

"I know." He laid her head against his shoulder and smoothed his hand down her back. "I recognized him, too. He was your brother."

# Chapter Four

"What do you think you're doing, you idiot? You can't come in here shooting up my kitchen!" Luke looked up into the florid face of the chef, who held a cleaver in one hand, the other curled into a fist.

"I'm a federal agent." Luke gently separated himself from Morgan. "I have to go," he said, to her, not the cook. "Maybe I can still catch them."

She nodded and pushed him toward the door. "Go. Hurry."

He raced past the gaping chef, skirted the fallen trash can and the lettuce shreds and potato peelings that spilled from it, and pounded into the alley. At the end he looked down the street filled with cars and pedestrians. Taxis and limos jostled for space with more modest sedans across four lanes of traffic idling at the red light on the corner. Half a block farther on, a light rail train blasted its horn as it pulled out of the station. His quarry could be anywhere by now—in one of the taxis or cars, on that train, or hiding in a dark alley nearby.

"You looking for those two who hightailed it out of there a minute ago?"

The raspy tenor voice came from a tall, thin black man who leaned against the brick wall a few feet to

Luke's left, one foot propped against the brick, a ciga-rette glowing in his right hand.

"Which way did they go?" Luke asked.

"Both ways. They split up. Which one did you plan on shooting?"

Luke realized he still held the gun in his right hand. He replaced it in the holster beneath his left arm. "The man with the short brown hair—which way did he go?"

The man straightened, both feet on the ground. "I didn't pay attention to what either of them looked like," he said. "I just know they were bookin' it. I thought I heard gunshots, so I figured I'd best stay out of the way for a while."

"Did you see either of them get into a car or taxi, or onto the train?"

"No. They were both running. I'd just stepped out for a smoke in time to see them leaving." He snuffed out the cigarette against the brick. "And now it's time for me to get back to work." With that, he sauntered back into an alcove and took the stairs down a level to a club, The Purple Martini, spelled out in purple neon above the door.

Luke had little hope of finding either Morgan's brother or his suspect now, but he had to make an ef-fort. He set out walking, past The Purple Martini and a string of closed shops. As he walked, he pulled out his phone and called Travis. "Our suspect got away. He took a shot at me, then ran out the back door. I'm going to show his picture around on the street, but unless we get really lucky, he's gone."

"I heard the shot, but by the time I got to the kitchen it was all over but the crying," Travis said. "The chef is ranting at anyone within earshot and Morgan looks like she's seen a ghost."

"See that she gets back to her hotel okay."

"What happened?" Travis asked.

"I'll tell you the story later. For now, I want to keep looking. It's possible the suspect is still on foot downtown."

"I'm on it."

He ended the call, then scrolled to his photo album. The picture he had of their suspect was a grainy image from a surveillance video, but it showed his face and general build. He approached a group of young people gathered on the corner, waiting for the light to change. "Have any of you seen this man around tonight?" he asked, holding out his phone.

"Who wants to know?" demanded a beefy blond whose flushed cheeks and bright eyes suggested he'd had a few drinks.

"FBI." Luke flashed his creds and the blond gaped, while his friends crowded close to study first the credentials, then the image on Luke's phone.

One by one they shook their heads. "Sorry."

"No, haven't seen him."

"What's he done?" the blond asked.

"We want to talk to him in connection with a case we're working on."

He moved on to others. Everyone studied the picture, frowning in concentration, but no one remembered seeing the suspect. About the results Luke had expected. Most people didn't really look at others. Even when they did, the details didn't stick in their minds the way they did for Luke.

Over an hour later, he'd covered the two-block area

on either side of the hotel with nothing to show for his efforts. He stowed his phone once more and headed back toward the banquet facility. He needed to talk to people there and find out what they knew. Other members of the team had probably already conducted interviews, but he wanted to hear the information firsthand. It was possible the suspect had made friends who knew where he lived. Certainly, they'd have a name, though whether or not it was the man's real identity was doubtful.

And he needed to figure out if Morgan's brother, Scott, had anything to do with the suspect. Maybe he was merely holding the door open for a coworker, but the two had fled together. Luke needed to know why.

A block from the hotel, a woman moved out of the shadows ahead of him. The streetlights shimmered on the blue of her dress, and a gusty breeze tugged at her short hair. Luke straightened. "Morgan, what are you doing here?" he asked.

"I was waiting for you." She moved in close beside him, almost but not quite touching him. She cast a nervous glance over her shoulder toward the front door of the hotel and Luke saw the reason for her nerves: half a dozen news vans crowded the curb and men and women with cameras and microphones filled the portico in front of the entrance, everyone jostling to report the big story of the night.

Luke took her arm and directed her across the street, to a bench at an empty bus stop. "We can talk here," he said. "How are you doing?"

"Okay," she said, though her pinched face and hunched shoulders belied the answer. "Did you find him?"

By "him" did she mean her brother or the suspect?

"They both had a big head start on me. I found a witness who said they split up at the end of the alley and ran in opposite directions."

"I'm sure Scott only ran because he was confused and frightened," she said. "He's never liked tense situations, but even more so since he's been diagnosed."

He nodded. "I'd like to talk to him and find out what he knows about my suspect."

"I talked to Gary and he said Scott had been working as a dishwasher only three days," she said.

"Who's Gary?"

"Oh, he's the chef. Gary Forneaux. After you left I offered to bring him a drink from the hotel bar and he calmed down quite a bit. He told me they'd needed extra help for the banquet, so they'd agreed to hire Scott on a trial basis."

"Do you think that's how he's been supporting himself—working temporary jobs in whatever town he's in?"

"Probably. Gary said Scott knew how to run the commercial dishwasher. And he gets along well with most people. He can be very charming when he wants to be. Gary said everyone in the kitchen liked him."

"I'm glad you found him," Luke said. Along with everything else that had happened, there was that one bit of good news for her. "At least you know he's all right."

"But it feels like I've lost him all over again," she said. "No one at the hotel knew where he was staying. Though he did use his real name. Tomorrow I'm going to start calling around to hotels and apartments, trying to find him."

"I hope you do," he said. Not just for his investigation, but because he knew how much being reunited with her lost sibling would mean to her. He would have given almost anything to see Mark again.

"What about the other guy?" he asked. "Did you find out anything about him?"

"His name is Danny. He was a day laborer from a temp agency. He was brought in just for tonight. Gary couldn't even remember his last name and didn't know anything about him."

"Thanks. We'll follow up on it." Though he didn't have high hopes that anyone at the temp agency would have more information. So far this guy had been very good at covering his tracks.

He glanced toward the hotel, at the bright lights and rumbling growl of the generators powering the portable satellite dishes for the news vans. "I guess I'd better get back there."

"Luke." Her hand on his arm drew his attention to her once more. The streetlight overhead cast a golden glow over her, glinting off her hair and shadowing her eyes against her pale skin. "I really don't think Scott knew the man who shot at you. I mean, I don't think they were friends or anything. He was just opening the door for him, not trying to help him escape."

He wrapped his hand around hers and held it to his chest. "I know you want to believe that, but you can't know it. We have to check out the connection, though I hope we don't find one."

"Will you tell me if you do?"

This was hard. He didn't like the thought of keeping anything from her. He knew how much any scrap of information about Mark would mean to him. But he had a job to do. And sometimes that job required making hard decisions. "I can't tell you anything I find," he said. "But I will tell you if we're able to clear your brother."

"So in this case, no news is bad news."

She almost smiled, and the burden of guilt he felt at having to keep things from her lifted a little. He marveled at her ability to maintain a sense of humor under the circumstances. She was stronger than she looked. "You've had a rough night," he said. "You should go back to your hotel and get some sleep."

"What about you?"

"I've still got work to do." He doubted he'd see his bed before morning.

"The first stage of the race starts tomorrow morning, in Aspen," she said. "I have to be up early to Skype into a press conference."

"They're going through with it?"

She nodded. "The UCI made the announcement about an hour ago. The vice president, Pierre Marceau, said it was what Monsieur Demetrie would have wanted."

"So if someone was trying to stop the race by poisoning President Demetrie, he didn't succeed," Luke said.

"Are they sure it was poison?" she asked. "The kitchen was swarming with police after you left. They took leftovers from every dish as evidence. Gary was very upset."

"We'll know by morning, anyway."

"Do you think this is even connected to the bombings?" she asked. "Poisoning seems so personal."

"That's something we'll have to find out." They could very well be looking into two unrelated crimes. He stood, and pulled her up with him. He hated to leave the oasis of this little bench, away from the crowds and all the unanswered questions, but his duty had to come before his personal feelings. "Will you be all right walking to your hotel alone? I can find someone to go with you, but I can't leave the investigation. I've stayed away too long as it is."

"I'll be fine. You've done so much already. Thank you."

"You don't have to thank me." If anything, he'd made things worse for her, placing her brother at the center of an investigation into international terrorism.

"Thank you for listening to me. For believing me— or at least pretending to. And for sharing as much information as you have with me."

"So you aren't afraid of me anymore?" He continued to hold her hand, reluctant to let go.

"No." She put her hand on his chest, the warmth seeping through his shirtfront. "I'm glad we met, in spite of the strange circumstances."

"Yeah. I'm glad, too." Maybe from the moment he'd first seen her in that video, he'd known he'd seek her out. Something in her called to him.

She tilted her head up and rose on her toes to bring her face closer to his in silent invitation—an invitation he wouldn't refuse. He'd been wanting to kiss her, hesitant only because of the tenuousness of their relationship. Her lips warmed beneath his, as soft and sensuous as he'd imagined they would be. He wrapped his arms around her to pull her closer and she slid one hand around to cup the back of his head, her fingers tangled in his hair. He stroked his tongue along the seam of her mouth and she opened for him with a soft sigh more passionate than any words would have been. Every nerve in his body was attuned to her, to the soft floral aroma of her perfume, to the taste of wine that lingered on her lips, to the curve of her breasts against his chest and the strong line of her spine beneath his hand. He deepened the kiss, lost in the sensation of her.

A flash of light to his left distracted him, and reluctantly he lifted his head to look around, a sleeper emerging from a wonderful, compelling dream. He saw nothing but the array of news vans and reporters across the street, though he couldn't shake the sense that something had happened that he should have paid attention to.

"I'd better go. Good night."

She slipped from his arms and he curled his fingers into his palms to keep from pulling her back. She gave him a shy smile, then turned and walked away, hips swaying in the blue silk as she walked briskly down the sidewalk. He watched until she'd disappeared in a crowd at the corner, then turned toward the hotel to face a long night of unanswered questions.

THE MEMBERS OF Search Team Seven assembled the next morning in a conference room in the hotel that had hosted the banquet the night before. Luke slid into the seat next to Travis and nodded a silent greeting to the other team members. They all looked as weary and frustrated as he felt. Across from Luke, Gus Mathers stared at his phone, his eyes half-closed behind his black-framed hipster glasses. Next to him, Jack Prescott's burly frame looked too big for the spindly folding chair. Farther down the table, the youngest members of the team, Wade Harris and Cameron Hsung, cupped hands around the takeout coffee they'd brought in. Even in their regulation suits, they managed to look like the college students they had been until only a few months before.

The door opened and Ted Blessing strode in. He'd flown in on a red-eye and wore the look of a man who wasn't happy about having his sleep disturbed. In his midforties, with mud-brown skin and closely cropped hair that showed no sign of gray, he favored tailored suits and had the ramrod-straight spine of the military officer he'd been before joining the Bureau. He laid a tablet computer on the conference table in front of him and studied his team, all of whom were now sitting up straight and at attention.

"How is it that this man keeps getting away, when there are six of you and only one of him?" Blessing asked.

The others cast furtive glances at one another. It wasn't a question that had a good answer—or any answer. As usual, Jack was the first to speak. "He's got to have accomplices, helping him get away," he said. "Someone with a car waiting for him, and a safe place for him to hole up."

"We're circulating his picture to all local law enforcement," Wade said. "They'll be on the lookout for him."

"He'll dye his hair or put on glasses and they won't recognize him if they trip over him," Cameron said. Such disguises rarely fooled the recognizers on the team—they memorized facial composition, mannerisms and other details that couldn't be hidden so easily.

"I don't want some local cop to nail him," Gus said. "I want to nail him."

The others murmured agreement. Blessing sat, hands

clasped on the table in front of him. "Let's go over what we know so far. Agent Steadman?"

Travis referred to the tablet in front of him. "We know our suspect was going by the name Danny in the hotel kitchen, but we're pretty confident that isn't his real name. We spoke with the day labor organization that supplies temp workers to the hotel. The supervisor tells me that a Danny Robinson, a sometimes homeless man with a history of alcoholism, was the man who was supposed to report for work in the hotel kitchen that night."

"His body was found wrapped in a tarp and stuffed in a culvert near Confluence Park, not far from downtown Denver." Cameron picked up the story. "His throat was cut. We believe our suspect murdered him and took the hotel job in his stead, in order to get close to UCI officials."

"The chicken that President Demetrie ate tested positive for potassium cyanide," Jack said. "We should have the autopsy results later this morning, but it looks like that's what did him in. There was enough potassium cyanide in the dish that only a few bites would result in death within minutes."

"Did cyanide show up on any of the other plates?" Blessing asked.

Jack shook his head.

"So President Demetrie was definitely the target," Gus said.

"We don't think so," Travis said. "The covered plates with the entrées were stacked on trays and sent out by table. So the poisoner had a reasonably good chance of knowing that this plate would go to one of the tables of dignitaries seated at the front of the room, nearest the dais. But without the cooperation of the server, there was no way to be certain who would get that particular plate."

"So maybe the server helped him out," Blessing said.

"I spoke to the man who served that table," Travis said. "He's a longtime employee at the hotel. He says he never met our suspect, and witnesses back up his story. We're still investigating, but if our suspect had help, I don't think it was the server."

"What about the other guy in the kitchen—the dishwasher?" Cameron asked. "He and the suspect left together, right?"

Luke shifted and all eyes turned to him. "The dishwasher's name is Scott Westfield," he said. "He's a former pro cyclist who had to retire due to a medical condition. Since then, he's traveled around, taking a series of odd jobs. He sometimes photographs races."

"What kind of medical condition?" Blessing asked.

"He was diagnosed with schizophrenia."

"So, we've got a former racer, possibly upset at being made to retire, who's mentally unstable." Jack ticked the facts off on his fingers. "Sounds like the kind of guy who'd be happy to help our suspect. Maybe he's even the one behind the bombings and our suspect is secondary."

"I don't think so." Luke hadn't meant to speak up in Scott's defense. After all, the evidence pointing to his involvement in the bombings was pretty damning. But Morgan's faith in her brother had swayed him. "I can't find any connection between Westfield and our suspect. Westfield had been working in the hotel kitchen a couple of days before our suspect hired on, and the rest of the staff didn't notice any particular friendship between them."

"That kind of thing is easy enough to hide," Wade said. "Westfield gets the job first to scope the place out, then our suspect joins him. The fact that they left together tells me they were working as a team."

"Maybe," Luke conceded. "We need to find Westfield and question him."

"Oh, we'll have plenty of questions for him," Blessing said. He leaned forward. "But let's not lose sight of the bigger picture here. We've got some intel pointing to a possible terrorist cell, possibly based here in Colorado."

"What kind of intel?" Luke asked, relieved that the focus had shifted away from Morgan's brother, at least for the moment.

"Some intercepted phone conversations that seem to point to a plan to sabotage transportation hubs in the region, and a report of suspicious activity at a private airport near Denver that was called in by a concerned citizen." Blessing's expression grew more grim. "Nothing concrete, but it's worth paying attention to. We've got people working to follow these leads. For now, your job is to focus on finding our suspect and Scott Westfield. Don't let them get away this time." He stood, signaling the meeting was at an end, and the others rose, also. "Someone bring me the local papers. I want to see what the press is saying about all this."

As Luke turned toward the door, Blessing stopped him. "Agent Renfro, stay and talk to me for a minute."

Travis gave him a sympathetic look as he filed out with the others, leaving Luke alone with his commander. "Sit down." Blessing indicated the chair to his right.

Luke sat. He could guess what this was about. Discharging his weapon in public was serious enough to warrant a private briefing if not disciplinary action. Filing a report about the incident was at the top of his to-do list today.

Blessing fixed him with a steady, calm gaze. "I know what others say happened in the kitchen last night, but I want to hear it from you. I expect your written report later, but tell me now, in your own words."

Luke shifted, as if there was any way to get comfortable on the receiving end of a grilling from his boss. "After the president's death, I went to the kitchen to question the staff," he said.

"You weren't alone."

"No, sir."

"Witnesses say you were with a woman. Who was that?"

"Her name is Morgan. Morgan Westfield. She's a magazine writer."

He could sense Blessing grow more alert, like a hound on the scent of a quarry. "Any relation to the dishwasher?"

"He's her brother. Though I didn't know that when I went into the kitchen."

"How do you know Ms. Westfield?"

"We met in the lobby of her hotel the day before yesterday. I recognized her from some of the surveillance videos from the races and decided to follow her."

"Do you think she's involved in the bombings somehow? Perhaps she and her brother are part of this cell we're looking for."

Luke shook his head. "I followed her because I wasn't sure of anything at that point. I just wanted to check her out." Not the entire truth but close enough.

"But now I'm convinced she was at the races for her job and nothing else."

"And you know this how?"

"Everything she told me checked out. She's at the races on assignment for *Road Bike Magazine*, and she's blogging for a website, CyclingPro.com." Though he hadn't contacted anyone at the magazine to verify that. Was he letting his attraction to Morgan—his desire for her to be innocent—get in the way of doing his job?

"What was she doing with you last night?"

"We sat together at dinner. She followed me into the kitchen."

Blessing's face betrayed no emotion, but Luke could sense his skepticism. "Go on."

"I recognized the man who was carrying out the garbage as one of our suspects. I spoke to him and he pulled a gun. I pulled my weapon and returned his fire. He fled out the door."

"Is that all?"

"No, sir." The truth was bound to come out sooner or later, if it hadn't already. Half a dozen people had been working in the kitchen last night and team members had interviewed all of them. "As I pulled my weapon, Ms. Westfield shoved me out of the way. We both fell to the floor, which gave the suspect time to flee."

"Why did she push you?"

"She didn't understand why I was shooting. She saw my gun and panicked."

"Or she knew exactly what you were doing and acted to stop you."

"Yes, sir. That is a possibility." One he couldn't idly set aside. He was trained to be skeptical and suspicious.

He couldn't set that training aside because of his attraction to Morgan.

"You realize what you've done, Renfro?" Blessing's voice held a sharp edge; Luke felt the cut. He said nothing but forced himself to look his boss in the eye.

"At worst, you've become involved with the very person you're supposed to bring to justice. At best, you've endangered a civilian and jeopardized this investigation."

"Yes, sir." Luke held himself rigid.

"I expect better of you. You're not some randy teenager controlled by your hormones. If this woman is guilty, she's playing you for a fool and possibly using you to help her commit acts of terrorism. If she's innocent, she's interfering with a critical investigation. You're here to work, Renfro, not enjoy yourself."

"Yes, sir."

A knock on the conference room door preempted anything else Blessing was about to say. "Come in," he barked.

Wade entered the room. As he passed, he gave Luke a sympathetic look. "You asked to see the local papers," he said to Blessing.

"Sir, may I get back to work now?" Luke asked, seeing his chance for escape.

"Yes, go," Blessing said. He unfolded the first newspaper on the stack. "But remember your focus here. Don't let yourself get distracted again."

"Yes, sir." Luke started toward the door. He had his hand on the knob when Blessing barked his name again.

"Renfro!"

Luke turned, heart pounding. "Yes, sir?"

"How do you explain this?" Blessing turned the

paper to face Luke, who stared at the picture at the bottom of the page, of him and Morgan standing in the bus shelter, wrapped in a passionate kiss. Love Amidst the Chaos, read the caption.

# Chapter Five

Morgan logged out of Skype after the UCI press conference. Interim President Pierre Marceau had delivered an impassioned address about the importance of continuing to uphold the honorable tradition of their sport in the wake of tragedy. He would not disrespect the athletes who had worked so hard to get here or disappoint the fans who had rallied around them. The death of President Demetrie might not even be connected to the previous bombings. It would be a mistake to overreact to what might only be an unfortunate accident. But even if the president's tragic demise was the work of those who had set out to destroy racing, the UCI would not give in to the threats of terrorists. The cycling community was stronger than the faceless cowards who had targeted past races. With heightened security and eternal vigilance they would all emerge victorious from this race.

The crowds gathered in Aspen for the start of the race had cheered wildly at the end of the speech, and the racers had set off on the first of what would be seven stages covering almost eleven hundred kilometers through some of Colorado's most scenic and challenging terrain. They would arrive back in Denver on Sunday for the final stage to determine the winner. Morgan had agreed to write a short article for a bicycling web-site about the death of UCI President Demetrie, and another piece about this morning's press conference, but she wasn't anxious to get started on that work. She couldn't sit still in front of a computer, knowing that Scott was so close—almost within her reach.

And she needed to find him before Luke or one of his fellow FBI agents arrested him for something he hadn't done. No way was Scott a terrorist. No matter what schizophrenia had done to his brain, she refused to believe her brother would ever harm anyone else.

At the hotel where the banquet had been held, she by-passed the front entrance and made her way to the alley and the door into the kitchen. The scents of cooking onion, garlic and peppers engulfed her as she stepped inside, making her mouth water. The chaos of the pre-vious evening had been replaced by a different kind of busyness. Sometime in the night, workers had cleared away all evidence of the police presence and restored order to the kitchen. The chef, Gary, presided over an army of men and women who chopped, sautéed, plated and cleared dishes for late-breakfast or early-lunch din-ers and room service orders.

But Scott was nowhere among the crowds of work-ers. A young woman with spiked hair had assumed his place in front of the commercial dishwasher. Trying to hide her disappointment, Morgan made her way into the kitchen. When Gary saw her, a grin split his face. "Hey, girl," he said. "What brings you back here this morning? You looking for a job?"

She managed a smile and shook her head. "I was hoping to see Scott," she said.

"He hasn't come in yet, and we could really use the

help. We got behind, what with dealing with the cops and all." His sunny expression clouded. "I can't believe those clowns. They practically accused me of poisoning that man. As if I would do something like that."

"So he *was* poisoned?" She moved to join him in front of the massive commercial range, where he sautéed mounds of chopped vegetables in a large skillet.

"Cyanide." Gary's eyes widened. "Can you believe? Nasty stuff."

"That is bad." And it explained why Monsieur Demetrie had perished so quickly. "Say, Gary, do you know how I can get in touch with Scott? Where he lives or a phone number or anything?"

"Sorry, sweetie, I don't." He added the contents of a measuring cup to the skillet and clouds of fragrant steam momentarily obscured his face. "I don't ask too many questions about the people who work for me," he said. "It's usually better that way."

That was probably why Scott had been drawn to kitchen work, she thought. He'd always been a very private person, and more so since his diagnosis.

"You have good timing," Gary said, looking over her shoulder. "Look who just walked in."

She turned in time to see Scott tying on a big white apron. He didn't glance in her direction—or at anyone else, for that matter, but moved to the sink and began rinsing the pile of dishes there.

She hurried to his side. "Hi, Scott," she said softly, afraid of frightening him away.

He cut his eyes in her direction and quickly looked away.

"It's good to see you," she said. He looked the same as he always had—thin and wiry, a bicyclist's body even two years after he'd stopped competing. "How have you been?"

"Okay." She waited for him to ask about her or their father and stepmother, but he didn't.

"I've missed you," she said. "Dad and Nicole miss you, too. I'd love it if you'd come home with me for a visit."

He jerked his head back and forth, almost violently. "No. Won't go back."

"You don't have to do anything you don't want to do," she said. "But why wouldn't you want to come home, just for a visit? To let Dad and Nicole know you're okay."

"I'm not supposed to go home. The demons tell me not to."

"Aw, honey." She stroked his arm. "We can find some new medication that will shut those demons up for good. Drugs without all the side effects you had problems with before."

He set his mouth in a stubborn line and said nothing, focusing on the dishes.

She tried another tack. "What brought you to Denver?" she asked.

"I came for the race."

"That's good. Have you seen some friends while you're here?"

"Some." His expression grew more troubled. "They're all busy. Still racing. I think it was a bad idea for me to come. I should leave."

"Please don't go before we've had a chance to catch up." She tried not to sound as desperate as she felt. If she talked to him longer, reminded him of how close

they had been, maybe she could convince him to ignore
the voices in his head and listen to her instead.

He switched off the water and turned to her, looking her in the eye for the first time. "What were you
doing with that guy last night?" he asked. "The guy
with the gun."

"I was looking for you."

"Why? Do you think I did something wrong? I
didn't." He flinched, clearly agitated, and began shaking his head again.

"I know that. You wouldn't do anything wrong. I
just wanted to see you. Because you're my brother and
I love you."

"That guy had a gun," he said.

She debated whether to tell Scott that Luke was a
law enforcement officer. Would that frighten him even
more? "He was looking for the man who was taking
out the trash," she said. "Are you a friend of his?" Her
stomach knotted as she waited for his answer.

"Danny?" He shook his head, then nodded. "I mean,
I didn't really know him. I ran into him in London. He
was watching the race. A fan, you know?"

"So he likes racing, too. That's something you have
in common."

"But we're not friends or anything. He scares me."

He switched on the water again and reached for a
dirty plate.

"Why does he scare you?" she asked. "Did he
threaten you or try to hurt you?"

"He put something on one of the plates last night.
He didn't think anyone saw him, but I did. And when
he looked around and saw me watching, he made a really mean face. It scared me."

"Hey, sweetie, I'm sorry to break this up, but you're gonna have to go." Gary joined them by the sink. "We're getting ready for the lunch rush and I need Scott to speed it up on washing these dishes."

She started to protest but thought better of it. She didn't want to get on Gary's bad side. "Okay, I'll go now." She pulled a business card from her pocket and scribbled the name of her hotel, her room number and her cell number on the back. "Come see me after you get off, okay?" she said, slipping the card into the back pocket of Scott's jeans. "We'll have dinner and just talk. Okay?"

He nodded, head down over the sink.

She wished he would look at her so she could see that he really meant to stop by later. But he clearly didn't intend to look up, and she could feel Gary growing impatient. She patted Scott's shoulder. "See you later."

She stopped at the door and glanced back at him. He'd looked up from the sink and was watching her. The haunted look in his eyes made her want to cry out and rush to his side to comfort him. But she knew doing so would only make him retreat further into his shell. So she settled for a brave smile and a wave, then hurried away, blinking back the tears that stung her eyes.

LUKE'S FACE STILL burned from the tongue-lashing he'd endured from Blessing when he finally exited the conference room. Fury churned his stomach and knotted his fists. He didn't know whether he was more upset with Blessing, the photographer who'd snagged the damning photo, Morgan for interfering with his case or himself, for getting involved in such a mess.

Travis caught up with him at the elevators. "What happened in there?" he asked.

Luke shoved both hands in his pockets. "I'm off the case."

Travis had the grace to look stunned. "Why?"

"Did you see the paper?"

"The picture of you and Morgan? Yeah. Some photographer's idea of being cute."

"Blessing is hot under the collar about it. Says I jeopardized the case, endangered a civilian. He's pulling me off."

"Off the team?"

"No." At least the commander hadn't gone that far. "He's shifting me to tracking down leads on the terrorist cell, trying to find a connection."

"Maybe you'll have better luck than we've had. Our guy has vanished, and Blessing isn't the only one losing patience."

"All the more reason why I should be out pursuing our suspect. I was the closest to him. I got the best look."

"You'll still be in the loop, so you can help us," Travis said. "Will you see Morgan again?"

"I still have a lot of unanswered questions for her." The elevator arrived and he stepped on. Alone after the doors closed, those questions played on an endless loop in his head. Was Morgan spinning a crazy lie for him? Were she and her brother somehow tied up in terrorist activity? Was she using him to keep tabs on the investigation?

The pain when she'd talked about her missing brother had felt so real to him. It was the same pain he felt when he thought of Mark. But was he letting his emotions interfere with logic? The other team members didn't have any trouble thinking of Morgan as a suspect—why couldn't he reclaim that same objectivity?

As if his thoughts had summoned her, when he stepped off the elevator, Morgan was standing there, waiting to get on. She grabbed his arm, practically vibrating with excitement. "I saw Scott," she said. "I talked to him. He agreed to have dinner with me after he gets off tonight."

Out of the corner of his eye he spotted Cameron, in line at the lobby coffee shop. He hadn't seen Luke yet, but all he had to do was turn his head to spot him talking with a woman the rest of them hadn't ruled out as a suspect. Luke hurried her out of sight, around the corner. "We need to go somewhere we can talk," he said. "Somewhere private."

"Have you found out something? Something about Scott? Or about Danny?"

"I'll tell you what I can when we're alone." He scanned the area. Any minute now, Blessing himself might walk around the corner and see them.

"All right," she said. "Do you want to come to my hotel? We'll have plenty of privacy in my room."

He knew she didn't mean anything illicit in the invitation, so why did his mind go immediately to images of them sharing a bed? As if that was the only reason two adults might be alone in a hotel room in the middle of the day. "All right," he said. "Lead the way."

LUKE SAID NOTHING on the walk over to Morgan's hotel, and as they rode the elevator up to her floor, he kept his eyes focused on the door in front of them. His silence and his refusal to look at her made the distance between them seem much greater than the few inches that physically separated them.

She led the way down the hall to her room, aware of his muffled tread on the carpeting behind her. "This is it," she said, stopping in front of the door, nerves making her hand shake as she slid her key card into the lock. She'd felt so at ease with Luke last night, but something had happened to change that. Not knowing what that something was made her uneasy.

Inside, she was relieved to see that the maid service had made the bed and provided fresh towels. Being here alone with Luke was awkward enough without an unmade bed to taunt them. And why did hotel rooms never have adequate seating? With only one chair, one of them was going to have to sit on the bed.

It didn't help when Luke took the Do Not Disturb sign and hung it on the doorknob. "I don't want any interruptions," he said.

A hot tremor raced up her spine at the words, as if her body insisted on seeing this meeting as a passionate tryst even though her mind knew differently. She backed toward the bed but didn't sit. "Is something wrong?" she asked.

"Why would you think something was wrong?" His words were clipped, his tone bitter.

"You're acting strange," she said. "As if you're angry at me."

"I'm angry at you. And at myself. And at pretty much everyone else involved in this whole fiasco of a case." He raked one hand through his hair and looked around the room, as if searching for something to punch.

"What's wrong?" She did sit then, her legs too shaky to support her. "What's happened?"

"I've been pulled off the case. I'm lucky I wasn't sent back to Washington, or to Timbuktu."

She had trouble breathing, and it was a moment before she could speak. "Pulled off the case? Why?"

The grieved look in his eyes wounded her. "You don't know? You can't guess?"

"Was it because I interfered with your capturing the terrorist?" The memory of that made her stomach hurt. "I feel terrible about that, but I didn't know—"

"Have you seen today's paper?"

She shook her head, confused.

He strode to the laptop set up on her desk and stabbed at the keys. After a moment, he angled the screen toward her.

She stared at the image that filled the screen, of them clinging together, bodies melded, lips joined. Her body responded with the same heat and intense desire she had felt in his arms, sensuous and visceral. Then the realization of what he was showing snapped her back to the present. "Someone took our picture? Why?"

"I thought maybe you knew."

"No, I... That was in the paper?"

"Front page. Love Amidst the Chaos." His scowl chilled her.

"I had no idea..."

"You swear you didn't know anything about this?" He jabbed his finger at the screen.

"Of course not. What? Do you think I arranged for someone to take our picture? Why would I do that?"

"You must have photographer friends. If you thought I was getting too close to information you didn't want me to have, you might use this kind of publicity to get me pulled from the case."

"Excuse me, but I don't recall holding a gun to your head and forcing you to kiss me. And what do you mean, 'information I didn't want you to have'? What are you talking about?"

"I'm talking about the way your involvement in this case looks when I lay out the facts."

She folded her arms across her chest. It was either that or give in to the urge to slap him. But she wasn't the slapping kind. "What facts are those?"

"When I went into the hotel kitchen last night to ask questions, you insisted on coming with me. Your brother, who you claim not to have seen for months, just happens to be there." He paced the narrow space between the bed and desk, ticking off his reasons on his fingers. "You say you didn't even notice the other man who was there, the one who tried to shoot me, but your pushing me out of the way allowed him to get away—and your brother with him. When I returned from searching for them last night, you just happened to be waiting to find out what I knew. And that kiss we shared got me pulled from the case, so I'm no longer part of the search for your brother or our other suspect."

"You're forgetting one very important *fact*. You're the one who approached me first. I came here to write a story for a magazine and the next thing I know, an FBI agent is following me. How, exactly, do you think I arranged for that to happen?"

Some of the stiffness went out of his posture. "Maybe you only saw your chance after I approached you."

"Right. Because, obviously, I'm a criminal genius. Then how about this? My brother really has been missing for ten months. You can check the missing person's report in Austin. Or talk to my parents, who are beside themselves because they haven't known where their son is. Or you could talk to Scott's doctors."

"You and your brother could have planned this all ahead of time." But even he didn't sound that convinced of the words.

"Fine. You believe all the lies you want to. But I'm not the one with the problem here—you are." She jabbed her finger at his chest. "Your trouble is you don't trust anyone."

"I've learned not to trust people. My line of work teaches us that trust is dangerous."

"Everything I did—all those *facts* you think are so incriminating—I did to protect my brother. If you had a brother, you'd understand."

"I do have a brother. And I understand more than you know." The weight of emotion behind his words froze her. She studied his face: aged by grief, the sadness in his eyes the same she saw in the faces of her parents and in her own reflection when she looked in the mirror during unguarded moments.

She carefully lowered herself to the bed once more, her outrage receding in the face of his sorrow, and patted the place beside her. "Tell me about your brother," she said.

He sat and leaned forward, elbows on his knees, head bowed. "His name is Mark. We're twins—fraternal, not identical. He's a physicist at the University of Colorado in Boulder. Or he was before he disappeared."

"Oh." The cry escaped her before she could repress it. "How long has he been missing?"

"Almost a year now. He went on a solo hike in the mountains and never came back. When search parties didn't find him, local authorities assumed he'd fallen or

gotten lost and perished. Others suggested he committed suicide. His wife had been killed in a car accident
six months before and he was still grieving for her."

"But you don't believe that." She touched his arm,
wanting to comfort him. More than one cop had suggested her brother had gone away somewhere to kill
himself.

Luke straightened. "No, I don't. For one thing, he
has a little girl he adored. Mindy is five. After his wife
Christy's death, she became even more important to
Mark. He would never have deliberately left her an orphan."

"Where is she now?"

"She lives with her godmother, Christy's sister. She
doesn't believe her father is dead, either. She told Susan,
her aunt, that she has dreams about him, and that she
knows he's going to come back to her."

Her hand tightened around his arm and she tried to
force down the lump in her throat.

"There's another reason I believe he's still alive,"
Luke said. "After he disappeared, I found out he'd been
receiving threats."

"What kind of threats?"

"Vague ones. Some of them threatened him, some
targeted Christy. They said harm would come to her if
he didn't cooperate." He shook his head. "I don't know
why he didn't tell me about them. Maybe he thought
knowing would put me in danger, but I could have in-
vestigated. I had all the resources of the Bureau at my
disposal."

"Were you able to find out anything more after he
was gone?" she asked.

"No. Although some of the messages seemed to suggest that Christy's death might not have been the accident it seemed. I tried to look into that, but I didn't get very far."

"Do you think he was kidnapped?" *Or murdered?* She didn't say those last words out loud. She wouldn't add to his burden.

"I think so. The worst thing is, I might have been in a position to stop it—or at least to find the people who did it." He turned to her, anguish written on his face. "I dropped him off at the trailhead the morning he set out on his hike. There was another car already there, with two men also getting ready to hit the trail. If I'd paid more attention—if I'd taken even a few more seconds to memorize their faces—I might be able to find them now."

"Don't do that," she said, her voice sharper than she'd intended.

"Do what?"

"Don't beat yourself up that way. I've done it and it doesn't do anything but make you feel worse. It doesn't help your brother. How many times do you think I've replayed my last visit with Scott over and over in my head? Why didn't I see how unhappy he was? Why didn't I offer to help him? Why didn't I find him the answers he needed? But none of us are mind readers. We can't see the future. Neither one of us had any way of knowing what would happen."

"You're right." He covered her hand with his. "Thanks for understanding. And I'm sorry I went off on you earlier. I shouldn't have taken my frustrations with the case out on you."

She gently slipped her hand from beneath his. For a moment she'd forgotten the rift between them and felt the closeness that had drawn her to him in the first place. "I guess I'd rather know you have doubts about me than be unsure of your feelings."

"No." He captured her hand in his once more. "Laying everything out like that helped me see the holes in any theory I might have had about you being part of this. I would have come to the same conclusion, eventually, if I'd been thinking clearly."

"But your colleagues still think I'm suspect."

"Right now, we're all in the mode of checking out any lead, no matter how tenuous, in hopes of finding a way to our suspect. We don't want more lives lost in another act of terrorism." He released her again. "I really need to talk to your brother, to find out anything at all he might know about this Danny character. Do you think you could persuade him to talk to me?"

"Maybe." She shifted, torn between protecting Scott and helping Luke. But somehow, in the past forty-eight hours, her feelings had grown to the point where she didn't think she could keep anything important from him. "He told me he knew Danny from before. Not well, but he said he'd run into him in London."

"Was he calling himself Danny there, too? Did Scott say what he was doing there?"

"He said Danny was a race fan, but I don't know how much interaction they had. Scott was at work, so we couldn't talk long. But he promised to come to my room after he got off work tonight so we could talk."

"I could question him."

"No. You'll scare him off. He's really suspicious of strangers."

"You could tell him I was a friend of yours."

She smiled. "He picked up on the fact that we were

together. I couldn't tell if he liked that or not. He's always been protective of me. But I'll try to persuade him to at least meet you. There's something else he told me—something that might be even more important to your case."

"What's that?"

"He said he saw Danny put something in the food on one of the plates last night, right before it went out to the servers."

"What did he put in there?"

"Scott didn't say. He said Danny saw him watching, though, and threatened him. Scott was really frightened, so that's something else that points to them not working together."

"Then it's even more important that I talk to Scott. We need to persuade him to let us bring him into protective custody."

"Custody? Why? He hasn't done anything wrong."

"No. But if the suspect knows that Scott could testify against him in this poisoning case, your brother could be in real danger."

She put her hand to her chest, pressing down on the stab of pain there, then realized she had stopped breathing. She struggled to take a breath, her heart hammering. "You think Danny might harm him?"

"If the man doesn't have any qualms about hurting dozens of innocent people with a bomb or poisoning a race official, he wouldn't blink at getting rid of a dishwasher he thought might cause him trouble." He put his arm around her and pulled her close. "I don't mean to frighten you. We'll do everything we can to protect your brother, but he has to cooperate with us."

She nodded, grateful for the strength of his arm

around her. "I'll talk to him. I'll try to make him see how important it is to trust us."

His phone vibrated, making her jump. He slipped the device from his pocket and glanced at the screen. "I have to take this," he said, and stood.

She rose, also, and went to the laptop, closing the window with the picture of her and Luke kissing, but not before studying it a moment longer. That had been such an intense, private moment. She felt a little violated, having their shared passion exposed to the world. All because some photographer thought it would make a nice—or maybe titillating?—contrast to the other scenes of violence on the page.

Luke grabbed her arm, startling her. "We've got to get over to the hotel kitchen right away," he said.

"What? Why?" She tried to resist as he tugged her toward the door.

"That call was from Travis. He just got word that one of the dishwashers is brandishing a knife, threatening to use it if anyone comes near him."

# Chapter Six

Travis met Luke and Morgan outside the kitchen after they'd rushed down the street and worked their way through a gauntlet of press, hotel employees and local cops. "What's going on?" Luke asked.

"One of the kitchen help, a dishwasher, lost it. He's holed up in an alcove by the sinks, brandishing a knife and threatening to cut anyone who comes near him."

Morgan clutched Luke's hand and let out a soft moan. He stayed focused on Travis but squeezed her hand to let her know he was aware of her distress. "Do you have a name on this guy?" he asked.

"Scott. Is that the guy who ran with the suspect last night?"

"He ran the same time as the suspect, not with him," Luke said.

"Scott is my brother," Morgan said. She was pale, but her voice was steady and she'd let go of Luke's hand. "I can get him to calm down, I'm sure."

"Has he ever done anything like this before?" Luke asked.

She worried her bottom lip between her teeth, then gave one quick jerk of her head. "Once. Before he was diagnosed. Not with a knife, but a couple of years ago, he barricaded himself behind a table in a pizza place where he used to hang out. He had a pool cue and told everyone they had to stay away."

"What happened then?" Travis asked.

"I convinced him to come out. The local cops—guys he knew—took him to a hospital. That's where he was diagnosed."

Travis glanced toward the closed kitchen door. "There are a couple of local officers in there with him now. I told them we had someone coming who might be able to help, so I think they'll let you talk to him, but it's their call."

Luke put a hand at her back. "I'll go in with you. If you can convince him to put the knife down and cooperate, he'll have to go to the hospital again." He didn't mention the possibility of custody and criminal charges; in any case, that wasn't his decision to make.

"The best thing for him would be to get help and medication," she said.

Luke nodded to Travis. "I think we're ready."

Inside the kitchen, they were met by a young woman in a black pantsuit and an older man with the build of a former football player. They introduced themselves as Lieutenant Litchfield and Detective Young of the Denver PD. "Detective Young is one of our hostage negotiators," Litchfield said.

"Does he have a hostage?" Morgan's voice carried a note of panic.

"Thankfully, no." Detective Young's hazel eyes assessed Morgan. "I'm here to try to talk him into putting down the knife and coming with us quietly," she said.

"This is Morgan Westfield," Luke said. "She's the young man's sister. She believes he'll listen to her and cooperate."

"Any idea what brought this on?" Litchfield asked. "Does he have a history of this kind of behavior?"

"He was diagnosed two years ago with schizophrenia." Morgan kept her gaze focused at the back of the kitchen, though the sink area wasn't visible from where they were standing. "He hears voices and gets upset about things sometimes. Please, let me talk to him."

"All right," Detective Young said. "But don't get too close until he agrees to put down the knife. We don't want this to turn into a hostage situation." She led them toward the back of the room. They turned a corner and the alcove came into view.

Scott crouched on the floor in front of the big sink, one arm hugging his knees. In his free hand, he clutched a chef's knife. His head jerked up at their approach, and he waved the knife, though he remained on the floor. "Don't come any closer!" His voice was high-pitched and agitated.

"It's me, Scott. Morgan." She bent over, leaning toward him. "I just want to talk to you."

"Go away!" he shouted.

"I will, if you really want me to. But, first, tell me what's wrong." Morgan's voice was gentle, full of sympathy.

"I just want people to leave me alone," Scott said. His face was angled toward her, his gaze unfocused, his eyes darting and fearful.

"Who is bothering you?" Morgan asked.

"Everyone. They keep looking at me and saying things."

"Is it the devils, Scott? Are they bothering you?"

He pressed his lips together and shook his head, then nodded.

"I think we can make them stop," Morgan said. She took a step toward her brother. Luke tried to pull her back, but she shook him off. "If you'll put down the knife and come with me, I promise to help."

"No. Don't come any closer."

She froze as he waved the knife. Luke kept his hands at his sides, poised to retrieve her if necessary. "You know I would never hurt you," Morgan said. "And I'd never let anyone else hurt you."

"Who's that?" Suddenly alert, Scott glared at Luke and jabbed the knife in his direction.

"That's my friend Luke. He wants to help you, too."

"He has a gun."

Detective Young gave Luke a questioning look, but he ignored her.

"Luke only uses his gun to hunt bad guys," Morgan said. "He knows you're not a bad guy."

He wished he did know that. For her sake, at least.

"Bad guy. Bad guy. Bad guy," Scott droned.

Morgan glanced back at them, beautiful even in her anguish. "Maybe I'd better take over," Detective Young said. She started to step forward, but Morgan waved her away.

"Just give me a minute more," she said. She looked back at Scott. "I was thinking about you the other day," she said.

Scott said nothing and gave no indication he'd even heard her. She took a step closer. "I was remembering when we were kids. Do you remember the neighbor we had—the old man who was so mean to all us kids?"

"Mr. Invin."

"That's right. We all waited for the school bus on the corner by his house and he was always accusing us of throwing trash in his yard and riding our bikes across his grass."

"And picking his pears," Scott said.

"Do you remember the time you were eating a pear while we waited for the bus and he accused you of picking it off his tree?"

Scott grinned, his face transformed. Luke could almost see the young boy he had been. "I brought the pear from home just to mess with him. He had such a fit. He said he was going to report me to the police."

"And then on the way home from school, you came up with the idea that we should pick all his pears," she said.

"We waited until after midnight, then went over there and picked every single pear off that tree. Then we waited at the bus stop the next morning to see what his reaction would be. He was furious! I was half afraid he'd have a heart attack, he was so stomping mad. He ran out there and started shouting about how we'd stolen all his pears." He laughed, a childish giggle. "I'll never forget the look on his face when I said, 'Do you mean all those pears on your front porch?' He turned around and there they all were, bags and bags that we'd picked and put there for him."

"He left us alone after that," Morgan said. "We made a great team, didn't we?" By this time, she was almost within striking distance of her brother. Luke tried not to focus on the sharpened blade, gleaming under the bright lights. "You know, I'm always on your side," she said. "I want to help you."

"You can't help," he said, all the joy gone from his face. "No one can."

"You have to let me try. It's in the sister handbook."

His smile was sad. "There's no such thing."

"Then maybe I ought to write one. I'll be sure to put that in."

Much of the tension had gone out of his body. "What are you going to do?"

She sat down, cross-legged, on the floor a few feet away from him. "Put down the knife and we'll both talk to some people who can help," she said. "New doctors who know about new medications. Ones that don't have the side effects you hated so much before."

"What kind of medications?"

While brother and sister talked medication and treatment options, Detective Young leaned over and whispered to Luke. "She'd make a good negotiator. She's good at defusing the situation."

"Unfortunately, she's had practice," he said.

"That's the thing about mental illness," Young said. "All the person's family and friends become victims, too."

A clatter drew their attention. Scott had dropped the knife and risen to his feet. Morgan stood also and went to her brother and hugged him. She said something to him and he nodded, then she turned to Luke and Young. "We're ready to go to the hospital," she said.

"We've got an ambulance waiting out back," Young said.

The three of them started toward the door to the alley, where they were joined by two uniformed officers. Scott halted in the door and turned to Luke. He looked more lucid now, though still agitated. "I ran away last night because I don't like gunshots," he said. "They scared me."

"I'm sorry I upset you," Luke said. "I wasn't shooting at you."

"I saw Danny after I left here. He said if I told anybody about what I'd seen him do, he'd kill me."

"Oh, Scott." Morgan clutched at her brother's arm.

*What did you see him do?* Luke wanted to ask. He needed to hear the accusation against Danny in Scott's own words. But he knew he would have to wait for the answer to question the young man further. He didn't want to risk upsetting Scott again. "Thank you for telling me that," he said. But there was one question he had to ask. "Where did you see him? I can pick him up and stop him before he hurts anyone else."

Scott shook his head, his expression clouded again. "I promised not to tell. He's a bad guy. A bad guy. A bad guy…"

An EMT opened the door to the ambulance. Morgan helped Luke inside, then started to step in after him, but one of the officers motioned her aside. "We can follow in my car," Luke said, as the second officer stepped up into the ambulance.

"All right." Morgan stepped back. "I'll be there as soon as I can, Scott," she called.

Luke moved to her side. "I'll drive you to the hospital," he said.

"Are you sure? I know you have so much work to do."

"I want to make sure you're all right, first."

"I doubt you'll get to question Scott today," she said.

"I'm not concerned about Scott right now." Not really. If the young man could tell him anything useful—and that was doubtful—he'd find out soon enough. Right now, Morgan needed someone to look after her. He was making that his job.

MORGAN HUNCHED OVER the laptop, reviewing Wednesday's blog for *Cycling Pro*.

The second stage of the race brought the challenges of 8700-foot McClure Pass and 9,900-foot Kebler Pass before a steep descent into the town of Crested Butte, where crowds lined the streets to welcome racers. I spoke with US Team Amgen leader Andy Sprague by phone at the close of yesterday's race. "This is a race that starts off challenging the riders right away," he said. "But conditions have been prime so far and the fans have been incredible."

Prerace favorite Victor Vinko of Spain's Team Contador suffered a nasty crash near the top of Kebler, tangling with team member Roberto Sandoval after losing control on a rough stretch of road. No word yet on whether Vinko and Sandoval will return to the race.

At the end of Stage Two, British racer Ian McDaniel of Team Sky is the surprise leader, having pulled out a superb effort just ahead of the American peloton. The Americans hope to reclaim the yellow jersey tomorrow, when racers navigate 155 kilometers — approximately 96 miles — between Gunnison and Monarch Mountain, including 11,312 foot Monarch Pass, where the weather forecast is calling for rain and possibly snow.

She finished reading and turned to Scott, who sat on the edge of the hospital bed, facing her. His shoulders slumped and he wore the blank expression of someone whose emotions were subdued under a fog of medication. But at least he no longer trembled or raged, as he had when they'd brought him into the psychiatric unit two days ago. "What do you think?" she asked.

"If those guys think Kebler Pass was tough, wait until they see Monarch this afternoon. It's two thousand feet higher, switchback after switchback."

"I meant about the article—though I think you're probably right about the race. I wouldn't even want to drive that pass, much less ride up it on a bicycle. What do you think of McDaniel's chances? You knew him in London, didn't you?"

He nodded, his expression unreadable.

She reached out and stroked his arm through the soft sweatshirt she'd brought him to wear instead of hospital scrubs. "I know you miss it," she said. "Racing." The doctors had encouraged her to talk to him about what he was feeling and experiencing. Learning to be more open about whatever was going on in his head was part of his healing.

He looked at her for so long without speaking she wondered if she'd made him angry. But finally he licked his lips and said, "I don't miss the pain or the training or the strict diet, but, yeah, I miss race days. I miss being good at something."

"You're a good photographer."

"There are a lot of good photographers out there. There aren't a lot of good racers."

She turned back to the computer. "I'm going to send this, unless you can think of something else I should add." The two of them had watched the coverage of yesterday's stage on the television in the unit's community room. Only one man had complained about their choice of television show, and an aid had escorted him to another area after a few moments.

Someone tapped on the door frame of the room and a male aide stuck his head in. "How are you this morning, Mr. Westfield?" he asked.

"I'm okay."

"You have an appointment with Dr. Chandra in the therapy room at eleven," the aide said. "We don't want to keep him waiting."

"We don't?" But Scott stood.

"I'll stop back by in about ten minutes to take you down there," the aide said, and left.

Morgan stood and began to pack away her laptop. "I'll see you this afternoon. We'll watch the wrap-up of the third stage together."

"You don't have to spend all your time here babysitting me," Scott said.

"I want to be with you." She was still managing to get her work done while he consulted various doctors and attended therapy sessions. At night, she returned to her hotel too exhausted to worry too much about Scott's future.

"What about your boyfriend?" The smirk reminded her of the old Scott—the teasing older brother.

"He's not my boyfriend. He's just a friend."

"Right. Since when do friends make you blush like that?"

She put a hand to her hot cheek. "There's nothing between us." She had thought there might be, but she hadn't seen Luke since he'd delivered her to the hospital

Tuesday evening. He'd called once while she was with Scott and left a message that he'd see her soon, but that was it. She didn't blame him for keeping his distance. Her brother's problems would scare off plenty of men, but she wasn't about to turn her back on Scott for the sake of romance. "He's very busy with work," she said.

Scott scowled. "Cop work."

"He's trying to find the person or group of people who've been setting off bombs at races," she said.

"And he thinks I had something to do with that."

"Of course not!"

"Don't lie to me. You're lousy at it." He shoved both hands into the pockets of his sweatpants. "Besides, I know the score by now. Always blame the crazy person."

"Don't say that. You're not crazy." She hated the word and all the implications that went with it.

"All right. I'm sick. Damaged."

Those words were even worse. "Sick people can get well," she said. "Damage can be repaired. You're doing well on the new meds, aren't you?"

He shrugged. "It's only been two days."

"But you're doing well. And you'll do even better."

"Are they going to let me out of here tomorrow? It's a mandatory three-day hold, right? That's over tomorrow."

"Seventy-two hours, yes." The maximum time they could legally hold someone for psychiatric observation. After that, would Scott be free to go? No charges had been filed—she wondered if she had Luke to thank for that. "I think you should wait and hear what your doctor has to say," she said. "If he clears you for outpatient treatment you can come stay with me. Or Dad and Nicole would love to see you."

"I talked to them on the phone last night. Nicole cried. Dad sounded like he was going to."

"They've been so worried about you." She'd called them from the hospital waiting room on Tuesday night. They'd been thrilled to hear she'd found Scott, but heartbroken to learn the circumstances and that he was back in the hospital. They'd agreed to wait and see him when he was able to travel back to Texas, trusting Morgan to take care of things in Denver.

"I don't think I could take their hovering over me," Scott said. "Like I was some toddler who was in danger of wandering out in the street. I can take care of myself."

"We'll work something out."

The scowl returned. "Little sister swooping in to save the day. Except you can't always do that."

The aide returned. "Ready for your appointment, Mr. Westfield?"

Morgan slung her laptop bag over her shoulder and kissed Scott's cheek. "I'll see you this afternoon."

"Don't feel obligated."

"I have to watch the races anyway. It's part of my job. It's more fun to watch them with you. You give me the insider's point of view."

"My opinion today is that the US team is going to take the yellow jersey again. They've got an advantage in this altitude."

"You'd make a good race analyst," she said.

"Right. People are lining up to hire me." He turned and left with the aide, but his words had sparked an idea in Morgan's head.

What if someone did hire Scott to analyze or provide commentary for bike races? As a former racer, he had the knowledge, and when he was well, he was very well-spoken and charming. It wouldn't hurt for her to call a few people she knew and talk to them. Maybe one of them would give him a tryout.

Excited by the possibilities, she hurried to her car. She was crossing the parking lot when her cell phone rang. "Ms. Westfield?" a woman's terse voice asked.

"Yes?" She shifted her laptop bag and juggled the phone and her car keys.

"This is Nurse Adkins. Could you please return to your brother's room?"

She dropped the keys, and almost dropped the phone. "Is something wrong? Is everything all right?"

"He's very agitated and he keeps asking for you."

"I'll be right there." She pocketed the phone, retrieved her keys and raced back into the hospital. What had happened to upset Scott in the few minutes since she'd left him? She pressed the up button for the elevator and waited, arms crossed, feet tapping. What was taking so long? Scott was on the ninth floor, or she would have risked the stairs.

At last, the bell dinged and the doors slid open. She had to step aside to allow an aide with a stretcher to exit, followed by an elderly man. She forced herself to be patient as he moved slowly after the stretcher, head down, taking short, shuffling steps. He took so long the elevator started to close behind him. She lunged for the door, catching it just in time and slipping inside. Then began the slow crawl upward, the car stopping on almost every floor.

When they reached the ninth floor, she burst from

the car and raced for Scott's room, skidding in the door, but the sight that greeted her made her stop short.

A large male orderly and a nurse who was almost as big leaned over the hospital bed where Scott lay. He thrashed against the restraints that held him and screamed obscenities, his face twisted in rage. The nurse looked over her shoulder as Morgan entered the room. "Speak to him," she said.

Morgan moved carefully to Scott's side and raised her voice to be heard over his shouts. "Scott! It's me, Morgan! It's going to be okay. Tell me what's wrong."

He quieted and stared up at her, eyes wide with fear, straining against the straps that held him to the bed. "I saw him," he said, his voice hoarse.

"Saw who?" she asked.

He flicked his gaze to the nurse, then pressed his lips together and shook his head.

Morgan turned to the nurse, fighting back rage at seeing her brother treated like some kind of animal. "Why do you have him restrained? What happened?"

Morgan's anger didn't faze the nurse. "He was on his way to the treatment room to see Dr. Chandra and he suddenly became very agitated," she said. "He tried to run away. When Carlos tried to calm him down, Mr. Westfield took a swing at him." She turned to the med tray on the table beside the bed. "His doctor has ordered a sedative to calm him down."

Morgan suppressed a shudder at the sight of the syringe. "Let me talk to him first, please." Not waiting for an answer, she leaned over Scott's stiff but now silent form. "What happened to upset you?" she asked, her hand on his shoulder.

"I saw him," he whispered, so softly she could scarcely make out the words.

"Saw who?"

"It was just one of the orderlies." The aide—his name tag read Carlos—spoke. "We passed him in the hall."

Her eyes met Scott's and he shook his head, though whether in denial or warning she couldn't tell.

"Which orderly?" she asked.

"One of the temps from the agency. Ricky or Rick—something like that. He walked past us, carrying a bag of dirty laundry, and your brother flipped. Started shouting that he had to get away."

"You have to get me out of here," Scott pleaded, and began straining at his bindings once more.

"That's enough, Mr. Westfield." The nurse took hold of his arm and inserted the needle. When she finished giving the injection, her eyes met Morgan's, but there was no warmth there. "That will calm him down."

Morgan realized any protest she made at this point was useless. "May I stay with him until he goes to sleep?" she asked.

"All right." Nurse Adkins picked up the medication tray. "Leave the door open and call if you need anything."

She and Carlos left. Morgan sat on the edge of the bed and stroked Scott's hand. "They don't believe me," he said. "No one believes me."

"I believe you. Why did seeing the orderly upset you? Did he do something to hurt you earlier?"

He turned his face to the wall. "It's all right," she said. "You can tell me. I'll do anything I can to help you."

"It was Danny," he said.

She blinked, not sure she'd heard him correctly at first. "What did you say?"

He looked at her once more, the sedative already beginning to relax his features and slur his words. "It was Danny," he said. "He was coming to get me." Then his eyes closed, and he slipped into unconsciousness.

# Chapter Seven

"Carmichael and I checked out the address where we got the tip about suspicious activity, but whoever was living there is long gone." Luke leaned back against his car, phone pressed close to his ear to shut out the sounds of passing traffic. A beep alerted him to another incoming call, but he ignored it.

"Did you talk to the neighbors? Business owners? The landlord?" Blessing barked the questions in rapid fire.

"We did. And no one knows anything. The landlord says the man he spoke to was named Smith. He paid three months' rent in advance, in cash, and he never saw him after that. The people who actually lived in the house—a woman and two men—were quiet, kept to themselves and didn't cause trouble. He thought their last name was Brown, but he wasn't sure."

"Any description?"

"Nothing we can use. According to the neighbors, both the men were average height and the woman was a little shorter. One of the men was balding. The woman was either a blonde or had light red hair, depending on who you talk to. One of the men wore glasses—sometimes. Are you sure the tip was legit?"

"They were getting mail from a contact we've been watching for a while and one of the men—whose name isn't Brown, but Brainard—visited a local machine shop and asked a lot of questions about explosives. The owner of the shop was suspicious enough to call in a report."

The incoming call alert sounded again. Probably Travis wanting to go to lunch. "Then somebody must have tipped them off, because the place is clean," he said. "And nobody saw them leave, or remembered the license plate number on their car, or took any pictures, or anything useful."

"We've got a photo of Brainard. Not a great one, but it's a place to start. I'll send it to your phone and you can show it around, see if you get any better answers. And I want you to talk to the machine shop owner, too. Maybe he's remembered something he didn't tell the local police officer who did the initial interview."

"Will do." He squinted across the parking lot toward a giant sculpture of two lanky dancers—five-story-tall modified stick figures all in white. There was an image he didn't necessarily want stuck in his head, but it would be there now, along with the faces of his suspects, who had all disappeared, the cashier at the burger place where he'd stopped for lunch, and the doorman at the hotel where he'd dropped Agent Carmichael after their fruitless search for the suspected members of a terrorist cell who'd rented the duplex in Denver's Five Points neighborhood. "Any news of our other suspect?" he asked.

"He's gone underground again. We got the autopsy back on Tuesday. Definitely cyanide poisoning. We're starting to think this might be unrelated to the bombings. Terrorists usually aim for a bigger impact. They want to take a lot of people out, not just one. This poisoning doesn't fit the pattern."

"Scott Westfield told his sister he saw Danny put something in one of the entrées waiting to go out to the dining room," Luke said.

"You should have said something before now," Blessing said. "We'll send someone to question him."

"I already tried that," Luke said. "His doctor won't hear of it until the end of his seventy-two-hour hold."

"Do you think Westfield is telling the truth? Is he making it up to get attention, or maybe to throw suspicion off himself?"

"I don't know. But I'd like the chance to question him. He's met me and I think he'd be more relaxed around me." He didn't know any such thing, but he thought it sounded plausible.

"I don't like it. Not given your relationship with his sister."

Luke stiffened. "Sir, there is no relationship." Not that he hadn't entertained the possibility, but the timing was lousy for both of them.

"Do you make a habit of kissing strangers on the street?" Blessing sounded almost amused.

Luke closed his eyes and suppressed a groan. He'd done his best to forget about that photograph. "There is no relationship," he repeated.

Again, the incoming call beep sounded. Luke ground his teeth together. *Go away*, he thought.

"I'll consider it," Blessing said. "In the meantime, see what you can get me on Brainard and company."

He ended the call and hit the symbol to check his missed calls. As he did so, the message alert popped up. *Morgan.* His heartbeat sped up when he saw her name on the screen. He punched the voice mail symbol and waited for the call to connect.

"You have one new message and three old messages," the mechanical voice intoned. "First old message..."

"Yeah, yeah, yeah." He clicked through the old messages. "First unheard message," the voice offered.

"Luke, please call me as soon as you get this message." Morgan spoke loudly, the words rushed together. "Scott saw Danny today. In the hospital. He's posing as an orderly, calling himself Rick or Ricky or something like that. Nobody believes him, but I know Scott's telling the truth. He's terrified and so am I. I'm staying with him until I hear from you."

He had his keys out and was starting the car by the time his call to Morgan connected. "Thank God, you called," she said, sounding out of breath. "The nurses made me leave Scott's room because morning visiting hours are over. I'm in a waiting room down the hall, but I can't see his room from here. Anyone could go in there. What if Danny tries to hurt him? He knows Scott saw him tampering with the food at the restaurant. What if he—?"

"Calm down. I'm on my way." He steered the car onto the street, past the giant dancers, toward the hospital where Scott was confined. "Have you contacted hospital security?"

"No. I didn't think they would believe me. The nurse and the other orderly didn't believe Scott. They think he's hallucinating or being paranoid. They wouldn't listen to me when I tried to talk to them, either."

"All right. As soon as I get off the phone with you, I'll call and talk to Security. Try to stay calm and I'll be there as soon as I can."

"All right. Thank you. Just talking to you makes me feel better."

The words pulled at something in his chest. "I'll see you soon." He ended the call, but instead of trying to find the number for hospital security, he called Special Agent in Charge Blessing. "Scott Westfield says he saw our suspect, Danny, at the hospital. The man is posing as an orderly and he threatened Westfield."

"Have you checked this out? Have you seen the orderly?"

"No, sir. I'm on my way to the hospital now."

"Luke, do I need to point out that Scott Westfield has a serious mental illness? He could be hallucinating all of this."

"He could be," Luke admitted. "But do we want to take a chance that he isn't?"

The only response for a long moment was silence. Luke pictured the team leader scowling across the desk, weighing his decision. "All right," Blessing said at last. "I'll send some men over there to check it out."

"You might alert hospital security. If they lock down the building now, we might be able to trap him."

"Do that, and we'll have the whole place in a panic. It's a hospital. If someone had a heart attack or a woman went into premature labor because they heard a terrorist was on the loose in the building, and it turns out to all be the delusion of a psychiatric patient, who do you think is going to get called on the carpet for it?"

"Sir—"

"You go down there and talk to Westfield. Assess the situation and come to me with some evidence that our suspect is there. Then I'll think about a lockdown."

"Yes, sir," he said, jaw clenched. He ended the call and took the exit for the hospital.

Inside the lobby, he headed for the reception desk. "I need to speak to hospital security," he said, and flashed his credentials. Wide-eyed, the receptionist pointed to a door behind her marked Security.

A stocky young man who didn't look to Luke as if he was old enough to order a beer looked up from behind a desk. On the wall to his right, an array of screens showed the parking lot, elevators and other areas of the hospital. "You've had a security breach in the psychiatric unit," Luke said.

"What?" The guard gaped at Luke. "Who are you? This is the first I've heard—"

"Luke Renfro, FBI." Luke showed his creds, then grabbed the guard by the arm. "Come with me. We might still have time to stop this."

The young man whose name badge read Cramer shook off Luke's hand but led the way to the elevators. He punched the button for nine, then turned to Luke. "What's this all about?"

"We have reason to believe one of the orderlies on the ninth floor is an imposter. He's a suspect, wanted for questioning in a case we're working on."

"Then why not just arrest him? Why all the drama?"

"He knows we're after him, so he's not likely to come willingly. He could be a very dangerous man."

"Huh." Cramer hooked his thumbs into his belt. "So what's he done?"

"He's threatened one of your patients, for one thing." The elevator doors opened. Luke scanned the hallway, then followed signs toward double doors. He tried the doors, but they didn't budge.

"They're kept locked," Cramer said, coming up behind him. "A nurse has to buzz you in." He pressed a button on an intercom beside the door. "Security. Open the doors, please."

A buzzer sounded and Cramer pushed open the doors. A tall, broad-shouldered nurse in pink scrubs met them on the other side. "Mr. Cramer, what is the meaning—"

"Agent Renfro, FBI," Luke interrupted. "Where is Scott Westfield's room?"

The nurse stared at Luke's badge and ID, but her expression only hardened. "You can't see him without permission from his doctor, no matter who you are."

"Luke!" Morgan hurried past the nurse to join him. "It's all right, Nurse Adkins," she said. "Agent Renfro is here to help."

"I don't care if he's Santa Claus or Saint Francis. Morning visiting hours are over and both of you need to leave," the nurse said.

"You've had a security breach," Luke said.

"We've had no such thing," the nurse said. She turned to Cramer. "Why did you bring him up here? It's against the rules and it's disrupting our schedule."

"He's FBI!" Cramer's expression grew as stubborn as hers. "I think that outranks either one of us."

"I'll show you where Scott's room is." Morgan took Luke's arm and pulled him down the hallway.

"You can't go in there," the nurse protested, but Luke pushed past her.

The room was a narrow cubicle with a chair, a rolling table and a hospital bed, where Scott slept on his back, his face slack. "He's sedated." Morgan smoothed the blanket over her brother's arm. "I don't know when he'll wake up."

Luke moved to her side and put his arm around her. She leaned against him, and he felt her gratitude at his presence without her having to say a word. "Tell me what happened," he said.

"I left to go back to my hotel and I hadn't even made it to my car when the nurse called to tell me Scott was freaking out. When I got here, they had him tied to the bed and were getting ready to sedate him. The aide said they'd passed an orderly in the hall and Scott freaked out. Scott told me the orderly was Danny, and that he made some kind of threat. And then the sedative took effect and he passed out."

"What did the aide say about the orderly?"

"That his name was Rick or Ricky and that he worked for a temp agency that supplies workers to the hospital. If Danny used a temp agency to get the job at the hotel, maybe he used the same ploy to get a job here. It wouldn't have been that hard to figure out that Scott was here, if he knew about the incident in the hotel kitchen and that this was where the city sends its psychiatric holds."

Luke squeezed her shoulder. "Give me a minute. I'm going to see what I can find out."

He left her and went to the nurses' station.

Nurse Adkins's expression was stern but professional. "What do you need now, Agent Renfro?"

"I need to talk to an orderly—Rick or Ricky."

Adkins looked over his shoulder and called to a passing aide. "Carlos, find Ricky and bring him here, please."

The intercom buzzed and the nurse answered the summons. "Who is it?"

"FBI. Let us in, please."

Frowning at Luke, she pressed the button to release the door. A few seconds later, Travis and Gus joined Luke at the nurses' station. "Agents Steadman and Mathers, Nurse Adkins." Luke made the introductions.

"You're beginning to worry me, gentlemen," she said. "What is going on that requires three federal agents on my floor?"

"We need to question one of your orderlies in connection with a case we're working on," Luke said.

"And we need to question Scott Westfield," Travis added.

"Mr. Westfield is sedated," she said. "Even when he wakes up, I don't know how much you'll get out of him. He's subject to delusions."

Carlos returned to the nurses' station. "I can't find Ricky," he said.

"I can page him." Nurse Adkins reached for her phone.

"Don't do that," Luke said. "We don't want to alert him that we're looking for him. We'll spread out and search for him. Cramer, you stay here with Mr. Westfield."

"Yes, sir." Cramer looked as if he was about to salute but thought better of it.

"I'll take the first three floors," Travis said. "Luke, you search the next three. Gus, take the parking garage and the attached atrium."

They split up and Luke stopped by Scott's room first. Morgan had pulled a chair up to the bedside and was holding her brother's hand. "I've got a couple of other team members here and we're searching the hospital for Danny," he said. "Call me if you see anything suspicious while I'm gone, or if Scott wakes up."

"I will. And thank you."

"You don't have to thank me for doing my job."

"No. But thank you for believing me, and for believing Scott, and for wanting to protect him from danger."

Nurse Adkins appeared in the doorway. "If you're going to search patient rooms on this floor, I have to come with you," she said.

"Fine. Just don't get in my way."

Luke had to admit that going room to room in the psychiatric ward was unnerving. Some patients stared at him blankly. Others smiled too brightly or glared or tried to start conversations. "Mr. Renfro is a hospital inspector," Nurse Adkins explained, before he could say anything. "He's verifying we're meeting all the regulations for our certification." Her eyes dared him to deny any of this.

"That's right," he said. "Have any of you seen this man?" He showed the picture of Danny, taken from the surveillance video of the London bombing, to a group of patients gathered in the day room. "He may have been dressed as an orderly."

"I saw him this morning," one young man volunteered. "He brought my breakfast."

"Why do you want to talk to him?" a woman asked. "Has he done something wrong?"

"We need to check his vaccination records," Nurse Adkins said.

"Have any of you seen him this afternoon?" Luke asked.

They all shook their heads or murmured no. He

moved on to the next room. "Vaccination records?" he asked Adkins.

"One of the state requirements is that all employees be up to date on their vaccinations and TB testing."

"Good thinking to allay suspicion," he said.

"One of my jobs is to keep everyone calm."

"Then I'd say you do a good job." They moved from room to room, questioning anyone they encountered. Most of them didn't remember any of the orderlies' names or faces. The few who did hadn't seen Ricky since breakfast.

They were almost to the last room when Luke's phone alerted him to a call from Travis. "What have you got?" Luke asked.

"I found a set of scrubs and a name badge in a stall in the men's room on the second floor," he said. "The name on the badge is Ricky. My guess is he changed into civilian clothes and left the building."

Luke swore under his breath. "I'll meet you in the security office, behind the reception desk in the ground floor lobby," he said. "We'll see if the security cameras show anything." He ended the call and turned to Nurse Adkins. "Call Security and ask them to send someone up to guard Scott Westfield. I need Cramer to meet us in his office."

"Saying please wouldn't undermine your authority, Agent Renfro."

He bit back a smile. "Point taken. Would you call Security, please?"

"I'll be happy to."

Travis met him outside the guard's room. "What are the chances Danny boy is still on the premises?" Travis asked.

"Slim to none," Luke said. "But maybe we'll get lucky and get video from the parking lot of his car or of him meeting someone."

"He hasn't slipped up yet," Travis said. "But anything can happen."

Cramer arrived and unlocked the door to the security office and led them inside. "Which cameras do you want to look at first?" he asked.

"I found the scrubs and the name tag in the men's room in the north wing of the second floor," Travis said. "Let's start there and see if we can pick him up."

"There's a camera at the end of the hall by the stairs, and one in the elevators," Cramer said.

"Start with the stairs," Luke said. "This guy is trying to keep a low profile."

Cramer sat at the desk and worked at the computer for a few moments. "How far back do you want me to go?" he asked.

"According to Morgan, her brother reported seeing Danny on the ninth floor about ten thirty," Luke said. "So go back to that time and roll forward from there."

A few moments later, a view of the door leading to the stairs on the second floor appeared on-screen. The timer on-screen showed that Cramer was fast-forwarding the video, but the view never changed. "Nothing on camera between ten thirty and now."

"Try the view of the elevator," Luke said.

A steady stream of people got on and off the elevator—hospital personnel in scrubs, men, women and children arriving and departing in groups as they visited patients, patients in wheelchairs leaving the hospital or being taken to other floors for treatments or testing. But there was no one who looked like their suspect.

"Wait. Freeze it there." Travis pointed to the screen and Cramer stopped the video. "That guy."

Luke leaned toward the screen and studied the solitary figure who waited for the elevator. A slight male, he wore jeans, sneakers and a gray hoodie with the hood pulled over his face. "That's our man," he agreed.

"How can you tell?" Cramer asked.

"His posture," Travis said. "The set of his shoulders. It's the same as the videos we have."

"Plus, the fact that he's wearing the hoodie to hide his face. Most people don't dress that way—not to visit a friend or family member in the hospital."

"Come on, turn around." Travis spoke to the figure in the video.

The elevator doors opened and the man in the hoodie got on. "I'll switch to the feed inside the elevator," Cramer said.

The screen flickered, and then they were watching their quarry step onto the elevator. Before the doors had even finished closing behind him, the screen went white.

"What happened?" Travis asked. "Did we lose the feed?"

"The camera is still rolling." Cramer tapped the screen, where the timer showed the seconds advancing. "I think he's covered the camera with something."

"He stuck an index card over the lens," Travis said. "Put double-stick tape on one side, tape a long straw to the back. Stick it up there and when you leave, pull it off. It's easy to conceal in a pocket and as long as you're alone in the car when you put it up and take it off, no one's going to notice. If the car gets full, you can leave it in place and walk away."

"Clever," Cramer said.

"Too clever," Luke said. "Why can't we get one step ahead of this guy?"

"Switch to the ground floor, outside the elevators," Travis said. "He's got to exit there."

Again the screen filled with snow, then cleared to show the lobby elevators. The doors to the left elevator opened and the man in the hoodie emerged. He moved quickly, head down, and, in less than five seconds, disappeared from view. "Give us the exit doors," Luke said. "The ones leading to the parking lot."

"Right. That's North Seventeen. Give me a sec. Here you go."

The screen showed the double doors leading to the parking lot as people of all ages and sizes entered and exited. But no man in a gray hoodie. "It's like he disappeared," Cramer said.

# Chapter Eight

"He didn't disappear." Luke rubbed his chin and continued to study the screen. "Back up the video and run it again. Half speed."

Cramer did so and they watched the flow of people toward the doors. "Freeze it!" Luke commanded. He pointed at the screen. "Now zoom in, here."

The image of a man in a white T-shirt and jeans, a red ball cap pulled over his eyes, filled the screen. "He's carrying the hoodie now," Travis said. "He must have had the cap in his pocket."

"I don't see how you recognize him as the same man," Cramer said.

"Would you recognize your mother if she walked across the screen?" Luke asked. "Even if she had her back to you and she'd changed clothes?"

"Well, sure. She's my mother."

"I know this guy's image like I know my mother's," Luke said. He hadn't asked for this particular talent, but he was going to use it to stop this guy from killing any more innocent people. "Zoom back out and let's see where he goes."

Cramer did so, switching to the parking lot surveillance when Danny moved too far from the building.

But a minute later, he had moved too far for even those cameras to see him.

"He's either parked down the street, or someone is going to swing by and pick him up," Travis said.

"What's the time stamp on our last image of him?" Luke asked.

"Ten forty-seven," Cramer said.

"He didn't waste time getting out of here once Scott made him," Luke said.

"What was he doing here in the first place?" Travis asked.

"Yeah," Cramer said. "What was he doing here?"

"He knows Scott saw him in the hotel kitchen Monday night," Luke said. "It's possible he wanted to find out how much he knew."

"Or, he wanted to make sure he didn't tell anyone what he saw," Luke said.

"How did he get past our security?" Cramer asked. "Even the temp workers have to have a background check and special credentials to work on the ninth floor."

"Who checks those credentials?" Travis asked.

Cramer looked puzzled. "I don't know. Human Resources, I guess."

"So, if someone shows up on the ninth floor with an official-looking name badge and acts like he's supposed to be there, everyone assumes he's been cleared by HR," Luke said.

"I guess so," Cramer said. "But he'd still have to have an ID. You have to scan it to get in."

"He probably stole it," Travis said. "People get careless."

"Yeah, I guess enough people hate their jobs that

they don't see why anyone would want to go out of their way to be here," Cramer said. "But you didn't hear that from me."

"I'll talk to Blessing, see if we can get someone over here to guard Scott Westfield and look out for Danny boy to come back."

"Danny?" Cramer asked. "I thought his name was Ricky."

"Don't worry about it." Luke put a hand on the guard's shoulder. "You've been a big help to us. I'll be sure to put in a good word with your bosses."

"Thanks. And maybe you could play up my role to Nurse Adkins."

"Adkins?" Luke tried to muffle his surprise.

"Yeah." Cramer grinned. "I've been trying to get her to go out with me. She's amazing."

Not the word Luke would have used, but there was something to be said for a tough woman. "I'll see what I can do."

He and Travis left the office and returned to the ninth floor. While Travis phoned Blessing, Luke slipped into Scott's room. Morgan jumped up from the chair beside the bed. "Did you find him?"

"No. But he's definitely out of the building." He moved to her side. "We're going to guard Scott's room until he's discharged," he said.

"So you believe he's in danger?"

"We don't want to take any chances. You should go to your hotel and try to get some rest."

"I have work I need to do. I need to watch the results of today's stage and write my blog entry for tomorrow." She glanced at the bed. "Scott and I had planned to watch the race results together."

"Would you settle for me watching it with you instead?"

She looked into his eyes, clearly pleased with the idea. "Don't you have a lot of work to do?"

"I need to write a report, and I have some other paperwork to review." He also needed to interview neighbors around the vacant rental that may or may not have been occupied by suspected terrorists, but he could delegate some of that work to others and postpone the rest. He needed time to review the situation and ponder his next move. Chasing after Danny— pursuing without a plan every time he appeared on their radar—wasn't bringing them any closer to stopping the terrorists. He wanted to analyze the guy's behavior thus far and see if he could spot any patterns or weaknesses.

And he wanted to spend more time with Morgan, especially when she needed him, as she seemed to now.

"Then, do you want to come back to my hotel with me?" she asked. "We could order in some lunch."

"That's a great idea," he said. And he hoped that, for the next few hours at least, his suspect wouldn't set off any bombs, commit any murders or generally cause trouble.

MORGAN HADN'T REALIZED how small her hotel room was until she was alone in it with Luke. Hanging out with him all afternoon while they both worked had seemed like a good idea at the hospital. He could distract her from her worries about Scott, and maybe she could even help him with his case.

He distracted her, all right, but not necessarily in a good way. At least, not good if she was going to focus on her work. "I'll just, um, let in some more light." She crossed to the window and pulled open the drapes.

Luke picked up the room service menu from the desk. "I'm starved. What do you want to order?"

"The deli on the corner will deliver, too," she said. "They have good sandwiches and salads. Their card is by the phone."

"Sounds good." They settled on club sandwiches, fruit and bottled water. Luke ordered, while she looked for some place to set up her computer.

"They said they'll have everything up in about fifteen minutes," he said, hanging up the phone.

"That's good," she said. "You know, if you'd rather, there are some rooms off the lobby we could use, with tables and more room to spread out."

"No, this is better. More private." He unknotted his tie, then slipped off his jacket. "We can make ourselves comfortable here." He unbuttoned his shirt cuffs and began rolling up his sleeves, and she had to look away. Something about his strong, tan forearms, lightly dusted with brown hair, was doing a number on her insides. She had to fight the urge to move over to him and finish unbuttoning his shirt.

"You take the desk," she said. "I'll take the bed." She fumbled with her computer cord, her cheeks hot. "I mean, it's where I usually work." That hadn't come out well, either. "I mean, on the computer."

He chuckled, a soft, sexy sound that made more than her cheeks feel hot. "I know what you mean. The desk works fine for me." He began to unpack his laptop while she kicked off her shoes and arranged pillows against the headboard. All she had to do was pretend the sexiest man she'd ever met wasn't sitting a few feet away from her. It was just like in college when she'd had guys over to study.

A flashback to a particularly hot and heavy study session from her college years filled her mind and she quickly pushed it away. Okay, so maybe not just like in college.

She'd just opened the file with her notes from yesterday's interview with American leader Andy Sprague when a knock on the door made her jump. "That's probably our food," Luke said. He crossed to the door and she saw that he'd removed his shoes, also.

"Let me get you some cash," she said, starting to get up.

"It's okay. I'll put it on my expense account. Your tax dollars at work." He winked—actually *winked*—at her. The only other person she could ever remember winking at her was her grandpa. This was definitely not a grandpa wink.

They both fell on the food like starving people, though she didn't have any faith that a sandwich and banana were going to do much to sate the hunger that was building inside her. When the meal was reduced to crumbs, she washed her hands and returned to her computer, determined to knock out the work she needed to get done. The complete blog post would have to await the results of the day's race, but she had plenty of other work to keep her busy.

Unfortunately, the intrigues of international bike racing couldn't compete with her interest in the man at the desk across from her. In between paragraphs, she found her gaze drifting to him. His hair was tousled, as if he'd been running his hands through it, and he slouched in his chair, long legs stretched out in front of him, the relaxed pose so different from the imposing agent who had first confronted her. The man she had come to know still had that sexy, dangerous edge, but he'd also revealed his vulnerability, his frustration at failing to stop the man he was pursuing and his grief over his own missing brother. She felt connected to him in a way she hadn't felt connected to anyone else in her life—ever. The knowledge both thrilled and unsettled her.

"What are you working on?"

His question startled her from her musings. Did he realize she'd been staring at him? She shifted her gaze to her computer screen. "I'm writing up an interview I did with Andy Sprague for a sidebar to accompany the feature I'm working on for *Road Bike Magazine*, and then I need to outline my blog post for tomorrow." Feeling calmer, she risked meeting his gaze. "What about you?"

"I'm analyzing every sighting we've had of Danny— where, when, what he was wearing, what he was doing, time of day. I'm trying to spot patterns."

"Are you having any luck so far?"

"No. He's being careful. Too careful for someone working alone."

She set her laptop aside and shifted toward him. "What do you mean?"

"No one can think of every possible danger. For that you need a team. Other people who can share their experience and ideas, what they've learned, and spot potential dangers."

That made sense. "So you think he has people helping him?"

"Almost certainly. He has to have other people to provide supplies, transportation, shelter."

"Are these just minions, or people he's hired, or do you think he's part of some organized group?"

"He could be part of a terrorist cell."

The words were straight out of a thriller novel or a spy movie. Sure, she'd read plenty of news stories about terrorism, but she still had a hard time wrapping her mind around the idea of terrorists living, working and organizing in this country. The knowledge made her realize how important the work of people like Luke really was. She moved to the end of the bed and studied the spreadsheet he'd pulled up on the screen.

"You realize this is all highly classified and I'm breaking all kinds of rules letting you see it." His voice was gentle, but all the same, he pressed a button to close the screen.

She could have complained that he didn't trust her but, honestly, in his job, how could he afford to trust anyone? And she had to give him points for telling her as much as he had. Better to make light of the moment. "I promise I'm not an enemy spy trying to seduce all your secrets from you," she said.

"Too bad." He moved his chair so that he was positioned directly in front of her, his knees bumping the end of the bed. "If anyone could distract me from my duty, it might be you."

"Could I distract you like this?" Tentatively—just in case she'd read him wrong—she leaned forward and pressed her lips to his. His arm came around her, steadying her and deepening the kiss. The sweep of his tongue across her lips made every nerve tingle and glow, and all thoughts of caution deserted her. All she wanted was for this kiss, this moment, to never end.

He was the first to pull away, although reluctantly. He traced the line of her jaw with one finger, his gaze searching. "There's nothing I'd like better than to turn off my phone and take you to bed right now," he said. "But I think we both know that wouldn't be a good idea."

"Because my brother is a suspect in your case." Saying the words made her feel cold. She withdrew her arms from around him and hugged herself.

"Not a suspect. But someone who might have important information that could help us."

"So you can't afford to get involved with me."

He caressed her shoulder. "If I was anyone else, in any other job, we wouldn't be having this conversation. We'd already be making love. But I'm not someone else, and, because of my job, I have to think about not only the circumstances that surround us now, but how those circumstances are going to look in a court case later. A defense attorney might be able to use an affair between us to discredit my testimony or your brother's, or to distract the jury from the important issues of the case. I've seen it happen before."

She nodded. How many times had she seen political campaigns derailed by personal issues or sexy stories trump real news in the headlines? "You're right." She sat back but couldn't resist giving him her most seductive smile. "But I'm warning you right now, when this case is over…"

"I'll be putting in for a long vacation. With you."

She laughed, though the heat of unrequited lust still simmered between them. Checking the clock, she was surprised to see it was almost two. "The race coverage started at one thirty," she said. "I try to catch as much of it as I can."

He handed her the remote. "Mind if I watch it with you?"

"Of course not." She switched on the TV and scooted back on the bed.

He moved his chair around to face the screen. "What is it you like about bike racing?" he asked. "I admit, I don't know much about it."

"I didn't, either, until Scott started racing. I got to know other riders and saw how hard they all worked and trained. The races themselves are grueling for the racers, but exciting, too. They're fast paced and there's a lot of strategy that goes into the races. It's both an individual and a team event. One racer may win a stage or a race, but he relies on his team to help him."

"Your brother must miss it."

"He does. He was very good at racing. When he had to leave it, he lost his focus. And he'd been in racing so long all his friends were there. I think he misses being part of that family. I've tried to encourage him to find new interests and make new friends, but he says it's too hard."

The screen switched to a close-up shot of the racers, straining to make the grueling climb up a mountain pass. The camera panned over the crowds of fans who lined the course, some holding signs, others waving flags. Luke leaned forward, his gaze focused on the television.

Morgan found herself watching him instead of the racers. "You're doing it now, aren't you?" she asked.

"Doing what?" His gaze remained fixed on the screen.

"You're looking for people you recognize from the other races."

"I'm looking for someone I recognize who is acting suspicious or seems out of place," he said. "Other members of the team are along the course. They're looking for any of our suspects, too."

"What happens if they spot someone?"

"They request that he—so far all our suspects are male—will come in to answer some questions."

"What if the person refuses to come?"

"Almost everyone does. We're good at giving the impression we won't take no for an answer."

"Yes. You definitely gave me that impression."

The television switched to a commercial and he turned to her, his expression grave. "I'm not in the habit of using my position to pick up women," he said. "I want you to know that."

"Then why did you follow me that day?"

"Partly because I was attracted to you, and I wanted to know more about you."

"And the other part?"

"I had a feeling. Call it instinct, or a hunch. After a while in this job, you learn not to ignore those feelings."

"Are you sure you aren't trying to justify your actions? Not that I'm complaining, mind you."

"Maybe I am. But finding you also led me to your brother, and I still think he could be an important link in this case."

Scott again. Would he always be a barrier between them? "Luke, no! I realize Scott has had his share of problems, and you probably think because he's lonely and drifting he'd be susceptible to people who pretend to be his friends, but Scott isn't that naive. He wouldn't

be taken in by terrorists, and he wouldn't hurt innocent people." Her voice broke, and she turned away, not
wanting him to see the tears that burned in her eyes.

"Hey." He moved from the chair to the bed and
pulled her close. "I'm not accusing Scott of being a
terrorist," he said. "But I believe he knows more than
he's been able to tell us. More about Danny. He could
be the one who helps us break this case."

"I hope he is," she said. "I want you to capture the
people responsible for all these deaths, but I also want
Scott to have something positive in his life. I want him
to see that his diagnosis and having to give up racing
don't have to be the end."

"Then I hope I can help him see that."

He kissed her temple, a gesture of tenderness and
comfort. But she needed more from him. Not everything she wanted—at least not now—but a reminder
of what might one day be between them.

She turned toward him, her lips angled to his. "Kiss
me," she whispered.

She closed her eyes and surrendered to the storm of
emotions his kiss stirred within her—passion and tenderness, wonder and worry. She wanted her feelings
for this man—the connection she felt for him—to be
real. But could she trust herself to love when so many
other things battled for her attention? Was she drawn
to Luke because he offered respite from the storm or
because he was the person she was meant to be with,
someone who was proving already that he would stand
by her for better or worse?

A loud ringing jolted them apart. "My phone," he
said, scowling toward the sound, which came from the
jacket he'd hung on the back of the desk chair.

"You'd better answer it." She sat back against the headboard, trying to control her breathing and slow her racing heart.

He snagged the jacket from the chair, then extracted the phone. "Agent Renfro," he answered, his voice crisp and professional.

He listened for a moment, the twin lines between his eyes deepening. Then he hung up, stood and began shrugging into his jacket.

"What is it?" she asked. "What's wrong?"

"We need to go," he said, and began to shut down his computer. "That was the hospital. Your brother has disappeared."

# Chapter Nine

Luke reached the hospital before Morgan and was grateful for a few moments to take stock of the situation before she arrived. Travis met him at the ninth-floor elevator. "What happened?" Luke asked.

"Another patient had what is politely known as an episode. He attacked a nurse and the officer assigned to guard Scott went to her aid. When he came back, Westfield's room was empty."

"Have you checked security footage?"

"Gus is reviewing it now. Did you notify the sister?"

"She's on her way." He and Morgan had agreed that coming in separate vehicles was less likely to arouse suspicion.

He followed Luke to Scott's hospital room. They had to squeeze past Carlos, who was righting an overturned cart, gathering up scattered syringes and meds. "You missed all the excitement, Agent Renfro," he said.

"What set off the patient?" Luke asked.

Carlos shrugged. "Who knows? They told me when I was assigned to this floor that I'd like the variety. I didn't realize they meant we can never really predict what these patients are going to do."

In Scott's room, the bedcovers were thrown back,

restraints were discarded on the floor and IV tubing dangled from a stand by the bed. "Was he still unconscious when the officer left him?" Luke asked.

"He said Westfield was a little restless, as if he was starting to come out of sedation."

"The sedative his doctor ordered was a mild one." Nurse Adkins stood in the doorway of the room. She had a stain on the front of her scrubs and a strand of hair had come loose from the bun at the back of her head. She looked much less intimidating than she had before.

"How long should that have put him out?" Luke asked.

"It's difficult to say," she said. "But these patients sometimes develop tolerances. Adrenaline, other drugs in their system and the way their bodies process medication can result in an increased or decreased effect in their systems."

"So Scott could have been coming out of sedation already?" Luke asked.

"Yes."

"Have any strangers been on the floor in the last hour?" Travis asked. "Did the temp service send over a new orderly to replace Ricky?"

She shook her head. "No one's been allowed on the floor."

"Someone could have slipped in while everyone was distracted by the other patient," Travis said.

The sound of someone running in the hallway made them all look toward the door. Morgan burst into the room, breathless. "Have you found him?" she asked. "Do you know what happened?"

"We haven't determined that yet." Luke touched her shoulder lightly, then moved away. He needed to distract her from her panic, get her focused on something active and useful. "Tell me if you notice anything missing from this room."

She scanned the bedside table, then walked to the small wooden cabinet on the wall and opened it. "His clothes are gone," she said. "The tennis shoes and T-shirt and pants he was wearing when they brought him here."

"His medication is missing, also." Nurse Adkins pointed to the top shelf of the closet. "The prescription was filled in anticipation of his release."

"So if someone did kidnap him, they took the time to get him dressed and to gather up his meds?" Travis shook his head. "I don't see how there was time for that."

"Let's check the surveillance tapes." Luke led the way to the elevator, followed by Travis and Morgan.

"Ms. Westfield, you need to stay here and let us handle this," Travis said.

"Let her come with us," Luke said. "Maybe she'll notice something we don't."

"Luke." The one word held a warning. Next would come the lecture about not letting personal relationships interfere with the job.

"She's his sister," Luke said. "She might be able to help."

Travis pressed his lips together but made no further objection. The three of them boarded the elevator and Luke pressed the button for the first floor. He glanced up at the camera. Its lens was uncovered, the green light on the front indicating they were being recorded. What had happened to Scott Westfield? Even if Danny had dared to return, how would he have gotten a reluctant, half-conscious or completely unconscious man out of here without someone noticing?

They found Cramer and Gus in the security office. Gus glanced up when they entered. "We've got him on tape," he said.

They crowded around the desk and Cramer worked the controls until an image of Scott filled the screen. Dressed in sweatpants and shirt, he carried a plastic bag and opened the door to the stairwell. "His other clothes were in a bag like that," Morgan said.

Cramer manipulated the controls, moving from camera to camera, following Scott down the stairs. He slipped into a bathroom on the third floor and changed into jeans and a T-shirt, then continued down the stairs and out a side door. The last image showed him at the edge of the parking lot, headed toward the street.

"How did he untie himself and get out of that bed?" Travis asked.

"Once he was unconscious, the nurse would have removed the restraints," Cramer said. "There are laws against keeping people confined for too long. They're supposed to keep people from hurting themselves or others in the short term, until they're under control."

Luke turned to Morgan. "Why did he leave?"

"Probably because he was scared," she said. "Seeing Danny really freaked him out. Once he woke up, he was probably worried Danny would come back. So he waited until the guard was gone and slipped out. He'd rather be on his own than trust the hospital."

"Where would he go?" Travis asked.

She shook her head. "I don't know. No one at the hotel where he was working could tell me where he lived." She stilled, then looked at him, her face more alert, almost hopeful, even. "I gave him my business card, with the name and address of my hotel on it. Maybe he went there."

"Go back there now and let us know the minute you see him," Luke said. "We need to talk to him and find out why he's so afraid of Danny, and what he knows that might help us."

She nodded. "Yes. I promise I'll call you as soon as I see him." She started to turn away, then looked back at Luke. "Thanks," she said. "For everything." Then she raced away, her shoes slapping on the tile lobby floor as she headed for the parking lot.

"I'll set someone to watch her hotel," Travis said, pulling out his phone. "Do you think he'll really show up there?"

"I don't know. They were close, but he's avoided her for the past year, so I'm not sure he'd have a change of heart now."

"Maybe he didn't run away to avoid Danny, but to join up with him," Travis said. "Maybe even to warn him of our suspicions."

"Danny already knows we suspect him. Even if he and Scott were partners at one time, Scott would be too much of a risk for him now. He's too unpredictable."

"Then Westfield is in danger either way you look at it."

"I hope we find him—or Danny—before we have another death on our hands." He didn't want to even think about the possibility of having to tell Morgan he hadn't been able to protect her brother. "Any news from the race?"

"An American won today's stage—Sprague? No sign of any of our other suspects. No sign of suspicious activity. If he's sticking to his pattern, he's waiting for the finale, when the biggest crowds and the greatest number of media eyes will be on the finish line."

"But he has to know there will be incredible security at the finish line," Cramer said. "I read in the paper they're installing scanners and the place will be crawling with cops and bomb-sniffing dogs."

"Some people see that kind of thing as more of a challenge," Travis said. "A call for them to up their game."

He and Luke left the office. "Now that we know Scott has left, I don't see any sense in staying here," Luke said.

"The hospital is in high security mode in case our suspect comes back, but that doesn't seem likely," Travis agreed. "We've put out an APB on Scott, so maybe one of the locals will pick him up."

"Soon, I hope," Luke said. "I think he knows more than he's telling us about our suspect."

"Did you get any information out of the sister when you went to her hotel room?"

Luke stiffened. "How did you know I went to her hotel room?"

"I might have overheard your conversation."

"I didn't go there to question her. She's not a suspect." He looked away, afraid he might reveal just how close he had become to Morgan in the short time they'd known each other.

"Until we solve this thing, everyone is a suspect." Travis spoke softly, but his voice was intense. "Even if she's not directly involved, her brother may be wrapped up in this some way. Don't compromise this case for the sake of your hormones."

"I won't compromise the case." What he felt for Morgan may have started out as pure physical attraction but went beyond that now.

Travis gripped his shoulder. "I shouldn't have said that. You're one of the best agents I know. But you know as well as I do that some people are very good liars. I'd hate to see you taken in."

He relaxed a little. "Morgan isn't lying." He started to add that Morgan wasn't like Travis's ex-fiancée, who had blindsided him when she broke off their engagement six months before. He didn't want to remind his friend of that hurt, though he knew it must be the worry behind Travis's warning to him. "But I'm still being careful. My focus right now has to be on the case."

"I'll keep you posted on this end of things," Travis said. "Where are you headed now?"

"I'm still trying to track down any leads on the suspected terrorists in that rental house in Five Points."

"Good luck."

"Thanks." They were all going to need a lot of luck to crack this case. For all the resources the Bureau was devoting to stopping these people, they kept slipping through their fingers.

MORGAN PACED HER hotel room—nine steps to the window, turn, nine steps back to the door. She stared at the cell phone in her hand, willing it to ring. She'd tried Scott's cell at least a dozen times last night before finally crawling into bed for a fitful night of half dozing and terrifying dreams in which Scott was in danger and she was unable to reach him.

This morning she'd fortified herself with coffee from room service and resumed her vigil again. All her calls had gone straight to voice mail. The thought of him out there alone, running scared through the city, made her too sad and jittery to sit down.

She turned to the television, where a local sports channel was showing live coverage of that day's race stage in Colorado Springs. Today's course was a circuit around the city, including a loop around the scenic Garden of the Gods. Apparently, one of the American team had just crashed into a fan who had stepped into the road to take a picture on his phone. Such accidents were becoming all too common at races these days. Race officials tried to publicize the dangers and urge people to stay back, but a long tradition of allowing crowds to get close to the racers made authorities reluctant to set up barricades.

The first jaunty notes of her ring tone sounded, and she yelped and hurried to answer the call.

"Hello," Luke said. "How are you doing?"

He'd called last night to check on her and reassure her, as well. Hearing from him made her feel less alone in all of this. "I'm going a little crazy, waiting and worrying." She sat on the end of the bed, shoving aside her laptop to make room. The hours she'd spent yesterday with Luke in this room had been such a sweet, welcome interlude from the worry and frustration, but now she struggled with guilt. If she had stayed at the hospital with Scott instead of returning here with Luke, could she have prevented her brother from running away?

"We're circulating Scott's picture to authorities," Luke said. "If anyone spots him, we'll hear about it."

"I checked with my dad and stepmom. They haven't heard anything." She hadn't shared that Scott might be in danger—telling them their son had disappeared again had been painful enough.

"The hotel where he worked hasn't heard anything, either," Luke said. "The address he gave them when he applied for the job is a men's shelter. They haven't seen him in three or four days."

"What is that address?" She reached for the notepad and pen by the phone. "Maybe I could talk to people there who knew him." Anything was better than sitting here doing nothing.

"Our people already interviewed everyone there." His voice softened. "I know you want to help, but the best thing really is to stay at the hotel and wait for Scott. We still think he might try to reach you."

"I hope so." Reluctantly, she set the paper and pen aside.

"Did he have a car, or credit cards?"

"I don't think so. He always rode his bike everywhere or used public transportation." When he was well, he was proud of not being tied to a car. "As for credit cards, if he was living in a shelter, working odd jobs, I doubt if he had much money."

"It was a long shot, but I had to check."

"I appreciate all you're doing." She knew he wanted to talk to Scott as a witness in his case, but she liked to believe at least part of the reason he was working so hard to find him was because of her.

"What are you doing besides worrying?" Luke asked.

"I'm watching the race coverage." She glanced at the TV, where a reporter stood on the side of the road, surrounded by a crowd of exuberant race fans. "I'll finish my blog post for tomorrow later. What are you doing?"

"I'm following some leads in another part of the case.

I'm going to be pretty busy for the next day or so, so I may not get to see you, but hang in there. And try not to worry. Your brother has been doing a good job of looking after himself for the past year."

"You're right. That's a good thing for me to remember." Scott was an adult, and when he was healthy, he was smart and savvy. It was his illness that made things so unpredictable.

They said their goodbyes and she moved her laptop to the desk and turned up the volume on the television. American racer Andrew Sprague had won the race's third stage the day before, just as Scott had predicted, with an impressive performance on the mountain passes that had blown away his closest competition. She watched the replay of an interview with Sprague at the finish line yesterday. The handsome racer in the yellow jersey had the same dazzling smile and charming manner she remembered from her previous encounters with him. He'd been one of Scott's chief rivals earlier in their careers. In Scott's last race, he had beat out Sprague by less than a second. The memory of that day was etched in her mind, a permanent image of Scott, in his racing jersey, lean and muscular, drenched in the champagne his teammates had sprayed over him in their victory celebration. He'd been so happy.

Two months later, he'd received the diagnosis that ended his career. At first, he'd brought the same determination that had allowed him to win races to his battle against his mental illness. But he was fighting an elusive enemy, one that tortured his mind, while the medications to control it tortured his body. She'd watched, helpless, as he sank further into despair. And then he was gone, vanishing from her life. Knowing he was alive, somewhere, but that she was unable to reach him, was worse in some ways than losing him to death.

She pushed the thoughts away and forced herself to write the blog post that was due tonight. Losing her job wouldn't help Scott any.

An hour later, she'd finished the article and was thinking about ordering in something to eat when her cell phone rang. Heart pounding, she studied the unfamiliar number on the screen, then hurried to answer it. "Hello?"

"It's Scott. Are you alone?"

"Yes. I'm alone in my hotel room." She tried to sound calmer than she felt, fearful of scaring him away if she acted too anxious. "Where are you? Are you okay?"

"I'm fine. I know you're worried about me, but don't. I'll be okay."

"Where are you? I can come get you. Why did you leave the hospital?" She couldn't keep back the flood of questions.

"It wasn't safe there. I had to get away. It'll be better now."

"Why wasn't it safe? Tell me where you are. Let me help you, please."

"You can't help me," he said. But the words didn't hold the despair she'd heard from him before. He seemed to be calmly stating fact. "You have to look after yourself."

"I can help you," she insisted. "If nothing else, at least we can be together. Please tell me where you are."

"I can't do that. It isn't safe."

"Who is trying to hurt you? Who are you afraid of?"

"You've got it all wrong," he said. "I'm not afraid for myself. But I have to stay away, to protect you."

"Me? Scott, please—I don't understand."

"Just—look out for yourself. Stay close to your cop friend."

"Scott, let me—" But he'd ended the call. With shaking hands, she hit the redial button. The phone rang and rang. "Come on, Scott. Answer me."

After a dozen rings a mechanical voice came on the line. "The party you are trying to reach is unavailable or out of service…"

She hung up and sat on the edge of the bed, replaying the conversation over and over in her mind. The Scott she'd spoken with just now had sounded strong and sure of himself—more like the old Scott, before his disappearance, and before his diagnosis, even. Though in recent years she'd slipped into the role of worrying about and taking care of him, when they were growing up he was the one who had protected and looked after her. If she was bullied at school, he dealt with the culprits. He vetted her boyfriends, helped her study for difficult tests, and was always there to offer advice and encouragement. She hadn't let herself think, until now, about how much she'd missed that side of her brother.

Believing she was in danger, he'd slipped back into the role of her protector. But why would he believe anyone would want to hurt her? She hadn't had any contact with Danny or anyone else associated with the bombings. How could she be in any danger?

# Chapter Ten

Luke was sure half a dozen pairs of eyes watched him as he approached the last house on the street. He'd spent the morning going door to door in the neighborhood, showing pictures of their suspected terrorists and asking if anyone knew them or knew where they went. The work was simple but filled with tension. Everything about him, from his car with government plates to his suit, pegged him as a fed. Every time he knocked on a door, he braced himself for a less-than-friendly reception. Agents had been gunned down for asking questions in the wrong neighborhoods.

But today's search had yielded nothing more than wary looks and denials that anyone knew anything about the former residents of the little white house on the corner. A few people would admit to having seen one or more of them or their car, but, as one woman put it, "they kept to themselves."

A young woman with a baby on her hip and a toddler clinging to her leg answered the door at the last house. She studied Luke's credentials with wide eyes and nodded when he showed the photographs. "I know who they are, but I don't know anything about them."

"So you never spoke to them, made conversation in passing or anything like that?" he asked.

"Why are you looking for them?"

It wasn't the first time he'd been asked that question. "We think they witnessed a crime we're investigating," he said. "Finding them could help us locate a murderer."

The word "murderer" invariably got people's attention. The young woman studied the photos again. "I talked to the woman once. She told me my little girl was pretty." She put a hand on the head of the toddler at her side. "She had kind of a Southern accent. Maybe from Georgia or someplace like that."

It wasn't much to go on, but it was something. "Was this at her house?" Luke asked.

"No. At the Gas N Go a block over. I get milk for the kids there a lot, because they put it on sale all the time, and I used to see one or all three of them in there a lot. I was buying milk and juice in there one afternoon and the woman was there. I smiled and said hello and she smiled back and said, 'Your little girl is so pretty. I always smile when I see her.'"

"What was she doing in the store?"

"I think she was buying a money card. You know, one of those credit card type things you can put cash on and send as a gift or something like that."

"Anything else you remember?"

The woman shook her head. "I think they moved out not too long after that. At least, when I walked by the house a week later, it looked empty."

"Thanks." Luke replaced the photos in his jacket and handed the woman one of his cards. "You've been a big help."

He drove to the Gas N Go and parked at the side of

the building. It was a typical neighborhood convenience store, with gas pumps out front and groceries, snacks, lottery tickets, gift cards and cigarettes for sale inside. This time of the afternoon, business was brisk. Luke waited until one of the two clerks on duty wasn't busy and approached the counter.

He identified himself and showed the photos to the clerk, a middle-aged African American man with a shaved head and a paunch, whose name tag identified him as Isaiah. "Yeah, they came in here pretty regular," Isaiah said.

"What did they buy?" Luke asked.

The clerk scratched the side of his face. "Well, you know, the usual. Cigarettes, soda, chips. Sometimes they bought calling cards, which seemed a little odd, I guess."

"Why was that odd?"

"Mostly we sell those to people who want to make calls overseas. Maybe they got a kid in the military, or they want to call home to Mexico or India or wherever. These three didn't look old enough to have kids in the service and they didn't strike me as foreign."

"Anything else?"

"They bought cash cards, sometimes, those Money-Gram things. You can put up to a thousand bucks on one. The woman mostly did that. She always bought the maximum amount on each card and paid cash."

"That didn't strike you as unusual?"

"It's none of my business how people spend their money or where they get it," he said.

Isaiah wore that closed-up look that told Luke he wasn't going to get anything else out of him, so Luke got his contact information and turned toward the other clerk, who was selling lottery tickets to a young couple.

"He can't help you any," Isaiah said. "He's only been working here three days."

The other clerk, Ray, shook his head and looked puzzled when Luke showed him the pictures of the three suspects. "Sorry, I can't help you," he said. Isaiah looked on, arms crossed, his eyes sending a clear message of *I told you so*.

Luke thanked them and started to leave, but on impulse, he took out his phone and pulled up the photo of Danny.

"Do either of you recognize this man?" he asked.

They leaned in to study the photo. Isaiah nodded. "Yeah. He came in with the other three one day."

"You're sure?" Luke tried not to let his excitement show.

"I'm sure. He wore a Boston Red Sox cap and I'm a Sox fan, so I said something about it, but he blew me off."

"Anything else you can tell me about him?" Luke asked.

"His friends called him Dan."

"Dan? You're sure?"

"I'm sure. Nothing wrong with my hearing."

"Any last name?"

"I never heard one. He didn't say much, you know."

"Did you know the names of any of the others?"

"No. They never said. At least, not while I was listening."

"Thanks. You've been very helpful."

"Why are you looking for these people?" Isaiah asked. "Is there a reward if I help find them?"

Luke handed the man one of his cards. "Call me if any of them comes in here again, or if you see them around. There just might be a reward."

Back in the car, he phoned Blessing to update him on his progress. "The woman had a Southern accent, maybe Georgia, and the clerk identified our bombing suspect as having been in the store with the three from the house at least once. He says he heard one of them call him Dan."

"It's not much, but it helps us start to build a profile," Blessing said. "Anything else?"

"The clerk said Dan wore a Boston Red Sox cap."

"A Sox fan named Dan. How many of those do you think there are?"

"I'll keep digging," Luke said, and ended the call.

Immediately, his phone beeped, alerting him that he had a voice mail. He clicked over to his mailbox and Morgan's voice, thin and shaky, said, "Scott called me. He said he's okay, but that I might be in danger. What is he talking about? Luke, I'm a little scared."

He started the car and hit the button to return the call. As he peeled out of the parking lot, she answered. "Luke, thanks for calling me back," she said. "Maybe I'm worrying over nothing, but…"

"It's okay," he said. "I'm on my way."

SCOTT FOLLOWED THE faint trail along the creek bank that led to the little clearing in the underbrush where he and Danny had been camping. Well, Danny had been camping there—he'd just let Scott spread his bedroll under the trees nearby and share the campfire for a couple of nights. The men's shelter wasn't bad, but he liked being out in the woods. It reminded him a little of the church camp he'd attended for a few summers when he was a kid.

Danny had been really friendly at first. He'd remembered Scott from London and he was the first person Scott had met in a long time who wanted to talk about cycling. Danny was a real fan. He knew the names of all the top racers and had watched a lot of the big races. But he'd never been to Colorado before, so he was eager for Scott to fill him in on details about the Colorado Cycling Challenge. It felt so good to sit with a friend and talk like that. Scott wasn't a weird crazy or even a has-been who couldn't cut it. He was a veteran racer who knew the sport and was happy to share his knowledge with someone who was interested.

But something had definitely changed back there in the hotel kitchen. Danny had been doing something with the food and he'd been angry when he'd caught Scott watching him. And then he'd pulled that gun and shot at Morgan and her friend... Remembering the gun made his stomach knot. What if Danny had the gun with him now? What if he decided to kill Scott?

He froze, wondering whether he should leave while he still had the chance. He'd stay away from Danny and avoid trouble.

But he couldn't get the way Danny had looked in the hospital out of his head. Disguised as an orderly that way. Worse, Scott couldn't forget what he'd said. When they'd passed in the hall, Danny had leaned over and whispered, "Keep quiet or I'm going to hurt your sister." The way he'd said that word—*hurt*—and the look in his eyes, sent a wave of panic washing through Scott, ice flooding his veins. It was as if one of the devils in his head had come to life and was standing before him, right there in the hospital hallway.

Scott was calmer now, and he was tired of being afraid. No person could be as bad as the devils in his head. The new medicine they'd given him at the hospital had shut up those devils, and he was feeling better. Stronger. But that might not last. He had to deal with Danny now.

He'd thought about this all last night and this morning, while he hid at various spots around the city. He and Danny had been friends. Scott could talk to him. He'd let Danny know that he knew how to keep his mouth shut—he didn't rat out his friends. But Danny had to leave Morgan alone. She had nothing to do with any of this.

He started forward again, moving slowly and quietly, damp leaves on the trail muffling his footsteps. He stopped at the edge of the clearing and waited, watching and listening. Danny's tent was there, on the other side of the clearing, camouflaged by the pine boughs he'd cut and draped over it. Behind that, more pine boughs covered the black metal footlocker. When Scott had asked about the footlocker, Danny said he used it for supplies, so the animals wouldn't get to them. A heavy lock on the front of the chest kept anyone else from looking inside. Once, when Scott had sat on the footlocker, Danny had yelled at him to stay away.

That was cool. Some guys were very particular about their things. And Danny had a lot of things—backpacks and a folding table and chairs, water jugs and pots and pans and lots of canned food. How did he get all that stuff here on foot? Someone must have given him a ride. The locker was really heavy—too heavy for one person to move.

When he was certain no one was around, Scott moved closer to the tent. It was zipped up tight. He checked the locker—still locked. The ashes in the rock-lined fire ring were cold. Danny had either left early that morning, or he'd spent the night somewhere else.

Scott looked at the tent again. What if Danny was in there now, asleep? What if he was sick? Or even dead? He rubbed his hand up and down his thigh, debating what to do. Maybe he should go inside the tent and check. If Danny wasn't there, he could leave him a note.

Heart pounding so hard it hurt, he crept to the tent and eased open the zipper. He let out a rush of breath when he saw the tent was empty. The sleeping bag was neatly rolled and tied to one side, and a backpack leaned against it.

A new backpack—not the one Danny had had before. Scott squatted in front of it and unfastened the top flap. Maybe the gun was in here. If he found it, he'd take it away and throw it in the creek so that Danny couldn't use it to hurt Morgan.

In the top of the pack, he found a map of the race route, and a program with the racers' bios and pictures, as well as lots of stuff about the history of the race. Scott stared at the brochures and began to get a queasy feeling in his stomach. The medicine he took sometimes made him feel sick, but this was a different kind of sickness. Danny had asked him a lot of questions about the race. He wanted to know the best place to stand at the end of the race, where the most people would be, where the cameras were. Something about those questions wasn't right.

"What the hell do you think you're doing?"

The harsh words made Scott jump away from the pack. He recognized the voice as Danny's, but all he could focus on was the gun pointed at him.

"What are you doing going through my things?" Danny demanded.

"I…I was looking for piece of paper to leave you a note," Scott said.

"Why aren't you in the hospital? Who have you been talking to? Who have you told about this place?" Danny fired the questions like bullets, sharp and rapid. Scott searched for answers.

"I haven't been talking to anyone," he said. "I didn't tell anyone anything. I left the hospital because…because I'm fine now. I don't need to be there anymore." He forced a smile, though it felt more like a grimace. "Now that I'm out, I thought we could hang together for a while. Maybe watch the race together. I could introduce you to some racers at the finish line."

Danny ignored the invitation. He jabbed the gun toward Scott. "Who was that man in the hotel kitchen? The one with your sister?"

"How did you know she was my sister?" Scott hadn't introduced them. Morgan hadn't said anything about knowing him.

"I make it my business to know things. Who was he?"

"Some guy she's dating. I don't know his name."

"You told her about me, didn't you? I saw her there in your hospital room. The two of you looked real close."

"I didn't tell her anything." He forgot about smiling. "She doesn't know anything. You need to leave her alone."

"Maybe I'll shut you both up," he said. "I'll kill you now, then kill her. I won't have to worry about either one of you saying anything you shouldn't."

What could Scott possibly say to that? He looked frantically around the tent for anything he could use as a weapon. Sleeping bag, backpack, clothes—everything was too soft and lightweight to stop a gun.

"Get outside." Danny gestured with the gun. "I'm not going to shoot you in my tent, get your blood all over my stuff."

Scott debated refusing to move, but he didn't think that ploy would work. Danny would only get more angry, and might decide to shoot him anyway. He had started to crawl toward the door of the tent when the alarm on his phone sounded, the ascending and descending electronic notes overly loud in the enclosed space.

"What's that?" Danny asked.

It was the reminder he'd set to take his medication, but Danny didn't need to know that. "Um, it's a text. Probably from my sister. I'm supposed to meet her for lunch. Her and her boyfriend—the cop."

Danny swore. "I knew he was a cop. Get out of the tent. Now!"

He backed away, the gun still fixed on Scott, who had to crawl through the door of the tent, then stand. "Over there, against those trees," Danny directed him.

Scott started toward the trees, but Danny put out a hand. "First, give me your phone."

Trying to control the shaking of his hand, Scott dug the phone from the pocket of his jeans and handed it over. Danny dropped it to the ground and stomped on it, grinding his heel into the screen. Then he kicked the pieces away. Scott swallowed against the nausea that climbed his throat.

"Get over there," Danny motioned to the trees once more.

A movie Scott had seen a long time ago came into his mind. A man—a detective or some other good guy—held at gunpoint by a villain. He threw gravel in the shooter's face and got away. Would that really work, or did that kind of thing only happen in the movies? If he failed, Danny would shoot him. He stared at the gun, fighting fear and paralysis. If he didn't try something, Danny was going to shoot him anyway. At least this way, he would die fighting.

He lunged forward, letting himself fall, bracing his arms to catch himself. His hand landed in the fire ring. Grabbing a handful of gravel, cinders and old coals, he flung the mess into Danny's face. The gun went off, the sound muffled, a single *pop!*

Scott didn't know if he'd been hit. He was up and running, terror propelling him back along the trail and up toward the highway on the other side of the creek. He splashed through the water and clambered up the slope, shots exploding in the dirt around him. All those years of cycling, of working out, had given him strong legs. He was fast. And he wasn't going to let this guy kill him.

He burst onto the shoulder of the freeway and didn't stop, running onto the pavement, hands in the air, screaming as loudly as he could, "Help me!" Horns blared and cars swerved around him. He reached the median and turned to look back.

Danny stood at the top of the slope, the gun no-where in sight. He bent and picked up something off the ground. Something white, like a business card. He read it and stuffed it in his pocket, then looked up at Scott and smiled—a smile like the devils in his head wore when they looked out of his eyes into the mirror sometimes. A smile full of evil and loathing, and Scott began to be afraid all over again.

# *Chapter Eleven*

Luke told himself he was going to Morgan's hotel to calm her down, but when she opened her door and moved into his arms, he realized how worried he'd been. "Thank you for coming," she said. "Scott sounded so certain when he said I was in danger—it really frightened me."

"Did he say why he thought that?" Luke asked, after he'd followed her inside and locked the door behind them. "Has someone threatened you?"

"He said he had to stay away to protect me. I thought maybe he was talking about Danny—that Danny was after him and he was afraid to involve me." She sat on the edge of the bed, hands clasped tightly in her lap. "I don't know what to think."

"How did he sound on the phone?" Scott pulled the desk chair so that he could sit facing her. "Were there any background noises that might give us a clue as to where he was?"

"I heard traffic, but almost anywhere in the city you'd expect to hear that. And he sounded good, actually. I don't mean happy, but he sounded stronger. More like the Scott he was before he got sick. He sounded more sure of himself, not as agitated. Which is funny, considering what he was saying to me. I mean, I think he was really afraid, but he wasn't panicking. Does that make sense?"

"I think so, yes. Maybe the time in the hospital did him some good."

"I hope so. I still worry when I don't know where he is."

"You've tried calling him?"

"Yes. But my calls go straight to voice mail." She glanced at the television. "The one thing that gives me hope is that I think he'll stay in town for the race finish on Sunday. He has a lot of friends and former teammates competing and I don't think he'll want to miss it. I'm hoping I'll be able to find him then."

"I'll be looking for him, too," Luke said. "I'll ask the other members of the team to keep an eye out for him, as well."

"Then I'm happy to take advantage of your talent for recognizing faces." On the TV, footage played of crowds gathered at the finish line in Colorado Springs. "I haven't heard anything about any threats or worries about bombings," she said. "Is that because you're asking the press to keep things low-key, or because the danger has lessened?"

"We haven't had any direct threats, but our intelligence tells us the bomber has targeted this race. The Union Cycliste Internationale has asked the press to soften reports of violence, not us. We're working with local law enforcement to make security as tight as we can, though it's difficult when the crowds are stretched out for miles. The UCI won't allow barriers or fences."

"It's against tradition. Cycling is a very fan-oriented sport."

"Except one of those fans might be out to kill people."

"We don't like to believe we live in a world like that." She switched off the TV and stretched her arms over her head. "I think I need to get out of this hotel room for a while. Being cooped up in here all day is making me nuts."

"Let me take you out. We can grab a drink, maybe a bite to eat. I'm betting you skipped lunch."

"How is it that you already know me so well?"

Her smile made him a little light-headed. He'd known she would be worried about her brother, and he knew just what that worry felt like. "I skipped lunch, too," he said. "And I'd like to spend some time with you that doesn't revolve around work."

"That's the best idea I've heard all week." She stood. "Give me a minute to change."

She retrieved some items from her suitcase and went into the bathroom. Luke stood and walked to the window, which offered a view of downtown streets filled with cars and bicycles. Pedestrians strolled the sidewalks or relaxed in a small park on the corner. The bright banners advertising the cycling challenge added color to the scene. He understood why people found it hard to believe others would want to destroy such peace and beauty. Yet he and his team and the other men and women like him who worked on the front lines knew the danger was all too real.

Every day they were getting closer to the terrorists responsible for the London and Paris bombings, but would they stop them in time—before they caused a tragedy on American soil?

The bathroom door opened and Morgan emerged, young and feminine in a flowered summer dress and silver high heels. "You look beautiful," he said.

"Thank you." She picked up her purse from the desk. "You aren't going to get into trouble with your boss for going out with me, are you?" she asked.

"I have a right to a personal life." Though Blessing might not see things that way. "Should we walk or drive?" he asked.

"Walk. It's a warm night and there are so many good restaurants downtown."

They found a bistro with outdoor seating and ordered craft beers and an appetizer sampler. She sat back in her chair and sighed. "I could live in Colorado," she said. "In Texas it's too hot to sit outside like this in August."

"One of the houses we lived in when I was a kid had a screened-in sleeping porch off the upstairs bedrooms," he said. "Mark and I slept out there all summer long— sometimes right up until the first snow."

"My dad would let Scott and I set up a tent in the backyard sometimes in the summer. We'd play tag in the dark, then sit around in the tent with a flashlight and scare each other with ghost stories." Her smile was wistful. "Whenever I see homeless people with packs and bedrolls, I wonder how many nights Scott has spent camping out because he had to, where there are so many scarier things than ghost stories."

Luke took her hand and squeezed it. "The not knowing is hard, I know."

"You do know, don't you?" She turned her hand over and twined her fingers with his. "I hope you find your brother, and that he's okay."

"I won't stop looking until I find him," he said. "And I won't stop looking for Scott, either."

The waiter brought their food and they fell into the

easy silence of two people who don't have to speak to communicate. "Would you like another drink?" he asked, when her beer mug was empty.

"I think what I'd really like to do is take a walk," she said. "Just to enjoy the evening."

"That sounds like a great idea." He paid the bill and they set out. When he held out his hand, she laced her fingers with his and bumped her shoulder against him, as if they'd known each other for years instead of only a few days.

They joined the pedestrians on 16th Street Mall, maneuvering around a clot of excited teens in matching T-shirts who were all talking at once as they took in the sights, then pausing to listen to a busker playing a guitar on the street corner. Morgan tossed a couple of dollar bills into the open guitar case before they continued down the street.

"We have to check out the Tattered Cover," she said, pointing toward the sign for the venerable Denver bookstore.

They waited for a mall bus that had stopped to unload passengers. Out of habit, Luke studied the faces of the people who stepped off the bus, looking for the familiar features of his suspects. Then the bus doors shut and the vehicle roared away. He focused his gaze once more on Morgan and opened his mouth to ask her what she liked to read. But the screech of tires on pavement and a woman's scream shattered the evening's peace.

He looked up to see a car hurtling toward them. He had an impression of black and chrome, roaring like a malevolent beast. He only had time to shove Morgan out of the way and go diving after her before all hell broke loose.

MORGAN RESISTED THE urge to pinch herself to prove she wasn't dreaming. This time with Luke had been a magical respite from the stress and worry that had wounded her heart for the past few days. How was it that, with all the things she had to be unhappy about, with him she could find such peace and contentment?

She had turned to him, to ask this question, when he shoved her hard. She fell, crying out as her knees struck the pavement, then Luke landed on top of her and they rolled together out of the way of the car that ran up onto the sidewalk. The roar of the engine was unnaturally loud in her ears and exhaust stung her nose. Screams tore from her throat and she clung to Luke, even as he pushed himself off her.

She struggled to a sitting position in time to see the driver's door of the car pop open and a figure in black leap out. Luke lurched to his feet and took off after the man, who was running like a wide receiver who had intercepted a pass, dodging and weaving, even leaping over obstacles as he raced down the sidewalk with Luke in pursuit.

"Are you okay, ma'am?" Two of the teenagers in green shirts that they'd passed earlier helped Morgan to her feet. The shirts, with black lettering and musical notes against the vibrant green, said something about a choral convention.

"I'm okay. Thanks." She let them help her to her feet and stood between them, staring in the direction the fleeing man and Luke had run. She could no longer see them for the press of people around her.

"That guy must have been drunk," someone said.

"I don't know," someone else said. "He looked like he was aiming right at that couple."

"Let me through, please." At the authoritative tone, the crowd parted and Luke returned to Morgan's side. He had his phone to his ear and was talking to someone even as he moved to her side. "Black Toyota Camry, Colorado Plate Kilo, Victor, Sierra, five, five, five. The driver was headed east on foot down Sixteenth. My guess is he had someone waiting to pick him up. Get a team over here to get what we can off the car. I'm going to take Morgan back to her hotel."

He ended the call and stowed the phone, then turned to her. "Are you okay?"

"Just shook up." She hugged her arms over her stomach. "What happened?"

He pulled her closer, his arm a warm, strong support holding her up and steadying her nerves. "I don't know, but we'll find out."

Local police arrived and Luke pulled her toward them. He identified himself. "The driver ran away," he said. "I can give you a description, but he was wearing a ski mask and gloves, so I don't think it will help much."

"The person who called it in said it looked like he deliberately tried to run someone down," the cop said.

Morgan gasped, then covered her mouth with her hand. Luke pulled her closer. "I've got a team on their way over to process the scene," he said. "We think this might be related to a case we're working on."

"What case is that?" the officer asked, but Luke ignored the question.

"If we find anything, we'll let you know," he said. He dug a card from his pocket and handed it to the officer. "Or if you hear or see anything… I'm going to take Ms. Westfield back to her hotel."

He led her away from the car, his arm still securely

around her. "Do you want to walk or take a cab?" he asked.

"I...I guess we'd better take a cab," she said. The memory of the car headed toward them made her stomach clench. "I mean, what if the guy comes back and tries again?"

He raised his hand to flag a passing taxi and helped her into the backseat, then gave the name of her hotel.

Neither of them spoke on the drive over, or in the elevator to her room. Her hand shook so badly trying to slide the key card into the lock that he took it from her and let them in. Once the door was safely locked behind them, he gathered her in his arms and kissed her, a fierce, claiming kiss that went a long way toward numbing the knowledge of how close they had both come to death.

For a long time, even after the kiss ended, they stood with their arms around each other, her head pressed to his chest and listening to the steady, reassuring beat of his heart. When she felt calm enough to speak, she looked up at him. "Do you really think the driver of that car was aiming at us?" she asked.

"We can't know for sure, but it looked that way to me."

"But why? Because the killer recognized you as an FBI agent?"

"Maybe. Danny saw me in the hotel kitchen, remember?"

"Do you think Danny was driving the car?" she asked.

"No. This guy was taller. Thinner. Maybe he's another member of the group Danny is a part of."

"Scott said I was in danger," she said. "Maybe this is what he meant."

"Until I can be sure you're safe, I won't leave you alone," he said.

Her eyes met his, and she felt again the tidal pull of attraction. "I'd like it if you stayed," she said.

"I can sleep on the floor."

He started to pull away, but she tugged him back. "I don't want you sleeping on the floor." She touched her fingertips to his mouth to stop his protest. "I know what you said before, about not compromising the case or anything, but no one has to know. Can't tonight just be for us?"

He looked into her eyes, and she saw the depth of his desire, matching her own. "Yes," he said. "All right."

They kissed again, but with the barely restrained urgency of two lovers who know the kiss is only a prelude to what is to come. She pressed her body more firmly to his, one hand gripping his shirtfront, the other kneading his shoulder. He slid one hand down her spine and caressed her bottom. "I've been dreaming about holding and touching you this way," he murmured.

"No photographers this time, I swear." Her breathlessness belied the teasing note she was striving for.

"I'm not sure I'd even care." He cradled her face in his hands and kissed her again, a thorough, claiming kiss that left them both just on the edge of control. A whole movie crew could have jumped out from behind the curtains and she wasn't sure she'd even notice.

He pulled away slightly, putting some space between them but continuing to cradle her face, one thumb stroking the side of her mouth. "You're sure about this?" he asked.

"I'm sure." She searched his face, trying to read the emotions there. She saw passion, and a concern that touched her even more than his lust. Luke was a man who cared deeply—she'd already seen that in his dedication to his job. Now she felt that same consideration focused on her. "All I want to know," she said, "is that right now, what we're feeling, doesn't have anything to do with your work or my brother. It's just about us. And who we are and how we feel about each other."

"This is about you and me." He brushed her hair back off her forehead. "It's all about the things you've made me feel since I first saw you in that surveillance video, before we even met."

"How I made you feel?" The idea intrigued her. How could you feel anything for a stranger? Someone whose name you didn't even know? "How did you feel about me?"

"It sounds crazy, but I felt a connection." He put his fist over his heart. "As if I'd found something—someone—I didn't even realize I was looking for."

The words would have made a beautiful dialogue in a movie, but nothing about them felt rehearsed to her. Luke was telling her the truth, and it touched her more than any fancy speeches or smooth lines could have. "That is crazy, but I feel it, too." She wrapped her fingers around the fist that covered his heart. "You're someone I can be myself with. I don't have to apologize for my nomadic job or my ill brother or anything else about me. I have never experienced that with anyone else. I always thought of relationships as tightrope acts. How much of myself could I really reveal? What was I going to have to compromise on? What were we going to end up fighting about because I wouldn't give in? I don't feel that way with you."

"I don't want you to change or give up anything," he said. "How could I, when my life is full of its own complications?"

"I admire your dedication to your job," she said. "And I understand your grief over your brother. But right now, I don't want to talk about any of that. I just want to be with you." She undid another button on his shirt. "Preferably naked, and under the covers."

"One more thing we have in common." He grabbed the hem of her dress and tugged it over her head.

After that, they couldn't get out of their clothes fast enough. While he cleared the bed, she went into the bathroom and returned with a condom. "I was prepared to go down to the gift shop and buy a box," he said, accepting the packet from her.

"I'm glad you didn't have an excuse to leave the room," she said. "I'd worry you might not come back."

"Oh, I'd have come back." He pulled her onto the bed beside him.

She laughed, then he smothered the sound with another kiss, his hands and his mouth skillfully stoking her passion to a simmer once more. He explored her body with the intensity of a detective examining a crime scene, as if he feared missing some crucial detail. She was equally determined to take her time and enjoy the sensation of him—the feel of his skin beneath her hands, the soap and musk scent of him, the play of light across his muscular body. She would only ever have one first time with him, and she wanted to fix the moment in her mind, not for comparison to future efforts, but as a foundation on which to build.

But their patience could only extend so far, and before too long, he levered himself over her and looked into her eyes. "Are you ready for me?" he asked.

"More than ready." And she pulled him to her.

Their lovemaking took on more urgency as they moved together, at first with the awkwardness of new partners, then with more assurance, driven by instinct and need rather than by conscious thought. Her climax thundered through her and he followed soon after, leaving her spent and shaken and more content than she could remember being in the months since Scott's disappearance.

Afterward, they lay in bed, his arm around her shoulder, her head cradled on his chest. He yawned and she playfully pinched him. "It's too early to go to sleep," she said.

"I'm hungry again," he said. "Maybe we should order in pizza."

"And after that?" she asked.

He slid down in bed and nipped at her neck. "After that, I'll be ready for dessert."

Laughing, she rolled toward him and sat up to straddle him. An old-fashioned telephone ring startled her. She glanced at the bedside phone, but it was silent.

"That's mine," he said. He sat up and gently pushed her away. "I'd better answer it."

She pulled the covers around her against the air conditioner's chill as, naked, he climbed out of bed, located his jacket on the floor and dug out his phone. "Hello? Yes. Where are you?"

Those suits he wore didn't really do his body justice. How had she failed to notice just how gorgeous he was? That pizza might have to wait...

Lost in a pleasant fantasy, she paid no attention to

the phone call, but the look on Luke's face when he ended the call and turned to her was like a bucket of cold water dumped on her head. "I have to go," he said.

"What is it? What's wrong?"

"A development in the case." He found his boxers and pulled them on. "I'm sorry, I can't talk about it." He looked around the room. "You should be okay here tonight. Call hotel security if you see or hear anything suspicious."

His cold tone and his refusal to look at her frightened her. "Luke, what is going on? What's happened?"

"I'll call you as soon as I can." Jacket and tie in hand, he bent down to kiss her cheek and then he was gone, leaving her alone and confused. Was this what life with a federal agent was like? Or had something more than a routine case development driven him away from her?

# Chapter Twelve

Luke stood at the edge of the clearing, out of the way of the crime scene techs, who were measuring, photographing and taking samples of everything from footprints to blood to bullet casings. The rush of water in the nearby creek and the thick screen of pines and oaks muffled the hum of traffic from the expressway half a mile away. If not for the presence of the techs and the yellow crime scene tape that marked off the area, this might have been an idyllic spot for a campsite. A tent, almost obscured by cut pine boughs, huddled on the opposite side of the space, and an ash-filled circle of rocks awaited an evening's campfire.

"A woman who lives in a subdivision back there called in to the emergency operator and said she'd heard gunshots." Special Agent in Charge Blessing, who had met Luke at the scene, pointed to the woods behind the tent. "A few minutes later, the operators got a call that a man had run out onto the freeway, dodging cars. Someone else called in that someone was chasing the man. That caller even snapped a couple of photos with a cell phone."

Blessing angled his phone toward Luke, who studied a grainy, much-enlarged close-up of a man wearing a Boston Red Sox ball cap. "It could be Danny," Luke said. "But it's not clear enough for me to be sure."

Frowning, Blessing pocketed the phone. "That's the same answer I got from everyone else on the team."

"Any photos of the guy he was chasing?" Luke asked.

"Nope. But the local cops did a good job. They brought in a dog, who led the investigators back in here. Looks like whoever was camped out here left in a hurry—didn't take much with him." In addition to the tent, the clearing contained two folding camp chairs, a five-gallon water jug and a plastic milk crate that held dishes and cooking utensils.

"Homeless people camp along the creek here, don't they?" Luke asked.

"Yeah, but this is no typical homeless person's camp," Blessing said. "There's too much stuff here, and it's all high-end. That tent retails for upwards of two hundred dollars, they tell me."

"How did we end up being called in?" Luke asked. Locals didn't like to share turf with the feds unless they had a good reason.

"That's where things get really interesting." Blessing indicated the techs processing the scene. "We're not getting much here right now because the Denver cops already did a thorough job. There was a lot of evidence at the scene." He indicated the orange evidence markers that dotted the clearing. "One of the first things they spotted when they came in was a cell phone on the ground. It was smashed up, but they were able to get a set of prints off it. When they ran them, they came up with a name we'd put out an alert for. The lead investigator was smart enough then to put the brakes on and call us."

A chill swept over Luke in spite of the warm night. "What was the name they came up with?" Though he thought he already knew.

"Scott Westfield." Blessing fixed his gaze on Luke, watching for his reaction. "He was here, probably not too long before those nine-one-one calls came in. From the description the Denver cops got from drivers on the freeway, we think he was the guy who ran out in traffic."

"The one the guy in the Red Sox cap was shooting at?"

"We think so."

"What happened to him? Was he hurt?"

"No. He managed to dodge the cars and disappeared. We've got the phone and we're going to see if we can get any call records, see who he talked to in the last couple of days. That might give us some leads."

Luke blew out a breath and looked around the campsite again. The chairs were lined up precisely beside the tent, which was zipped up tight. Neatly split logs formed a pyramid beside the fire ring. "Were there any signs of a struggle here—other than the smashed phone?"

"A couple of bullet casings, some scuffs in the dirt—that's about it. Whoever was here, they were the meticulous type. We haven't even found any food wrappers or apple cores or other garbage."

"Maybe he took it with him when he left, afraid we'd search it for DNA evidence. Can you tell if one person or two was living here?"

"There's only one sleeping bag in the tent, but maybe our shooter took the other one with him. There are two chairs, and enough supplies for half a dozen people."

A trio of men in bombproof suits filed down the path to the clearing. "What are they doing here?" Luke asked.

"The dog indicated explosives in that footlocker, so we thought we'd better bring in some experts before we tried to move it." He pointed to the tent and this time Luke noticed the black footlocker in its shadow.

"Come on." Blessing nudged his arm. "We'll leave them to it." He walked away and Luke followed, all the way down the path to the dirt lot where they'd left their cars. Blessing leaned back against his black Camry with the government plates and faced Luke, arms folded across his burly chest, an expression on his face that reminded Luke of the look his father had given him when he confronted him about a detention in school. "I heard you had an interesting night," the commander said.

The Denver police must have shared the information about the incident on the 16th Street Mall. "You heard about the car that tried to run me down," he said.

"I also heard who you were with."

Luke stiffened but said nothing. Blessing was sure to quash any defense he made.

"Your personal life is none of my business," Blessing said. "Except when it might jeopardize a case. What were you doing with Morgan Westfield last night?"

An image of a naked Morgan, beneath him in bed, flashed into his head. The scent of her still clung to him. The memory of her touch was still imprinted on him. But he wasn't about to share that with his boss. "We didn't discuss the case," he said.

"Agent Renfro, I shouldn't have to tell you that you cannot be involved with the sister of a suspect in this case." He held up a hand to cut off Luke's objection.

"We don't know Scott Westfield's role in all this, but he's clearly up to his neck in something."

"Danny was chasing him," Luke said. "He may have fired shots at him. That doesn't sound like they were on the same side."

"Maybe they were partners and they got into an argument," Blessing said.

Luke looked at the ground. He couldn't argue with his boss's logic, but he resisted the idea that Morgan was a danger to him or to this case.

"Has Ms. Westfield heard from her brother since he left the hospital?" Blessing asked.

"He called her yesterday afternoon, before she talked to me. He told her she was in danger and that it wasn't safe for him to see her."

"So she called you and told you this?"

"Yes."

"Anything else?"

"He told her to stick close to her cop friend—to me." The memory of this detail strengthened his confidence in her, and in Scott. He wouldn't have told her to stick close to the cops if he was working against them.

"Did he say that because you'd keep her safe, or because he wanted her to keep an eye on you?" Blessing's gaze was shrewd, assessing.

Luke stifled a sigh of frustration. "I don't know. I didn't hear the conversation. I only know what she told me." And what he believed in his gut.

"We'll have someone watch her to see if she contacts him, but you have to stay away," Blessing said. "If you don't, I'll send you back to Washington so fast you'll get a nosebleed."

Luke squared his shoulders and looked the commander in the eye. "Yes, sir." No matter how much it would hurt to break the news to Morgan, he'd sworn an oath that, if necessary, he would forfeit his life in service to his country. Right now, that meant forfeiting the desires of his heart, as well.

THE FIFTH DAY of the Colorado Cycling Challenge took the riders from the small community of Woodland Park, outside of Colorado Springs, to the popular ski town of Breckenridge. Morgan sat on the end of the bed in her hotel room and watched French rider Gabrielle Martiniere claim the yellow jersey for that day's stage, as crowds of onlookers pressed around him, waving French flags and shouting in a cacophony of languages.

She switched off the television and stared at her laptop screen, where she managed to write a halfhearted summary of that day's action for the blog. The race had been an exciting one, and Martiniere's surge in the last few miles to take the lead had been a surprising development, the kind of thing that was sure to have race fans talking into the night.

But she felt none of that excitement now, and worried her lack of enthusiasm would come through to her readers. No matter how hard she tried, she couldn't distract her mind from worrying about Scott and Luke.

She hadn't heard anything from Scott since their cryptic conversation yesterday afternoon. Her calls to his phone had gone straight to voice mail. Luke hadn't contacted her or answered her calls, either. Of course, he was busy. When the man you loved was occupied with saving the world you didn't expect him to call you every hour to whisper sweet nothings. But Luke's attitude when he left her last night had been so odd. She could practically see him erecting an emotional wall between them.

She'd scoured the papers and internet for any news that might explain Luke's silence but had come up with nothing. The absence of any news about the search for the bomber struck her as a little creepy. The Union Cycliste Internationale had pointedly refrained from any mention of the terrorist activities that had marred the Paris and London races. From their press kits to television interviews granted by UCI officials, they emphasized that the races were safe and that the United States was taking extraordinary security measures to protect both racers and spectators. Then they quickly changed the subject, preferring to talk about the scenic route, the exciting competition and the integrity of the race rather than the horror that made Morgan more and more uneasy as the race neared its finish.

The press had, for the most part, gone along with the charade of pretending that nothing was out of the ordinary about this race. The cause of Alec Demetrie's death had not been released and authorities had allowed speculation that the UCI president had died of natural causes to flourish. If asked about the bombings or any fear they might have for their safety, the racers brushed off or outright ignored the question. Spectators always expressed optimism; perhaps anyone who was afraid stayed home. And certainly the government wasn't saying anything. Maybe they took the view that the fewer people who knew about their activities, the less the chance that information would get back to the wrong person.

She checked the clock. Almost five. Was it too much to hope that Luke would call and ask her to dinner? Or that they'd be able to spend another night together? She hated this aspect of new relationships. Should she wait for him and risk being seen as dependent or clingy, or assert her independence and maybe come across as cold and indifferent? She wanted to be the serene, mature woman who didn't need a man to complete her, but the truth was, she wanted to be with Luke. She wanted to make love to him, but she also simply enjoyed his company, talking with him, working alongside him, simply being in his presence. That didn't make her weak or dependent. Maybe it only made her in love.

In love. A crazy idea, considering the short time they'd known each other. But how else to explain the closeness she felt to him? She wasn't a person who gave her heart easily, but somehow she'd handed it over to Luke Renfro without question.

She snatched up her phone and scrolled to his number before she could change her mind. This time, he answered on the third ring. "Morgan. I was just going to call you," he said.

*Then why didn't you?* she thought, but she refrained from voicing the snarky question. "Are you busy with work?" she asked.

"Yeah. Really busy." Silence stretched; she thought she heard traffic noises behind him.

"Where are you?" she asked.

Instead of answering her question, he said, "I'm afraid I've got bad news."

His tone of voice, as if he had to force out every syllable, as much as the words themselves, sent a shock wave through her. She couldn't breathe. "Scott?" she managed to whisper.

"As far as I know, he's fine. This isn't about him. At least, not directly."

"Then what is it? What's going on?" He didn't sound like himself, the confident, in-control agent. "You're scaring me."

"I can't see you anymore. Or at least, not until this investigation is over."

At first, she wasn't sure she'd heard him right. "What do you mean? What's happened?"

"I can't talk about it. I've said too much already. Just—I'm sorry. I've asked the local police to keep an eye on you, just in case. I have to go now. Take care."

He hung up. She stared at her phone, wishing more than anything that the technology was available that would allow her to reach right through the screen and shake him. She hit the redial button, but her call went straight to voice mail. "Coward," she said out loud, though she could think of a dozen less-complimentary names to hurl at him.

She tossed the phone onto the bed and began to pace, replaying the conversation over and over in her head. One of her journalism professors, a long time ago, had told her that the key to analyzing an interview was to look at what wasn't said as well as what was said. Luke hadn't sounded angry or indifferent just now. In fact, he'd spoken like a man who was struggling to keep it together. Not having visual clues didn't help, but she couldn't equate the man she'd come to know with a cad who would toss a woman aside after he'd spent the night in her bed.

No, this had to have something to do with his work. He'd said he couldn't see her until after the investigation. Maybe his boss had learned he'd spent the night with her and threatened to fire him if he didn't give her up. As romantic as it might be to picture a man giving up his job for her, that wasn't a particularly smart or practical thing for a guy to do. And when your job was protecting the country, giving it up for almost any reason might even be seen as a dereliction of duty.

Great. The man she loved was...maybe...putting the safety of his country before his personal feelings? This didn't make her feel any better. Why couldn't she have fallen for a chef or scientist or even a fellow journalist? None of them would be able to get away with canceling a date because they had to save lives instead.

And what about when the investigation was over? Would this fire between them have cooled to the point where he would have lost interest?

Or what if she was wrong about all of this and he was really just being a jerk? She kicked the desk, making her computer jump and her toe throb. Men! Why did they have to make her life so difficult?

## Chapter Thirteen

Scott waited across from the convenience store until the parking lot was empty and he was sure the clerk was alone. The midday sun beat down on the pavement and he could smell the mouthwatering aroma of onions and roasting lamb from the Middle Eastern restaurant next door. He remembered eating shish kebab and flatbread at a similar place with Morgan one of the last times he'd seen her in Austin. He'd teased her about the young waiter, who flirted with her; the memory of her laughter brought a sharp sadness to his chest. Would the two of them ever be so comfortable with each other again?

Sure that the coast was clear, he crossed the street slowly, just a dude strolling over to get a soda and a bag of chips. He kept his head down, shoulders hunched to hide his face, aware of the camera aimed at the door.

Inside the store, a plump older woman with a blue streak in her hennaed hair looked up at him. "Hello," she said, regarding him warily. "Can I help you?"

"Yeah. You sell phones?"

She pointed to a display of pay-as-you-go phones on a rack by the register. He scanned the display, skipping over the more expensive smartphones and settling for one that would allow him to text and call, for fifteen dollars. He laid it on the counter. "I'll take this one."

"You need to buy minutes to activate it," she said.

"Oh, yeah." He knew that. He chose the cheapest airtime card—an hour for twenty dollars. He pulled his wallet from the back pocket of his jeans and checked his cash. This wasn't going to leave him much for food or anything else until he could work again.

The woman scanned the phone and the card. "You know how these work?" she asked, not as if she thought he was an idiot, but because she had that motherly attitude he'd seen in a lot of older women.

"Yeah, I'm good," he said, then added, "Thanks."

"That'll be thirty-seven dollars and fifty-two cents," she said.

He handed over his last two twenties and waited while she made change, his foot bouncing.

"You okay?" she asked. "You look kinda pale."

"Yeah. I'm just in a hurry."

"All right." She studied him. Maybe she was trying to memorize his face. Or maybe she was remembering seeing his face on the news—if the police had put it out there. He hadn't seen a television since he'd left the hospital, so he didn't know. He grabbed the phone and card and his change and ran out of the building. When he looked back, the clerk had picked up her phone and was holding it to her ear, staring after him.

He made himself walk along the sidewalk until he was out of sight of the store, then he raced into an alley between a dentist's office and a women's resale boutique. With shaking hands, he tore the phone from the package. If the clerk had turned him in to the police, he might not have much time. The plastic that encased the phone sliced the side of his hand, drawing blood. He sucked on the wound, which made him think of vampires. He looked around the shadowed alley. If he was a vampire, this would be the kind of place he'd hang out.

His hands shook so badly he had to try half a dozen times to punch in the right code numbers to activate the phone. The charge showed only 25 percent power, but there wasn't anything he could do about that. It wasn't as if he had anyplace to plug it in out here. Maybe later he could find a library and hang out there for a while.

He slipped the phone card into his pocket, in case he needed the numbers again, and felt the punch card of medication he'd brought with him from the hospital. He couldn't remember when he'd last taken his pills. Without the phone alarm to remind him, he had lost track.

He wished now he'd gotten a Coke or some juice from the convenience store. Swallowing the pills without any liquid was hard, but he made himself do it. Then he took a deep breath and punched in Morgan's number.

One, two, three… By the fifth ring he was ready to hang up when she answered, sounding out of breath. "Hello?"

"Hey," he said. Then, in case the one word wasn't enough for her to recognize him, he added "It's me. Scott."

"Scott!" The way her voice soared, as if she was so happy to hear from him, made his chest tight. No one else ever greeted him that way; he realized how much he'd missed it. "It's so good to hear from you," she continued. "I've been so worried. Are you okay? Where are you? Can I see you? Do you need anything?" The words rushed out, like air escaping from a punctured balloon. The anxiety in her voice ratcheted up his own nervousness, and he bounced his leg again. He felt as if he had Ping-Pong balls ricocheting off the inside of his chest and stomach.

"I'm okay," he said. "You don't need to worry about me."

"Of course I'm going to worry, as long as I don't know where you are and what you're doing." Wind noise filled his ear, or maybe she was shifting the phone around. He heard the murmur of voices, as if she was in some public place. "Scott, please be honest with me," she said. "Are you in trouble? If you are, I promise to help you, but you have to level with me."

"I'm not in trouble." At least, he didn't think he was. He hadn't done anything wrong. He'd left the hospital before he was supposed to, but that was because Danny was after him.

"Have you seen Danny?" Morgan asked.

He hesitated. How much should he tell her?

"Scott, have you seen Danny?" she repeated.

"I heard you." He chewed the inside of his mouth, struggling with how much to tell her. But that's why he had called, wasn't it? "We had a fight. I went to his camp to talk to him—to tell him to leave you alone. He tried to shoot me."

"Scott!" Her voice rose, too loud in his ear.

He held the phone away. "Don't yell at me."

"I wasn't yelling at you, I just… Are you hurt?"

"No. He missed." He stood up straighter. He felt good about that. He'd been too fast. Too clever. Or maybe Danny was just a lousy shot. "I ran away."

"Where are you calling me from? This isn't your number."

"He smashed my phone. I had to get a new one. Listen, I don't want to talk about my phone." He needed to conserve his minutes. "I called to tell you to be careful. Danny is really bad. I didn't realize how bad. He's got a gun and…and I think he might want to hurt racers. He acts like a fan, but I don't think he really is."

"Scott, do you know anything about the bombs that went off at the races in London and Paris? Was Danny involved in that?"

"I don't know. I just saw him in London—I didn't know him. But I get a bad feeling about him. You have to stay away."

"I promise I won't go anywhere near Danny," she said. "But you need to tell all this to my friend Luke. He's with the FBI and they're trying very hard to catch Danny and stop him from hurting people."

"Is Luke the cop I saw you with?"

"Yes, and he is trying hard to find Danny. You could help."

"I don't see how I could help. I don't know where Danny is. I haven't seen him since he tried to shoot me."

"You can tell Luke everything you know—where you saw Danny last, what he was doing, things like that. It might help save a lot of lives."

"I don't know." He looked around. Despite the meds he'd taken, his anxiety was ramping up. He had to get out of this alley. "I've got to go now." He needed to be alone, so he could think.

"Wait. Let me give you Luke's number. Call him. He can help you."

"I don't have anything to write on."

"Fine. When we hang up, I'm going to text the number to you. Promise me you'll call him."

"Maybe. I don't know. I just want you to be safe. I have to go now."

He ended the call before she could try to talk him into doing something he wasn't sure was right. Before he had gotten sick, people had always said he had good judgment. That he'd been smart. A good person. But no one had said that about him in a long time. It was as if the devils in his head were determined to steal who he really was. He had to fight them, to hang on to himself for as long as he could.

MORGAN STARED AT the phone, dragonflies battling in her stomach. All this time, Luke had been saying that Scott could be the key to stopping a killer; now she knew he'd been right. But she wasn't sure if Scott realized yet how important the information he had could be. He hadn't exactly promised to call Luke himself, and they were running out of time. The race ended tomorrow. In Paris and London, the bomber had attacked at the race's finish line. Scott might be the only one who could help stop a similar tragedy here in Denver.

Morgan would have to put aside her hurt over the way Luke had ended things between them and call him. Maybe he could track down Scott through his new phone number.

Afraid he might ignore a call from her cell phone, she used the phone in her hotel room. "Agent Renfro," he answered, his voice brisk, all business.

"Luke, it's me, Morgan. Please don't hang up. I just heard from Scott. What he told me might be important."

"I wouldn't hang up on you," he said. "You didn't stop being important to me just because I have to keep my distance for a little while."

His words, and the warmth behind them, washed over her like a soothing balm, easing some of the tension in her shoulders. She wanted to tell him how good it was to hear his voice and how much she'd missed him, but they didn't have time for those personal feelings, not with so much else at stake. "Scott said he saw Danny. Yesterday, I think. He went to talk to him, to tell Danny to leave me alone. He said Danny shot at him." Her voice caught on these last words, as the enormity of what her brother had told her hit.

"Neighbors heard the shots and called it in," Luke said. "We didn't find any evidence that Scott was hurt."

He'd known about this and hadn't told her? She pushed aside the feeling of betrayal. She didn't like that Luke's job meant he had to keep some things from her, but she had to learn to accept it. "He said he was okay, physically, at least. But he thinks Danny may be mixed up in the bombing."

"Did he say why he thought that?"

"Danny was asking him a lot of questions about the race and the racers, but Scott said they weren't the kind of questions a real fan would ask. I gave him your number and told him he needs to call you and tell you what he knows."

"He needs to contact me soon," Luke said. "We don't have much time."

"That's why I called," she said. "I have his new phone number."

"We found his smashed phone near where the neighbors reported gunfire. We wondered what he and Danny were doing together."

"Is that why you said you couldn't see me? Because you'd discovered evidence that Scott and this Danny guy knew each other?"

"We didn't know what their connection was," he said.

She wanted to argue that there was no connection, but how did she really know that? The most important thing was for Luke to find Scott and talk to him. Then he'd know for sure her brother was innocent. "Will you call him?" she asked. "Or maybe you can track him somehow, using the cell number."

"We'll try. What's the number?"

She read off the number. "Thanks," Luke said. "I'll do my best to reach him. If you talk to him in the meantime, try to find out where he is and I'll go to him."

"If you find him, will you arrest him?" she asked. "He swore he didn't know Danny before a few days ago, though he had seen him in London."

"He hasn't been charged with any crime," Luke said. "We only want to talk to him and find out what he knows. But if he doesn't come forward voluntarily, it could look bad for him, since we know he and Danny know each other."

"It's hard for me to hear you say things like that," Morgan said.

"I know. But you and I are on the same side, truly," he said. "And I'm glad Scott wasn't hurt and is all right."

"He's not all right. He's out there alone and scared and a terrorist wants to kill him. You have to help him."

"I promise I will. I know this is hard," he said. "Especially with things so unsettled between us. But you need to trust me. I'm good at my job. I'll look after Scott, and I'll look after you, too, even though you may not always see me or know that I'm there."

"I do trust you." In spite of everything—years spent looking after herself, his suspicions about Scott and this new distance between them—she did trust him. Perhaps from the moment they had met, she'd known Luke was a man she could depend on.

## Chapter Fourteen

"Our suspect is going to make his move soon. We need to be prepared." Ted Blessing faced the members of Search Team Seven, his brow furrowed with grim determination. Late-afternoon sun slanted through the windows of the hotel conference room illuminating the drab surroundings. The finish of the Colorado Cycling Challenge bike race was less than twenty-four hours away and Luke doubted any of them would sleep before then.

"Maybe we've scared him off," Jack Prescott said. He sat back at one end of the table, tie loosened, an open can of Red Bull in one hand. "When he abandoned his camp, he left behind all those explosives. He might not have time to assemble more."

"Two pounds of C-4." Cameron Hsung read from the report they'd all received earlier today. "Blasting caps. Maps of the race course."

"He didn't get all of that by himself," Travis said. "Someone probably picked him up from the hotel the night of the banquet, and we don't think he was driving the car that tried to take out Luke and Morgan. We need to be alert for any accomplices."

"We got a match from IAFIS on fingerprints inside the footlocker." Blessing passed around a sheet with a photo of a clean-cut young man in military fatigues. "His name is Daniel Bradley. Thirty years old, honorably discharged from the United States Army in 2011 after service in Iraq and Afghanistan. No priors. No known association with terrorist groups. Though that doesn't mean he hasn't hooked up with a group we don't know about."

"That's the guy we've been looking for," Travis said. "What's his beef with bicycle races?"

"We don't know," Blessing said. "But poisoning the UCI president and the attack on Agent Renfro and Ms. Westfield shows an escalation of violence."

"We've got enough evidence to put this guy away forever," Cameron said. "Knowing we've got that would make most crooks think twice."

"Maybe," Blessing said. "But it could also make him even more determined to complete his mission."

"He can get more explosives," Luke said. "Maybe not high-grade C-4, but an old-fashioned pipe bomb can still do a lot of damage."

"He may already have all the material he needs." Blessing tossed a computer printout onto the table. "I just heard from our friends at the Denver Police Department. Jefferson County Sheriff's Office reported the theft of ammonium nitrate and fuel oil pellets— ANFO—from a quarry sometime early this morning. The thief disabled the security camera, cut off the lock and was in and out before the night watchman at the place had finished his rounds."

"Could be our guy," Travis said. "Or it could be some other nut."

"What I want to know is why can't we catch this

guy?" Luke asked. "We've got all the resources of the United States government behind us, and every law enforcement agency in the state is looking for him. And he's making us all look like a bunch of idiots."

"What about his friends who had the house in Five Points?" Jack asked. "Maybe he's hiding out with them."

"Every indication is they left the city," Blessing said. "We have one lead that suggests they may be operating on the western slope. Possibly near Durango. We haven't been able to pinpoint anything solid but we're still looking. Right now we're focusing our resources on the race. Agent Mathers, give us the rundown on the schedule for tomorrow."

Gus stood and directed their attention to the screen behind him, which showed a map of the downtown area. "The racers will leave Boulder about twelve thirty," he said. "They'll travel toward Golden via Highway 93." He traced the route, from Golden, over Lookout Mountain and into Denver. "After three laps of the downtown area, they'll come up the 16th Street Mall to Union Station, to the plaza behind the station, over the underground bus transit center. The first racers should start arriving between three thirty and three forty-five. The winner's podium and press area are here." He indicated an area of the plaza, between the historic Union Station building and the orange neon sign that proclaimed Travel by Train and the new transportation hall, with its swooping white canopy and glass walls. "There will be grandstands set up on the plaza here." He indicated an area next to the commuter rail tracks. "This entire area will be barricaded. The only way in or out is through a metal detector."

"Except if you're a rider," Luke pointed out.

Gus's pointer stilled. "Yes, except if you're a rider."

"Do you think he'd try to pass himself off as one of the racers?" Travis asked.

"How would that work, unless it's a suicide bomb?" Cameron asked.

"We can't rule out the possibility of a suicide bomb," Blessing said. "But can our man pass himself off as a racer?"

"All the top riders—the ones expected to arrive at the finish line first—are pretty well-known," Travis said.

"But he could wait until later in the race, when the less-well-known racers started to arrive," Luke said. "There would still be plenty of people in the grandstands and press and other racers milling about."

"We can't frisk every rider who comes into that plaza," Jack said. "The UCI would have a cow. And the press would have a field day, too."

"We stop them before they get to the press, before they get into downtown, and search them then," Blessing said.

"It won't keep someone from sneaking into the race after the checkpoint," Travis said.

"We're going to blanket the course with security," Blessing said. "No one is going to get in or out."

"The UCI won't like it," Jack said.

"They won't," Blessing agreed. "But I think the specter of a third bombing, which could very well destroy their sport, will persuade them." He turned back to the map. "Each of you will be stationed somewhere in this area, tasked with searching for Danny and any of the others on our suspect list. This guy and his friends aren't going to get anywhere near the race course." He turned back. "Try to get some rest tonight. We're going to be on the job early, at 6:00 a.m. I'll keep you apprised of any new developments between now and then."

Luke and Travis left the room together. "Do you really think any of us will sleep tonight?" Luke asked.

"I'm going to try," Travis said. "Need to be alert for tomorrow. You?"

"I'm going to keep trying to reach Scott Westfield. I can't help thinking he knows where Danny is—even if he doesn't realize it."

"He won't answer your calls, huh?"

"No, and he hasn't been in touch with Morgan again, either."

"Have you seen her?"

"No." But they'd stayed in touch. He'd kept the conversation focused on Scott and his job. He was sticking to the letter of his agreement with Blessing. He didn't know where the case would end up, but he wanted to leave the door open for Morgan. She was too special for him to lose without a fight. "She promised to let me know if she heard from Scott. I tried to put a trace on the phone, but didn't have any luck. We just don't have enough time left."

"It's making me crazy that this guy keeps giving us the slip," Travis said. "It's like he can turn himself invisible or something. I mean, the whole point of this team is to see people, the way other people don't see them. But we're not stopping him."

"I drove around the area near the camp for over an hour last night, hoping to see Danny or Scott." Luke shook his head. "No luck."

'"Gus says the key is to go all Zen and think like these guys do, but that doesn't seem to be helping him any."

"I'd try anything if I thought it would work," Luke said.

"Pray that we catch a break tonight or tomorrow," Travis said. "I have a feeling that's the only way we're going to stop this guy."

They parted at the street, Travis headed for his car, Luke to walk downtown. While he scanned the faces of those around him, he tried to puzzle out where Scott might be. He'd left the camp on foot, running. He was concerned for his sister and wanted to stay close to her. To watch over her, even. And he felt a connection to the racers and the bike race. So maybe he would stay close to the course, also. The people Luke had interviewed at the men's shelter where Scott had been living seemed to think he and Danny had met at the shelter. And Scott may have been sharing Danny's camp down by the creek. So he wasn't a loner. He sought out the company of others on the street.

He set out walking in the direction of Union Station, but instead of heading toward the upscale restaurants and high-rise apartments that flanked the transportation hub, he detoured to a soup kitchen he'd seen advertised on a church sign. Half a dozen men lounged on the steps of the church in the sun. A sign advertised the kitchen would open in another hour.

A definite chill set in when he approached the group. Even if he hadn't been dressed in his suit, he knew everything about him screamed "cop" to these streetwise men. "I'm looking for a friend of mine," he said. He scrolled to his photo of Scott and held it toward them. "His name is Scott. Have any of you seen him around?"

"What you want him for?" A burly black man with a beard fixed a hard stare on Luke.

"He hasn't done anything wrong," Luke said. "His sister is worried about him and she asked me to look for him. I only want to talk to him and make sure he's okay."

The only answer he received was stony stares and silence. If he told these men that the lives of dozens, even hundreds, of people might depend on him finding Scott, would they believe him? Would they even care?

"I seen him yesterday, down by the tracks." A younger man, thin with a pockmarked face, spoke up.

"The tracks? The train tracks?"

"Light rail. Perry Station. He was sitting under a tree. Might be he stays around there."

Luke thanked the man and took off at a trot for the light rail station on Eighteenth. He scanned the route map and hopped on the next W train to arrive. Ten minutes later, he got off at Perry Station. New apartments fronted a green space beside the station, next to a neighborhood of older homes in various stages of renovation. A bike path next to the creek led past a playground and basketball courts.

Luke set off along the path, searching for any place a man might camp for the night, out of sight of cops and nosy neighbors but still close to the trains, which would make it easy to get around the city. After ten minutes of walking, he found what he was looking for—a dirt path that led into the woods behind a gutted factory. A sign beside the factory announced it was being transformed into lofts.

He followed the trail through the woods, noting the empty whiskey bottles, beer cans and fast-food wrap-

pers that littered the underbrush. Before long, he came
to a dirt clearing, where an old sofa and a trio of folding chairs were arranged around half a metal barrel.
Two men occupied the folding chairs. Scott lay on the
sofa, eyes closed.

The men were already standing and moving away
when Luke approached. "I'm not here to bother you," he
said, and walked over to Scott. He shook the young man
gently. "Scott, wake up. It's me, Luke. We need to talk."

THE SIXTH DAY of the race consisted of time trials in
the mountain town of Vail. American Andy Sprague
claimed the yellow jersey for this stage, and was a favorite to win the race tomorrow, as well. Morgan, sick
to death of her hotel room, watched the race results
from a tavern on Seventh, surrounded by noisy race
fans who cheered on their favorites. She wondered what
Scott would think of today's results. In time trials, each
racer competed against the clock. They couldn't draft
off team members or trade off positions with someone
on their team, to allow each other to rest. Scott had always preferred the camaraderie and strategy involved
in team racing, but some racers saw time trials as the
true test of a racer's ability, so every big race these days
incorporated both approaches in the various stages.

The bartender switched the television to a baseball
game and Morgan paid for her drink and left the bar. It
was too early to return to her room, which had begun
to feel more like a prison. She decided instead to walk
down toward Union Station, and the finish line. Maybe
she'd find inspiration there for the article she had yet
to write, summarizing today's race results. And she

could scope out the best location from which to watch the finish tomorrow.

The area around Union Station was undergoing a transformation, with work crews hanging colorful banners from every lamppost down the street leading to the finish line. Flags from every country participating in the race snapped in the breeze around the broad plaza, where more workers were assembling a podium and grandstand. Someone had even hung a banner over part of the station's iconic orange neon sign, so that the legend would read Travel by Bike.

She crossed the street at Fourteenth and started toward the grandstands, but she hadn't gone far before a blue-uniformed police officer stopped her. "Excuse me, ma'am, but this area is closed to the public."

"Oh, I'm sorry." She stepped back. Behind him, she could see crews setting up shining metal barriers.

"You can go through the bus station." He pointed up the block. "Go in the doors of the transportation hall, and downstairs. There's an elevator at the end that will take you up to street level on the other side of the plaza."

She glanced at the barriers. "I guess this is all part of security for the race tomorrow."

"Yes, ma'am. We want everyone to enjoy the race safely."

"Thank you." She retraced her steps down the street. This time, she noticed the extra police on duty, and signs notifying race-goers that they must pass through security before taking their place along the final route or entering the plaza. Luke was out here right now, doing his part to keep people safe, too. If only she could contribute more to the efforts.

She rode the escalator down to the bus station beneath transportation hall. The area was packed with people waiting for or disembarking from city buses. She wove her way through the crowd and had almost reached the exit on the opposite side when someone jostled her.

"Excuse me," she said, and tried to move away, but a strong hand grabbed her arm.

"Don't scream," a voice whispered in her ear, and something sharp jabbed at her side.

"What? Who are you?" Fighting panic, she tried to turn her head, to see her attacker, but the knife jabbed, and a sharp pain went through her.

"Walk," the voice commanded, and pushed her forward.

She walked, the man's arm wrapped around her, holding her close, like two lovers making their way through the crowd. Except that one hand gripped the back of her neck to keep her from turning her head or looking at him, and the other held what she guessed was a knife to her side.

He led her, not outside, but to a door marked Custodial. He pulled this open, shoved her inside and then everything went black.

# Chapter Fifteen

Morgan's head throbbed. What had she done to end up with such a headache? Was she coming down with the flu or something? And why was this bed so uncomfortable? She opened her eyes and stared at gray concrete. She tried to move her arms and couldn't, then realized she wasn't lying on a bed at all, but on a hard floor. She rolled over again and kicked her feet, trying to get free. She had a dim memory of walking through the transportation hall, of someone grabbing her and then…nothing.

"I wouldn't thrash around so much if I were you. You don't want to blow us up. At least not yet."

She whipped her head around and saw a man standing in front of a door. He was dressed all in black—black boots, black pants, black long-sleeved T-shirt and a black ski mask over his face. At the mention of blowing up, she gasped. "Who are you? What are you talking about?"

He knelt beside her and adjusted something on her chest. Some kind of vest. It wasn't too tight, but it was definitely heavy. "There are five pounds of pelleted explosives in this vest, as well as several sticks of dynamite," he said. "It's wired to go off at a signal from me, but you should probably lie still, just in case your movement happens to trigger a stray spark. It would be a shame to waste all my efforts before the big day."

He spoke calmly, with an unaccented but definitely American voice. His hands, the only part of him she could see, were white. "What are you talking about?" she asked. "You sound crazy."

"Your brother is the crazy one. It's a shame, really, I watched some footage of him, racing. He was good. Though probably as corrupt as all of them."

His mention of her brother made her break out in a cold sweat. This had to be Danny. The man who had killed the UCI president. The man who had shot at Scott. The person Luke suspected of being responsible for the bombings in London and Paris. She had to learn as much as she could about him. "Were you a racer, too?" He didn't really have the build for it—he was too soft. "Or was someone you loved a racer?"

"No."

"Then what do you have against racing?"

She felt his gaze on her, though she could see little of him in the ski mask. "Racing represents everything corrupt about this country," he said after a moment.

"I don't understand what you mean."

"I don't require you to understand."

What an odd choice of words. What did he "require" from her? "What are you going to do with me?" she asked. She wasn't sure she really wanted to know the answer to that question, but if she had any chance of surviving at all, she needed to know what was going on in his head.

"The problem with people today is they don't listen." He tightened a strap on the vest and stood once more. "I told you, this is a suicide vest. It's wired to explode at a signal from me. It will kill you, and everyone around you."

"What did I ever do to you that you'd want me to die?" she asked, hating the way her voice shook on the last words.

"You didn't do anything in particular," he said. "But as my mentors have taught me, the best way to get back at the people you hate is to target their loved ones. Your brother and your cop friends are making my life very difficult right now. They're interfering with plans they have no business trying to stop. They must pay for their mistakes, so I'm going to destroy what they love most. You."

Did he really think Luke loved her that way—that he'd be destroyed by her death? She closed her eyes and swallowed back tears. Maybe he did feel that way about her. She knew for sure that she cared for him enough to not want to see him hurt this way. And Scott—to have her death associated with the bicycle racing he still loved could be enough to send him into a madness from which he might never recover.

She opened her eyes and tried as best she could to hide her emotions from his scrutiny even though, as Luke had pointed out, she was a lousy liar. "What are you going to do?"

He took something from his pocket—a purple cell phone she recognized as her own. "First, I'm going to take a picture." He held up the phone. "Smile."

She stared at him, rigid with fear. The digital shutter clicked and he studied the results on the screen. "That will do," he said. "You look suitably horrified."

"Why do you need a picture?" she asked.

He pocketed the phone. "I'm going to send this to

the media, so they'll see what I have planned. But they won't know where or when."

Clearly, he was nuts. She had to get away from him, any way she could. "Fine. You have your picture. You can take the vest off now."

"No." He moved to her side and pulled a bandanna from his pocket. He stuffed it in her mouth as she fought against him. "Remember what I told you about the explosives," he said as he taped the gag in place. "You don't want to set them off too early." He moved to the door and flicked the switch to shut off the light, plunging the room into darkness. "I'll be back in a little while to move you into place," he said.

*What then?* she wondered.

He anticipated her unvoiced question. "Then, I'll blow you up." The last thing she heard was a choked sound, as if he was chuckling to himself while he shut the door behind him, leaving her alone in the dark.

"I WAS GONNA call you," Scott said. He sat on a bench next to Luke, under a streetlight in a park not far from the sofa where Luke had found him. Ace and Dinky, the guys he'd been hanging with, had left. They didn't want to hassle with a cop. Scott didn't want the hassle, either, but he figured he had no choice. When Luke suggested they walk over here to the park, Scott had followed. He was tired of running, anyway. "I just had to think how to do it," he said. "I don't want to get into trouble."

"You're not in trouble," Luke said. "But I really need your help. I need to know everything you can tell me about Danny."

"Where's Morgan? Is she okay?" Scott had been counting on Luke to look after his sister when he couldn't. If Luke was here with him, that meant Morgan was alone.

"She's fine. I talked to her yesterday."

"Why aren't you with her?" he asked. "I thought you'd look after her."

Luke shifted on the bench. He looked...guilty. "I've been busy," he said. "With work."

"I thought with a cop protecting her, she'd be all right. She could be in danger." Scott fought down his rising agitation.

"I asked the local cops to keep an eye on her."

"That's not the same as having someone looking out for her who really cares."

Luke's face reddened. "Morgan will be okay," he said. "But we have to stop Danny. Do you know where he is?"

Scott shook his head. "I saw him this morning, in the bus station. He didn't know I was watching, but then the crowd cleared out and I was afraid he'd see me. But he left before I did. He got on a bus and I didn't see him any more after that."

"Do you know which bus?" Luke had pulled his phone out of his pocket and was typing something into it.

"No. I didn't see. I got out of there fast. I didn't want him to see me."

"What time was this? I can have someone check the bus schedules."

"Maybe two o'clock? It was after lunch, and before I ran into Ace and Dinky and came here."

Luke nodded. "What else do you know about Danny? Do you know his full name?"

"He never said. And I didn't ask. I mean, it wasn't

like he was a good friend or anything. We just…hung out, you know."

"Did you stay at his camp by the creek?"

Scott looked away. The camp was supposed to be a secret.

"We know the two of you argued there. He smashed your phone and he shot at you. Neighbors reported the shots and drivers on the freeway saw you running away."

"I told him he had to leave Morgan alone and he didn't like that."

"What can you tell us about the camp? What kind of things did he have there?"

"Just, you know, camping stuff. But good stuff. New."

"What kind of things?" Luke asked.

"Just…a tent and a sleeping bag and some blankets. A couple of chairs and dishes and food and water. And he had a footlocker, where I guess he kept his clothes and stuff. Or maybe he had money in there. He kept it locked and he didn't like me going near it. Once I made the mistake of sitting on it and he almost bit my head off."

"Did you ever see him open the trunk?"

Scott shook his head. "Not while I was there, but I only stayed there a couple nights, after we left the men's shelter."

"Why did you leave the men's shelter with Danny?"

"Well, you know…he asked me to." He began jiggling his right foot. "I was staying there a couple days and then one day Danny walks in. I sort of recognized him, but couldn't remember him—not really. I thought he was just another homeless dude I'd seen around. But then he comes over and starts talking. He reminds me we saw each other at the bike race in London. He was a fan and he wanted to talk racing, which was cool, you know? Not many people care about racing. But they got mad at us for talking about it. Some of the guys complained and the people who ran the shelter said we had to either shut up or leave. So Danny said we should leave, that he had a nice place down by the creek."

"If he had the place by the creek, why did he come to the shelter at all?" Luke asked.

"I wondered that, too," Scott said. "But he said he came to take a shower, and to ask about day labor jobs. He thought maybe the shelter folks could help him out."

"Okay, so you went to his camp," Luke said. "Did anyone else come with you?"

"No. He didn't ask anyone else."

"Why not?"

"I don't know. Maybe because a lot of those guys are older than us. And Danny said he wanted to talk about racing. They didn't care about that."

"So you talked about racing."

"Yeah. He asked a lot of questions at first. He remembered that I had been a racer and he wanted to know what that was like. He knew a lot of the top racers' names and he asked about them."

"Like a fan would," Luke said.

"At first, yeah. You know, things like 'Is Victor as intense as he seems when he's racing?' and 'Is Andy a good teammate?' But later, he asked other questions. Things that didn't sound so odd to me at the time, but later, when I thought about them, they didn't seem like the kind of things fans would want to know."

"What kinds of things?"

"He wanted to know about the end of the race. How long would it take the top riders to get from Boulder to the finish in downtown Denver? How many of them would arrive at once? How close would the fans be able to get to the winners? How many people would be there? Would the crowds be bigger at the beginning of the finish or did most people stay around to see the end? He wanted to know what kind of security they had at races, what the racers did after they finished—did they leave right away or did they stay to mingle with fans? Some of the questions I didn't know the answer to, but if I couldn't answer them, he'd get angry."

"What did you do then?" Luke asked.

"I started to make up things. And sometimes I lied, just because he annoyed me. He made me feel like he didn't care about me, he was just pumping me for information."

"What did you tell him?"

"I told him all the racers stayed until the end, and the crowd stayed, too, so by the end it was this big, wild party. I told him if he wanted his picture taken with the winners, all he had to do was ask. That's sort of true at some races, though usually you have to be a pretty woman for them to say yes. I didn't tell him that."

"Were you staying at the camp with Danny the day you broke down in the hotel kitchen and were taken to the hospital?" Luke asked.

"I don't know where I would have stayed that night if I hadn't ended up in the hospital," Scott said. "When I told Danny that morning that I was going to work, he got mad. He said I didn't need to go back there. I told him it was a good job and I liked it and the people were nice. I wanted to see Morgan again, too. Danny got really upset. He told me my sister didn't care about me and none of the people at the hotel cared about me—but that he and I were a team. We needed to stick together."

"What did you say to that?"

"Nothing. I just grabbed my stuff and told him I was going to work. He yelled at me not to tell anyone about him. I told him I wouldn't, but I could tell he didn't believe me. So I'd already decided not to go back."

"Except you did go back," Luke reminded him.

"Well, yeah. But only because I was worried he would hurt Morgan. I needed to tell him to leave her alone."

"He had threatened Morgan?"

"In the hospital." Scott's stomach hurt, remembering the menace in Danny's voice. "He said if I didn't keep quiet he would hurt my sister. And I could tell he really meant it. You get a feeling about people sometimes, you know?"

Luke nodded. "Yeah, I know." He looked at his phone. "I'm going to call in a report that Danny was seen in the bus station this morning. That's very near where the closing ceremonies for the race are going to be held tomorrow."

"Do you think Danny is the one who planted those bombs in London and Paris?" Scott asked. "Do you think he'll try the same thing here?"

Luke hesitated. Scott thought he was deciding whether or not to trust him with the information. "He was in London," Scott said. "And he's been acting so strange here. I heard the UCI president died—that he was poisoned. I saw Danny doing something with the entrées that night. He'd lifted the lid on one and he really didn't have any business being around the food.

When he saw me watching him, he moved away, but he also told me he'd hurt me if I told anyone I saw him. If Danny is the one who poisoned President Demetrie, then he must hate racing."

"We think he could be the bomber," Luke said. "Your coming forward may help us stop him before he kills more people. Thank you. It took a lot of guts to do this."

Scott looked away, trying to control his emotions. "I hate that I can't race anymore, but I still love the sport. Someone trying to hurt the sport—and hurting innocent people that way... It's a lot sicker than I'll ever be."

"You're right." Luke turned to his phone, which sounded a trio of descending notes. "It's a text—from Morgan."

He thumbed the text icon. Scott wasn't looking at the phone, but at Luke, and the FBI agent's face blanched as white as his shirt.

Scott sat up straight. "What's wrong? Are you okay?" Luke looked like he was about to pass out or have a seizure or something. Did Scott remember the CPR he'd learned the summer he was a lifeguard in high school?

"It's Morgan." The words came out choked. Luke turned the phone toward Scott, who stared at the image of his sister. She was tied up and lying on a dirty concrete floor, her eyes wide with terror.

"What's that on her chest?" Scott asked, pointing toward what looked like a radio or a bundle of old highway flares.

"It's a bomb." Luke stared at the picture, some of the color returned to his face now. "The message says, 'I've got a friend of yours. She's going to celebrate the end of the race with a real bang.'"

# Chapter Sixteen

Morgan didn't know how long she lay on the floor in that bus station storage room. With her arms bound behind her back and the vest a heavy weight on her chest, she could find no comfortable position. At first, she could see nothing in the dark room, but as her eyes adjusted, she could make out a thin band of light at the bottom of the door. The muffled, hurrying footsteps of people passing through the transportation hall ebbed and flowed with the arrival and departure of the buses, along with scraps of words she couldn't assemble into any coherent conversations. "So he said…The report… Anthony, wait up!…Nowhere…Did you see?"

After a while, she closed her eyes and turned her attention to trying to get out of the ties that bound her wrists. The plastic or wire or whatever Danny had used cut into her flesh, drawing blood when she struggled too much. She inched on her back toward the door. Maybe she could pound on it with her feet and someone would hear her. But the first hard kick at the metal sent such a shock wave through her that she gasped, sure she had set off the bomb. After that, she was too afraid to try again. She'd have to wait until Danny returned and try to get away from him then.

If he did return. The thought that Danny might not made her choke on the gag, and she had to force herself to calm down. But maybe he had left her here for good. He would set off the bomb when he was ready. The bus station was right under the transportation hall, next to the plaza. If the explosives were powerful enough, he could do a lot of damage by detonating the bomb here.

But no. He had said he would return. Hadn't he? She was so terrified she couldn't be certain what was real and what was fearful imagining.

Long after the bus station fell silent, the door opened. She startled, not having heard his footsteps. She saw the baggy gray uniform pants first, and a powerful hope made her try to sit up and to cry out from behind the gag. One of the janitors had found her. She was saved.

But then Danny looked down on her, much of his face hidden by oversize sunglasses and a knit cap pulled down low over his forehead. "It's time," he said, and hauled her to her feet.

He pulled her roughly toward a large garbage cart by the door, then, without warning, he picked her up and stuffed her into it. She tried to fight him, but the bindings around her ankles and wrists, as well as his viselike grip, kept her immobilized. He shoved her down into the trash cart, her knees to her chest, then dumped a trash can full of loose papers over her. "One peep from you and you're dead," he ordered, and switched off the light.

He rolled the cart out of the janitor's closet. The tinny strains of classical music and the echoing footsteps of passing people told her they were in the bus terminal. One of the wheels of the garbage cart gave off a high-pitched squeak. Through the screen of papers, she could see the arching canopy of the terminal.

The cart stopped and a fresh load of trash rained down on her—paper coffee cups and food wrappers, old newspapers and soda cans. She ducked her head and closed her eyes against the worst of the onslaught. They continued on, stopping two more times while her captor emptied trash onto her.

Finally, the cart reversed direction. She could no longer see out of the top of the cart, but she listened for any clues about where he might be taking her. After a few minutes, they stopped, and she heard the familiar *ding* of elevator doors opening.

Inside the elevator, Danny leaned over and pushed the trash aside. He grabbed her by the arms and hauled her out of the can and propped her against the metal handrail that encircled the car. The elevator car was glass on all four sides, with chrome supports. Though enclosed on this lower level, at the plaza level it was a striking glass-and-chrome rectangle that provided handicapped access to the facilities below.

But her captor didn't order the elevator to ascend. Instead, he produced handcuffs from his pockets—two pairs. He untied Morgan's wrists and attached one set of handcuffs to each one. Then he attached the other ends of the handcuffs to the railings on adjacent sides of the elevator. She was trapped in the corner of the elevator, facing the door.

"This elevator is now officially out of order," he said. "This afternoon, when the time is right, I'll send a signal via the building's computer controls to activate the elevator and tell it to ascend. The glass here will give everyone a very good look at you, but before they can do anything, I'll make the call to detonate the bomb and you'll go boom."

*Why are you doing this?* Silenced by the gag, she tried to telegraph the question with her eyes.

"We live in a corrupt world and violence is the only way to force change," he said. He checked the cuffs to make sure they were securely fastened. "Don't waste your time struggling. You can't save yourself now." He replaced the gag in her mouth and tore off a fresh strip of duct tape. "And neither can your brother or Agent Renfro."

LUKE AND SCOTT arranged to meet the rest of the team in Union Station's security offices, deep in the bowels of the historic train terminal. Antique clocks lined the hallway leading to this sanctum, each showing the time in a different part of the country or the world. But the only clock Luke cared about was the one ticking until the race ended later today, and what could be the end of Morgan's life.

Outside the door to the security office, he stopped and turned to Scott. "Don't say anything unless someone asks you a question," he said. "Some people aren't going to like that I'm involving a civilian at all. You may be asked to leave for part of the meeting, but don't go far. We need your help on this."

Scott nodded. He looked calmer than Luke felt, something he hadn't expected. Maybe he was numb to what was really going on. Or maybe he had it together a lot more than people gave him credit for.

Inside, he found the others crowded into a small conference room to the left of the door. The others scarcely glanced up when Luke and Scott slipped inside. They were too focused on the image of Morgan that Luke had emailed to Blessing, who had it projected onto a screen on the back wall. "Do we know it's a real photo, not a fake?" Jack asked.

"That bomb looks real enough to me," Travis said. "And that's definitely Morgan."

Behind Luke, Scott made a strangled sound in his throat but kept quiet.

"The big question is, how is he going to sneak a woman wired with a bomb onto the scene?" Cameron asked.

"Put her in a muumuu, a raincoat, a minivan. There are probably a hundred ways," Blessing said.

"He'll never get her past a metal detector, with all that hardware," Jack said.

"He'll use a disguise," Luke said. "He's done it before. First, he was a dishwasher in the hotel kitchen. Then he was an orderly at the hospital. He knows how to blend in."

"So what disguise?" Blessing asked.

"Someone who doesn't have to go through the metal detectors. A cop," Travis said.

"A security guard." Cameron nodded toward the guards in the next room. "There must be a dozen of these guys all over this building," he said. "It would be easy enough for a skilled operative to knock one out and change clothes with him."

The image on the screen switched to a blueprint of the plaza area. "Mr. Westfield."

Blessing's deep, commanding voice made Scott jump. "Y-yes, sir?"

"You know Danny better than any of us. Where do you think he would put his bomb?"

"I don't know him that well," Scott said. "I just met him."

"I'll amend my statement then. You have spent more time with him than the rest of us, and you've spoken to him more. I want to know your thoughts."

Scott studied the map of the plaza, his brow furrowed. "He wants to go after the bikers. He has a grudge against the racers. And…I think he wants attention. He asked a lot of questions about when the most people and the most press would be around the finish line."

"That fits with his previous pattern," Blessing said. "And bringing an innocent person into his plan fits with the psychologist's prediction of escalating violence."

Luke stared at the plaza map. "We're missing something," he said. "Some flaw in our security that he's going to take advantage of."

"We need to get to Morgan before he brings her to the finish line," Travis said.

"The picture he sent doesn't give us any clues where he's holding her," Cameron said.

"What if he sent the picture to distract us," Gus said. "He wants us to focus our resources on rescuing her, while he sneaks in behind us and wreaks havoc."

"Or what if he has two bombs?" Jack said. "One for Morgan and one for the race?"

"I forwarded this image to our explosives experts at Quantico," Blessing said. "They're going to look at close-ups of the bomb and see if that will tell us anything."

"We know he was in the bus station this morning," Luke said. "Do the surveillance videos show anything?"

"I'm already on it." Wade spoke up from the other end of the conference table. "I downloaded the video for the last twenty-four hours. We were able to pick him up leaving about 2:00 p.m., but we can't spot when he came in. He may have come in on one of the buses that arrived before then. It would be pretty easy to get lost in the crowds."

"And you're sure he hasn't been back?" Blessing asked.

"He hasn't shown up on film," Wade said. "And he'd be easy to spot this time of night. The last bus departed at 9:00 p.m. The station is closed until tomorrow at 6:00 p.m. for the bike race. The only people in the hall now are a security guard, and the janitor who went through about an hour ago."

"You're sure of the identity of the guards and the janitor?" Blessing asked.

"I'm one step ahead of you," Gus said. "I already checked with the head of security. He identified every employee we saw on the screen. And I'd have recognized our guy if he was one of them."

Blessing's phone beeped. He answered the call, listened a moment then disconnected. "That was the explosives tech at Quantico," he said. "He thinks the bomb Morgan is wearing in the photo would be remotely detonated. The most common way to do that these days is with a cell phone. And he reminded me they think the London bomb was remotely detonated, as well."

"Can we block the signal?" Luke asked.

"Yes," Blessing said. "At our first security meeting with the UCI, we suggested it. They objected. People don't like being disconnected—whether we're talking the racers, the fans or the press. We backed down, but now I'm going to ask for a cell phone signal block within a two-mile radius of this station."

"You're betting on the bomber not having an alternate way to set things off," Luke said.

"The explosives tech says the alternatives would require Morgan to manually trigger the bomb, or the bomber would have to get close enough to do it himself." Blessing clapped him on the shoulder. "We're doing everything we can to find her and to stop him."

Luke nodded. "I want to take a look at the bus terminal again," he said. "See if I spot anything." The terminal was the last place they definitely knew Danny had been. If they only had some way to retrace the bomber's steps.

"All right," Blessing said. "Let us know if you spot anything."

Luke turned to leave. Scott joined him at the door. "Can I come with you?" he asked.

Luke had thought he wanted to be alone, to worry and brood over the case. But Scott's offer gave him a way to avoid what would probably be a pointless exercise. "Yeah. You can show me where you saw Danny last."

They headed outside and crossed the plaza, which was lit up like midday by the portable light towers surrounding it. Half a dozen uniformed officers guarded the space, and the streets leading to the station were already blocked off. Bus and light rail service to the area had been halted until after the race.

"I don't see how anyone could get past all those guards," Scott said.

"We've got spotters in the hotel watching the plaza, as well," Luke said, nodding toward the high-rise hotel that flanked one side of the plaza. "But this Danny guy seems to have a knack for slipping past every trap we set."

The escalators leading down into the bus terminal were shut off. Luke flashed his ID to the guard at the top of the stationary steps, then led the way down into the cavernous space. Their footsteps echoed on the concrete, against a background of piped-in classical music. "You think they would at least shut off the music," Scott said.

"People don't like silence," Luke said.

"It's because they don't like to hear what's in their own heads." He gave Luke a half grin. "You don't have to be schizo to know that."

Luke nodded. The more time he spent around Scott, the more he liked him. He'd been dealt a bad hand but was doing his best to cope.

They walked the length of the terminal, surveying the empty bus bays and benches. Posters advertised an upcoming musical or advised of bus route changes. Midway down the hall, the handicap elevator bore an out-of-service sign; like the escalators, it was shut down in anticipation of events that afternoon.

Across from the elevator was a door marked Custodial. Luke tried the knob and it opened to reveal a closet that contained a large trash can on wheels, a couple of push brooms and a shelf of toilet paper, soap and other restroom supplies.

"Guess the janitor's already gone home," Scott said.

They exited the other end of the terminal and headed back toward the train station. "There's something we're not seeing," Luke said. He turned to look back at the silent, floodlighted plaza. Flags popped in the night breeze and the podium and grandstand awaited tomorrow's celebration. This was how he'd felt when Mark disappeared. He'd returned to the trailhead again and again, certain that he was missing some important clue that could help him find his brother. But no matter how hard he drove himself, he always came up blank. A man who never forgot a face couldn't remember those two hikers who had been at the trailhead when he dropped Mark off. And now he couldn't spot the clue that would lead him to Danny and to Morgan. What good was a skill like his if he couldn't use it to help the people who mattered most to him?

"Wherever she is, she knows you're looking for her," Scott said.

Luke nodded and turned back toward Union Station. As he and Scott walked back to the security center, the line of clocks taunted him. Only eleven more hours to find a killer. Only eleven more hours to save the woman he loved.

LUKE SNAGGED A few hours of restless sleep on a cot just off the conference room, but at five he was back in front of the computer, staring at diagrams of Union Station and the plaza, trying to put himself in the mind of a killer.

Scott slid a cup of coffee in front of him, then sagged into a folding chair at his side. "Did you sleep any?" Luke asked.

Scott shook his head. "I don't know whether it's because I'm worried about Morgan or because it's a race day. Even though I'm not racing anymore, I still get that rush of anticipation the night before. I never slept well the night before a race. I raced on nerve and adrenaline. By the time the day was over I was completely wiped. I remember one time I collapsed walking off the winner's podium. My trainer and Morgan hauled me to my feet and sneaked me out by some back elevator so no one would see."

"The race was over. Why did you care if anyone saw?"

"Because when something like that happens, the judges think you must be on something. All I needed was more water, food and rest." He leaned over and pointed to the handicap elevator behind the winner's podium. "That would have been convenient that day. Right by the podium."

The words struck Luke like a hammer blow. He stared at the X within a cube that marked the elevator on the diagram and had an image of the out-of-service sign on the door in the bus terminal. Why would someone bother to put a sign on the elevator when the whole building was closed?

The image in his mind shifted to the janitor's closet across from the elevator. The garbage cart inside the door would be big enough to hold a person.

"Gus!" He whirled in his chair and shouted to the agent across the room.

"What?" Blinking, Gus looked up from his computer.

"Do you still have those security recordings from last night?"

"Sure. What do you need to see?"

"The janitor. Let me see that janitor."

He and Scott hurried to stand behind Gus, who scanned through the videos, fast-forwarding through the arrival and departure of the last few buses of the night. Finally, he slowed and zoomed in on a figure pushing the garbage cart.

The janitor, a stooped man in a baggy jumpsuit with

a black stocking cap pulled low, exited the custodian's room with his cart and proceeded through the terminal, pausing now and then to empty a trash can. Finally, he headed back toward his closet. But instead of stowing the trash can there, he crossed the hall and pressed the button to open the elevator. He pulled the cart in after him and the door closed.

Luke swore and pounded his fist against the table. "How could we be so stupid?" he said. "That's Danny. It has to be."

"Come on." Gus pointed to the screen. "This guy is older and fatter. And the security chief here swore it was the regular janitor."

Travis and Blessing joined them in front of the monitor. "What's going on?" Blessing asked.

"I've found Danny." Luke indicated the figure on screen. "He's wearing those baggy coveralls and he's walking stooped to make us think he's old, and he's keeping his head ducked so we can't get a good look at him. But it has to be him, and I'll bet he's got Morgan in that cart. Why else would he go into the elevator? There aren't any trash cans there."

"Maybe he was taking the trash up to a Dumpster," Gus said.

"Run the video forward," Luke ordered.

They watched and, after ten minutes, the elevator doors opened and the janitor emerged, pushing the trash cart. Keeping his head down, he crossed to the closet. He came out seconds later and stuck the out-of-service sign on the elevator door, then shuffled away.

"Mark the time, then give me the camera on the elevator up top, in the plaza," Luke said.

Gus scrolled through files on the computer until he

came to the right one. "Here we go. Nine thirty-eight," he said.

The three of them leaned close to study the image on the screen. For five minutes they watched as little on the screen changed.

"He never took the elevator up," Travis said, breaking the silence.

"No. He left Morgan in there, I'm sure of it," Luke said. The image of her, trapped in that elevator all these hours, made his chest constrict. Only years of training prevented him from rushing to pull her out right away.

"Later today, probably not long after the first racers arrive, he'll send the elevator up top and detonate the bomb," Travis said.

"Except we're blocking cell phone signals, so he won't be able to detonate," Gus said.

"We have to get Morgan out of there before then," Luke said.

"We can't take a chance he's got the elevator wired to blow if someone tampers with it," Blessing said.

"Can't we get some explosives guys down there to figure that out?" Luke asked.

"Maybe." Blessing looked grim. "And then we miss our best chance to get this guy—and maybe to get all the people who are helping him, too."

Luke stared at him. "So what are you saying? We wait for her to die?"

"We let him make the first move and send the elevator up," Blessing said. "He chose that elevator on purpose—not just because it's close to the action, but because it's glass. It's like Mr. Westfield said—he wants people to see what he's doing. A pretty woman with a bomb wired to her is the kind of image they'll reprint in every paper in the country and show on every television station. He'll make sure everyone has enough time to get a good look. That's when we make our move."

"I don't like it, letting him call the shots," Luke said.

"Maybe we can find a way to throw off his timing," Travis said.

"How do we do that?" Blessing asked.

Luke looked to Travis, then Gus. Like him, they appeared to be fresh out of ideas.

"He thinks the racers will start to arrive about two forty-five," Scott said. "It's what I told him, and what the papers say, too. He'll want to wait until everyone is busy celebrating the victory before he brings up the elevator."

Blessing nodded. "Go on. How do we use that to our advantage?"

Scott licked his lips, and shifted from foot to foot. "We could come in earlier, before the real competitors arrive," he said. "Maybe one forty-five. Make him think the race is ending sooner. Throw off his timing. I could pose as a racer. Dress me up like the leader, with the yellow jersey. Put some agents on bikes as racers and we can get right up to the elevator, before the real winners come along. When he raises the elevator, the agents can move in."

Blessing was shaking his head before Scott finished speaking. "We can't involve a civilian," he said.

Scott met the commander's fierce gaze, his jaw set in a stubborn line. "You're the civilians to the racing world," he said. "I was one of them. I know the route, I know how to ride and I know how to make the victory look real."

"Danny knows you," Luke said. "Won't he spot the trick?"

"Most people aren't like you," Scott said. "They don't really remember people they don't know well. And he knows Scott the crazy dishwasher. He doesn't know me as a racer. He won't expect it. Besides, he's not a fan, even though he pretended to be. He doesn't care about the athletes. To him they're just a bunch of skinny guys in spandex, helmets and goggles. If we come in before he's expecting us, we'll force him to send the elevator up early. Agents will be right there to get in."

Blessing rubbed his chin, then nodded. "All right. We'll go with your plan. We don't have time to execute anything better. I assume you'll need bicycles and uniforms?"

"I've got a friend here in town with a bike shop," Scott said. "He'll help us out. And the UCI can supply official gear."

"What about the real racers?" Travis asked.

"We'll set up a checkpoint a couple of miles away to hold them off until we've cleared the area. Gus, you take care of that," Blessing said. He turned to Travis. "Get with the Denver Police. Tell them we'll need a SWAT team to come in on light rail. We'll position the cars on the tracks nearest the plaza and they can deploy from there when we give the signal. Luke, you go with Mr. Westfield to make the arrangements for the equipment he needs."

"What about Morgan?" Scott asked.

"She'll have to wait a little longer, but we'll get her out of there as soon as it's safe to do so," Blessing said.

## *Chapter Seventeen*

Morgan didn't know when her fear gave way to numbing calm. At some point in those hours of darkness inside the elevator she'd sunk into a kind of stupor. Maybe she was in shock, or simply exhausted and dehydrated. Her thoughts drifted to scenes of her life with her parents and Scott, then settled on replaying the time she'd spent with Luke. He was looking for her now. She was as sure of that as she was certain of her own name. The knowledge gave her strength. As impossible as her situation seemed, she wasn't going to give up hope. Danny thought he held all the cards, but she had Luke and his team fighting for her. She had to keep fighting, too. Right up until the very end.

She knew when morning came because of the increased sounds of activity overhead. She imagined the crowds gathering, the news trucks staging. Where was Danny? Was he watching it all from one of the expensive hotel rooms overlooking the plaza? Was he listening to race coverage and preparing to make his move?

More time passed and then, without warning, the elevator lurched and began to rise. Heart pounding, she looked up as the car emerged into the plaza. The sunlight blinded her, so that she had to view the scene through eyes closed to slits. She had an impression of crowds of people, of movement and bright colors.

As her eyes adjusted to the brightness, she could make out a group of riders beside the podium. One of them looked so much like Scott she knew she must be hallucinating. He wore the yellow jersey of a winner and looked so fit and confident, just as he used to.

A booming voice on a loudspeaker, audible even through the thick glass, ordered people to move away. A woman screamed, and, desperate to be free, Morgan strained against the handcuffs that bound her to the railing.

Then the elevator doors slid open and she stared across the now-vacant plaza. A row of helmeted men with heavy shields stood facing her, a hundred yards or more away. Then a single figure stepped out in front of them.

Luke, dressed in black, with a helmet and tactical vest, started walking toward her. As he drew closer, he lifted the visor on his helmet and his eyes locked to hers. The pain of the previous hours receded in the warmth of his gaze. Despite the bonds that still held her, she felt strong and safe again.

"Stop! Don't go any closer!"

The voice, loud and echoing against the stone and glass of the surrounding buildings, froze Luke in mid-stride. Morgan turned her head toward the sound as Danny stepped out from behind a concrete barricade, a scoped rifle braced against his shoulder. "One shot and I'll detonate that bomb," he said, continuing to move closer. "Even if you shoot me, you won't kill me before I've destroyed you and everyone around you."

Luke faced Danny, arms held out at his sides. "Is your life really worth this?" he shouted.

"It is to make people see that these dopers and frauds are a big part of what's wrong with our world today." He gestured toward the empty podium and grandstand. "People celebrate their lies and ignore the real wrongs."

"Blowing them up won't change anything," Luke said.

"You're wrong." Danny settled the rifle more firmly against his shoulder and lowered his head to peer through the sight.

Morgan stared, as if encased in ice, unable to move, to scream, to prepare herself for the death her brain told her was coming. Time seemed frozen, too, and then with a jolt, everything unstuck, events happening so fast they were a blur of movement and color and noise.

A slim figure in a yellow jersey raced toward the shooter. "No!" Scott shouted, and launched himself at the man.

Danny turned toward her brother and in that moment Luke drew his gun and fired. The first shot caught Danny in the shoulder. The second hit him in the head. He let go of the rifle and dropped to his knees. Scott stood over him, panting, and then the SWAT team rushed in and surrounded them both, obscuring them from view.

Luke holstered his gun and ran to her. He embraced her, holding her up, and gently removed the gag from her mouth. "I knew you'd come," she said, as he cradled her face and kissed her.

"I love you." He looked into her eyes. "I wasn't about to let you go when I'd finally found you."

"You don't ever have to let me go again."

"Sir. We need you to move back now." A helmeted man with a backpack in one hand and a pair of bolt cutters in the other moved in beside them. "We've still got work to do."

Reluctantly, Luke released her. "I'll go check on Scott," he said. "But I'll be back. I promise."

"I know," she said. "You're a man who keeps his promises." The kind of man she could trust with her life—and her heart.

TWO DAYS AFTER what the newspaper dubbed the end of the Bicycle Bomber, Morgan stood before a gathering of press, city officials and law enforcement and read from a prepared statement. "I'm very grateful to the law enforcement personnel who worked tirelessly to rescue me and stop a tragedy." She looked up from her notes to find Luke in the crowd. When he grinned at her, she couldn't keep back a smile of her own. Since her rescue, they'd been inseparable.

Had it really been only two days since that horrible ordeal? So much had happened since then. In the midst of almost unrelenting attention from the media, she'd been offered a staff job with a Colorado biking magazine. Best of all, Scott and she were growing close again. The new medication he was on was doing a good job of controlling his symptoms. But more than the medicines, the ordeal had summoned up a new strength and determination within him. The man who had launched himself at a madman in order to save her wasn't the tormented, rebellious man who had hidden from her for almost a year.

She turned and squeezed his shoulder before yielding the microphone to him. He cleared his throat and looked out at the crowd. "Some people have called me a hero for what I did," he said. "But the real heroes are the men and women in uniform who serve and protect the rest of us every day. I was simply a big brother who wanted to save his sister."

He paused for applause and cheers from the crowd, then looked back down at the paper he clutched. "I want to thank the mayor and city council for recognizing me with their service award. I also want to thank the other people and organizations who have reached out to me. I hope that I have helped others see that having a mental illness does not automatically make a person bad, or prevent him from being a contributing member of society."

He stepped back from the podium, only to be surrounded by the friends from his biking days who had rallied around him in the past forty-eight hours. He had been offered a coaching position, work as a trainer and even a book contract to write his story.

As the press conference ended, Luke found Morgan in the crowd and pulled her aside. "You looked beautiful up there," he said.

"I'm glad it's over," she said. "I'm ready to go back to being an anonymous journalist."

"I guess the new magazine job will keep you here in Denver," he said.

"As long as I stay in Colorado, I'm good. Scott is going to be here in Denver."

"Oh? What are his plans?"

"He's decided to take a job with the bicycle shop that supplied the gear for your agents in the race. The work will be enjoyable but low stress, and he'll be close to his new doctors."

"That's good." He glanced toward where her brother stood, talking with his bicycling friends. "I'm glad he's doing so well."

"What about you?" she asked. "What are your plans?" She held her breath, waiting for the answer to that question.

"I got my new assignment this morning. Looks like I'm headed to Durango."

"Searching for the people who helped Danny?" In their time together since the bombing attempt, she'd learned a lot more about his work.

"Yes. Taking out Danny may have slowed them down, but I doubt it will stop them for long."

"Maybe I can find a way to visit," she said. "I know it's tough for you to get time off while you're on a case."

He took both her hands in his, his expression tender. "I was hoping I could persuade you to come with me."

Did he mean for a visit or something more permanent? "What, exactly, are you asking?"

"I meant it when I said I have no intention of losing you again." He pulled her close. "We have something special between us. You know that, don't you?"

"Yes." From the moment they'd met, they'd shared a connection and the events of the past week had only drawn them closer together.

"Then let's make it official," he said. "I'm okay with a long engagement, if you need that, but I want you to be my wife."

"This is crazy," she said, laughing.

"Is that a yes?"

"Yes." Before the bomber had kidnapped her, she would have said it was too soon to make such a commitment— that she and Luke didn't know each other well enough.

But facing death head-on had made her realize how fragile and unpredictable life could be. Luke had risked everything for her. She could take a few risks to be with him. To love him forever.

\* \* \* \* \*

*Cindi Myers's series*
THE MEN OF SEARCH TEAM SEVEN
*continues next month with*
*LAWMAN ON THE HUNT.*
*Look for it wherever*
*Intrigue books are sold!*

**"My daughter is on her way to you now. I need you to promise to keep her safe. Don't forget she's just a child."** Cassidy turned toward the windows. **"A child who should not have to make this choice."**

"She will be with us for her Sunrise Ceremony."

"Are there drugs involved? Peyote or some such? Because I will bust you, all of you, so fast."

Clyne rolled his eyes. "You see. This is the trouble. You don't know anything about us."

"I know it's illegal to give drugs to a minor."

"We won't."

"Fine. Dress her up in feathers and beads. It won't change her." She stomped across the room and then back, her arms flapping occasionally. Finally she stopped before him. "I can't believe I kissed you."

He gave her a satisfied smile. "Well, you did."

# NATIVE BORN

BY
JENNA KERNAN

First Published in Great Britain 2016
By Mills & Boon, an imprint of HarperCollins*Publishers*
1 London Bridge Street, London, SE1 9GF

© 2016 Jeannette H. Monaco

ISBN: 978-0-263-91908-0

46-0616

Our policy is to use papers that are natural, renewable and recyclable products and made from wood grown in sustainable forests. The logging and manufacturing processes conform to the legal environmental regulations of the country of origin.

Printed and bound in Spain
by CPI, Barcelona

**Jenna Kernan** has penned over two dozen novels and has received two RITA® Award nominations. Jenna is every bit as adventurous as her heroines. Her hobbies include recreational gold prospecting, scuba diving and gem hunting. Jenna grew up in the Catskills and currently lives in the Hudson Valley of New York state with her husband. Follow Jenna on Twitter, @jennakernan, on Facebook or at www.jennakernan.com.

For Jim, always.

# Chapter One

If Cassidy Walker had known what would happen that Monday morning, she most certainly would not have worn her new suit. As an FBI field agent, Cassidy had drawn the short stick on assignments today or perhaps this was her boss's idea of humor. He knew there was no love lost between her and Tribal Councillor Clyne Cosen. Yet here she was watching his back.

Did her boss think it was funny assigning her to Cosen's protection or was this still payback for her bust in January? Was it her fault he was skiing in Vail when she and Luke had found both the precursor and the second meth lab? He'd gone back to the Organized Crime Drug Enforcement Task Force to report his agents had made the bust, but he hadn't been there.

Another feather in Cassidy's cap.

She glanced over at her supervisor, Donald Tully. Because of his dark glasses, she could not see his eyes. But his smirk was clear enough. The man could hold a grudge.

Cassidy adjusted her polarized lenses against the Arizona sun. From her place behind the speaker, she scanned her sector for any sign of threat. Her assignment was to protect the speaker from harm. This was not her usual duty, but today the stage was filled with a mix of state and national officials and that meant all hands on deck.

Outdoor venues were the most dangerous, but the Apache tribal leaders had insisted on staging the rally here in Tucson's downtown river park.

As the next speaker took the podium she tried hard to ignore his rich melodious voice and the fine figure he cut in that suit jacket. The long braid down his back had been dressed with leather cords and silver beads. His elegant brown hands rested casually on either side of the podium. He had no speech. Clyne Cosen, tribal councilman for the Black Mountain Apache, didn't need one.

She gritted her teeth as she forced her gaze to shift restlessly from one person to the next, looking for anyone lifting something other than a cell phone. Judging from the wide-eyed stares from most of the women in the crowd and the way they were using up their digital storage snapping photos of the handsome tribal leader, it seemed she was not the only one who admired the physical presence of this particular speaker.

Cassidy glanced at the cheery arrangement of sunflowers just before her feet and resisted the urge to kick them off the stage. She had a personal grudge with this speaker and was struggling to maintain her focus.

The next up would be Griffin Lipmann, the president of Obella Chemicals. The Bureau had already suited Lipmann in body armor as this latest spill had made him public enemy number one in the minds of many. He was the main reason the Bureau had lobbied to hold this rally indoors. Of course Clyne Cosen and his band of Apache activists wanted to be right beside the river that was now an unnatural shade of yellow.

Cosen knew the power of the television cameras and social media. Until he finished speaking, he was her damned assignment and the way he was going on and on, it didn't look like he'd be stopping anytime soon.

She tried to set aside her personal issues with him and do her job. But her teeth kept gnashing and her hands kept balling into fists. Soon she'd be meeting Clyne in a personal capacity, him and all his brothers. Damn that Indian Child Welfare Act. It had left her with no options, no more appeals. Nothing but the judge's final ruling. For the first time in her life she considered breaking the law and running for Mexico.

She glanced back to Clyne Cosen, who now motioned toward the ruined water. She knew he had spotted her before he took his place because his usually sure step had faltered and his generous smile had slipped. Did it make him nervous to have her behind him, watching his back? She hoped so.

Her gaze shifted again, from one face to the next. Watching the expressions, keeping track of their hands. The sunlight poured down on them. It was only a little past ten in the morning but the temperature was already climbing toward eighty. March in Arizona, her first one and hopefully her last. She'd planned to take the first assignment out of here, Washington hopefully or New York. She'd certainly earned a promotion after her last case. But now, if her daughter would be here she might… If they won, would she even be allowed to see her?

Cassidy jerked her attention back to her assignment. How she hated the outdoor venues. There were just an endless number of places to secure.

A woman wearing a cropped T-shirt reached into her purse. Cassidy leaned forward for a better look as Clyne lifted his voice, decrying the carelessness with which Obella Chemicals had released the toxic mix into their water. The woman lifted a silver cylinder from her bag and for one heart-stopping moment Cassidy thought it was the barrel of a gun. She reached under her blazer, gripping her pistol as the woman fumbled with a white cord. She plugged the cord into her cell phone and the other end into the cylinder. A charger, Cassidy realized and relaxed.

That was when the three-foot-tall vase of sunflowers beside the podium exploded.

"Shots!" she shouted, and took down her assignment, diving on Clyne's back as other agents moved before the line of dignitaries on the stage, making a human shield.

Griffin Lipmann, the representative from Obella Chemicals, hit the stage unassisted. His personal security force sprang before him an instant later, hustling him off the stage.

Her weight pitched Clyne forward, but he kept his balance, spinning toward her and then hitting the second flower arrangement before toppling backward onto the stage with her sprawled on top of him. She pushed off his torso and drew her weapon.

He tried to sit up.

She pressed a hand into his chest.

"Down!" she ordered, ignoring the firm body beneath her as she lifted her weapon and rolled to a kneeling position.

Two more agents stepped before them. Below the stage the audience members screamed and many turned to run.

"What's happening?" Clyne asked.

She didn't know. It could have been a shooter or some kid with a slingshot.

"Up," she snapped. "That way."

Cassidy followed the plan, tugging Clyne up and

guiding him off the back of the stage, pushing him before her. He was two steps down the staircase and she had reached the top step when something struck her in the back. It felt like someone hit her with a Louisville Slugger right below her left shoulder blade. The impact was so strong that it pitched her forward onto Clyne Cosen's back. He staggered. Then he grabbed both her forearms and kept running, making for the cover of the side entrance of the waterfront hotel. Cassidy tried and failed to draw a breath. The blow had knocked the wind right out of her and all she could manage was a wheezing sound.

He carried her along like a monkey on his back, never slowing as he stretched his long legs into a full-out run that made the wind whistle in her ears. Those Apache moccasins he wore were tearing up the ground faster than any cross trainers she'd ever owned. Local law enforcement held open the door. Cassidy glanced backward as they charged into the corridor.

The crowd erupted into chaos as men and women scrambled to clear the riverfront park that had turned into a shooting gallery. A bullet struck the building beside the exit and a chunk of concrete flew into the air. The officer holding the door moved to cover as Clyne grasped the closing door and hurtled inside.

Cassidy peered over his shoulder as the striped wallpaper and heavily painted desert scenes flashed past. She wanted to tell him to put her down or to make for the safe room. But she still hadn't succeeded in drawing a breath and now feared she was going to faint.

Finally he slowed, moving to the wall and swinging her around as if she were a dance partner instead of a rag doll. He made her feel small by comparison. Clyne Cosen had to be six-four in his flat footwear.

He lowered her to the ground in an alcove beside one of the restrooms. She slumped against the wall. Only then did she regain her breath. It came in a tortured gasp. Her eyes watered but she could see he'd gone pale.

Dignitaries and FBI agents rushed past them toward the rendezvous point. Cassidy still gripped her pistol.

"I think I'm hit," she said.

Clyne pulled off her blazer, sticking his finger through a hole in the back as he did so.

"Damn, that was Armani," she said.

"The shooter?" he asked.

She shook her head. Clearly Councillor Cosen did not know fashion. He dropped the blazer in her lap and she stroked the gray pinstripe like a sick cat. Then she holstered her weapon.

He expertly unclipped her shoulder holster and she grasped his wrist.

"Don't touch the gun," she said.

He met her scowl for scowl.

"Fine. You do it." He lifted his hands as if he was surrendering to her custody.

She did and the motion made her wince, but she managed to slip out of her holster and draw it down into her lap. When she finished she was trembling and sweat glistened on her skin.

Cosen tugged her blouse from the waistband of her slacks. A moment later she heard a rending sound as he tore her pristine white blouse straight down the center of her back. Then he leaned her forward to drag her blouse down off both shoulders so they puddled at her wrists. She now sat in only her slacks, practical shoes, body armor and her turquoise lace bra.

She flushed the color of ripe strawberries, a hazard of those with fair skin and felt her face heat as his eyebrows lifted. He hesitated only a moment and muttered something that sounded like "none of the guys in my unit wore lace."

She felt the pressure of his hand on her back.

"Perforation," he said, pressing on the sore place on her back. "Got you here."

She bit her lip to keep from whimpering. More people ran past in the corridor but she could see only trousers and dark shoes.

"Get me up," she said.

He ignored her, splaying a hand over her chest and pitching her forward like a ventriloquist's dummy. A moment later his other hand slipped under her vest at the back, rooting around.

"Vest is distorted right over your heart," he said. He released a long breath. "Didn't penetrate," he said. His hand stroked her back, skimming over her bra and out from beneath her vest. "No blood. Your vest caught it."

He eased her back until she leaned against the wall. He was propped on one knee as he looked down at her, his eyes were the color of polished mahogany.

"Still need a hospital," he said.

She flapped her arms, now decorated with what was left of her Ann Taylor white blouse. He'd torn the collar right off the back as if he were tearing tissue paper.

She tried for a full breath and didn't make it.

"Hurts like hell, doesn't it?" he asked.

It did.

How did he know that?

But then she remembered. Clyne Cosen was a former US marine. His jacket didn't mention that he had taken lead.

His smile held and she felt herself drawn in. Three

words from his character profile bounced around in her head like a Ping-Pong ball dropped on concrete.

*Charismatic.*

*Charming.*

*Persuasive.*

"Took one here and here." He pointed to his stomach and ribs. Making them part of an elite club, she supposed. The two of them. Only she was the one struggling with her breathing.

"A vest saved my life once before."

She didn't understand. He hadn't been hit. She'd kept him from that, protecting him like she was in the secret service and he was the president.

"Before?" she asked.

He pressed his open palm over her middle, his fingers splayed over her abdomen and she swore she could feel his touch even through the body armor. He met her stare.

"Agent Walker, you just saved my life."

# Chapter Two

"You can thank me later," Cassidy said. The bullet meant for Cosen had struck her in the back. She'd done her job, acted like a human shield and was trying very hard not to feel pissed about it.

Who wanted him dead? she wondered.

Cassidy slipped the shoulder harness over her right side and winced as she reached to get that left arm through. She managed it.

"Let me help," he said, reaching for the buckle.

"Did I warn you about the gun?"

He drew back. Once she had it clipped she was sweating like a marathon runner. But she still managed to drag her gray pinstripe blazer over her body armor, removing the view of turquoise lace from Clyne and any of the persons in the hallway. The tattered remains of her sleeves peeked out from the cuff of her ruined jacket.

She pushed off and he helped her up. Cassidy resisted the urge to bat his hand away.

"You're uninjured?" she asked.

"Yes. But you need to see a doctor."

"You carrying?" she asked, trying to surmise if he wore a holster under his blazer or clipped to the belt that sported an elaborate turquoise and red coral buckle.

Her gaze dipped south of his buckle and she flushed. And wouldn't you know it, when she lifted her gaze it was to find Cosen's gaze intent and his body perfectly still. Only now the tension in his tightly coiled muscles seemed sexual and arousing as all get-out.

"Sorry," she said.

He made a sound in his throat that fell somewhere between a growl and an acknowledgment.

She shook her head to clear the unwelcome arousal that stole through her. "Rendezvous point. Come on. Not safe here." Man, it hurt to talk.

Cassidy motioned for him to proceed down the hall. They'd made it about halfway when two of the field agents from her unit, Pauling and Harvey, appeared in the hall. Pauling came first, jogging so the sides of his suit coat flapped open to reveal both the shield on his belt and the butt of his pistol under his left arm. Keith Pauling was young, hungry and a former army ranger, with neatly trimmed hair and a hard angular face that screamed Fed from a hundred yards. Behind him came Louis Harvey, more experienced, heavier set but the haircut was a dead ringer.

"She's been shot," said Clyne.

Harvey took charge of Clyne and Pauling flanked Cassidy as they ushered them to the rendezvous room and her supervisor, who no longer looked smug.

"Walker. What took you so long?" he asked.

"She's been shot," Clyne said again.

Cassidy cast him a look. She didn't need him as her mouthpiece. Her ribs were feeling better and she'd be damned if she was going to spend the afternoon in the hospital when they had a shooter out there.

Clyne was herded away. He gave her one last long look over his shoulder, his braid swinging as he went.

He was one of the most handsome men she had ever met and for just a moment, the confident mask slipped and she saw her daughter's face. The resemblance took her breath away.

Amanda. The arch of the brow, the worry in those big brown eyes. And then he was gone.

She scowled after him. If she had saved his life, then he had also protected hers. When other speakers on stage had run or fallen or flattened to the platform, Clyne had acted like a soldier, recognized that she was injured and carried her to safety.

She hated to owe him anything and wondered if he felt the same. She had met him before this. On a snowy evening on the Black Mountain reservation while investigating a meth ring. And again in court when her attorneys succeeded in delaying the process for challenging her daughter's adoption.

Cassidy saw a medic first, who decided that her ribs were bruised. The slug that they dug from her vest appeared to be a thirty caliber. She declined transport and borrowed an FBI T-shirt from Pauling that was still miles too big for her. The navy blue T said FBI in bold yellow lettering across the front and back. She covered what she could with the blazer.

Her people had already found the location of the shooter, now long gone. He'd left at least one rifle cartridge behind, despite taking two shots.

"He was on the roof of the adjacent hotel," said Tully. Her new boss peered at her with striking blue eyes. His hairline had receded to the point that it was now only a pale fringe clipped short at the sides of his head, but his face was thin and angular with a strong jaw and eyes that reminded her of a bird of prey.

She knew from his previous comments that he liked

running their unit and didn't like that she wanted out. He took it as some kind of black mark that she was not satisfied to bake out in this godforsaken pile of sand called Arizona. But Cassidy wanted to join a team that chased the big fish, not the endless flow of traffickers and illegals that ebbed and flowed over the boarder like a tide.

Tully plopped her down before a computer and made her write her report. While the others moved out to investigate; she sat in the control room. The reporting didn't take long. After she finished, she went over the footage of the event with one of the techs, watching her movements when the vase exploded from the first blast and then the proceeding mayhem. They had not stationed on the roofs because the threat was not deemed great enough to warrant the added security. If they had, her people might have been in place when the shooter arrived.

Her partner returned. Luke Forrest was Black Mountain Apache and Clyne's uncle, though as she understood it, he was Clyne's father's half brother and born of a different father and clan, though she didn't understand the clan system very well. Luke had not applied to the Bureau, but had been recruited right out of the US marines.

"How you feeling?" he asked.

"Bored," she said.

He laughed, his generous smile coming easily on his broad mouth.

"Well, there's worse things," said Luke.

His hair was short, his frame was athletic and slim and he only vaguely resembled Clyne around the eyes and brows.

Cassidy stared at Luke and wondered what Clyne's

mother had looked like because she was Amanda's biological mother, too.

"What?" said Luke.

"Did you know Clyne's mother?"

"Of course."

"What was she like?"

He gave her an odd look, but answered. "Beautiful. Strong. Protective of her kids."

Cassidy nodded. Strong and beautiful, just like Clyne, she realized.

Why was she comparing everyone to Clyne Cosen? With any luck she wouldn't have to see him again. Her stomach twisted, knowing from her attorney that she would lose. Clinging to the only loophole allowed in the Indian Child Welfare Act. Thank God her daughter had turned twelve last June. Of course neither had known her real birthday until recently and had always celebrated on her adoption day on February 19.

"Where've you been?" she asked.

His eyes did that thing, the quick narrowing before his face returned to a congenial expression.

"Luke?"

He chuckled. "I must be losing my edge. I was with Tully and with Gabe Cosen. They're both on the joint task force."

She knew that Gabe had been invited belatedly to the joint drug enforcement task force that had been behind the operation to find the mobile meth lab and precursor needed to make the drugs. They had done an end run around Gabe, the chief of the tribal police force, and her partner because they were both Black Mountain Apache and therefore also suspects. Reasonable precaution, she had thought at the time. Now she felt differently.

"Listen, I'm sorry they left you out of the loop," she said.

"Yeah. Me, too." He gave her a long look. "You sure you're okay? You had a close call today."

"Yeah." Cassidy waved away his concerns as if they were smoke.

She refused to think about it, refused to consider that her daughter might have been left without a mother, again. Would Amanda then be turned over to her birth family?

She focused on what Luke had said. "So does Tully think this has to do with the bust on Black Mountain?"

"It might. Might be someone after Obella Chemicals. Hell, it might be someone *from* Obella Chemicals."

"In other words, they have no leads."

Forrest shook his head.

"Tully said that he thinks Clyne Cosen was the target. Gabe Cosen agrees and wants his brother to have added security detail when off the rez."

"Reasonable," said Cassidy.

Forrest rubbed his chin and Cassidy knew he was holding back.

"Spill it."

"Your name came up as a possibility, too." He gave an apologetic shrug.

Her first reaction was indignation but she reined that in. "They figure how I shot myself in the back?"

Forrest chuckled. "Yeah, that did put a chink in their theory."

"Anyway, we're trying to get Clyne to accept protection. He's resisting," said Forrest.

"You think Tully will pick you?" Luke Forrest would make sense. He spoke Apache, knew the culture and the tribe. He'd blend in while the other agents would stick out like flies on rice.

"Don't know. Doesn't matter if Clyne won't take us up on the offer. Plus we're still on cleanup with the Raggar case."

Which was proving much easier now that Gabe Cosen was on board. They had the meth lab and the precursor and were working on shutting down the distribution ring, run by mob boss Cesaro Raggar, currently in federal prison. She knew this because she'd been pissed not to get that assignment herself, when she was the one who'd responded to Gabe Cosen's call for backup once the precursor had been located. "How's the youngest brother doing?"

"Kino?" Luke rubbed his neck reflexively in the place his youngest nephew had taken a bullet. "Healing. And back to work on the tribal force."

As a tribal police officer, she knew. He'd also been a Shadow Wolf working on the border, tracking smugglers with his brother Clay. The Shadow Wolves were an elite team of Native American trackers working under Immigration and Customs Enforcement to hunt and apprehend drug traffickers on the Arizona border.

"Anyway, Gabe mentioned to Tully about the petition to overturn."

Cassidy's gaze flashed to Forrest and held.

"You should have told him, Cassidy. He's talking about pulling you off the Raggar case."

Which was exactly why she had not told Tully about the custody battle.

"That has nothing to do with me doing my job. Damn it, Luke. I've been on this since the beginning. I've put in the time and I deserve to see it through." Plus she knew bringing down Raggar and Manny Escalanti would give her the commendation she needed to earn a promotion to a major field office. Escalanti was the leader of the Black Mountain's only gang, the Wolf Posse. He'd managed to insulate himself on the reservation and by using others to run his errands. Cassidy wanted him bad.

Forrest shrugged. "It's a problem."

Clyne burst back into the room with her boss and his brother Gabe Cosen on his heels. Gabe scanned the room, met her gaze and did a quick clinical sweep before moving on. He kept his gun hand clear and immediately stepped out of the doorway to a position where he could see anyone approach the entrance. She smiled in admiration. The man would make a good agent, she decided, thinking that being the chief of police on the rez seemed a waste of his talents.

"Councilman Cosen, please," said Tully. "We can't guarantee your safety."

"Your guarantee. We all know what a guarantee from the federal government is worth."

Man, she could see the chip on his shoulder from clear across the room. If she had it right, his tribe was one of the few that had remained on their land because they had succeeded in making a deal with the federal government that had been kept.

"It would be easier with your consent," said Gabe. "We are only talking about the times when you come down off Black Mountain."

"I'd rather have you," said Clyne, his dark eyes flicking to his younger brother.

"Well, I already have a job on the rez. These folks are much better prepared to watch your back, as evidenced by Agent Walker here."

Clyne came up short when he spotted her.

Gabe's comment forced Clyne to look at her. Cassidy sucked in a breath and felt the twinge at her ribs. Why did the simple connection of his gaze and hers make her skin buzz with an electricity? Oh, this was really bad.

He looked away and Cassidy exhaled. Unfortunately her skin still tingled. It was his charisma. Had to be. Because she refused to consider that she was attracted to Clyne Cosen.

"It's bad enough that you've got DOJ and these agents swarming all over Black Mountain," said Clyne. She knew that he didn't like Department of Justice or FBI, really any federal agency, on Indian land. But his words lacked the authority of a moment before and his gaze slipped to meet hers again before bouncing away. He wiped his mouth. If she didn't know better she would say he was rattled.

"Yes, and one of them died taking that load of chemicals. And you didn't mind them using their helicopter to transport Kino to the hospital down here."

Cassidy had arrived on scene just after the shooting Gabe mentioned. Kino had been hit in the neck. He would have bled to death if not for the transport.

Clyne scowled and damn if she didn't find him even more appealing. Now Cassidy was scowling, too.

"I won't object to protection for gatherings off the rez," he said at last. "Are we done?"

It seemed Clyne was as anxious to be away from them as she was to see his back.

"Almost," said Gabe. "I want to request a new DOJ agent be appointed to the joint task force to replace the fallen agent, Matt Dryer."

"Easily done," said Tully.

"And," said Gabe glancing first to his brother and then to Cassidy. He held her gaze as he spoke. "I request that Luke Forrest and Cassidy Walker be assigned to Black Mountain to assist in our investigation and report back to the joint task force."

"No," said Clyne.

Gabe turned to his elder brother as the two faced off. Clyne was slightly taller. Gabe slightly broader.

"I am required to notify tribal council of the presence of federal authorities on the reservation. I am not required to obtain their permission. This is your notice."

Clyne's teeth locked and his jaw bulged. Cassidy had to force herself not to step back. If the man could summon thunder it would surely have been rumbling over his head.

"Perhaps an agent other than Walker?" suggested Tully.

Gabe shook his head, his gaze still locked on Clyne. "Her."

Cassidy swallowed. She didn't understand why Police Chief Cosen would make such a play when his brother was against it. Her boss looked leery as well, likely because he now knew of the custody battle boiling between them. But she wanted the assignment because she wanted to continue her investigation and there was only so much she could do from Phoenix when the main player, Manny Escalanti, never left his nest on Black Mountain.

But why would Gabe Cosen want her? It didn't make sense and she suspected a trap. Was he trying to gain some advantage in the adoption battle? If so, she couldn't see it.

Clyne now leaned toward Gabe with a hand on his hip, which was thankfully clear of any weapon. Gabe settled for folding his arms over his chest and smiling like a man who knew he had won this round. Cassidy didn't think it was over, because Clyne looked like a bull buffalo just before a charge.

Their uncle Luke Forrest stepped between them, placing a hand on the shoulder of each brother.

"It won't be so bad," he said to his nephew. "Just like I'm visiting. And I sure won't mind sitting at your grandmother's table a time or two."

Tully glanced at her with an open look of assessment. She thought he was trying to puzzle this out as well and had also come up empty.

"All right, then," said Tully and pointed at Cassidy. "Agents Walker and Forrest, you are reassigned to Black Mountain until further notice."

Clyne glared at her and her wide eyes narrowed to meet the challenge in his gaze.

"Yes, sir," she said.

# Chapter Three

"But why would he choose me?" Cassidy asked.

"Damned if I know," said Tully. "Because you saved his brother's life?"

Her partner, Luke Forrest, spoke up. "Don't you see a conflict of interest here?"

"It's Chief Cosen's call," said Tully. "One thing I know about Agent Walker is that she does her job. She proved it again today."

She couldn't tell if he was proud of her or still annoyed. But it was true. If she wanted Clyne Cosen dead, that had been her chance.

"Yes, sir." It was automatic, her response. Inside her head she was shouting, *No!* But that was the voice of emotion. The one that she ignored whenever possible.

"Walker. Forrest. You are assigned to the Organized Crime Drug Enforcement Task Force."

"Yes, sir."

Cassidy groaned. She didn't need to be on another committee. Especially one made up of state, local and federal authorities. What she needed was to be in the field. They'd been getting close to Ronnie Hare and that bust might be all she needed to gain her transfer.

"Since you are Apache, I expect you to be able to do some recon and find out if there is anything going on up there that would lead someone to take a shot at Tribal Councillor Cosen."

"Yes, sir," said Agent Forrest.

Her daughter. The basketball game that she'd promised she would attend.

"I need to make arrangements for my daughter."

"Go on, then."

Clyne's scowl deepened.

Cassidy moved to the far side of the room to make a call to her mother-in-law. After Cassidy's husband, Gerard, had been killed in action, Diane Walker had moved west to help her pick up the slack. Cassidy had no family of her own, and Gerard had been Diane's only child. She made the call, apologized and disconnected. It was not the first time she had been unexpectedly sent on an assignment. It was the first time that that assignment was challenging her custody in federal court.

Cassidy glanced back to the waiting three men. She had one more important call to make to Amanda, the only thing more important than her job.

"Hi, pumpkin. You at school?"

"Mom, school ended hours ago. I'm at the rec center. The game. Remember? Where are you? Warm-up is almost over."

She glanced at her watch and saw it was nearly four in the afternoon.

"Right. You all warmed up?" she asked, turning her back on the men.

"Where are you?" asked Amanda.

"I'm still in Tucson." Her daughter groaned. "Grandma is on the way."

"Oh, Mom!"

"Listen. There was some trouble. You'll see it on the news."

"Mom?" Her daughter's voice was now calm. Unlike some of her fellows, she had never hidden what she did from her daughter. "Are you okay?"

"Yes, fine. But I'm still in Tucson."

"Did you see my brothers?"

She glanced to Gabe and then to Clyne. "Yes." She gripped her neck with her opposite hand so hard that her back began to ache.

"I want to meet them!" Her daughter's voice filled with longing.

"Maybe soon."

And maybe forever. Cassidy's heart ached low down and deep, reminding her of a pain she had not felt since she'd discovered her husband had been killed in action.

She needed to get them out of Arizona. If only that would work. But she knew that moving wouldn't protect Amanda from one particular threat. The ICWA, Indian Child Welfare Act. Sovereign rights. Tribal rights.

"Are you listening to me?" asked Amanda.

"What was that, pumpkin?"

"I asked if you will be back in time for Saturday's game?"

She glanced to Clyne, the newest of the tribal council and enemy number one in her book. Oh, if she could just find something to bury them but all she'd come up with was something ancient on the third brother, Clay. She stiffened. A brow arched as she looked at Clyne, who narrowed his eyes at her.

"I'll try, pumpkin."

"Oh, Mom!"

From the phone, Cassidy heard the sound of a scoreboard buzzer.

"I've got to go."

Cassidy pictured her in her red-and-white basketball

uniform, her dark hair pulled back in a ponytail, her lips tinted pink from the colored lip gloss her daughter had begun wearing. It was her last year of elementary school. Her last year of eligibility in the youth basketball league. Next year Cassidy would have a teenager on her hands. She hoped.

"I love you," said Cassidy.

"You, too." The line went dead.

She held the phone to her chest for just a moment, eyes closed against the darkness that crept into her heart. What would she do if they took her daughter away?

"Was that her?"

The gruff male voice brought her about and she faced Clyne, who had snuck up on her without a sound.

Cassidy straightened for a fight with Clyne—her daughter's eldest brother and the first name on the complaint petitioning to have her daughter's closed adoption opened and overturned. She knew he'd win. He knew it, too. She saw not an ounce of pity for her in those deep brown eyes. Just the alert stare of a confident man facing a foe.

His face was all angles where her daughter's was all soft curves and the promise of the woman she would soon become.

An Apache woman. Not if she could help it. Amanda would be whatever she wanted and not be limited to one place and one clannish tribe who clung to that mountain as if it were more than just another outcropping of stone. Cold as his heart, she suspected. What did he know about Amanda, anyway? Nothing. According to his records he'd been deployed with the US Marines when his sister had been born and hadn't been discharged until after the accident that took his mother.

"Was that who?" she asked. But she knew. Still she made him say it.

"Jovanna?" he said, breathing the word, just a whisper.

Her skin prickled at the hushed intimate tone.

"Her name is Amanda Gail Walker."

"Amanda?" Clyne spat the word as he threw up his hands. "I've never met an Apache woman named Amanda."

"And you won't meet this one if I have any say in it."

"We are her family," said Clyne. "Her *real* family."

"Hey, I'm just as real as the family that didn't even know she was alive for twelve years."

"Nine," he corrected. Nine years on July 4 since his mother had died in that auto accident.

"If it were up to you all, she would have been raised in a series of group homes in South Dakota."

"You are not a mother. You're a field agent."

"And?"

"You have no husband, no other children."

"What's your point?"

"You are alone raising my sister and you have a very dangerous job. You were shot today! You could get killed at any moment. A good mother doesn't put her child at that kind of risk."

"It's an important job."

"So is motherhood," said Clyne. "So is teaching her who she is, who her people are, where she comes from. She belongs where her tribe has lived for centuries. You move her around like she's a canary."

"You finished? Because it isn't up to you. It's up to the judge. Until then I do my job and you keep away from *my* daughter."

"Walker!" She turned to see her boss closing in. "Outside. Now."

She followed him out into the hallway.

"What was that?" asked Tully.

"Custody battle," she said.

"I know all about that. What I'm asking about is why are you fighting with a tribal councilman?"

"Perhaps I'm not the right one for this assignment," she said, hating herself for saying it. She'd never turned down an assignment before.

"I agree. But I need an agent up there on Black Mountain. One who is not Apache and Chief Cosen just gave me an in. So you're it. Find out what's going on up there. You got it? We've got permission for two agents on that rez. That's never happened before. So shut your mouth and do your job."

"Yes, sir." Cassidy had a thought. "Do you think the Cosens might be involved with the distribution ring?"

"How do I know? That's for you to find out."

Cassidy's mood brightened

If she were up there, in his home, in his community, perhaps she could find some chink in the Cosen armor, something to make them unfit to raise a twelve-year-old child.

But if that were so, then why in the wide world would Chief Gabe Cosen allow her up in his territory?

She had a terrible thought. What if the Cosen brothers wanted her up there, away from the protection of other agents, so that something bad could happen to her? That would remove her from the equation when it came to the custody of her daughter.

Cassidy drew in a breath and faced her boss. It was a gamble. But it was the only way she could see to keep

Amanda without putting her daughter in the position to choose.

A twelve-year-old should not have to choose between her mother and her brothers. It wasn't fair to ask a child to make such a choice. But Amanda would have to, if it came down to that.

Cassidy squared her shoulders as if she were still at attention in lineup. Then she met the analytical gaze of Donald Tully.

"If I do this, will you put in that recommendation for my transfer to DC?" she asked.

Tully's mouth went tight, but the glimmer in his eyes showed he knew she had won. "You know we do some good work here, too."

"Answer the question."

"Yes, damn it. I will."

"All right. I'll do it."

HIS BROTHER ANSWERED on the first ring.

"I got her!" he said, his voice full of jubilation.

"You sure?" asked his brother, Johnny.

"Gray Volvo station wagon, right?"

"That's what I said."

Johnny had tailed her the day she'd shown up in court to testify on a big case. She'd lost the tail easily but now they knew the make and model of her personal vehicle.

"She heading to the hospital?" Johnny asked.

"Don't know," he said.

"Damned, I hit her dead center. Should have knocked her down, at least. Then I would have had another shot," said Johnny.

"We need to get that tungsten ammo."

"We don't. Common caliber will get the job done."

"If it's a head shot."

"It was a head shot," said Johnny. "She moved. Jumped on him."

"What about a bigger caliber or a hollow point?"

"We buy that and we might as well wave a red flag in front of the Feds' eyes. No reason to buy that ammo but one."

"No guts, no glory," he said, using Johnny's favorite expression.

"Hey, I'm all about hitting the target. Just don't want a spot next to Brett's."

"What do you mean?"

"In the cemetery, stupid," said Johnny.

"Right," he said. Johnny was always the smart one. "She's heading for the interstate."

"Heading home, maybe. That'd be a break. Get her address if you can," said Johnny.

"Sure. Sure."

"Hey, kid? Finding her car? Ya done good."

He basked in the praise. Truth was, he didn't mind a cell next to Johnny's. Just so long as he took care of business first.

# Chapter Four

Seemed you only needed to get shot to get the rest of the day off. Cassidy's boss sent her to the hospital. But she didn't go. Instead, she went home to her daughter. The drive from Tucson to Phoenix took three hours, but it didn't matter. She made it in time for supper.

She arrived with pizza and found Diane waiting with the table set. Amanda bounded off the couch and accepted a kiss and then the boxes, which she carried to the kitchen dinette.

Gerard's mother retrieved the milk from the refrigerator for Amanda and then took her seat. Diane had many good qualities. Cooking was not one of them. But she was the only other family Amanda had. Cassidy gritted her teeth at the lie. The only family that Cassidy wanted her to have. Was that selfish?

"Finally," said Diane. "I'm starving."

Diane was sixty-three, black and didn't look a day over fifty. She had taken an early retirement from UPS five years ago when her only son had been killed in action. Her skin was a lighter brown than her son's had been and she chose to straighten her hair, instead of leaving it natural, as Gerard had.

When Cassidy had transferred from California to Arizona, Diane had joined them. Her decision to help raise Amanda had allowed Cassidy to take Amanda out of the school keeper's programs and allowed Cassidy to move into fieldwork, which she truly loved.

Cassidy excused herself to change. Using a mirror, she checked the sight of the impact and noted the purplish bruise that spread across her back. She took four ibuprofens and slipped into a button-up blouse because it hurt too much to lift her arms over her head. Then she rejoined her mother-in-law and daughter.

After dinner it was past nine on a school night. Amanda headed off to bed. Cassidy joined her, sitting on the foot of the twin bed, trying not to look at the photo of her husband on his second deployment that rested on Amanda's nightstand.

"You're leaving again, aren't you?" said Amanda.

Cassidy stroked her daughter's glossy black hair away from her face. Clyne's hair had been just this color. Gabe and Kino kept their hair so short it was hard to compare and she had yet to meet Clay, the middle brother.

"Yes, doodlebug. I have to pack tonight. I'll be gone before you get up."

"We have another game on Wednesday."

"I'm sorry."

"Where?" Her daughter knew that her mother couldn't say much about her assignments. But this time, somehow, it seemed important that she know.

"Black Mountain."

"On the reservation?" Her daughter's voice now rose with excitement. "Oh, Mom. Why didn't you tell me?"

Because she tried to keep her daughter away from the people who were attempting to take Amanda away from her.

"Can I come?"

"Of course you can't come."

Her daughter continued on and Cassidy wished she had not mentioned the location of her assignment.

"Are you going to Pinyon Fort? Will you see the museum? There are two hotels on Black Mountain, the ski resort and the casino. Where will you stay?"

It was like watching a train pick up speed and having no way to slow it down.

Ever since Cassidy had told her daughter that she was not really Sioux, as they had been told, but Apache, Amanda had been Googling the Black Mountain tribe's website and studying Apache history.

"I'm not sure yet." Cassidy pressed a hand to her forehead.

"You have to tell me everything, what it's like. They had snow there today. I checked. I haven't seen snow since we left South Dakota. I wish I could come, too."

Cassidy stroked her daughter's head and forced a smile.

"Maybe next time."

"Will you see them?"

"Yes."

Amanda's eyes widened. "Oh, I want to go!"

"I know."

"What if the judge says I have to go with them? Wouldn't it be better if I had at least met them?"

Cassidy's heart ached at the possibility of losing her daughter.

"They can't take you for long. Even if the judge overturns my custody, you remember what I told you?"

"I'm twelve."

Cassidy nodded.

Amanda recited by memory. "Twelve-year-olds can request to be adopted away from their tribe."

"That's right."

Amanda frowned. Ever since they'd discovered who she really was and that she had another family out there, Amanda had been increasingly unhappy. Of course the opening of her adoption and the challenge for custody upset her. Why wouldn't it?

"They can't win," said Cassidy. "Because you are old enough to choose."

Amanda moved her legs restlessly under the covers and seemed to want to say something.

Cassidy waited.

"Can you at least take a picture of them?"

"What? Why?"

"So I can see if they look like me?"

How she wished she could go back to the time when they both thought she had no one but her mom and dad and Grandma Diane. When there was no one else.

"I don't think that's a good idea," said Cassidy.

"Please?" asked Amanda.

Cassidy tucked the covers back in place. "I have to go pack and you have to go to sleep. Good night, sweetheart."

Amanda kissed her mother and then flopped to her side. She said nothing more as Cassidy walked to the bedroom door and waited.

She was about to give up when Amanda flopped back to face her.

"Be careful up there, Mom."

"I will. I love you."

"You, too."

Cassidy closed the door and headed to her bedroom to pack. She was good at packing. A tour of duty with the US Army had taught her that. And also how to fly helicopters. She'd put in for a transfer from her first assignment with the FBI after Gerard died because she couldn't stand to live in the home they had chosen together. They'd ended up in Southern California.

After she had finished in her room, she carried her suitcase, briefcase and duffel down to the hallway. She told Diane all she could about where she was going. But she didn't tell her that after this assignment she would finally get her transfer. Would Diane come with them or would it be just the two of them again?

She didn't know. What she did know was she needed the custody decision so that Amanda could tell the judge she wanted to be adopted again by her mother. Then she needed to get away from this part of the country. As far as possible from the Apache tribe. Until then, she was keeping her daughter away from the Cosen brothers.

"So you won't change your mind?" Clyne asked Gabe.

"Do you know how many officers I have?"

Clyne did, of course. Twelve officers for twenty-six hundred square miles. Only it was eleven since he'd lost a man in January.

"I need help, Clyne. Not just on processing evidence in the Arizona crime labs. I need investigators. Because if you think this is over with you are mistaken. All we did was slow them down. They'll be back and I don't want my guys killed in gun battles with Mexican cartel killers."

Clyne did not want that, either.

"But why her?" He meant Agent Walker.

"Do you know anything about her?"

"All I need to know."

"That's bull. She's highly qualified and she knows what she is doing. She knows all the players. You have to trust me on this."

Clyne tried for humor. "She's a real company man, huh? She probably wears that FBI T-shirt to bed."

That gave him a strong image of pale legs peeking out from beneath a navy blue T-shirt that ended right below her slender hips.

Clyne growled. He stood with his four brothers, all now wrapped in blankets and perched as close to the fire as possible as their uncle Luke added the stones to the fire. The stones were among the Great Spirit's creations and so had a life force and power like all things in nature. Luke would be tending the fire and passing the hot stones into their wikiup for the ceremony of purification. Their uncle was the only one dressed appropriately for the chilly night air, warm enough to unzip his parka and remove his gloves.

"When will she be here?" he asked.

His uncle took that one. "Tomorrow morning. Late morning, I think. In time for the BIA presentation."

Their people had a love-hate relationship with the Bureau of Indian Affairs, who oversaw business on the reservation for the federal government. But the BIA had money Clyne needed for their water treatment facility so he would do his best to play nice.

Luke poked at the coals, judging the heat. "Almost ready."

Clyne began to shiver and Clay was now jumping up and down to keep warm.

Kino nudged between Clay and Gabe. He still had a white bandage on his throat. A visible reminder of how close they had been to losing him. Clyne remembered Gabe's words about not wanting to lose any more officers to this war with traffickers. He knew from Gabe that his men had been outgunned. The cartel killers had automatic weapons and the tribal police force was issued rifles, shotguns and sidearms. It was not a fair fight.

Clyne looked from Gabe to Kino. Would the FBI presence on the rez help keep them safe or put them at greater risk?

"Will she bring Jovanna?" asked Kino.

Gabe cast him an impatient look. "She doesn't want her to meet us."

"But the attorney says we'll win," said Kino. "Any day and we'll win."

"And she'll slap a petition to allow Jovanna to choose to be adopted," said Clay. "Our attorney said so."

"Nothing we can do about that," said Gabe.

They all looked to Clyne, as they had since he'd came home from the endless fighting in the Middle East to assume his place as head of this household.

"We have a petition, too. I spoke to our attorney yesterday."

Before he was almost killed. She wouldn't do something like that. Set him up, would she? Killing him wouldn't stop this. She must know that.

"Our sister can't make a fair choice unless she has had an opportunity to meet us," said Clyne.

Clay grinned. "Think that will work?"

"I do. It's logical. It's appropriate."

"How long will we have her?" asked Kino.

A lifetime, Clyne hoped. His sister belonged here with them in the place of their ancestors.

"I've asked for a year," said Clyne.

Kino gave a whistle.

Luke poked at the stones. "You boys ready?"

They shucked off their blankets and ducked into the domed structure. All of the brothers had built this sweat lodge. The stone foundation lined the hollow they dug into the earth and the saplings arched beneath the bark-and-leather covering.

Clay and Kino moved to sit across the nest of fresh piñon pine and cedar branches. Clyne was glad the two had somehow managed to leave their pretty new wives for the evening to join their elder brothers in the sweat lodge.

Outside the entrance to the east, the sacred fire burned. Their uncle would stand watch, providing hot stones, protecting the ceremony.

Clyne sat in a breechclout made from white cotton. Both Gabe and Kino preferred loose gym shorts and Clay sat in his boxers, having forgotten his shorts. Luke passed in the first stone, using a forked cedar branch. Clyne moved it to the bed of sage, filling the lodge with the sweet scent. More stones followed as Clyne and his brothers began to sing. When the stones were all in place Luke dropped the flap to cover the entrance and the lodge went dark, black as a cave, the earth, a womb, the place where they had come from and would one day return. Here their voices joined as they sang their prayer.

Gabe used a horn cup to pour the water of life over the stone people, the ones who came before Changing Woman made the Apache from her skin.

Steam rose all about them and their voices blended as sweat ran from their bodies with the impurities. Clyne breathed in the scent of sweet pine and cedar and prayed for the return of their sister.

# Chapter Five

Cassidy Walker called ahead so the tribal police wouldn't pull her over like they did the last time. She made it to Black Mountain but did not have time to make it to her room at the Black Mountain Casino. This was one of two hotels on the property. The other was clear up in Wind River where the tribe had a ski resort, but that was too far from Clyne's home.

From her former partner, she knew the Cosens all lived near the main town. Clyne and Gabe lived with their mother Tessa's mother, Glendora Clawson. Both the younger brothers were newlyweds and had their own homes. Kino was expecting his first child.

*Amanda is about to become an aunt.*

The realization came like a kick to her gut.

It didn't matter, she told herself. That petition would hit the minute the judge ruled. A week or two up here in the hinterland and she'd have her promotion. The judge would rule against her but the petition would reverse Amanda's placement. In six months she and her daughter would be living in DC or lower Manhattan. One thing was certain, Amanda would have an education and opportunities she would not likely receive on the reservation. Amanda would have the chance to become whatever she wished.

The ringing phone made her jump clear out of her seat. The ID said it was Tully. She hit the speak button on her phone.

"Good morning, sir."

"You there yet?"

"Nearly." She had decided to catch a few hours' sleep at home and leave at five in the morning, rather than drive up last night as Tully had suggested. "Anything on the shooting?"

She couldn't help stretching and then winced. Sitting made her ribs hurt. Breathing made her ribs hurt. Talking made her ribs hurt. She glanced at the ibuprofen bottle and then the clock. One more hour before she could have another dose.

"Yes. One shooter, .30 caliber. Positioned on the Star of Tucson Hotel. We now have three cartridges. Forensics has everything we could pull from up there. Garbage mostly, we think. But maybe we'll get a hit."

"Let's hope," she said.

"Change of plans for today."

Cassidy tensed. She didn't like surprises and so tried to be ready for every eventuality. But she hadn't seen this assignment coming. That was certain.

"Gabe Cosen called. His brother has a groundbreaking on the rez today. He wants you and Forrest on hand in case there is trouble."

"I thought we were up here to pursue leads to apprehend Ronald Hare and investigate the—"

Her boss cut in. "Yeah. Yeah. But today try to be sure Cosen doesn't get shot." He provided her with the coordinates given to him by Police Chief Cosen. "Clyne Cosen has another rally off-reservation in Phoenix on Wednesday. Damned victory tour. You and Forrest are accompanying him from Black Mountain to the rally."

"Does he know this?"

"Not yet."

Cassidy grimaced. This wasn't going to be good. She knew Clyne Cosen well enough to know that. But she also didn't like the bait and switch. She was here to investigate the ongoing drug activity here. Not play nursemaid to a bristly Apache who didn't want her within a mile of him.

"We'll be on-site for the next rally. This one is indoors, so no BS. Love to find the shooter before then."

"You and me both." She couldn't help but twist to check the sore muscles and ribs. Yup. They still hurt. "I'm here. Gotta go."

"Check in after the event."

"Yes, sir." She disconnected and said, "And keep that transfer request front and center."

Cassidy pulled into the barren patch of ground her GPS had brought her to. She would have been certain she was off course but there was a series of fluttering triangular flags flapping briskly in the March breeze. She dragged her winter coat from the rear seat. Down in Phoenix it was sixty degrees. But up here fourteen thousand feet above sea level there was ice on the ground.

"That's why they call themselves Mountain Apache," she muttered.

A leaning white sign advertised the future site of the Black Mountain water treatment facility. *Whoo-hoo*, she thought and climbed from the vehicle. The wind tore a strand of hair from her ponytail and no amount of recovery could make it stay in place. Her chin-length hair was just too short for a pony and she'd be damned if she'd be seen outside the house in either pigtails or a headband.

She glanced at her watch and saw she'd arrived forty-five minutes early. That gave her time to check the perimeter and to wish she had worn thicker socks. The open field left few places to hide and the lack of any obvious vehicle was encouraging. But with a scope, a shooter could easily be in range. Clyne had agreed to wear body armor for this event. Cassidy adjusted hers, her backup. The one without the distortion over her heart.

Back at her sedan, Cassidy was just lifting her phone to call Luke when a line of vehicles, mostly pickups, arrived in a long train of bright color. The wind pushed her forward and she had to widen her stance to keep from losing her footing. The sudden movement made her ribs ache.

She watched the men and women emerge from their vehicles. Clyne was easy to spot. She didn't know exactly why. Perhaps his height or the crisp way he walked. He joined some men dressed in trenches, walking with them along the flapping flags.

Luke walked slightly behind them. She knew the instant Clyne spotted her because his ready smile dipped with his brow. Then he turned his attention back to his conversation with his guests.

She heard him say, "Self-sustaining and by using local labor we expect to come in below the estimate."

She fell into stride behind him, ignoring the heady scent of pine that reached her as Clyne passed. He'd smelled like that yesterday, she recalled, when he had carried her into the hotel. Cassidy inhaled deeply, enjoying the appealing fragrance.

"Hey," said Luke.

"How was last night?" she asked.

"Quiet. You?"

"Good."

"What did they say at the hospital?"

She didn't answer.

"Cassidy?"

She fessed up. "I went home."

Luke's smile seemed sad. He had met Amanda more than once in the times before she knew he was her uncle. Amanda's father's half brother. If it were only him, she wouldn't mind Amanda getting to know him better. Luke, she knew and trusted.

"I got Gabe to put someone on Manny Escalanti. Told him our office would pick up the overtime."

Manny Escalanti was the new head of the Wolf Posse, the Apache gang operating on the rez. It had been this gang that had held the chemicals for production and moved the mobile meth labs to keep them ahead of tribal police.

"We need ears on him, too. Do we know if the Mexican cartels are still working with them?"

"DOJ says that they are working with both the Salt River gang and the Wolf Posse."

In January, the cartel had decided to move operations to Salt River but failed to capture the chemicals needed because Gabe and his very connected fiancée, Selena Dosela, had succeeded in stopping them. Selena was also Black Mountain Apache and her father, Frasco, had ties to the Wolf Posse and American distributor, Cesaro Raggar. Good thing Dosela was working with them now.

"What do you think of Selena?" she asked.

"I think she's very brave and very lucky."

"I mean, do you think she is working with the cartels?"

"No. Not at all."

His answer was a little too quick as if that was what he hoped to be true, rather than what was true.

"Her father was recruited by Raggar."

Raggar was the head of the American distribution operation running the business from federal prison.

"And Frasco went to DOJ and made a deal."

"To save his hide," said Cassidy.

"It's a valid reason to come to us. Kept his family safe and got them out of the operation."

"Unless Raggar retaliates."

"Gabe is very worried about that. Even asked me about witness protection for Selena's entire family."

That was new information.

"But her father won't leave the rez."

The sentiment seemed endemic up here, she thought.

The group formed a rough circle around nothing she could see other than that this was the place that their tribal councilman had chosen to stop moving forward into the barren field.

She and Forrest stepped back, just outside the circle, scanning the audience and the surrounding area.

"Too far from cover," she said to Forrest.

"Too cold, as well. We won't be out long."

But it didn't take long for a bullet to travel through a person's flesh and bone.

Cassidy scanned the faces, checked the hands and listened to Clyne lift his voice to describe the fantastical water treatment plant as if it were some shining tower sitting on a hill instead of a pit that strained excrement.

Cassidy scanned the faces and realized that she and the two representatives from the BIA, Bureau of Indian Affairs, were the only white people in the gathering.

Clyne spoke loud enough for the gathering to hear and she had to admit his argument for the funding was

eloquent, thoughtful and timely, but perhaps wasted on
the men who were wearing the equivalent of raincoats in
the unceasing wind. They stomped their feet restlessly
as she swept the crowd, impressed with the practical
clothing of the rest of the gathering.

Clyne finished and the men all shook hands. Photos
were taken for the Black Mountain webpage and Cassidy made sure she was not in any of them. The procession retreated to the string of vehicles that reminded her
of a wagon train for some reason. She shadowed Clyne
to his vehicle where he stopped to glare at her.

"Would you like me to follow you or accompany
you?"

"Neither," said Clyne.

"Then I'll follow." She stepped away so he could
open his door. "Shouldn't Gabe be here, too?"

He smirked at her and just that simple upturning of
his mouth made her insides twitch in a most unwelcome physical reaction to a man in whom she refused
to have any interest.

"He is here. He told me to tell you that you did a
pretty good job of scouting the perimeter. Though not
too good, obviously." With that he climbed in the navy
blue pickup and swung the door closed.

The truck rode high, leaving her at shoulder level
with the decal of the great seal of the Black Mountain
tribe that was affixed to the door panel and showed a
chunk missing at the top right. The seal included Black
Mountain in the background with a pine tree, eagle
feather and something that looked like a brown toad-
stool in the foreground.

"Try and keep up," he said and led the procession
back toward town, leaving her to scurry along the icy
shoulder to reach her vehicle. Her time in South Dakota

had taught her about driving in snow, but she still skidded on the icy patch as she pulled into place. Clearly Clyne was as thrilled at her current assignment as she was. Somehow she didn't think that commonality would bring them any closer together. If she could just find something that would connect the Cosens to the mobile meth ring or something that made their home unfit, she could challenge custody, collect her transfer and be on her way.

She made the drive at the end of the snake of cars, parked in the lot beside tribal headquarters and followed the remains of the procession inside, where she was asked to present her credentials, sign in and wear a paper name badge.

*Hi, My Name Is... Pissed Off,* she thought.

Gabe Cosen appeared through the doors and paused only to speak to the receptionist in Apache before coming to meet her.

"Agent Walker. Nice to see you again."

She accepted his offered hand. The handshake was firm and brief. Chief Cosen stepped back from her. Gabe had none of his brother's swagger. He had bedroom eyes that made Cassidy uneasy and the same full mouth as Clyne. But his gaze was completely different. She saw no hint of distain or banked resentment.

"Chief Cosen. I understand this isn't the first time you have seen me today."

"That's true." Chief Cosen grinned and she felt nothing. Why did Clyne's attention stir her up like ice in a blender?

Chief Cosen removed his gray Stetson and gave it a spin on one hand. His hair was cut very short, which was so different from the long, managed braids of his older brother.

"Police headquarters is right across the street. I'm going to get you and Luke set up right after lunch. Say one o'clock?"

"That's fine."

"I've got to speak to Clyne. Would you mind?" He motioned for her to accompany him.

She forced a smile. Why had she been hoping she would not have to see Clyne again today?

Cassidy kept pace with Gabe as they walked down the hall and through the outer offices of the tribal council. She resisted the urge to look at Clyne through the bank of glass that skirted the door to his office.

Gabe paused before the assistant's desk. The Apache woman sat with her legs slightly splayed to accommodate her swollen belly. Cassidy thought she looked ready to deliver at any moment. The woman held the phone wedged between her ear and shoulder as she wrote something on a memo pad. She still had time to lift a finger to Gabe in a silent request that he wait.

Gabe stepped back and faced Cassidy.

"You settling in?" asked Gabe.

"I haven't been to the casino hotel yet."

"Oh, it was my understanding that you would arrive last night."

"Personal business. Delayed."

His smile faded. "Of course. How are you feeling?"

She shifted testing her ribs and felt the sting of healing muscle. "Fine."

He peered at her from under his brow and she felt he did not quite believe her.

"Well. On behalf of myself and my family, I want to thank you personally for protecting our older brother yesterday."

The display of manners, so divergent from those of his older brother, shocked her into speechlessness.

"Ah," she struggled. "You're welcome."

"Strange, don't you think, that you would be the one responsible for his protection?"

Was there an accusation there or a hint of suspicion?

"It was a rotation."

"Yes. So I understand." Gabe didn't try to hold on to his smile.

"I thought you'd be more present today," she said.

"Clyne didn't want the BIA feeling unsafe."

Had she and Luke been too obvious? She didn't think the BIA officials even noticed her.

"He's been courting them for months and was afraid my force would raise questions about security. He has another rally tomorrow. Phoenix this time. Then Friday, some folks from a home-building charity visiting. Another outdoor gathering, touring the proposed building site here on Black Mountain."

"So you don't want help with the investigation. You asked for us to protect your brother?"

"No. I need investigators. But someone just tried to kill Clyne yesterday. I could use the help keeping him safe."

"But why me, specifically?"

He watched her for a moment that stretched on to eternity.

"Can't you guess?"

"I don't like guessing games, Chief Cosen. Any games, really."

"Miss Walker, you have been a mother to my sister for most of her life. Perhaps the only mother she remembers. It seemed to me that we should know something about you and that you might want to know something about us."

She knew all she needed to know about them, or wanted to. "This has nothing to do with the investigation."

"It does. But two birds, so to speak."

"Do your brothers feel the same?"

Gabe rubbed the back of his neck and she had her answer.

"Gabe!" Clyne's voice was much louder than it needed to be when he called from the open door.

"Excuse me." Gabe stepped into his brother's office and shut the door.

She could hear their words but did not understand Apache. The angry voices and the flailing arm gestures were clear enough as both men engaged in an epic battle of wills.

Gabe eventually reached for the knob. Clyne stood with both fists planted on the surface of his desk. Gabe cleared the threshold and planted his hat on his head. His breathing was fast and his nostrils flared as he turned his attention to her.

"My brother would like to take you to lunch," he said.

The office assistant lifted her brows at this announcement and glanced from Gabe to Cassidy still waiting.

"I was meeting Luke for lunch."

"He told me that he will see you after lunch," said Gabe.

Cassidy reached for her phone and sent Luke a text. The reply was immediate.

C U after lunch.

Cassidy squared her shoulders and marched into the lion's den.

## Chapter Six

Clyne looked back to Field Agent Walker, who glared at him from the outer office, her eyes now glinting like sunlight on a blue gemstone. She held her navy parka in her lap, because he had not offered to hang it and wore a blazer, presumably a different one. One without a bullet hole in the back. Her drab gray button-up shirt did not quite hide the flak jacket beneath, and her practical lace-up nylon boots showed salt stains on the toes. Fully erect, she didn't even reach Clyne's chin. Her blond hair had again been yanked back into a severe ponytail but the March wind had tugged the side strands away and they now floated down about her pink face. If she were Swedish, he did not think her skin could be any paler. Outwardly, they were completely different, but they had one thing in common. They were both fighters. So why did his chest ache every time he forced himself to look at her?

She seemed ready to spit nails. He lifted one of the fists he had been braced upon from his desk and motioned her forward as a Tai Chi master summoned his next challenger.

Walker's fine golden brow arched and her pointed chin dipped. He lowered his chin as well, as one ram does when preparing to butt heads with another. He thought he welcomed the fight, but her proximity raised a completely different kind of anticipation. He identified the curling tension of sexual desire and nearly groaned out loud. Not for this woman. No. Absolutely not.

Her stride was staccato and devoid of any female wiles. So why was he breathing so fast?

Now he noticed how her eyes seemed not quite sapphire, but more ocean blue and flashing like a thunderstorm.

She marched into his office with her coat clutched at her left hip, leaving her gun hand free.

"Just so we are clear," said Clyne, "I haven't changed my mind."

"Good afternoon to you, too, Councilman."

He ground his teeth. Something about her made him forget his manners. He had a reputation for charm but this woman stripped away that veneer like paint thinner on varnish. He felt about as enchanting as a prickly cactus. He glared at her, deciding if he should retreat, advance or return her greeting.

"I don't need protection," he said.

"I have a slug in my body armor that says otherwise."

"That was down there in your world."

She lifted a brow. "Well, I really don't own the whole thing. I'm just a renter."

He scowled because if he didn't he feared he might laugh.

"So do you want to tell me if your problem is with my world, the FBI or just me?"

"You don't have that kind of time."

"Try me." She folded her arms and braced against the door frame.

"Well, let's start with single white women adopting poor little Indian children."

She sucked in a breath as his first blow struck home. "I was married when we adopted our daughter."

That announcement set him back and he didn't think he hid the surprise. Clyne quickly reevaluated. He'd assumed she was one of those career women who wanted it all and had decided that if she didn't want the physical inconvenience of being pregnant, she could just buy a baby.

"Was?" he said.

FBI personal records were sealed. Even Gabe, the tribal police chief, could find very little information about her. That put him at a disadvantage here because she likely knew a great deal about him. Perhaps his brother was right. They should know what kind of a woman had raised their sister.

Was she one of those modern women who thought life came as an all-you-could-eat buffet? Clyne knew better. Life was all about difficult choices.

Should he press or drop it? He studied her body language, arms folded, legs crossed at the ankle as she braced against the solid wooden frame. She was in full-out protective mode. But he was off balance now, fighting with a hand tied behind his back.

"Yes, was," she said.

"So you are now unmarried?"

She inclined her head like a queen consenting to give a response.

"But you have sole custody. Jovanna's only guardian?" asked Clyne, refusing to use the word *parent* as he considered the possibility of having to go through another custody battle with her husband.

"Guardian? I'm her mother. And yes, I am her sole guardian."

"Then you should take a desk job," he said. Her flashing eyes made it clear what she thought of his suggestion.

"Risk comes with living. Your mother's death should have taught you that. And this reservation doesn't have magic properties. You're not safe hiding up here on this mountain, either."

"We aren't hiding. We're living and we choose to be separate. To preserve our culture and teach our children where they come from and who they are." Even to his own ears his words sounded like a speech given from rote.

She had uncrossed her arms and now tilted her head. Her hair shone yellow as corn silk. He saw something in her eyes.

"Doing fabulously well by all accounts. What's the teen pregnancy rate now?"

"Irrelevant."

"Not if you have a teenage daughter it isn't. And where you come from is not as important as where you end up," she said. He'd heard the sentiment before, frequently from those who did not know where they came from or needed to forget. Which was she? A terrible childhood or one without roots?

"Does she even know about us?" he asked.

Her eyes narrowed and that cool demeanor slipped. "She does."

"And about the challenge?"

"Yes, again."

What did Jovanna think about that, to learn she was not an orphan but had an entire family waiting for her? Did she feel betrayed that they had not come for her sooner?

They had gotten little information from their attorney about their sister's life. Mainly facts. Nothing that would tell him how she felt or if she had been happy.

Jovanna had been removed from the vehicle after their mother's death by a state trooper, who had turned her over to child welfare, who had seen her in her dance competition dress and turned her over to BIA. The trooper's writing, "One survivor," had been transposed to read "No survivors" and they had learned, incorrectly, that they had lost both their mother and sister to a drunk driver.

Jovanna had disappeared into the system. Only after their grandmother had insisted they place a stone lamb on Jovanna's grave to mark her tenth birthday, had they learned that only their mother was buried in that grave. The search had begun. He had flown to South Dakota and hired an investigator. Gabe had used his badge to get more information. Kino had followed the procedures to open the adoption and Clay now waited for a ruling from the judge on their motion.

But during those nine years, Jovanna had been listed as a member of the Sweetgrass tribe of Sioux Indians. No kin had come forward, so she was placed in an orphanage at age two and then in a foster home with a Sioux family at age three. Then Jovanna had been adopted just after she turned four.

"We want to meet her," said Clyne.

Her hand settled on the grip of her pistol and her eyes met his. "No."

"Why not?"

"Because it will only make it harder when we leave."

Leave? Where was she going? And then he remembered what his uncle had said about his new partner. A hotshot. A firecracker. Destined to be promoted and transferred to a major field office. And if that happened, they might lose Jovanna again.

"You're leaving?" he asked.

She nodded. "Just as soon and as far from here as possible."

He took a step in her direction, leaving the authority of his desk. She sidestepped until she was beyond his grasp. He lifted his top from the coat rack, his attention still on her. She rolled those crystal-blue eyes at him and exhaled.

"My brother says I am to take you to lunch."

Cassidy did not like the twinkle in his eyes one little bit. But she was a guest here and if Chief Cosen wanted her to dine with his brother, she could do that. She wondered if anyone else found that funny.

"You ready?" he asked.

She lifted her arms, still bundled in her jacket. "Seems so."

He motioned to the door but she waited. "After you, Councilman."

Clyne turned to his assistant. "I'll be at Catalina's," he said and headed out the door, leaving Cassidy no choice but to follow.

In the large foyer before the great seal she paused to zip her coat, realized she would not be able to reach her weapon and left it unfastened.

"Who is Catalina?" she asked.

"Not who. What," he answered.

"I'll drive," she said.

"Why?"

"Everyone knows your SUV."

He made a sound that could have been a laugh. "They all know your dark federal-issue sedan, too, Agent Walker. Besides, it's only across the street."

"Walking out in the open. Bad idea," she said.

"You want to drive? Go ahead."

"I want you inside a vehicle and eating in a securable location. I don't know this place and we have no protection there."

"Oh, but I have you, Agent Walker," he said.

"You can call me Cassidy."

He shot her that wary look again.

"If you want."

Clyne looked like he didn't want to call her by her first name. But he nodded and then set out the door.

She followed his directions to Catalina's, which turned out to be a little diner tucked across the street and behind the main road so as to be invisible to outsiders. The exterior was humble enough, with peeling paint and large tinted windows. Cassidy knew that she would have been apt to avoid entering had Clyne not marched up the stairs, leaving her to follow.

The first thing that hit her was the aroma of frying bacon, onions and coffee, all mingled in an enticing mix that made her stomach rumble. She paused on the welcome mat to scan the room for potential threats. The place was alive with working men, seated at the counter, in booths. Men and women ate breakfast and lunch at the center circular tables. The interior was bright, large and had a central wood-burning stove that warmed the room and filled the air with the inviting scent of wood smoke.

The waitress called a greeting that she could not understand and Clyne responded in kind. He paused to speak to most of the men at the counter, patting some on the back and joking with others. But he spoke in Apache, leaving her unable to follow what was said. Each man turned to glance at her, stone-faced, eyebrows lifted. In all her travels, she had never felt so aware of her white skin, pale hair and European lineage. Clyne worked the room, settling at last in a central table by the woodstove.

The waitress arrived with a smile for Clyne and a scowl for Cassidy. She thought it was Clyne's inten-

tion to unsettle her, so she scanned the room once more
and then studied the menu. It was in Apache. She blew
away her frustration and set it back behind the salt and
pepper shakers.

"That's what it feels like for us out there," he said.
"Being a cultural outsider, feeling apart."

"But you choose to live apart."

His smile was cold, so why did it warm her insides?

"Well, don't take it personally."

She couldn't hold his gaze. It was too intense and
made her all jittery inside. This was just terrible. In all
her years she'd never had a crush on her assignment.
But Clyne was different from anyone she'd ever met.
Seemingly charming, but beneath that *protective* exterior, she sensed danger and inner strength. A heady
combination, she admitted.

She lifted her gaze to catch him watching her in a
way that made her insides tense.

"What would you like? I'll order for you."

She told him and he placed the order. The waitress,
an older woman dressed in jeans and a T-shirt that de-
picted a string of armed Apache warriors and read
Homeland Security, Fighting Terrorism Since 1492.

Their coffee arrived and Cassidy sipped the strong
brew and sighed.

"You have me at a disadvantage, Cassidy," Clyne
said. "You know a great deal about me. I know little
about you."

"I thought you didn't want to know anything about
me."

"I didn't. But Gabe is right. You have raised my sister."

"I'm not talking about Amanda."

"Fine. Your ex-husband, then."

He'd picked the topic that cut most deeply into her heart, but she'd be damned if she'd show him that.

"What about him?" She braced for the barrage.

"Why did you two decide to adopt?"

*Personal business.* But she answered. "We couldn't have children. We tried. Saw someone. But he couldn't…" She shrugged. Gerard was infertile. It had been hard to believe, so hard, when he was so virile and so… She flushed as she realized Clyne was watching her again.

"So you two decided to adopt an Indian child."

She met Clyne's gaze and held it as she delivered the next part of her answer. "We wanted a baby, like everyone else. Boy or girl, we didn't care."

"So why Jovanna? She wasn't a baby."

"They said she was between three and four."

Cassidy thought back, remembering the little girl she had been. She had looked at Gerard and then at Cassidy and made up her mind. How could they say no?

"She came up to us when we toured the facility. She was outgoing even then. And charming, like you."

His eyebrows lifted. She hadn't meant to say that.

Cassidy sipped the coffee and tried again. "She walked right up to Gerard and took his hand. She said… well, it doesn't matter. She picked us and stole our hearts all in the same instant."

Clyne cocked her head. "What did his family think about his adopting an Indian into his Anglo family?"

Now it was Cassidy's turn to scowl. She reached in her coat and withdrew her billfold. She didn't carry a purse. Just did like her fellows. Wallet, cell phone, personal weapon, handcuffs and shield. What else did a girl need?

She drew out the photo she kept of Gerard's official portrait taken just before his second deployment.

She liked this one because he'd managed to sneak a slight smile in past the army photographers. She also liked it because he was in his captain's uniform. Cassidy slipped it from the vinyl shield and passed it to Clyne.

"This is Gerard."

She watched as his eyes rounded and his gaze flicked to her and then back to the photo. "He's...an army captain."

She chuckled at how he'd avoided saying "black." Then she accepted the photo. It still hurt to look at Gerard's image, but the hurt was softer now, like a tug on her heart instead of a knife blade. She tucked away the photo.

"Captain and a tank commander. And to answer your question, Gerard's mother loved Amanda on sight. Diane moved out here to help me."

She had a grandmother, he realized. Two. His and Gerard's.

"When did you two break up?" asked Clyne.

She scowled, refusing to answer that one. He waited and then tried again.

"Why did you choose the name Amanda?"

Back on less rocky ground, Cassidy gave him a reply.

"She's called Amanda because that was what she called herself when she arrived into the care of the BIA."

"She never could say it right. Avana. That's what she called herself."

"Avana. Amanda," said Cassidy.

"What did she say to you that first meeting?"

She had said that she didn't want to speak of Amanda and here they were talking about her. She resisted but something in his gaze, something like pleading that he would never voice, made her relent.

"She hugged Gerard's leg and called him 'Daddy.'
You should have seen him melt. Then she took his hand
and my hand. I looked at Gerard and he nodded. We
signed the papers that day."

"Just like that?"

"No. We also turned down the three-month-old we
came to see. We didn't pick Amanda. She picked us."

He seemed about to say something when their meal
arrived. Clyne handed back the photo.

The waitress set Clyne's food before him and slid
hers over, letting Cassidy know that she was not happy
to serve her.

She thanked the waitress, who said nothing to her.
Then Cassidy surveyed the offering. She'd stuck to the
familiar, eggs, bacon, fried potatoes and white toast.
She inhaled and glanced at Clyne's meal. Before him
sat a large bowl of a rich aromatic stew and something
that looked like the fried dough from the Italian festival
she and Amanda once attended in San Diego.

"What's that?"

"Fry bread. Traditional Apache food. Try it."

"Is it sweet?" she asked, thinking of the powdered
sugar that covered the Italian fried dough.

Clyne made a face. "No. Sometimes we put chili or
other foods on top, like this beef stew. It's best hot." He
motioned for her to take some.

She lifted her knife and fork preparing to cut away
a bit as if it were an oversize pancake. He batted her
hand away and took hold of the golden brown amor-
phous bread before tearing it into two pieces.

"Like this." He dipped it in his stew and took a bite.
Then he dipped the smaller piece and offered it to her.

She took it and their hands brushed. Cassidy felt the
tingle of awareness dart up her arm and right to her

center. Her eyes widened and her gaze flashed to his to see his jaw had gone rock hard. His brow sank over his beautiful eyes and the tingling awareness squeezed her heart.

What the heck was this?

Clyne pulled away, leaving Cassidy holding the bread in the air as if it were a telegram portending bad news. She lifted the fry dough to her mouth and took a small bite. He watched her chew and swallow. The veins in his forehead appeared. Her mouth went dry.

"It's very good." Cassidy noticed the silence. She glanced about to see the room was also watching. Judging her?

Clyne turned his attention to his meal.

"I'm glad you enjoy it."

Cassidy focused on her meal as well, finishing in record time under the watchful stares of their audience.

The check arrived and she made a grab for it. Clyne was quicker and her hand landed on his. She drew back so fast her chair rocked. It didn't matter. The contact still made her insides twitch. This had happened once before, with Gerard, but it had developed slowly, over weeks. This was more visceral and much more immediate.

Cassidy stared at Clyne Cosen.

*Oh, no. Please not this man.*

# Chapter Seven

Clyne left Cassidy at the tribal police offices across the street. For reasons he did not wish to examine, he walked her in to Gabe's office. He told himself it was only to prove that he had done as he promised, kept a civil tone and shared a meal with Agent Cassidy Walker. He didn't understand why Gabe thought this necessary. But it occurred to Clyne that instead of fighting Gabe on this, he should try to figure out what his brother, who had good reasons for his actions, was thinking.

Unfortunately his uncle and Gabe's second in command, Randall Juris, were both there. Detective Juris glanced at them through the glass windows that fronted his brother's office. Juris looked from Clyne to Cassidy and his brows lifted. Juris had once been a Hollywood stuntman and extra in various movies that needed Native American actors. His big barrel chest, dark skin and classic features made him the perfect foil to the Texas Rangers, settlers and scouts he had failed to best on camera. The truth was he could have bested any of them.

Cassidy paused outside the door to make use of the watercooler to assist in downing three brown tablets. She made a face and then shifted her shoulders. It was the first time that she'd given any indication that she'd taken a bullet yesterday. He knew how that felt, with and without a vest.

"Is that because of yesterday?" asked Clyne.

Cassidy shrugged and winced. "Just sore."

"Well, here she is!" The female voice came from behind them.

Clyne recognized the familiar new arrival and groaned. His grandmother was bustling across the room toward his open door. Cassidy turned toward this smiling stranger, noted she was the target of his grandmother's advance and wisely retreated two steps. She had time to crush the paper cup in her hand and drop it into the basket on the floor before his grandmother reached them.

Glendora Clawson was sixty-nine but looked somewhere in her fifties. Her hair, which was mostly black, brushed her shoulders and she had a wide grin on her broad face. Her pink snow coat was open, revealing a plump body dressed in black slacks and a cardigan sweater with a silver dragonfly pin affixed to her powder-pink blouse.

Cassidy backed into the wall of windows in her attempt to avoid his grandmother's arms now wrapping her up like a mama bear. Clyne smiled in amusement as Cassidy Walker stiffened. Behind her the audience of Forrest, Juris and his brother watched the unfolding drama like fans in a skybox.

Clyne met Gabe's eye and thought his brother was smiling. Clyne had a sneaking suspicion that this was also his brother's fault.

Glendora stepped back, her dark brows lifted high on her forehead. Then she turned her attention to Clyne.

"Why didn't you call me? I had to hear from Gabe that Cassidy was here." She said the name so casually as if she had the right to call Agent Walker by her first name, as if they were old acquaintances.

"She is here on business," said Clyne. None of them had told their grandmother that someone had shot at him yesterday. The woman had lost her husband and her only daughter. That seemed enough pain to them all.

"Nonsense. You are both coming for supper tonight. I'm making a roast."

"We can't," said Clyne, but the sinking feeling already gripped him. He'd rather face a nest of rattlers than have this woman seated at his family table.

"You will," said Glendora, lifting a brow in his direction.

Cassidy looked from one to the other. Cassidy shrugged and he nodded. Her face went grim for a moment but then she forced a smile and turned to his grandmother.

"I'd be honored," she said.

It was exactly what she should have said in this situation and Clyne knew it could not have been easy for her. His interest increased as he watched her with his grandmother.

"Gabe and Selena will be there. Lea and Kino. Clay and Izzie."

And he and the FBI agent that wanted sole custody of his sister. Seemed like a date from hell to him. His only consolation was that it would be worse on Cassidy.

He had to give Agent Walker some credit. She was cordial and warm to his grandmother. Her smile changed her entire demeanor and had him scowling. It was just not possible for him to find this fierce little warrior woman attractive. But he did. Damn it, he did.

Gabe sauntered out and joined the conversation as Clyne wondered again how his neat world had started to spin so badly out of its orbit. Cassidy Walker's arrival in Black Mountain was acting like the impact of a meteor to the surface of the earth. He couldn't breathe past the billowing smoke his grandmother and Gabe were both blowing. He made his excuses and tried for a graceful exit, but his grandmother took a hold of him and extracted a promise that he drive Cassidy to their home.

"She can find it," said Clyne. "She has GPS."

"Which doesn't work half the time out here. You know that. I want you to bring her."

Clyne surrendered and fixed a smile on his face that felt as tight as drying wax. "My pleasure, then, Grandmother."

She patted his cheek, making him feel about six years old and making him flush. He spun and retreated as his grandmother called out a time for him to pick up Agent Walker. He lifted a hand in acknowledgment and escaped to his offices, where he spent much of the afternoon distracted by the clock that ticked down the time until he had to pick up Walker.

As the time approached to head for his home he grew more agitated. Here was another way Agent Walker would know them when he knew little about her. He didn't want to know her or did he?

He wanted his sister back and Cassidy Walker gone. But Gabe had said that to take a child from her mother was a terrible thing.

Didn't Gabe want his sister home?

At the appointed time, he returned to the police station and Yepa, Gabe's assistant, directed him to the conference room.

"What do you think of her?" asked Yepa.

"I don't think of her."

That made her cock her head and give him a strange look followed by an annoying quirk of her mouth.

Clyne reached the conference room and knocked. Someone called him in and he entered. There they sat, laptops open, files and folders strewn across the table. Juris sat beside Luke, who sat beside Cassidy. To Cassidy's left sat Gabe and beyond him, Sergeant Salvo. Gabe peered over Cassidy's shoulder at her laptop. Clyne narrowed his eyes at the position of Gabe's chair. It seemed far too close to Cassidy. Clyne felt something inside himself growling. Gabe glanced up and his smile of greeting wilted to one of bewilderment. But he moved his chair away from Cassidy, who still stared at her screen.

"You about ready?" asked Clyne.

He noted the change in her body language the instant she heard his voice. Her expression tightened from relaxed to tense and her shoulders stiffened. She did not look at him but closed her laptop and collected her papers, tucking them into a briefcase. She rose and said her farewells. Luke told her he'd see her at Glendora's.

She followed him out, stopping at her car to relieve herself of her briefcase. She carried no purse, which didn't really surprise him, though it was unusual for the women in his acquaintance.

"I'll follow you," she said.

That suited him fine.

"Why did you agree to come?" he asked.

She seemed as if she would not answer. "Curiosity. And my daughter asked me if I've met her brothers. She wants to meet you." It was clear from her tight expression that she did not want this. But he knew that it was only a matter of time. There was no avoiding the inevitable. Jovanna was Indian and so she would be returned to her birth family and tribe.

"And we want to meet her."

Cassidy said nothing to this. She hesitated beside her vehicle.

"How did they get separated, your mother and your sister?"

Clyne drew in a breath and braced to tell the tale as quickly as possible.

"My sister was a very good dancer, jingle and fancy shawl."

She gave him a blank look.

"Those are types of dances. At powwows?"

She nodded half-heartedly.

"There is money in it, if you win. Just like rodeo." Which was how he and then Gabe had made money to help support the family.

"There's a big powwow up in South Dakota on the Sweetgrass reservation. She was bringing Jovanna to her first competition. They got hit head-on by a drunk driver. My mother was killed instantly and Jovanna survived. They were wearing their regalia and my mom's ID was still at the campsite. She was listed as a Jane Doe. It took them a week to even tell us about the accident. By then she was already buried up in the Sweetgrass reservation cemetery."

"But why didn't they ID Jovanna and send her back to you?"

Clyne swiped a hand over his face.

"Because the report said 'no survivors.' We were told she had died with our mom."

"But how?"

"Penmanship. The state police officer wrote one

survivor and it got transposed into no survivors on the report."

Cassidy thumped back against the side of her car as she absorbed this.

"How did you figure it out?"

"The cemetery records showed that they buried only one body. We were trying to place a stone lamb on Jovanna's grave and discovered the mistake."

Cassidy swiped a tear from her cheek. Clyne's throat felt tight.

"We better go," he said.

She nodded and slipped into her dark government-issue sedan and started the engine. He trudged to his SUV and led the way. Cassidy followed him in her sedan with the tinted windows. She followed him to the door of his grandmother's home, where she met the first member of their family, Buster, a rather old and partially deaf sheepdog who, at twelve, was the most senior one of them.

The family hound was a mix of several breeds with the long snout of a collie and the mismatched blue and brown eyes of a husky. Buster's legs and face were a buff color and his back showed the blanket common in some collies and shepherd breeds. His full, bushy tail wagged as he reached them.

His walk was stiff but he still bowed a greeting to Cassidy, who offered her hand for Buster's inspection. His white muzzle and clouding eyes revealed his age. Buster was gentle but protective, which was why he was surprised to see him lick Cassidy's hand.

She followed the shepherd mix to the living room, where his grandmother made introductions to his brothers and their wives and Gabe's fiancé. Uncle Luke arrived for supper. He was wise enough to know that Glendora's cooking was not to be missed. Finally, Cassidy followed him to the table, where they posed for a photo, taken by Luke, and then all sat.

He didn't want her here. So why did he keep looking at her?

His grandmother's table was round so there was no head of the table. But she had placed Cassidy next to him. Better, he thought, for he could keep an eye on her.

In deference to their guest, the family spoke in English. Only the prayer of thanks was offered in Apache. The meal smelled delicious, but the scent of Cassidy kept intruding. She smelled of summer flowers and baby powder and he wanted to tuck her under his arm and inhale.

Cassidy listened as Kino and Clay spoke of their time with the Shadow Wolves on the Arizona border. Gabe relayed tales of when he and Clyne rode the rodeo circuit together. Finally Glendora steered the conversation to Cassidy. She started with Luke, asking how they had met and what it was like working together. Luke's comments were far too glowing for Clyne's taste.

Clyne focused on his meal but his heart wasn't in it. Cassidy's presence was ruining his appetite.

His grandmother left the table to retrieve the dessert, two fresh-made pecan pies. Kino's wife, Lea, rose heavily to her feet to help serve. Her hand went occasionally to her round belly, caressing the place where her first child grew. Only one more month and Clyne would be an uncle.

Once all the plates were full, Glendora resumed her seat and turned her attention to Cassidy.

"Cassidy, do you have any family out here?" asked Glendora.

Clyne did his best to pretend he wasn't listening.

Cassidy swallowed her mouthful of pie and returned her fork to her plate, correctly judging that the interrogation had finally reached her. "I'm an only child, but both my parents are gone."

"Oh, I'm so sorry. How many brothers and sisters have you, Cassidy?" asked Glendora.

"None."

Glendora blinked as she absorbed this. Clyne knew that his grandmother wanted more children but also had had only one, his mother.

"I see," said his grandmother. "Where's home?"

"I'm an army brat. Moved around a lot. New England, DC, then up in Alaska for a little while. I also lived in Germany."

"Heavens. A world traveler."

*Rootless*, thought Clyne. With no home and no people. Only herself and her stolen daughter.

"How did you choose the FBI?" asked Gabe.

Now his brothers were getting into the action. Clyne glanced at his watch, wishing the evening away.

"I enlisted in October of 2001," she said.

Clyne's head jerked up because that was when he had joined the US Marines. Back then he had felt the need to defend his country. Now he only wanted to defend his people and their land.

"I met my husband in basic training. He was deployed before me."

Glendora blinked, her gaze shifting to Cassidy's left hand but their guest wore no ring. Many FBI officers did not.

"You're married?" asked Glendora.

"I was. For seven years. He was a tank commander until he died in Afghanistan in his second deployment, March 4, 2011."

There was a moment of absolute stillness. Cassidy had successfully silenced his grandmother. Clyne did the math and realized Jovanna had been adopted when she was about four and she had been seven when Walker had died. The US tank commander had been her father for only three years. How many occasions had he been home during that time? They would have given him leave, of course. But army tours were two to six years each. Had Walker re-enlisted to support his family?

Cassidy met his gaze with a challenge and held it, those flashing eyes now reminded him of seawater, as blue and deep as the Pacific Ocean. And now he realized what made her different from every other woman he had ever met. She was a warrior and she was a survivor. A veteran who, like him, had lost someone important. Not comrades, though perhaps she had. She had lost her husband.

He looked at her with new eyes, his head cocked as he wondered if he dared to ask if any of the men and women in her unit had been lost.

"He signed for a second tour?" asked Clyne.

"Yes. I stayed home with Amanda and Gerard re-enlisted for another four years. I joined the bureau after my daughter started school. Gerard came home whenever he could."

Clyne's head dropped. He'd made so many assumptions and felt ashamed of himself. He'd even asked her when they had divorced. He rubbed his hand over his forehead and prepared to apologize.

"But I'm not the only veteran at the table. Clyne was in the US Marines. Also enlisted after 9/11. Deployed to Iraq." She turned to him with a sweet smile. "A sharpshooter, right? Thirty-six confirmed kills."

He sucked in a breath. All eyes turned to him as if

suddenly he was the stranger at the table. He'd never told them.

Clyne stood and grabbed Cassidy by the arm and hustled her out of the room. She went along but once in the foyer she tugged away, breaking his hold with such ease it startled him into stillness. He'd forgotten that Walker was a fighter, too.

"What's your problem?" she asked.

"I don't talk about that time."

She snorted. "Maybe you should."

He tilted his head to one side, wondering where she got the nerve to tell him what he should do. "What would you know about it?"

"Not much. We were just the ones who had to clean up your mess."

Suddenly he needed to know about her time in the military. Had she seen action?

"Where were you deployed?"

"I flew birds, Black Hawks. Medical transport mostly."

The hairs on his neck lifted again.

"Afghanistan?"

"Iraq, 2003. Don't worry. I didn't transport you. I checked."

So she knew he'd been wounded. He didn't like that she knew so much about him.

How many broken, bleeding bodies had she carried to safety?

"You want me to go back in there?" She glanced toward his waiting family.

He shook his head.

"Call it a night."

She glanced at her watch. "Fine. See you at 0800."

For some reason he wanted to talk to her. Ask her about her tour of duty and maybe learn how she could still carry a gun and enforce the law and fight the bad guys when all he wanted was to stay here where things made sense.

"You know how to find the hotel?" he asked.

"My GPS does. Good night, Cosen," she said. "Please thank your grandmother for the meal. She's an excellent cook."

THE FOLLOWING MORNING, Cassidy left the tribe's casino in the wee hours of the morning, passing through the din of ringing bells and the flash of colored lights that was way too bright for this early in the day. It seemed that most of the guests were white men and women, older, overweight and mesmerized by the whirling wheels and bright digital displays. They sat immobile on the wide stools with coffee and liquor waiting at the ready, their casino players' cards connecting them like umbilical cords to the machines.

Once outside the sun showed no hints of appearance but she paused to savor the clean air. She had spent a lonely night in her vacant hotel room with far too much time to think. Much to her chagrin, her thoughts lingered on Clyne and how he had cared for her when she had been shot. He'd been more than professional; he'd shown a kindness and concern that disquieted. One soldier looking out for another, she told herself. It had to be, because she was not willing to accept that the attraction she battled was mutual.

She reached her vehicle and paused to admire the fine lacy pattern of ice crystals that frosted the windshield. Then she used her gloved hand to scratch an area big enough to peer through. March and still they had frost up here. It was the altitude, she knew, but the terrain was so different from Phoenix. Lovely, really.

She had told Amanda all about her brothers last night. Even sent her the photo that Luke had shared.

Today they would not be investigating Manny Escalanti or searching Salt River for Ronnie Hare because Clyne was heading to Phoenix for another rally against Obella Chemicals. That event would take place at 11 a.m., indoors this time in the civic center. Luke had point, Gabe accompanied Clyne and she had rear security. That meant another three-hour drive by herself behind Clyne's vehicle where her only job was to watch for possible attack from every vehicle they passed. Oh, joy.

At least they had a phone tap on Escalanti. She was considering how to place a camera and microphone in his crib as the procession departed.

Cassidy peered through the gap in the frost as she drove until the defroster softened the edges of the ice, and she attacked the retreating edge with the wiper blades. By the time she reached Black Mountain the window was clear. By the time she reached the Cosen residence, the darkness receded to reveal a gray cloudy morning.

She waited in the drive for the two men. Clyne cast her a glance. He cut a striking figure in his topcoat. She ignored the spark of interest, crushing it out like a cigarette butt.

Luke stopped at her driver's side. "Everything good?"

"All set."

"You got coffee?"

She lifted the paper cup with the casino logo. Luke nodded, grinned and headed to the large SUV that held the tribal seal on the front door.

She pulled out behind them and the small procession started down the mountain. She wished she had her he-

licopter. Her stomach growled and she fantasized about
a piece of Glendora Clawson's pecan pie and the table
that had been so full of life and energy. She'd never been
at a dinner like that. When she was young she usually
ate with her mother. Her father ate on base or after she
was in bed. She shifted uncomfortably as she thought
of all the dinners that she shared with Amanda over a
white pizza box or containers of takeout. The comparison was glaring and not very flattering.

Last night she had met them. The Cosen family. And
they were not some terrible monster of clannish bump-
kins. They were bright and friendly and connected in
ways she could not understand. Being among them
made her long for something she had not even known
she still wanted. Brothers. Sisters. And the real possibility of nieces and nephews.

Was she wrong to deny her daughter this family?
Was she really operating on what was best for Amanda
or what was best for Cassidy Marshal Walker?

Gradually the sun emerged; the day brightened and
warmed as they wound down the mountain past the
rocky outcroppings and red rock.

Cassidy snapped back to focus on the road. When
the dash clock read six forty-five she dialed home and
checked in with Amanda, who was using digital flash
cards to cram for a science test.

Once she reached Phoenix, Cassidy turned her attention to the event. Another rally. Cosen was an ac-
tivist of the first order, delivering poignant speeches
and garnering support for his causes. They were important causes, she admitted, but her main objective
was Cosen's safety, second only to finding something
to incriminate him.

They finally reached a two-lane highway and soon

afterward arrived at the downtown Phoenix City Center. Then she trailed Luke's vehicle to Phoenix Convention Center and then into the underground parking facility.

She parked in the first available spot, diagonally across from Forrest's vehicle, and climbed stiffly from her sedan. The drive had tightened all her back muscles into one giant ball of muscle spasm. Stretching helped a little.

The air in the parking garage smelled of gasoline, rubber and rotting garbage. The comparison between this and Black Mountain was startling and she began to see what was so appealing.

Agent Forrest and Cosen were out of the SUV and she headed in their direction as they turned toward the entrance to the convention center.

An engine revved. She caught motion in her peripheral vision. A dark pickup truck took the corner so fast the tires squealed. The truck sped toward them, halogen lights blinding in the subterranean garage. She had time to dive for safety. Instead, she charged forward into Clyne, rushing him out of the way.

"Move," she shouted.

Forrest jumped clear of the front passenger tire. Clyne wrapped an arm about her and together they dove. They landed on the curb. The jolt of pain shot through her healing ribs like a sledgehammer. She caught the blur of a rear tire inches from her face. She grunted and rolled to her back, reaching inside her open blazer for her gun. By the time she scrambled to her feet, Forrest was already up, but the truck had made the turn and disappeared.

"I got a plate," he said.

She turned to Clyne, who lay on his back. He braced himself up on his elbows. His dark trench coat flapped open, revealing the pale denim shirt unbuttoned and, at the throat, a leather cord tied about a small leather pouch. What was that?

"You all right?" she asked.

"Thanks to you, again."

"Who wants you dead, Clyne?" she asked.

"Besides you?" He grinned.

Forrest pulled out his phone. "I'm calling local police." He placed the call and then met Cassidy's gaze. "Almost looked like he was aiming at you, Walker."

"Me?" she asked, her voice filled with disbelief, and then the disbelief ebbed and she fixed her attention on Clyne, who had come to his feet. She scowled at him.

"Did you arrange that?" she asked.

## Chapter Eight

Now they were both frowning.

"Me? Why would I do that?"

"Because it's cheaper than paying attorney fees."

"Then the same goes for you, I guess," he said, rolling easily to his feet and standing to dust off his coat.

Cassidy turned to Agent Forrest. "Plate number?"

He lifted the phone from his mouth and gave her the number.

"We get Clyne inside, then I'll run the plate," she said.

Cassidy took Clyne to the security station, such as it was. They at least had offices with good solid doors and locks. Once she had Clyne secured, she began her investigation, calling the office to have them run the plate while Luke coordinated with venue security and the local police on-site. Reinforcements were en route. Registration information was sent to her mobile and showed the vehicle belonged to a member of the Black Mountain tribe.

Cassidy felt him before she saw him and turned to discover Clyne leaning over her shoulder.

"I know him," he said. "Works for the Cattle Association."

"Step back," she ordered.

"I'm not armed."

"I am."

He stepped back.

Forrest joined them. "No sign of the driver yet."

She showed him the registration information and Luke gave a low whistle.

"I'll call Gabe."

The head of the convention center security reported that they had footage of the driver. They all hovered around a large computer screen to watch.

"I know Dale Donner," said Clyne. "He's the tribal livestock manager and would no sooner run me down than run over a child."

"His truck," said Forrest.

"Not the driver. Stake my life on it," said Clyne.

The driver was male but that was about all they could tell. He wore a ball cap, large sunglasses and possibly a false beard. They printed the images.

"Not him. Too thin," said Clyne.

Over the next hour they made some progress on finding the driver, as the rally participants began to arrive.

Gabe called Clyne to report that Donner was still at home and did not know the truck was missing. Her boss had been notified and he had recommended more agents, a request that Clyne Cosen had quickly declined.

Luke's contact with PPD told them that the police had recovered the truck only three blocks away, illegally parked by a hydrant. Their CSI were processing Donner's truck for latents and physical evidence, which Cassidy knew could take a while. Long enough for the would-be assassin to make another attempt.

It seemed the driver had vanished.

"He followed us all the way from Black Mountain," said Luke.

And she'd never seen him, she realized.

Luke left them to meet with local PD in the hunt for the driver. Phoenix PD was given the description and set out in hopes of getting lucky. Cassidy didn't feel lucky.

Particularly not when she was the one left guarding Clyne Cosen, yet again.

Cassidy turned to Councilman Cosen. She was still unsure if he was the target or if Agent Forrest was correct and the shooter in the truck had been aiming at her. For now, she would act as if Clyne was the objective. But if she could find a connection between him and that driver, it would only strengthen her custody argument.

"You should cancel this appearance," she said.

His answer was immediate. "No."

"Would you consider modifying your schedule? Appearing by video feed?"

"No."

"Canceling the press conference or future outdoor rallies?"

His eye ticked. It was the only evidence she had that he was rattled. "No. Obella Corporation needs to take responsibility for that chemical spill."

"Fine. Send someone else."

"No."

"You are a hard man to keep alive. You realize that?"

He said nothing, just checked the time on his phone. It occurred to her that perhaps Clyne was more interested in causes than breathing. That troubled her.

"You need body armor," she said.

He went pale and wiped his upper lip with the palm of his hand, rubbing it back and forth over his mouth as if trying to stifle nausea. Finally his hand dropped. But it was shaking.

"No. Not again."

Funny, she thought. Getting shot at and nearly run down had not rattled him. But the mention of body armor made him tremble.

He was a puzzle. Seemingly strong, proud and capable, he had a definite soft spot when it came to his military service. His uncle had mentioned that Clyne used to love to hunt. She wondered if he still did?

"I hear the hunting is great up on Black Mountain," she said.

He eyed her warily, no doubt wondering about the sudden change of topic.

"It is. We have some of the largest elk in the country."

"And guides."

"Yes."

"Would you be willing to guide me?" she asked.

He flinched at the request and turned half-away to collect himself. Then that hand went to his mouth again. He really ought to see someone about this. His behavior had PTSD written all over it. Seeking help was no shame.

She'd taken advantage of a grief counselor after Gerard had died. It had helped. But Amanda had helped more. Her daughter gave her a reason to get up and make breakfast and go outside and reengage with the world. Eventually the joy had returned. What would happen if she lost Amanda?

"I don't guide," said Clyne, now apparently recovered. "But Clay is an excellent guide. I'm sure you would have some luck."

She nodded her head and smiled. It was good to know your enemy's weakness.

His eyes narrowed right back.

"Have you ever killed a man, Cassidy?"

That question did not come out of the blue. He was

probing her weaknesses, just as she had done to him. Still, she didn't entirely keep herself from reacting. Her heart rate increased as she sucked in a breath. She held it and then let go in a long easy release. She wasn't going to let this particular man rattle her.

Cassidy knew this was the sharpshooter speaking. Seeking another connection with her that transcended the physical.

"Have you, Cassidy? Have you looked down your sights and taken his life? Stolen him from his family and from all future generations?"

She had. Twice. Cassidy looked at Clyne.

Thirty-six confirmed kills.

"I took down an armed bank robber in Phoenix. The guy had hit over eleven banks. And when we got to number twelve, he had hostages. I didn't feel bad about it. Not even afterward, I wasn't the only one who shot him, but it was my bullet that killed him. At least that's what the ME said. There was also a kidnapper in Chandler." She glanced away, swallowing down the gall rising in her throat. She stopped talking as her stomach tensed. She remembered him, Brett Parker, the man who had snatched a toddler right out of the child's bedroom window. A few days later, she'd been there to take him down. The arrest went bad. He had killed the child almost immediately. Never meant to ransom her. Now she carried the memory of that dead girl and also her finger on the trigger when she sighted Parker. She remembered the recoil of her gun, the training that included everything but how to watch a man you killed die before your eyes. That moment entangled with the discovery of the child, submerged in that stream. They lived in her mind, repeating like a spliced video loop until she'd come to accept that she would never forget them, either of them, killer and victim. Wolf and lamb. Couldn't. It was emblazoned on her memory, etched like the bullet from the barrel of her gun. She glanced at Clyne, met his steady gaze. Thirty-six kills. Thirty-six memories he could never erase. She scrubbed her hands over her face and shook off the horror.

"It was unavoidable," she said, her voice straining. "And he can't hurt anyone again."

"Because you stopped him."

As he had stopped thirty-six. Had any of them been women or children? She couldn't ask.

"Yes," she whispered. "I stopped him." She met his gaze, seeing the dangerous glitter in the eyes of a dangerous man.

"You should cancel your speech."

Clyne's face showed nothing but determination.

"Not a chance."

Cassidy was relieved to see the reinforcements from her department arrive. Security was tight for the rally and Clyne, minus his body armor, spoke to a crowd of energetic activists. She was so busy watching for threats that she almost did not hear his speech. But his rich baritone did break her concentration, rumbling through her like a far-off locomotive.

After the rally, Clyne met with local officials, was interviewed by the media and finally headed back to security, where he could not be convinced to allow additional agents onto his sacred land. So it was Cassidy and Luke again, winding back up the mountain at midday. Gabe met them at the border of the reservation with another officer, who escorted them to tribal headquarters. Luke left them there and she followed Clyne back to his offices, where it seemed the entire tribal council and half the police force waited to greet them.

She filled Gabe in on everything that had happened while Clyne busied himself with his computer.

Both their phones awoke simultaneously, hers beeping and his pounding some tribal drum ring tone. She retrieved hers first and saw the name and image of her attorney appear on the screen. Her jaw dropped and she glanced to Clyne. He was scowling at his phone and then his eyes met hers.

His attorney. She was certain.

They both held their ringing phones in statuesque silence for one more instant. It could mean only one thing. The judge had made a ruling on her appeal.

They both turned, giving each other their backs as they took the calls.

Cassidy punched the answer button.

"Hello?"

# Chapter Nine

Her attorney continued as Cassidy tried to understand what he was saying.

"But she's twelve," said Cassidy. "By law, Amanda is old enough to choose to be adopted outside her tribe."

Her attorney's breath rattled across his phone's mic sounding to her like static. "The judge felt it was not a fair choice for Amanda to make since she does not remember her family."

"*I'm* her family," Cassidy snarled into the phone. Why did this have to happen in the center of tribal headquarters, in front of half his tribe?

"I'm sorry, Cassidy. Child Protective Services is on their way now to pick her up."

"Now?"

Cassidy was on her feet. She didn't remember clearing the doorway or leaving her assignment. She just found herself in the parking area, rummaging for her keys as she clutched the phone to her ear.

"I'm coming."

"No. Don't," her attorney said.

"But they can't just take her," she said.

"They *are* taking her. I'll head over there now. But I can't stop them."

"How long?" she asked.

"Six months," he said.

She sucked in a breath.

"Can I go with her? Help her with the transition?"

"No."

She'd see about that.

"I have to go." She hung up and then fumbled to pull up her contact favorites list on her mobile but her fingers weren't working right and the screen blurred. She swore and tried again.

Amanda was at school, of course, and could not pick up. Her daughter was allowed to carry her phone but could use it only at lunch and before and after school.

Cassidy was calling Gerard's mother when she received a text reply from Amanda. The phone began to ring as Amanda's message popped up.

?up

Cassidy translated her daughter's message. *What's up?*

Gerard's mother answered. Cassidy's voice cracked as she rushed to tell Diane the situation.

"Should I go to the school?"

Cassidy didn't know. Diane couldn't stop them from taking her granddaughter, but she could speak to Amanda first.

Amanda's next message popped up.

mom u there? w/b

Cassidy translated her daughter's message. *Mom? Are you there? Write back.*

"Yes. Please tell her."

"Can she come back here, pack some clothing?"

"I don't know. Bring her some things. But hurry. Diane. Hurry. They'll be there soon."

She disconnected and saw Clyne alone in the lot, heading her way with his phone glued to his ear. He didn't have the look of triumph she had expected. Why hadn't she anticipated that when they served the judge Amanda's notarized request that something like this could happen?

The Indian Child Welfare Act was very clear. There were only three reasons a Native American child could be adopted outside their tribe. If the adopting parent was the biological parent. If no member of the child's tribe was willing to adopt and finally, if the child had attained the age of twelve years and chose to be adopted outside the tribe. It was this final stipulation that Cassidy's attorney had argued. And received a conditional denial because Amanda had been only two when she left her birth family.

Cassidy had been aware of the ICWA when she adopted Amanda but as her daughter had no kin, the issue seemed moot. During this challenge, her attorney had been so certain that, regardless of the ruling, Amanda, since she was now twelve, could just choose to be adopted away from the Cosens.

If she'd had even an inkling this might happen, she would have been home guarding her daughter instead of up here on Black Mountain.

What was a conditional denial anyway?

Cassidy didn't know what kept her upright. The pain in her chest was swelling like a balloon. She could hardly breathe. She tried to text but her fingers, clumsy on the tiny keyboard, made a mess. She swiped at the tears and checked Clyne's progress. She had to get a message to Amanda.

thr comeing. Judge rules U going 2 biological family
6 mo. today.

Clyne reached her. She turned away, clinging to her
phone. Her lifeline to her daughter.

WDYS? Mom? WDYM? ?U@

Cassidy interpreted her daughter's text. *What did
you say, Mom? What did you mean? Where are you?*
Cassidy tried again, typing madly. Wishing she had
learned more slang so she could write faster. Her phone
dinged again.

cnt tx. po po <3 u. *4

Cassidy read the message. *Can't text. Police. Love
you. Kiss for...*
*4U. Kiss for...*you.* It was how Amanda ended all her
texts. But her daughter had not had time to finish. They
had her phone. They had her. Cassidy burst into tears.
Clyne touched her shoulder. "Cassidy, I'm sorry."
She didn't resist as he dragged her in and held her
right there before the tribe members streaming by on
the way to headquarters. She should pull away and tell
him she didn't need his sympathy. Instead she clung
and sobbed.
"They're taking her."
"I know."
"I'm not there with her."
"It will be all right."
She clung, burying her face in his topcoat, smelling
wool and the faint aroma of cedar and sage, and gave
voice to her deepest fear.

"Six months!" she sobbed.

Clyne stroked her head. "Come on. We have to go back in."

She pushed back. "No. I can't."

"All right, Cassidy." He glanced back toward the tribal headquarters and his brother Gabe. "Let me get you away from here."

She let him guide her to the passenger side of her sedan. She slipped into the seat and he closed the door. Clyne took the driver's side and asked for her keys. She pressed them into his palm.

"They have her," she said, her voice just a whisper.

"I know."

"Will you let me see her, just for a minute, to explain?"

Clyne gave her a look of pity. He'd won. He could afford to be gracious or not. By the time she had her tears reined in, she realized they were pulling into the casino hotel. Clyne guided her through the lobby. She should be looking for threats, but she ducked her head, like a coward and allowed him to lead her along. Even after Gerard's passing, she had never felt so lost.

Of course Clyne knew everyone at reception and several of the folks working the floor. Even in the elevator he met an acquaintance. She was happy her dark glasses covered her eyes but knew they didn't mask the tears running down her cheeks or the pink nose that always accompanied her waterworks. She hadn't cried since Gerard's funeral and then only after his family had departed, Amanda had retired and she was alone in her bedroom.

Clyne helped her with her key card. She remembered to lock the door behind them and throw the latch.

He said nothing to this precaution as they made their

way into the room. He crossed to the window and drew back the curtains. She sank into the love seat.

"Got a view of the mountain," he said. "That mountain is sacred to us. We believe that we are related to the stone, trees and wind. The mountain is a relative and there are spirits that live there. They are called Ga'an."

She cradled her head in her hands, trying to stop her shoulders from shuddering as she listened to the soft melody of his voice telling her the origin of his people.

He sat on the long rectangular footstool, his legs splayed on either side of hers. He rested a hand lightly on her knee.

"In our ceremonies, Apache men dress as the Ga'an, Crown Dancers, summoning the mountain spirits to help protect our people from disease and evil. I have been a Crown Dancer. All my brothers have been. Together we have danced for our people. There are five spirits, four Crown dancers who are painted all in white and one sacred clown in black. During the dance, they *are* the spirits. Their dance protects the tribe. Perhaps you have seen photos of men in masks with large wooden headdresses?"

She shrugged, thinking she had not.

"Well, that is the embodiment of the Ga'an. The headdresses are made by powerful medicine men and blessed in a sacred ceremony. When the Ga'an dance together, they are powerful. But more powerful still is Changing Woman. She is a goddess who makes the land and people fruitful. Every spring she is young. In the summer she is fertile. In the fall she is bountiful and in winter, she grows old. But come spring she is young again. Once she grew so lonely that she made man and woman out of a piece of her own skin."

Cassidy lowered her hands from her eyes, mesmerized by his voice as much as his words.

"When a child is born, Changing Woman will dance. She is also called White Painted Woman. We have ceremonies for births, weddings and to bless a home. She also dances at the coming of age ceremony for girls. It is like a sweet-sixteen party, wedding and New Year's festival all mixed together. But also like a christening, because it is when a girl is welcomed to the tribe as an adult. The ceremony takes four days."

"Four?"

"Yes. Much of this time the girl must dance. Apache girls must prove they are strong enough to be Apache women. Part of the ceremony involves painting the child white. By doing so, she becomes the embodiment of Changing Woman. Her dance is sacred. All girls look forward to their Sunrise Ceremony."

Cassidy's suspicions stirred. "You didn't tell me this to distract me."

"No. I did not."

"Why, then?" But she was certain she already knew.

"My brothers and I have dreamed of dancing at our sister's Sunrise Ceremony. My grandmother has made her dress and moccasins."

"When does a girl become a woman?"

"In the summer she turns thirteen."

"Amanda is only twelve and a half."

Clyne shook his head. "She will be thirteen this summer. The ceremony takes place on July 4 each year. It will be good for this to be a day of celebration."

And they would still have her then. She could become Changing Woman and afterward she would be an Apache woman. And then, she would have to choose between the family of her birth and the one she had made that day when she took Gerard's hand.

Cassidy stood and excused herself to wash her face and repair her hair. She gave up on her hair and left it down. Another month's growth and she could resume her low ponytail.

She found Clyne standing by the window. She slowed, hesitated and considered retreat. He turned to her and smiled. The upturning of his mouth transformed his face from statuesque beauty to a man with more sex appeal than any one person should possess.

"There is so much I need to tell you about her." She came to stand beside him. "She is allergic to kiwis and she hates spiders. She loves animals. Always wanted a dog. She loves sports and she is a really good skier. Surfer, too, but I can't see…"

He pressed a finger to her lips. She was babbling.

"She's our sister. We will take care of her." His finger slipped over her bottom lip and away, leaving a soft sexual tingle in its wake.

She looked up at him. He nodded.

"We will."

She let her shoulders sag and accepted what she could not change.

"All right, then."

They stared for a moment and her skin began that tingling itch, an awareness that did not need touch to come alive. Just to be near him made her entire body quicken.

"I really wanted to hate you," she whispered.

"Don't you?"

She shook her head. "I think your family is wonderful and that Amanda will be very lucky to have you all as brothers."

She didn't say the rest aloud. Amanda would have

the big family she had always wanted, the kind of family Cassidy had once fantasized of having when she was a lonely little girl moving with her parents from base to base.

"I'm not giving up. I still want her to pick me."

His mouth quirked. "Of course."

He stepped closer, lifting his hands and gently held her at the shoulders. He pressed his lips together as if trying to keep himself from speaking. Bit by bit his mouth relaxed into the full sensual wonder it was.

"I think she is very lucky to have a mother like you. Strong, capable and it's clear you love your daughter."

She lifted her brows, half expecting him to qualify his words. He didn't. Instead he used a crooked index finger to lift her chin. His gaze dipped to her mouth and she knew he was going to kiss her.

*Oh, no, no, no*, cried her mind. *Yes*, whispered her heart.

Cassidy rocked forward, moving to meet the soft brushing of lips. It was just a whisper of a kiss yet it dropped inside her like the first domino to fall, sending the rest toppling in turn. Her arms went about his neck, keeping him from escape as she lifted to her toes and rocked closer, taking his mouth against hers.

It had been so long. So damned long and she never ever thought to find this kind of electricity, had never expected it to strike twice.

His hands splayed across her back. One high and one low at that place where her back became her backside. He pressed and she yielded, letting her hips drop against his and finding what she had expected, hard male flesh. She wanted this, wanted him. And there was no doubt that he wanted her.

# Chapter Ten

Clyne had only meant to comfort her. But deep down, underneath his compassion, something stirred. Something dangerous.

Clyne breathed in as the sweet fragrance of coconut and hibiscus rose to greet him. Walker smelled more like Hawaii than Arizona.

He drew back to look at her and immediately recognized another mistake. She was captivating. Her fine hair now brushed her shoulders, accentuating her beauty. Her face was heart-shaped and her cheeks and lips a becoming pink. She wore tiny diamond studs on her earlobes. They flashed when she moved and drew attention to the graceful curve of her neck. Field Agent Walker had a lovely complexion. Pale, but lovely.

She was a head shorter than he was and her build was slim and athletic. Clyne preferred more curves and a darker complexion. He'd dated a few white women, but never for long and never a blonde. Yet here he was, alone in her room, thinking of what she would taste like.

No. He should walk away. But he didn't.

If he could just figure out what the attraction was, perhaps he could stop it or kill it. Because he was not getting tangled up in a relationship with Cassidy Walker.

She'd been married. She carried a gun. She was a

federal officer. And she had adopted his sister. Any one of those made good cause for him to stay the heck away from her.

"We shouldn't," he said.

She stiffened and her fingers, laced behind his neck, slipped to his shoulders, then dropped away.

"It's a huge mistake. I don't want this," she said.

"Neither do I."

He stared at her Pacific-blue eyes and knew he was a liar. He wanted her. He just didn't want what came along with her. A white woman. It wasn't in the plan. He was going to marry a woman who shared his culture and his heritage. This woman was a complication—a trap.

"You and I, you're an assignment. I'll be gone in a few weeks."

"Yes. I know." But instead of being a reason to step away, her words gave urgency to his desire. They lacked the luxury of time and the knowledge that it could not last made the connection even more tempting.

She stepped back and away, facing the windows. Clyne eyed her and knew that whatever was between them, words and distance would not staunch. Would bedding her put this behind them both or would it only open the floodgates wider?

He was usually wise. He was usually cautious. Usually.

Clyne advanced. Cassidy lifted her phone.

"I have to check in."

He smiled. "Yes. Me, too."

She called his uncle and Clyne realized that Luke likely knew a great deal about Cassidy. They had worked together on several assignments.

Cassidy's conversation broke into his musings.

"Where?" she asked and there was a pause. "You

want me along?" Another pause. "All right. I understand. I'll go over the audio here. Yes, I'll do that. Call
if you find him." She tucked away the phone.

Clyne asked the question without words.

She made a face, clearly not inclined to tell him the
subject of her business.

"Luke has a lead on Ronnie Hare."

Ronnie Hare was the parole officer who had been
running messages from the cartels to the Wolf Posse.
Gabe had nearly caught him in January, but he had escaped.

"That's good," said Clyne.

"Yeah. His cooperation would help us make a case
against Escalanti, for sure. The police on Salt River
Reservation had his family under surveillance but there
has been nothing. So we suggested watching a few of
his parolees. We got a possible hit."

"You going?"

"Tomorrow, maybe. I was hoping…"

He didn't jump to her rescue but made her ask him.

"I'd like to see Amanda."

Clyne considered the wisdom of having the girl's
adoptive mother there when she arrived.

"No."

She looked as if he had punched her in the face.

"What if she's frightened?"

"Jovanna is my sister. I'll protect her with my life."

"I'm not talking about protection. I'm talking about
a child being taken from everything that is familiar."

"She's Apache. She's strong."

"She's a little girl whose favorite color is still pink."

Clyne set his jaw and hardened his heart to her pleas.
Cassidy threw up a hand, stormed away, spun and

retraced her steps. Then she folded her arms before her, jutted one hip and worked a brow.

"Do you know what music she likes to listen to when she's going to sleep? Or her favorite foods or the names of her closest friends?"

He didn't, of course. "Those things will come once she takes her place in her family."

Cassidy's jaw twitched. "She's not a clock for your mantel. She's a little girl who still leaves a tooth under her pillow for the tooth fairy."

Clyne remained unyielding, though the doubt cramped his belly. What if she was unwilling to know them? Angry at being forced from the home of this fierce little woman?

"I will bring you to see her. But only if she is not aware of your presence."

Two HOURS LATER Clyne sat in the darkness in his SUV beside Cassidy Walker. The two floodlights in his grandmother's driveway illuminated the yard and road beyond. Glendora Clawson and her husband, Hex, had not waited for Housing and Urban Development to assign them a residence like many on the rez. Instead they'd built a four-bedroom home that had been larger than they needed to raise their only daughter, his mother, Tessa.

His phone rang and he took the call from Gabe. Cassidy watched him as if she were on surveillance until he hung up.

"They reached Black Mountain. She should be here any minute."

Cassidy directed her attention to the road. A few minutes later a string of three cars turned in. Kino led the procession in his tribal police cruiser. Next came the dark Ford sedan from Child Protective Services and Gabe had the tail in his white SUV.

Cassidy leaned forward as doors opened and the two Cosen brothers appeared. Next came a woman from the rear seat of the Ford. She wore a green down coat that made her look like a walking sleeping bag. The driver emerged, a white man in a black woolen topcoat and red scarf. Finally he could see his sister.

Jovanna slipped from the backseat and into the circle illuminated by the floodlights. She wore a pink nylon jacket unzipped and the floppy sheepskin boots popular with young girls. Her face reminded him of his mother's in the photos of Tessa as a girl. Only the smile was missing. She had wide brown eyes and a soft round face. Her dark hair had been dyed blond at the tips and strands hung over her face like a shield.

"She's here," said Cassidy and reached for the door, before remembering that she was to stay in the car. She sunk back into the seat, then rebounded to lean so far forward that her forehead struck the window.

His grandmother was out of the house now, flying down the stairs, her arms flung wide. Jovanna had time to straighten before Glendora had her in her arms. Clyne smiled as Amanda all but disappeared in the bear hug. His grandmother was weeping, of course. Jovanna's hands came up and she wrapped her arms about her grandmother. Glendora tucked her grandchild under one arm and motioned to her grandsons. Gabe came forward, Stetson in hand, and leaned to touch his forehead to his sister's. Kino repeated the greeting and then gave Jovanna a hug.

Jovanna, now sandwiched between his youngest brother and his grandmother, was ushered toward the door, where Kino's wife, Lea, stood with a hand on her protruding belly beside Clay's wife, Isabella. Clay stepped from the house holding the collar of a large sheepdog.

Buster she remembered. The dog strained and jumped to be free of Clay's grip. Clay released the shepherd, who flew down the steps and right to Jovanna. His sister took a step back and lifted her hands to ward off attack but Buster threw himself to the ground, rolling and kicking like a submissive puppy. Then he sprang to his feet and tore away and back to Jovanna before throwing himself down again.

Clyne felt a catch in his throat. Buster remembered the lost member of their family. Jovanna knelt beside their family pet and buried her face in the warm coat.

"She always wanted a dog. Talked about a big shaggy dog. How old is Buster?"

Clyne found his voice held a telling quaver when he spoke. "He's twelve."

Jovanna's face now received a thorough licking as she laughed and straightened. Clay stepped forward to greet Jovanna by touching foreheads and his sister seemed to already have adjusted to this traditional form of greeting.

Clay introduced his wife and then his sister-in-law. Clyne now wondered why he had agreed to bring Cassidy. He was not there to greet his sister as he should be and Cassidy did not seem comforted judging from the tears now streaming down her face.

"She looks like them. Like all of you." Cassidy's words were choked with emotion.

"She looks like our mother," he said. "Her name was Tessa."

The door opened and the gathering filed inside, Buster sticking to Jovanna's side as she crossed the threshold. Gabe glanced toward Clyne's SUV and nodded before closing the door.

Clyne started the engine and drove Cassidy back to her hotel. Right now Glendora would be showing Jovanna the room they had repurposed for her with the blanket that had once graced his mother's bed.

Cassidy was silent during the drive except for an occasional choking sound. Clyne did not like to see a woman in pain even if it was the woman he had fought in court for the past eight months.

"I'm sorry," he said. "My family owes you a great debt."

That seemed to stiffen her spine. "Don't you dare thank me. I haven't lost her yet."

Once at the casino entrance he tried to walk her in but she stopped him with an outstretched hand.

"Leave me be, Clyne."

He watched her walk away and wondered why he felt compelled to follow her rather than return to his family. She was messing with his head and making him question what he knew to be true. Jovanna belonged with her tribe and her family. And Cassidy was once a soldier. Surely she understood collateral damage.

Clyne forced himself back into his car. Jovanna was home, where she belonged. He'd won. So why did his chest hurt?

## *Chapter Eleven*

When Clyne arrived home, the late supper was nearly ready and he could not understand why he did not feel the satisfaction he had expected to experience at this moment.

Glendora ushered Jovanna over to him and he looked down at the girl he had dreamed of since he'd learned she survived. He compared her against the little child she had been. He had not been there when she was born because he'd been on a rooftop in Iraq. And on the day his sister had left them for her first competition in South Dakota, he'd been riding the rodeo and sending all he could from his winnings back to his mom, who had just separated from their dad. He had seen his sister briefly, then almost two, on visits home. Kino, the youngest of the brothers, had been nine when Jovanna was born.

Jovanna stood and accepted the touching of foreheads and then the greeting in Apache that she did not return. The spark of fury ignited. She'd been robbed of her native tongue, her culture and her family. All because of a stupid bureaucratic mistake. If not for that mistake Cassidy would have a Sioux baby who had no other home and his family would never have lost Jovanna. But then he would never have known Cassidy.

That didn't matter. It couldn't.

"Jovanna, do you remember me?" Clyne asked.

She gave her head a little shake and her silky hair slipped over her shoulders. He stared at the blond tips that he now saw had a distinctive pink tint.

He lifted a strand and scowled at the cultural intrusion. This little girl was now as much white as she was Apache.

"Well, perhaps in time," he said and released her hair. "We welcome you back to your home. Our people have lived in this place for thousands of years."

She looked around and then back to him. "Doesn't seem big enough for all those people."

Kino burst out laughing. Jovanna had a sense of humor. He quirked a brow not sure if that was good or bad.

"Supper time," announced Glendora.

Jovanna rested a hand on Buster, who accompanied her to the table and sat at her feet. It seemed this shepherd was not going to let this sheep out of his sight again. He looked at Clay with his bicolored eyes as if to say, "You lost her."

It was only an ordinary Wednesday but his grandmother had made it a holiday with a pot roast cooked with potatoes and root vegetables. Nothing too exotic. But when they sat to eat, after the prayer to thank the food, Clyne noted that Jovanna did not take any of the meat.

Glendora noted the same thing and glanced to him in confusion. His sister's plate consisted of bread and green beans.

"Is there something wrong?" asked Glendora.

"Um. No, everything is fine," said Jovanna, looking very small surrounded by her brothers and their wives.

"You don't like pot roast or potatoes?"

"I love potatoes. It's just…"

Lea took up the conversation. "I couldn't eat meat when I first got pregnant. Just the smell." She rolled her eyes.

Clay looked at Jovanna and hazarded a guess. "You're a vegetarian?"

Jovanna nodded. "Yes."

"What? You're Apache. We've raised cattle for hundreds of years. We all have cattle in the communal herd. This is from our herd," he said motioning toward the meat.

"I don't eat anything with a face," she said, but her voice now trembled.

Glendora placed a hand on Clyne's arm, a signal to stop talking.

"The potatoes don't have a face, unless you count the eyes."

Jovanna smiled. "But they were cooked with the meat. I'm sorry, Grandmother. I don't want to be rude. I just think animals should not be food."

"That's ridiculous," said Clyne.

Jovanna's eyes went wide and glassy.

His grandmother rose from the table and disappeared into the kitchen.

"We're hunters and ranchers," said Clyne, lifting his hands in frustration. "We have some of the best trout fishing in the country not twenty minutes from here." He pointed east toward Pinyon Lake.

Jovanna seemed to grow smaller in her seat.

His grandmother returned with a jar of peanut butter and jelly.

Jovanna smiled as a look of relief lifted her features.

Clyne's scowl deepened. Peanut butter and jelly, on the dinner table.

He continued to glower as Kino took up the conversation, recalling tales of his childhood of which Clyne had no recollection because he had already been in the service at that time. Kino told stories that involved Jovanna. When he mentioned the time she had used a green marker to color the family dog and herself, Jovanna straightened.

"I remember that!" She looked at her hands as if seeing the green marks. "I remember that. How old was I?"

Kino's smile was sad. "You just turned two. It was right before the contest. Mom was furious because she didn't think the ink would come off before then."

Clay broke in. "I was supposed to be watching you, so it was my fault. Boy, was she angry." He smiled.

"She scrubbed me in the tub." Jovanna pointed to the bathroom. "Here. In this house." And she inhaled and looked around as if for the first time. "I lived here!"

"That's right," said Glendora. She expertly made a peanut butter and jelly sandwich and offered it to Jovanna.

"Why did we live with you, Grandma?"

The men went quiet but Glendora replied. "Your mom and dad were having some trouble."

Some trouble, thought Clyne. His dad had been a drug trafficker and his mom had been right to get his siblings clear of him. It was what Clyne had used his signing bonus on. Money for his mother and siblings until she could get her feet under her.

"Where is he?" she asked.

Kino went pale. He'd been there, hiding under a kitchen table in their dad's home when their father's contact had murdered their dad. Thankfully a tablecloth had kept him from seeing Kino but also kept his little brother from seeing the killer's face.

"He's gone, too, sweetie," said Glendora. "He died a long time ago."

"Oh," said Jovanna, and her expression of joy dropped.

His sister would never know their father. Clyne didn't know if he should be heartbroken or relieved. Both, he decided.

The somber moment passed when Clay launched into stories of their mother. How she sewed contest regalia for powwow dance competitions and danced. Jovanna munched her peanut butter sandwich and drank her milk. After the meal they shared a cake with Welcome Home Jovanna written in blue frosting on the top.

Everything went well until Kino and Clay said goodnight and left with their wives. Gabe announced the ongoing investigation and took his leave shortly afterward. His grandmother took Jovanna down the hall to the bedroom and he and Buster trailed along. His sister had only her school backpack, so Glendora offered a worn flannel nightie that looked miles too big for her granddaughter. On the bed, Glendora had placed some of the stuffed animals that had belonged to Jovanna a lifetime ago. Buster left Clyne's side to sit at Jovanna's bedside, resting his head on her knee.

Jovanna sat on the bed and lifted a lavender elephant with wide felt eyes. She studied the toy she once called Fafa and tucked it under her arm. Then she set it aside and rested a hand on Buster's head.

"Do you have a Wi-Fi code?" asked Jovanna.

"A what?" asked Glendora.

"To connect to the internet. I want to write my mom."

Glendora glanced to him. He shook his head.

"I'm sorry, sweetheart. We don't have that here."

"Oh." Jovanna did not quite hide the crestfallen look.

From there it all fell apart. It must have struck her that she was going to spend the night in a strange house with these strangers who were her family.

Her lip trembled and tears sprang from her eyes. She sank to the floor and wrapped her arms about Buster. Her words where more wail than speech.

"I want my mom!"

Glendora spent the next hour trying to comfort Jovanna while Clyne paced up and down in the hallway.

In his mind, Jovanna's return had gone much differently. Jovanna would remember them and slip back into her old life. Now he saw the problem with that plan. He'd never really considered his sister's feelings. Only what was best for her.

Gabe had tried to warn him. Even said flat out that their sister had already lost one mother and that making her lose another would be cruel.

Cruel.

That was something Clyne never intended. He knew it was best for children to be raised by their tribe. He knew in his heart that without that heritage the Indian part of them died. But his philosophical and moral stand did not take into consideration the pain of his sister's tears.

Her first night back with her family and Jovanna was sobbing into Buster's damp fur.

Glendora stepped out into the hall. She held the doorknob as she met Clyne's gaze.

"What do we do?"

"Only thing to do is let her cry. She's homesick."

"But this is her home," said Clyne.

"She's not a cactus. You can't just plop her down anywhere and expect her to grow."

"She belongs here."

"She does. But she was just escorted from her school by police officers and dropped here like a sack of laundry. She wants to be a part of this family and to have her big brothers around her. But Clay and Kino won't be here for her. They're starting families of their own. Gabe is going to marry Selena.

Which was a mistake. He'd already told Gabe that Selena's connections to illegal doings would be nothing but a problem to him and his reputation.

"Where is Agent Walker staying?" asked Glendora.

Clyne's heart sank.

"The casino hotel. Why?"

"Maybe she could come by. Tuck in her little girl."

"That's a bad idea."

"Why?"

"Because we won custody but only for six months. Then Jovanna will have to choose. If I let Walker in here, she might pick her."

"You're thinking what to do in six months." Glendora inclined her head toward the door and the sobbing that came from within. "I am thinking of a little girl missing her mother."

"She is not her mother."

Glendora looked ready to cry herself. Her daughter, his mother, had lost her life and her chance to raise her baby girl.

Clyne dragged in a long breath and let it go.

"I'll go get her."

Glendora turned the knob and reentered the room, leaving the door ajar.

"Honey Bear, your brother is going to fetch your mama."

Jovanna's face came up from her pillow and stared at Clyne. Then she lifted the dragging hem of her nightgown and rushed to him, wrapping her arms about his middle and clinging like a monkey.

"Thank you, Clyne. *Ixehe*."

Clyne stroked Jovanna's hair. His sister had just thanked him in Apache. Did she recall the language of her birth or had she learned it before returning to them?

He looked to Glendora, who was crying now. He just knew he was going to regret this. But he whispered to his sister in Apache that he would take care of her and that everything would be all right.

# Chapter Twelve

Cassidy had just finished a call with Luke. They'd successfully followed one of the Salt River gang members to a remote location where he had left food and supplies at a drop. They were feeding someone and he believed it was Hare. He was staying on surveillance for the night.

"I have the calls from Escalanti," she said.

"Anything good?"

"I don't know. The tech guys couldn't provide transcripts. It's all Apache."

Luke made a sound in his throat. "Gabe, Kino or Clyne can translate. Clay, too. Any of them."

Like she'd ask them.

When she didn't respond Luke spoke again.

"Cassidy. Don't be stubborn. There might be something there. Get it translated."

"I will," she promised.

Luke said good-night and she ended the call. She was heading for the shower, dressed only in her underwear when the knock sounded on her door. A firm rapping, unlike the polite tentative rap of housekeeping.

Cassidy stepped into the bathroom to retrieve her pistol. She wasn't going to stand in front of that peephole and ask who was there after the two attacks.

"Who is it?" she called from the security of the bathroom.

"Clyne Cosen."

She lowered the pistol. Cosen? At this hour. Her suspicions peaked. Had he come to finish what they'd started? Her body came alive, tingling all over. That made her scowl. His timing sucked. She'd just finished up another round of tears before Luke phoned.

The nerve of hitting on her when he knew she would be sad and vulnerable. What a jerk.

"I'm not that lonely."

"Open the door, Cassidy. Jovanna needs you."

She shoved the pistol into her holster as she left the bathroom, and threw back the metal latch, released the lock and tugged open the door. The breeze from the hallway reminded her that she was wearing only a fuchsia lace bra and matching panties.

Clyne's eyes widened as he swept down the length of her, reversed course and lingered at the swell of her breasts. The lace cups of her bra did not include a lining, and she felt her nipples pucker up under the contact of nothing more than his stare.

When he finally met her gaze his eyes were glittering with an unmistakable intensity that had her backing up. Her ears tingled with the rest of her.

"Lace?" he said.

Cassidy ducked into the bathroom and grabbed a white bath towel winding it around herself. It covered her from beneath her armpits to just below her hips.

Her throat had gone dry and a glance in the mirror showed her that her skin was flushed nearly as pink as her underthings.

"I was about to take a shower," she said.

Clyne remained in the hallway as if refusing to take the step that would lead him again over her threshold.

"Yes, I see."

He certainly had.

"You said Amanda needs me?" He'd actually said Jovanna. But she refused to speak that name. The only person who could make her say otherwise was her daughter.

"She's crying. My grandmother sent me to fetch you."

Cassidy let the towel drop as she rushed back into the room to retrieve her trousers. She slipped into her blouse and fumbled with the buttons, noticed they were out of alignment and left them that way as she reached for her coat. By the time she had her boots on and holster clipped Clyne was using a bandanna to wipe his brow.

"Hot?" she said with a wicked smile. The temperature in the hall was anything but. March up in the mountains felt more like January to her.

"Yeah," he said, casting her a doleful look. "Ready?"

Cassidy slipped her phone into her pocket with the charger and scooped up her computer. Everything else she could live without.

He walked with her through the casino, greeting various members of his circle as he escorted her out and to the large SUV.

"Should I follow you?"

"I'll drive you back." Her radar went up again as she imagined Clyne walking her to her room late at night, lingering outside her door with that big empty bed inside.

"I'll take my car."

"Fine."

He drove her to the lot, following her directions. When she told him to stop, he did and then turned to her.

"Did you really think that I'd come back for…"

She closed the door because she was sick of him seeing her turn pink every time he asked her a question.

"Listen, I'm sorry about that."

"Would you have let me in, Cassidy, if I had been there for that?"

"What do you think?" She tried for a look of impatience but her stomach was tightening and her toes curled in her boots as she looked at his appealing features and that wide, full mouth. Her mind flashed an image of that mouth fixed on her breast, his tongue working against the lace cup of her bra.

His mouth quirked and she lifted her gaze to meet his. His eyes held the glitter of desire that fueled her own.

"Let's go," she said and pulled the latch before slipping out into the crisp evening air. She was afraid cold air would not be enough to cool her heated blood but she kept walking.

CLYNE STOOD LIKE a silent sentinel as Cassidy spoke with her daughter. Their reunion had tugged at his heart and made him question his decisions to end her custody.

It was clear that Cassidy loved Jovanna and that Jovanna adored her mom. He considered for the first time that Jovanna would not choose to remain with her brothers after the six months were over. Even his grandmother didn't think Jovanna would pick them. She might learn to love them, but she already loved Cassidy Walker.

Now Clyne had to think of a way to keep Jovanna here, even if his sister chose Walker. His gaze flicked to the woman in question. There was no doubt what she wanted. She had told him. She was going to get her promotion and move east. She was going to take Jovanna. He had to think of a way to stop her.

Cassidy looked up at him and smiled. Her gratitude shone clear on her face. Jovanna's eyes were drooping. Cassidy moved to stand.

Jovanna roused herself. "Mom. Where are you going?"

"Back to the hotel."

"No, stay."

She stroked her daughter's dark hair off her forehead. "All right. I'll stay until you fall asleep."

"No. All night." Jovanna glanced at him and Glendora hovered in the doorway. "In case I have that dream."

Cassidy glanced to Glendora, who nodded her silent consent.

Clyne looked from one woman to the next, miffed that he had not even been consulted.

"All right, doodlebug. I'll stay." She glanced to Clyne and this time she had the smug smile of a poker player holding the winning hand.

CASSIDY STRETCHED OUT on the narrow bed beside her daughter and listened to Amanda tell her about her day from the moment Child Protective Services scooped her up to this moment.

"I'm sorry this is happening to you," said Cassidy.

"It's okay now, Mom. I want to be here. But I want you here, too."

"That's not the way it works. The court has ordered you to stay with them. I'm not allowed to stay here. It's just that your grandmother thought I could help. You understand. It's just for tonight."

Amanda clung tighter. She stroked her daughter's hair and Amanda settled. Her breathing grew steady and her eyelids drooped.

"Don't leave, Mom. Don't sneak out when I fall asleep."

"All right. I'll stay."

"Promise?" asked Amanda.

"Promise."

Amanda drifted to sleep and Cassidy lay in the room that smelled like wool, cedar and old dog. Were these scents familiar to her daughter? When Amanda rolled to her side, Cassidy slipped off the bed and across the room. She needed to find a bathroom.

Buster lifted his head at her departure but did not move from the rug beside her daughter's bed. Cassidy regarded him, trying to decide if he was a threat. Finally she retrieved her gun and holster from the bookcase near the door and slipped the holster on before retreating to the hall. She closed the door softly behind her.

"Is she asleep?"

The male voice made her jump clear off the ground. The corridor was dark and he stood in shadows, leaning against the opposite wall. A shaft of light stabbed across the runner in the hall, supplied by a lamp in the living room.

Clyne, she realized. Now her heart accelerated for a different reason. She pressed a hand over her racing heart and felt the strap of her lace bra beneath her blouse. A tingling ache grew inside her.

He stepped forward, his face all shadows and hard angles.

"Yes."

"Are you staying?"

"I promised that I would."

He nodded and motioned to the door behind him. "I put your things in here. Coat. Briefcase. It's Gabe's room but he's at the station tonight. And…I gave you one of my T-shirts because my grandmother said you would need it."

"Thank you." Why wasn't she moving?

"Do you need anything else from me?" he asked.

She felt the question was intentionally leading, an offer to finish what they had started in her hotel. She took a little too long answering and his nostrils flared as if catching her scent.

"Nothing," she managed to say, her mouth now dry as dust.

He lifted his chin and she wondered if he was brave enough to take what they both wanted but also knew was just a really rotten idea.

"Thank you for the shirt."

"Bathroom is right down there. My room is there." He pointed and she wondered if this was another invitation.

"I'll be sure not to mix them up."

He lifted his brows. "My grandmother is on the other side of the house, past the living room. So if Amanda has a bad dream, I don't think she would hear the noise."

She didn't take the bait. "I'll be with her."

"Protecting her at night and me all day." He lifted a hand and stroked her cheek. "Chasing away bad dreams."

Her body trembled but she managed to hold her ground. Unfortunately she didn't step past him or retreat into the spare room. What kind of game was he playing?

"We're talking about Amanda's nightmares. Right?"

He glanced away. Suddenly she didn't think Amanda was the only one who was afraid.

"Gerard had them. I did, too. No shame in it."

"You?" he asked.

"I got some help. No shame in that either. But if you're asking me to tuck you in, I'm going to have to say no."

"I want more than that, Cassidy. I think you do, too."

"What about your reputation?" she asked. "Pillar of the community. Tribal leader. Bastion of Apache culture." She hoped he heard the contempt in her words. She didn't like being treated like an undesirable merely because of her race.

"I will need to choose soon. There are several women who are interested. All Apache women."

"So why point out your bedroom to me?"

He stepped closer. "Because you are different."

She flipped her blond hair. "I'll say."

He took hold of her arm. "No, Cassidy. I don't mean the way you look or the way you smell or your choice of undergarments, which are…memorable. And though you are a beautiful woman. It's deeper than that. You know. You understand what it was like."

And then it made sense, the thing that none of the other women of his tribe could offer. They had not seen action in the Middle East. They had not experienced a war and survived and none of them had lost loved ones to that terrible war.

"How do you do it?" he asked.

"What?"

"Keep fighting?"

"Because it's not over," she said.

"It will never be over," he said. "Just like the battle to keep our land and our heritage. The struggle stretches through generations."

He looked away, staring into the darkness.

"That's true," he said at last.

"Luke says you don't carry a personal weapon. That you don't hunt."

"I have done enough hunting for a lifetime."

"But someone is trying to kill you. You should take some steps to protect yourself."

"No."

"You might die."

"Yes. But I will not die with a gun in my hand."

They shared a moment of silence as each considered their choice. To wear a gun. To set it aside forever.

"Do you remember them all?" she asked.

He met her intent gaze. "Every one. And that's not all. I remember the weather, the location, the moment just before I squeezed that trigger." He sighted an imaginary rifle and looked through his imaginary scope. Then he moved his index finger and made the sound of the discharge. Cassidy flinched. He lowered his hands to his sides.

"You?"

"I remember. The second one was worse. Parker refused to put down his weapon. He pointed it toward me and I fired twice to mass."

He took her hand.

"And I remember the smell of blood and the sound of him trying to breathe with two punctured lungs."

"It's easy to take a life," he said. "Hard to live with, though. You understand that."

This was what attracted him, he realized. What made her different from all the rest of the women in his life. Cassidy knew what it was to fight to defend her life and live with the aftermath.

"But I saw someone afterward. A counselor. It helped, Clyne. You should try it."

His hand slipped from hers. "I don't think so."

"They have a program, some of the counselors are vets. They've seen action. They understand. They don't judge you. Just help you talk it out. I have a connection there."

He hesitated, actually considering it. Then he shook his head.

"I'd go with you if you'd like."

He checked to see if there was some joke associated with her offer, some smirk or facial expression. All he saw was earnestness and compassion. It was his undoing.

Clyne turned away, giving her his back.

She came up beside him, rested a hand on his shoulder. "You did as you were ordered, Clyne. You did what you had to and you came home alive. That has to count."

He turned and lifted her chin with the crook of his index finger.

"Part of me didn't come back," he said and dropped his hand to his side.

She gave him a fragile smile. "Most of you did."

He thought of her husband, the tank commander. He had not been so lucky. He'd lost his life and his family and this beautiful compelling woman standing so close he could feel the heat of her body.

"Clyne, I know you had a terrible assignment. Gerard did, too. He killed people with those tanks. Maybe more than you did."

"He didn't have to look at them."

"Yes. He did. From inside his armored vehicle, he did. I know because he told me. And I saw some of them, too. The wounded. Transported some along with our soldiers."

"Did we make any difference or did we just make more enemies and orphans?"

She had asked herself that very thing. "We made a difference and enemies and orphans. They're still out there, coming for us, Clyne. They still want to do what they did in New York. That's why I still fight. That's why I want to get to out east. I want to stop that from happening again. I want to stop them from killing another American."

Clyne cocked his head. "Are you fighting for a cause, Cassidy, or for revenge?"

She drew back. "Does it matter?"

"Only to me. I had a brother who once sought revenge."

She knew exactly who he meant because she had read his file. Kino Cosen had joined the Shadow Wolves of Immigration and Custom's Enforcement and tracked smugglers but he was there to find his father's killer.

"He got him, too. The very man who took your dad. Must have felt good."

Clyne's mouth tipped down. "He said it didn't feel good. He told me that he didn't kill that man. In the end he forgave him and made his peace."

"The report said…" She thought back, recalling the autopsy report. Snake venom. Why had she thought Kino had killed the Viper?

"Seems I can't forgive myself and you can't forgive the men who took your husband."

That was about it, she realized. "You think sleeping together will clear all that up, do you?"

"No. But it's a connection. That is rare enough." He stroked her cheek. "Takes it beyond the physical. I'm tired of sleeping with women who do not know me inside. They see a leader. I see a killer. You at least recognize me for what I am."

"You were a soldier, Clyne. So was I. It's no shame."

"I thought if I came home and if I did enough for my people that I could again return to the Red Road."

"Red Road?"

"It is the proper way to live and die. Indian people follow this path, the natural way."

"Killing one's enemies should be part of that way." She cupped his jaw in both of her hands. "You might not ever forgive yourself, Clyne. But I forgive you and I thank you for fighting."

The hot tear rolled down his cheek and seeped between her fingers and his jaw.

Then she lifted up on her toes and gave him the kind of kiss she had dreamed of giving her husband when he returned from overseas. A kiss to welcome a soldier home.

# Chapter Thirteen

Clyne deepened the kiss as he dragged Cassidy against him. She molded to him as if this was where she was meant to be. Then he realized it was his longing he felt, his need for this woman, too long denied because he knew that she could not be so easily set aside. Because Cassidy knew the warrior's way. She had made an unusual choice and she had continued the fight. Nothing was more important to her except her daughter.

"Do we know what we're doing?" he asked.

She shook her head. "I don't think so."

She stroked his shoulders, her fingers kneading the muscles there, wordlessly seeking contact.

Suddenly he felt like some dreadful cliché. Tarzan with his Jane, King Kong entranced by Fay Wray, the cover of every one of those romance novels that showed a naked warrior gripping a nearly naked blonde and had the word *savage* emblazoned on the cover.

"I don't date white women."

She cocked her head. "This isn't a date."

He still felt the need to qualify. "I'm going to marry an Apache woman. Someone who understands our culture and our ways and can help me lead our people."

She shrugged.

"I didn't want you to think…" His words fell away at the open look of invitation she cast him.

"I don't."

She raked both hands through her fine hair that fell immediately back to place. "I have been without a man for a long time, Clyne. And I haven't missed it. You make me miss the heat and the friction. You make me wonder and fantasize. Maybe it is because we are alike or because we are different. But this attraction is something new. I've never had a battle like this before."

"Is this a battle we need to fight?" he asked.

"Yes, because I'm not sure sleeping with you will make this need go away."

"It might," he said.

"What if it doesn't?"

What, indeed.

The tingle of danger mixed with his arousal increased the ache.

The connection of Jovanna meant they would never be totally rid of each other. Unless his sister chose to stay with Cassidy. That was what Gabe believed would happen. It was why he pushed so hard to have Cassidy here on Black Mountain.

Clyne thought of Jovanna's tears. Gabe had been right.

His brother didn't see the battle. He saw the compromise. Clyne was a master of compromise. Why hadn't he seen it with this woman?

Was it only because he wanted her and so needed her as far away from himself as possible?

Her eyes beckoned, issuing an invitation he could not resist. Her arms circled his waist.

"This will not solve anything," he said.

She agreed with a nod and stepped closer, offering her mouth. "It will make everything worse."

She was right. Whatever it was between them was strong and growing stronger. And he knew the best way to get rid of this kind of unwelcome physical need was to get it over with. The rodeo circuit had taught him that much. Lots of tension. Lots of heat and lots of mornings creeping from a hotel bedroom with his boots in his hands.

She could stop him if she wanted. This woman looked at him as many women did. But the difference was that he wanted her, too.

His mouth descended. She met him with a kiss filled with passion and need. Her fingers raked over his shoulders as her tongue danced with his. The urgency and the heat surprised him.

He captured her, pressing them together. Cassidy broke the contact of their kiss and turned away. Her eyes closed and he saw the fine blue veins that threaded across her lids.

"We're in a custody battle," she said as if she needed to remind herself as much as him.

"We are."

"Opponents. I'm not doing anything that will hurt my case."

He drew back. "Cassidy, in six months Jovanna will have to choose. Sleeping with me won't change that."

But she was already slipping from his arms. He let her go.

She disappeared into the bathroom. He heard the water run, the toilet flush and the water again. He should go, but he lingered like the love-sick calf that he was.

Clyne did not want to think about why she made him

ache all over. Not just in the obvious places, but down deep in his gut and up in his chest. This was about more than sex. That alone should send him running in the opposite direction.

The door opened and she slipped past him again and into Gabe's room. He watched her go and wondered if he was falling for this little white warrior woman. She reappeared with the shirt she had given her, neatly folded and clutched to her chest. Then she eased Jovanna's door open and cast a glance back at him, then into the room. He saw her stiffen and reach. A instant later she held her pistol.

CASSIDY CAUGHT MOVEMENT and reached for the gun as she retreated a step. Her gaze pinned on the possible threat. The dark shape squatted beside her daughter's bed.

And then her brain made sense of the image. Not some person creeping on the floor, she realized, but the dog. He stood and stretched, performing that unique bow used only by dogs. He sauntered to her and used his head to brush her hand. She stooped to thump him on the side.

"Good dog, Buster," Cassidy whispered and holstered her gun.

Behind her, Clyne filled the doorway, blocking out the light and casting a long shadow across the floor.

Buster preceded her to Amanda's bed, then turned in a tight circle on the rug and curled upon the floor. The dog sighed and then lowered his head, allowing Cassidy to approach her daughter's bed.

Amanda slept on her side, facing the wall, her breathing even and deep and the stuffed elephant clutched to her chest. A toy of her childhood. The childhood that Cassidy had no part of.

She sensed rather than heard his approach. She turned to find Clyne halfway across the room, tall and imposing. His presence a comfort.

"Everything all right?"

She nodded, smiling and was rewarded with one of his in return. If possible, it only made him look more appealing.

"I forgot Buster was in here," she whispered. "She never had a dog. Always wanted one."

"She remembered Buster."

Cassidy believed that was so. He drew closer.

"She okay?" he whispered, moving to stand beside her. It reminded her of Gerard, somehow, coming to stand beside their new daughter's miniature bed after they brought her home. In those few precious months between his first and second deployment, they would stand together and watch Amanda sleep.

Cassidy felt her throat constricting at the losses. Clyne's family losing this child and she losing her husband. Was it possible to give Amanda the home she deserved away from the family that loved her? She suddenly did not know what to do and that frightened her.

"Will you promise to keep her safe when I'm gone?"

"You going somewhere?"

She glanced at him but found his expression unreadable. "Well, I can't stay in Amanda's bedroom forever."

He neither argued nor affirmed her comment. Just stared at her with dark, unblinking eyes.

"Don't forget she's just a child," Cassidy whispered. "A child who should not have to make this choice."

Her eyes closed and she held her hands laced together before her mouth as if in prayer.

Cassidy opened her eyes and exited the room, waiting for Clyne to follow. He met her in the hallway and she closed the door.

"When she chooses me, and she will, you will let her go? Drop all your attempts to take her from me?"

His jaw went hard and the muscles of his chest bunched. She held her ground, determined as a badger facing a wolf. His size didn't intimidate her. She'd fight him to the last breath if she must.

"She would lose everything," he said. "Her connection to a people and a place. Her identity. Her legacy. She is Bear clan. Born of Eagle."

"I don't know what that means."

"Exactly my point. You don't. Jovanna must relearn the language of her people. Begin her training so she will be ready for her Sunrise Ceremony."

Cassidy's eyes narrowed. "The womanhood thing? She's a girl. She just bought her first tub of pink lip gloss, for goodness' sakes."

"So it's already begun, her transition to a woman."

"Hardly." But the signs were there. The interest in boys and her abandonment of the childish toys that once were so important.

"I spoke about Changing Woman. Jovanna will become her during the ceremony. Not pretend to be her, she will be her. And she will dance and pray. We will all pray for her to become the best possible woman."

"Are there drugs involved? Peyote or some such, because I will bust you, all of you, so fast."

Clyne rolled his eyes. "You see. This is the trouble. You don't know anything about us."

"I know it's illegal to give drugs to a minor."

"We won't."

"Fine. Dress her up in feathers and beads. It won't

change her." She scowled at him. "I just want my daughter back so I can get her out of here."

Now Clyne scowled. "What is so wrong with Black Mountain?"

"Let's see." She lifted her hand to tick off the reasons on each finger. "Unemployment rate. Dropout rate. Teen pregnancy rate. Violence against women." She ran out of fingers. "Oh, yeah, and a major drug syndicate."

Clyne's expression fell. "But she belongs in this place. You can't take her away from here."

"Not yet I can't. But once this ridiculous separation is over and she makes her choice, I surely can and you can't stop us."

"Why? Why is it so important to take her away from the place of her ancestors?"

"Because I need to get to a real field office. One where I can do some good instead of busting bank robbers, kidnappers and drug traffickers."

"Real? What does that even mean?"

"Where the bad guys are. The important ones."

"You mean Al-Qaeda, ISIS?"

"Yes."

"In other words, terrorists."

One brow lifted and he considered her for a long moment. "You know that the illegal immigrants have included members of both of those organizations, right here in Arizona."

"And the cases are made in NY and DC. I need to be a part of that."

"Why?"

She didn't answer. She'd already told him too much. Cassidy turned to leave him but he took hold of her elbow, urging her to face him.

"Why, Cassidy. Why ISIS and Al-Qaeda?"

She threw the words at him, hurling them from deep down inside herself where she had kept them alive, burning like a coal ember.

"Because those are the men who killed Gerard."

She slapped her hand over her mouth as her eyes rounded. She had not meant to tell him that.

He reached for her and she shuffled back, letting her hand slip from her mouth.

"Good night, Clyne."

He stopped his advance. "Cassidy, wait."

She didn't, instead she made a quick march back to her daughter's room. Sometimes retreat was the best course of action.

Cassidy closed the door and lay her pistol and shoulder holster on the book shelf. Then she quickly undressed, leaving on only her panties and then slipping into the overlong T-shirt. The cotton was soft and clean and smelled of soap. It wasn't until she was standing beside the closed wooden door that she looked down at the T-shirt he had provided for her. It read: I ♥ Rez Boys.

Cassidy let out a groan. She forced herself to march across the room and slipped in beside her slumbering daughter. She forced herself to stillness as she recalled Clyne's earthy scent and his words. Why was it so important to take her away from her home, her people and her tribe? To say she slept would be a mistake. Dozed, roused, listened, dozed, from well after midnight until the early hours before morning.

She woke to a noise similar to the high-pitched whine that alerted her to one of Amanda's nightmares. She was already halfway out of bed when she realized she slept beside her daughter. The whine became a shout. But it was not Amanda. That was the voice of a man and he was screaming.

Cassidy's ears pinned back at the ferociousness and she crept across the floor to retrieve her pistol, removed the safety and headed for the door.

## Chapter Fourteen

Cassidy slipped into the hallway. Someone was already there. The light flicked on and Cassidy recognized Glendora, her expression startled as she took in the picture of Cassidy in the hallway gripping her pistol.

"What is that sound?" asked Cassidy. Then she realized that the shouts came from Clyne's room.

"He has nightmares ever since coming home," said Glendora, motioning to Clyne's room.

Cassidy slid the safety back in place and lowered her weapon. Glendora shuffled past her and knocked on the door.

"Mama?"

Cassidy recognized her daughter's voice coming from her new room. She went to her daughter, finding her sitting up wide-eyed in bed. Buster was no longer on the floor, but sitting beside her daughter on the mattress as Amanda clung to his shaggy coat.

"It's all right, doodlebug. Your brother Clyne is having a nightmare."

It was the first time she'd called him Amanda's brother and the realization brought her up short.

"He has nightmares, too?" Amanda's grip on Buster loosened.

Cassidy sat on the bed.

"Are they about breaking glass?" Amanda's therapist thought the breaking glass dream stemmed from some early childhood experience. Now Cassidy understood, it was the car crash. Amanda had been in the accident that had killed Tessa Cosen.

"I don't know. Maybe you can ask him tomorrow."

The shouts stopped and the house went quiet. A few moments later she heard Clyne's door shut and Amanda's open.

"You two all right?" asked Glendora.

"We're fine, Gramma," piped Amanda.

Glendora offered another good-night and left them.

Cassidy stretched out beside her daughter. "What do you think of them?" she asked Amanda.

"I love them," she said instantly. They were quiet for a time and she thought Amanda had dozed off when she spoke again. "Mama?"

"Yes."

"Would it... Could you... Will you call me Jovanna from now on?"

Cassidy felt the stabbing pain as some deep part of herself began screaming.

"Why do you want that, doodlebug?"

"Well. It's my name. The name my first mother gave me."

"Oh, I see." She held back the burning in her throat and thought her words sounded almost normal. "Well, I can try. But you might have to remind me sometimes."

"Okay. Thank you, Mama." Her arms came around Cassidy's neck.

Cassidy held her daughter, wishing that Amanda could have her brothers and her grandmother and still stay with her forever. She thought of Clyne and his insistence that he marry an Apache woman. Of Gerard promising to come home. Things didn't always go as you hoped. Amanda's arms slipped from her neck as her daughter cuddled in her bedding, settling for sleep.

Cassidy might be different from other women in his life and she understood some of the issues he faced as a vet. They might even share a physical connection that she knew was unique. But there was one thing they did not share—his heritage. And no matter what she did, there was just no way she could ever become Apache.

CASSIDY WOKE AND checked her watch. It was a little past six. She eased from her daughter's bed and headed for the hallway, pausing only to retrieve her pistol from the bookshelf. Then she continued to the bathroom at the end of the hall. She opened the door and paused at the billowing steam and the scent of soap and shaving cream. Clyne stood naked before the bathroom mirror with a white towel slung over his neck and his bronze skin made even darker in contrast to the white shaving cream covering one side of his face. He held a razor in one hand and the other gripped the sink.

Cassidy squeezed the doorknob as her entire body leaped from drowsiness to tingling awareness. Clyne Cosen naked was a better stimulant than a double shot of espresso.

"I'm sorry," she muttered.

Clyne startled and then whipped the towel off his shoulders and threw it around his hips.

"I didn't know. It wasn't locked." She forced her gaze to his face.

He gripped the towel with one hand and pressed the other to his chest.

"Didn't hear you." He blew out a breath. "Thought it was Jovanna for a minute."

She tore her gaze away and looked at the door, seeing there was no latch.

"No lock?" she asked.

"Shut is occupied in this house. I'm sorry no one told you." Cassidy retreated so fast she stumbled into the hall. Clyne tucked in the edge of the towel, fixing it in place. He was naked except for a narrow band of terry cloth. She thought he looked even more appealing with his muscular frame damp from the shower and his wet hair clinging to his wide shoulders. He showered with that small beaded leather pouch, she realized. She had seen the sodden leather nestled just below the hollow of his throat. Something else she didn't understand, she realized.

"Do you carry that thing everywhere?" he asked, pointing his razor at her pistol.

"Nearly."

"I'll be out in a second." He let his gaze sweep down her exposed legs and then returned his attention to her face. The look he gave her could have steamed the mirror.

"We're in trouble. Aren't we?" she asked.

Clyne didn't look at her. "Cassidy, am I the guy you want to introduce to your family?"

His tone was sarcastic. Her answer was not.

"I don't have any family except Amanda."

When he looked at her again, the heat was gone, replaced by a look of pity.

"No one?" he asked.

She swallowed but the lump continued to rise in her throat, so she shook her head in answer. Then she closed the door, removing the sight of his jaw dropping open. Of course he couldn't imagine that, no clan or tribe or community. No huge loving family. No place that was home.

She didn't care. Home wasn't a place anyway.

Cassidy returned to her room and dressed, waiting until she heard Clyne leave the bathroom and the sound of his bedroom door clicking shut before she ventured out into the hall and into the bathroom.

It still smelled like soap and aftershave.

When she reached the kitchen a few minutes later it was to find Clyne dressed in polished, elaborately stitched cowboy boots, dark jeans and a deep blue button-up shirt cinched at the throat with a chunk of turquoise the size of a quail's egg. The long wet hair was now contained in a neat braid secured with a bit of red cloth. His gray blazer sat on the back of the chair.

He glanced up at her and motioned to the seat across from his. His presence so captivated her that she hardly noticed his grandmother, dressed in black knit pants, white blouse and pale blue cardigan sweater.

"How you like your coffee?" asked Glendora, sliding a mug before her.

"Black," said Cassidy. "Thank you."

Glendora nodded. "Same as Gabe and Kino. I think all police drink coffee black. No fuss. Right?" She motioned to her eldest grandson. "This one drinks it with milk. Lots of milk. Good thing I still have some cows!" She turned back to the stove. "I'm making potatoes, scrambled eggs and bacon. But then I remembered that Jovanna doesn't eat meat. So I don't know what to do. I never cooked for a vegetarian before. I generally use the bacon grease for the potatoes and eggs."

Cassidy stood, tentatively approaching the stove. "I can make her breakfast. She likes fried eggs and toast."

They spent a few minutes discussing her daughter's diet until Glendora felt more comfortable.

"Last night, she asked me to call her Jovanna," Cassidy announced.

Clyne and Glendora stared.

Glendora clasped her hands together. "She did!"

"She said that was what her first mom named her."

"First mom?" Clyne said, his brow lifting as he replaced his coffee to the table. "That's what she called her?"

Glendora bustled as she spoke. "The lady from Child Welfare will be here soon. She's taking Jovanna to school and she said she'd be back after school to check in, too."

Buster appeared and stood by the back door. Clyne let him out by opening the door without moving from his place. A moment later Amanda emerged in the doorway. *Jovanna*, Cassidy corrected herself.

She had already dressed in the same clothing she wore yesterday. She accepted greetings from them all and sat between Clyne and Cassidy. Buster scratched at the door and spent breakfast eating the crusts of toast offered by Jovanna.

Her daughter munched her toast and sipped her milk. Then she eyed Clyne and said.

"Are your nightmares about breaking glass?"

Clyne choked on his coffee, narrowly missing spilling on his pristine shirt.

"Did I wake you?" he asked.

"Yes. I was scared, but Mommy came right in. I have them, too. I hear glass breaking and screaming and I wake up."

Clyne looked to Glendora. Had they both correctly

guessed at the root of this particular dream? Clyne turned his attention back to his sister.

"Mine are about the time I was a soldier."

"My father was a soldier, too. He was killed in action by an IED. That's an…"

"Improvised explosive device," said Clyne.

"That's right!" said Jovanna.

Clyne's complexion had taken on a green tinge. He knew IEDs. That much was certain. Had he seen one detonate or stopped someone who carried one?

"I wish he was still alive. You two could be friends."

Clyne and Cassidy exchanged a look. It was doubtful that Amanda's father and Amanda's brother would have ever been friends.

"Right, Mama?"

"I think they have a lot in common."

Amanda munched her toast, slipping another crust under the table, where it vanished. The sound of Buster chewing came an instant later.

Child Welfare arrived on time and Cassidy kissed her daughter goodbye. She called Diane to check in and asked her to overnight a box of clothing to Clyne's address and Diana said she had sent a box yesterday to her hotel address. They should arrive today. That was a relief because her daughter was not wearing the same thing to the reservation school tomorrow.

Buster scratched at the door, and Clyne let him out and then called to Glendora.

"I think Buster is following Jovanna to school."

Cassidy looked out the back door and saw Buster tearing down the drive and out onto the road.

"I'll go after him," he said and turned to Cassidy. "Want to see the school?"

She did. They left together in her car. On the way

she asked if he would be willing to translate some of Manny Escalanti's phone conversations and he agreed. They finished the lot before reaching the school.

"What do you think?" she asked, regarding her careful notes.

"Well, the brown rabbit might be his way of speaking about Ronnie Hare. He said he'd gone for a run and that he was a bad swimmer."

"Swimmer?"

"Might mean he's not willing to cross back over the Salt River to our reservation or that he's not willing to leave the reservation to go to Mexico."

"He said his cousins are taking care of the rabbit," said Cassidy. "Is that bringing him supplies or is that an order to kill him?"

Clyne gave her a long look. "I don't know. But if it were me, I'd want Ronnie Hare dead. He was the messenger between Escalanti and the Mexican drug lords."

"Who is bringing messages now? I wonder."

"Good question. Either way, you guys better bring him in quick." Clyne pulled into the school lot. There sat Buster, before one of the string of windows on the side of the building. "There he is."

"Is that her classroom?"

"If Buster says so. That dog lost her once. He's not letting her go a second time."

Cassidy thought that Clyne and Buster had a lot in common.

Clyne called Buster but he had to carry the dog to the car.

Cassidy stood beside her vehicle staring at the window Buster had chosen. How many times had Amanda had to begin again? Be the new kid who started months after everyone else with a new teacher and a new set of requirements? Six? Seven? How many more times was she going to pick up her daughter and move her like, what had Clyne said, as if she was a canary?

Six months. It wouldn't be enough to set down roots. Not the kind that sank deep, those that took a lifetime to grow. And her daughter had only—

"Six months," she whispered.

Clyne stood beside her, holding the giant dog as if he were a puppy instead of a senior citizen with a white muzzle.

"Cassidy, it's fair. Six months with us after nine years with you. Give your daughter a chance to know us."

"It's too much. A child shouldn't have to choose between two families." She should never have to choose. She should be able to have her mother and her family. But how?

"The courts make them do it every day. You know it. I know it."

Cassidy looked at him with big blue eyes, brimming with tears. It hurt to look at her, but he couldn't look away. Clyne knew the face of grief, intimately.

"What if she chooses you?" she whispered.

And there it was, the reason she had fought so hard to keep her child.

"She's all I have, Clyne. You have brothers, their wives, your grandmother. Your whole tribe." She looked away. "She's all I have in the world."

"Gabe says you are a part of Jovanna, because you raised her. That's why he wanted you here."

"And maybe for me to see the family I am keeping her from," said Cassidy.

Clyne gave her a lot of credit for admitting that.

He opened the door and let Buster into the backseat.

Then he opened her door and waited for her to take her seat. She handed over the keys.

She didn't recall him starting the sedan, but the speed bump leaving the school grounds snapped her back to the present. She looked at him and he glanced to her and back to the road. Behind them Buster panted and paced across the backseat.

"Is it a good school?"

"I went there. My brothers, too. Lots of our kids go on to college. Jovanna can take advanced classes at the high school later on."

"She won't be here that long."

He said nothing to that.

"Tell me about the Sunrise Ceremony," she said.

Clyne looked out at the road as he tried to think back to the last ceremony he attended instead of the woman beside him. Cassidy had moved past a distraction. She hadn't even mentioned their exchange last night. But he couldn't stop thinking about her, them. He was in trouble. Big trouble.

"Clyne?"

"Yes. I'm thinking." About the fuchsia underthings worn by this field agent and former army evac pilot.

He described the ceremony that took place each July Fourth. He did not tell her that it was the same day that his mother had died and his sister had been lost.

Instead he described the chanting prayer and the drumming of the males of the family and all of the families coming from other reservations. The gifts given and received. The feasting and music and dance. The sacred objects and the bee pollen to be sprinkled on Jovanna by the medicine man to bring prosperity, fertility and health. But there were gaps. Parts of the ceremony were secret to outsiders and others secret from the Apache men. Even he did not know what Jovanna's mentor would teach her during their time of seclusion, only that it involved the mysteries of womanhood.

"She will dance through an entire night and greet the rising sun, still dancing."

Cassidy frowned. "Isn't that too much to ask of a little girl?"

"No. It's a test of strength and she won't be alone. Others will dance with her. Her mentor, grandmother and sisters. Then she'll sleep a little and there will be feasting. Finally the Crown Dancers will dance when she becomes Changing Woman."

Her voice turned wistful. "I'd like to see Amanda dance."

He didn't correct her or call his sister by her given name, but he thought that Cassidy should be there. That Gabe was right to want to include this woman in Jovanna's inner circle. Did it make them less her family to have Cassidy as her mother?

He wondered what his own mother would advise him? He knew that she would want what was best for Jovanna. But what was that?

# Chapter Fifteen

Luke called that afternoon to announce a major break. Cassidy was reviewing the transcripts from Manny Escalanti with Chief Cosen when Luke reported that he had caught Ronald Hare at the food drop he'd been scouting in Salt River. They now had in custody a man who could testify against several of the big players on both reservations and confirm exactly which cartel they were dealing with. That was *if* he was willing to play ball. If not, he was going to prison.

Cassidy knew that it would be up to the Salt River tribal council whether to try Hare in tribal court or turn him over to federal jurisdiction. Now the transcripts she was accumulating on Manny Escalanti took on new urgency. Luke had made certain that Hare's arrest was public because he wanted to see the rats scatter.

Late in the afternoon, she collected a large box from the hotel. Amanda's clothes. She breathed a sigh of relief.

Now she had an excuse to stop by the Cosens' again. She glanced at her watch. Amanda would be home from school by now. Cassidy was dying to hear about her first day.

Perhaps she could stay the night again. A perfect image of Clyne naked except for that white towel burst across her mind like the finale of a fireworks display. He was that breathtaking.

Eventually she would have to move back to the hotel.

Six months without Amanda. How would she do it? Of course she had to eventually move back to Phoenix and she wasn't about to move to DC or New York with Amanda being a captive of the Apache tribe.

Bear born of Eagle, he had said. What did that even mean? Clans, she supposed.

Clyne stopped by to speak with Gabe but as he entered his brother's office, his gaze moved immediately to her. She stood as he paused, noticing every last detail about him. His hair was in one braid today, wrapped in maroon cloth overlaid with a crisscrossing series of leather cords. She could barely manage a clip in her hair and he'd managed that.

He lifted his gaze and it locked with hers. Her stomach twitched and her skin turned to gooseflesh in excitement. Who was she kidding? She wasn't stopping this man from walking across the hall and over her threshold. Not for long. It was just a matter of time. He knew it and she knew it.

This was bad.

She dragged her gaze away and met Gabe's speculative eyes. His gaze flicked to Clyne and then back to her. She could see the suspicion solidifying to certainty. He lifted his brows and her ears went hot.

Clyne finally noticed his brother's scrutiny. The corners of his mouth drooped.

"What?" Clyne said.

"Nothing," said Gabe. Then he lifted his finger and aimed it at his older brother. "But I don't want to hear one more word about Selena's father and how marrying her will ruin my reputation."

"I don't know what you're talking about," said Clyne. But his color rose with the denial.

"No? Maybe I don't need to sleep on my office couch tonight. Maybe my bedroom is free."

Cassidy looked to Clyne to see how he wanted to play this.

"It's not free," he said.

"But it might be?"

Clyne didn't deny it.

"Oh, great!" said Gabe. "Just great." He pointed at Cassidy and kept his eyes locked with Clyne's. "This is the kind of thing I'd expect from Kino or Clay. But you? I don't believe it. She's a federal agent. She's white. She's fighting us for custody."

Clyne rounded on his brother. "You're the one who said to bring her here. Include her in our family."

"I didn't mean you should sleep with her!"

"I haven't," he said.

"Yet," said Gabe.

Heads in the squad room snapped up. She wished she could sink through the floor, and Clyne seemed to have turned to stone. His eyes shifted to Gabe and just his hand moved as he closed the door to his office.

"What do you think you're doing?" Clyne asked.

"What, you think it will stay a secret? Your assistant already told Yepa that you took her to lunch."

Cassidy had met Yepa, Gabe's personal assistant.

"You were seen with her at the casino hotel, leaving her room. Plus Yepa's brother drives the school bus and saw her car in the drive a little too early this morning."

"Jovanna didn't take the bus," said Cassidy.

Gabe shook his head as she missed the point. Black Mountain was a small community and they had already made the list of interesting doings here.

What was that buzzing sound?

Cassidy's phone vibrated across Gabe's desk. Conversation stopped. The phone buzzed again. She lunged and scooped up the device.

Phone in hand, Cassidy checked the ID and saw it was her boss.

"Agent Walker, here."

Tully skipped the pleasantries and got right to business.

"We pulled a partial from the rifle casing on the roof in Tucson and got a match."

Cassidy stuck a finger in her opposite ear to better hear the results. This caused both brothers to shift their attention to her. Clyne and Gabe moved in.

"Who?" she asked.

"Johnny Parker."

"Parker?" She raked her nails through the hair at her temple as the pieces still did not fit. "Should I know that name?"

"He's the brother of Brett Parker. Your case. Kidnapping."

Brett Parker. *That* name she knew immediately. Johnny was the kidnapper's brother. She turned to Clyne to see his brow furrowed.

"Why would Johnny Parker want to kill Clyne Cosen?"

"He wouldn't. Cassidy, we don't think Cosen is the target. He's after you."

Cassidy clutched the phone as she reeled from this new information.

"Me?" she asked.

Clyne moved beside her. Gabe returned to his desk, his attention fixed on her. Cassidy pressed the phone to her ear.

"Not Cosen?" She shook her head at Clyne.

"We think Johnny Parker picked you up at the Tucson rally. He might have guessed that there would be a strong FBI presence and got lucky. After all, you were right up there on stage."

"How would he know me?"

"We aren't sure. He could have been in court any of the times you testified. Our guys are looking at court surveillance video now."

"The truck. In the garage in Phoenix. Forrest said—"

"I know. He told me. But someone picked up that truck in Black Mountain. He knows you are up there. We need you to get to the safe house. Hare is in custody and Forrest is en route to you. He will meet you there. We're sending our people to you."

"All right." A burst of terror bolted through her. "Wait! My daughter!"

Her eyes locked to Gabe. He picked up his desk phone and started pushing buttons.

"He couldn't have her location," said Tully. "It's not possible."

Cassidy pressed a hand to her forehead. "It *is* possible. I didn't go to the hospital after the shooting. I went home to my daughter."

"What?" Her boss's voice was a roar.

Gabe dropped the handset back to the cradle and headed out the door, scooping up his gray Stetson as he passed the coat rack. Cassidy followed him out with Clyne on her heels.

"And last night. I was at the Cosens'. He could have followed me. He could know where she is."

"Hold on."

She didn't listen and instead broke into a run. She

could hear Tully shouting orders to his staff. Then he came back on.

"We're bringing her in."

"She's not at home."

"Where is she?"

"Here on Black Mountain Reservation. Cosen residence. They won temporary custody." She followed Gabe out the squad room, passing him as she ran down the hall. Clyne reached the door first and shouted that his car was closer.

Donald Tully spoke again. "I'll call their police chief."

"He's already on his way to her. I'm en route," she said.

"Cassidy. No. Get to the safe house, now."

"En route," she said.

"You're the target! You might draw him right to her."

Cassidy froze, phone pressed to her ear and stared at Clyne, who with his longer legs had beat her to the car and stood with the door open.

"Go to the safe house," ordered Tully. "We're coming to you."

"No! My daughter. I have someone for protection."

"Who?"

She looked at Clyne, who nodded his consent.

"A US marine sharpshooter."

"Are you talking about Clyne Cosen? He's not protection. He's a civilian. Cassidy, I need you—"

She hung up.

"Get in," said Clyne.

Cassidy shook her head. "You have to get to her. Amanda. Jovanna, I mean. There is someone after me, but they could have followed me to her."

He closed the door. "What about you?"

"I'll go right back into the station."

Clyne swept the parking lot and street with his gaze and then pinned it back on her.

"All right."

Cassidy did something she had never done. Something she knew was against every rule in the book. She removed her personal weapon and offered it to Clyne butt-first. He looked at it as if she had offered him a live rattlesnake. He gave a rapid head shake as he backed away. Then he turned and retreated to his SUV. She watched him pull away and then slipped her weapon back into its holster. She withdrew her cell phone and dialed her daughter.

"Hi, Mom." Her daughter's voice rang like a musical instrument. "What's up?"

"Where are you?"

"At Grandma's house." Her voice was more hesitant now as she picked up the note of panic in her mother's voice.

"Inside?"

"Yes. Mom, what's going on? Is it the Child Protection people again?"

"Put Grandma on."

There was a pause and she heard Jovanna speaking. Then Glendora came on.

"Hello?"

"Glendora. It's Cassidy. Gabe and Clyne are on their way. There is a current active threat against Jovanna. Get to a back bedroom and lock the door. Get on the floor, away from windows. Do you understand?"

"Yes."

"Go."

She heard Glendora speaking to Jovanna. And, bless

her heart, her voice was calm and even as she gave instructions. A few moments later Glendora spoke.

"We're locked in. Gabe is calling on my phone," said Glendora. "Here."

There was a brief pause and Jovanna came on again.

"Mom, what's happening?"

"Just wait there. Your brothers are on their way to you. They'll explain."

"I hear sirens," said Jovanna.

Cassidy closed her eyes and breathed a sigh of relief and when she opened her eyes she realized she was standing in the open on the sidewalk before the parking area. Her gaze flicked about, taking in the numerous places where a shooter could hide. Her hand went to her vest and she recalled she had left it in her hotel room last night in her rush to get to her daughter.

Cassidy now stood, unprotected and vulnerable to a shooter. She lowered the phone and ran toward tribal police headquarters.

# Chapter Sixteen

There was no one in the yard and the eerie emptiness of the house gave Clyne a chill. He and Gabe pulled in right behind Kino and Clay. Gabe reached the steps and flew into the house, gun raised, shouting for their grandmother. He cleared the entrance as he heard the reply.

"We're here. In my bedroom."

Gabe had reached their grandmother's door and held his gun pointed at the ceiling.

"You both all right?"

Clyne stood shoulder to shoulder with Gabe as Glendora replied. From beneath the door came a familiar huffing sound that Clyne recognized as Buster sniffing them from beneath the door.

"Yes. We're all fine."

"Jovanna?" called Clyne.

"I'm here, too!" she piped, her voice sweet music to his ears. "And Buster."

"You want me to unlock the door?" asked Glendora.

"No," said Gabe. "Stay on the floor. I have to check the area."

He was on his radio now. Kino and Clay remained outside and Gabe ordered them to scout the exterior for any sign of intruders. Clyne knew that there were no better men for the job. Kino and Clay had been excellent trackers before they went down on the border as Shadow Wolves. Now they were the best on the reservation.

Gabe looked to Clyne. "Will you take my shotgun?" he asked.

Clyne felt that cold sweat at just the thought of holding a weapon.

"Never mind. Just stay here until I get back." Gabe darted down the hall.

He watched his brother go and thought of what might have happened. The horrors of the past mingled with the potential threat against his sister. They'd only just got her back. He couldn't lose her again. Yet he wasn't strong enough to pick up a gun to defend her. His mind gave all the rational reasons to go down the hall to Gabe's gun closet, the one in his bedroom. He even made it to the locked cabinet. But he couldn't open that lock. Oh, he knew where Gabe kept a second key. That wasn't the trouble. The trouble was one particular gun. He thought he might be able to hold a shotgun. But he knew what else was in there because he'd placed it in Gabe's care when he came home. His long-range rifle, the one with thirty-six confirmed kills. Three dozen lives. Most of the ghosts stayed away. But some haunted him. Especially the boy who died with a claymore in his hand, the detonation coming just after Clyne squeezed the trigger and before the youngster could throw the bomb at the US forces. Clyne knew he had to take the shot. But the age of the boy made it wrong in his heart.

Maybe Cassidy was right. He needed to talk to someone.

"Clyne?" called Glendora.

He retreated to his grandmother, his palms slick with sweat. "Cassidy wants a report."

His mouth twitched. "Tell her we are checking the perimeter."

"Okay."

In a few minutes Clay appeared. "Nothing. No tracks and no sign of an intruder. Gabe wants Kino and me to get Jovanna to the safe house."

"Cassidy?" asked Clyne.

"Gabe wants you to bring her." Clay knocked on the door and then spoke in Apache. "Grandma. Open the door."

The lock clicked and Glendora peered out at them. She ushered her granddaughter out. Buster pushed past him, hugging Jovanna's leg as she moved into the hall. Clay took charge of his sister, guiding her down the hall with Clyne covering their back.

Gabe waited on the front step and Kino held open the door to his police car. Clay scooped Jovanna up as if she were still that two-year-old girl they had lost and ran her to Kino's police cruiser, ducking into the backseat with her. Buster jumped inside before Clyne had the door shut.

"Grandma, you're in the front with Kino," said Gabe to Glendora.

"Let me get my coat."

Gabe waited and then guided his grandmother across the muddy yard to his brother's unit. He saw Glendora seated in the front.

"Luke is en route from Salt River," said Kino to Gabe.

"Good. Take off," ordered Gabe and closed the door.

Clyne watched Kino pull out, lights flashing but without his siren.

Gabe looked to Clyne. "Cassidy?"

Clyne nodded. "I got her." Gabe swept behind the wheel and Clyne climbed into his SUV. A moment later they were off.

CASSIDY WALKED WITH Clyne up the steps of the safe house. She knew the drab exterior was an illusion. This place had a safe room, supplies and enough communication equipment to make the Apple Store jealous.

It also had weapons. Lots and lots of them.

She entered the code and waited for the door to click. Her daughter called to her and leaped off her seat in the dining room. But Gabe got a hold of her arm, keeping her from charging into the open until Cassidy got Clyne inside and the door shut and bolted.

Buster greeted them first, and then Gabe let Jovanna go. Cassidy met her daughter halfway across the room with a hug so tight she didn't think anything or anyone could break it. Gradually she eased away.

"Are you all right?" she asked.

Jovanna nodded and motioned to her brothers. "They all protected me."

Cassidy tried for a smile as she looked from Glendora to Gabe, to Kino, to Clay and finally to Clyne. But her lip trembled, and she and her words quavered.

"Well, that's what families do," she managed.

Buster nudged between them and used his head to encourage Jovanna to pet him.

"Oh, and Buster, too. Of course," said Jovanna and laughed.

Jovanna and Buster lead her through the dining room. "They have a machine here that makes hot cocoa! Do you want one?"

"Maybe just coffee."

The group moved to the kitchen, where a large couch

flanked the counter set with four stools. Kino and Clay took the stools, and Glendora and Clyne sank into the couch. Gabe remained on guard by the metal door that led to the garage, where two vehicles waited, gassed and ready to go.

With Buster beside her like a guard dog, Jovanna showed her mom to the marvelous machine that dispensed coffee and hot cocoa. "Were you scared?" asked Cassidy.

"Only a little. When we were on the floor. But Grandma told me stories about Changing Woman. Did you know she had two sons?" She held up two fingers and ticked them off. "Child of Water and Monster Slayer." She glanced to Glendora, who nodded at this correct reciting. "He's also Killer of Enemies and he made the world safe for us. I wonder what monsters he killed."

The only monster Cassidy cared about right now was Johnny Parker.

"Then Changing Woman got lonely and made the Apache people out of her own flesh." Jovanna gave a little wiggle as if this thought was repellant and Cassidy smiled, thinking that all children are made of their mother's flesh.

"During the Sunrise Ceremony, I'll be Changing Woman and my dance will be a blessing. But first I have to learn a lot of things and start my real education."

Cassidy lifted a brow at Glendora. Jovanna's grandmother certainly had been a busy bee.

The coffeemaker whirred and spit black liquid. Cassidy passed the first cup to Gabe with her thanks and then took orders from the rest of the Cosens. When she finished, she sat at the counter with her daughter, facing Kino and Clay.

"Grandma showed me the buckskin dress," said Jovanna. "It's the most beautiful thing I've ever seen!"

Cassidy smiled at the excitement in her daughter's animated gestures as she described the wonderful garment.

"I'm jealous," said Clay. "Boys don't get to wear something like that. But we'll all dance at your ceremony."

"You will?" She looked from one brother to the next. "All of you?"

"All," said Clyne.

"We'll be dressed as the Ga'an," said Kino, "the four spirits of the mountain."

"But there are five dancers," said Jovanna. "I read about it and watched it online. The crowns are huge! One will wear a white hood. Who will be the fifth?"

They all turned to Clyne for the answer.

"I was going to ask your uncle Luke."

Jovanna smiled and clapped her hands. "Yes!"

Buster settled beneath Jovanna's stool with a slight groan before resting his head on his white-tipped paws. She wondered vaguely what kind of sheepdog he was and decided it didn't matter. He was a good one.

"And your brothers will also beat the drum while you sing."

"Only one drum?" asked Jovanna.

"Only one. But it's a big one," said Glendora. "My grandsons are really good drummers and they have wonderful voices. You'll hear them all singing just for you."

And Kino and Clay's wives and Gabe's girl will all dance with you through the night. Keep you company and encourage you when you get tired."

"My mentors?"

Now how did her daughter know about that, wondered Cassidy and her gaze flicked to Glendora.

"You will have only one mentor."

"Who?" asked Jovanna.

"Well, she can't be a relative and she must be strong and wise and an Apache, of course," said Glendora.

Cassidy realized all her grandsons were looking to her.

"I would like to ask Selena Dosela."

Clyne's jaw dropped and then snapped shut. Gabe grinned and stood a little taller. A controversial choice, thought Cassidy, recognizing that Clyne was less than pleased. Selena was Gabe's fiancé, but she had also been the driver of the chemicals needed to supply the meth lab in January. Working with Department of Justice, but only because the cartels had threatened her family. Cassidy considered what she would be willing to do to protect Jovanna.

"I like Selena," said Cassidy. "She's nice."

Clyne thought he might need to discuss this choice with his grandmother, but not here or now.

"Three of my boys have found good women."

He met his grandmother's gaze. He knew the look. He had no woman to bring to the ceremony.

Thirty-two was hardly over-the-hill. He had time still. Time to rise to council chairman and time to choose a wife who would help him lead the tribe with honor and dignity. Rita was a good choice, or Paulina. They were both professional women, accomplished, modest. Karen was the most knowledgeable about their cultural history. They were all suitable and all had made their interest known. So why hadn't he chosen?

His attention strayed to Cassidy. Their gazes locked and he felt the tingle of awareness that made him itch to bring her into his arms. He broke the contact and stared at his coffee and then to his brothers. Clay was watching him with a curious expression.

Glendora was speaking about Clay's wife, Izzie.

"I knew she was the girl for him. Why it took him so long to realize it, I'll never know." She pushed Clyne and he had a time keeping the coffee from sloshing out of the mug onto the arm of the couch. "This one has yet to choose because he's working all the time."

Jovanna giggled at her older brother.

"The oldest. He should set an example and marry a nice Apache girl."

"I will, Grandma," he said, but his gaze fixed on Cassidy. Her expression was a frozen mask, her smile tight as the grip on her coffee.

"You work too hard. That's why you don't have a girl. You need to dance more and sing more and play the drum like you used to."

It couldn't be Cassidy. He would not allow it to be her.

"I still play the drum and sing."

"At ceremonies. What about your flute? You used to play all the time."

What had happened to his flute? He didn't even know. In a box somewhere with the things his mother had packed when she moved his belongings from their father's house while he'd been deployed in Iraq. Despite the hot coffee in his hand, Clyne felt cold.

His grandmother noticed something immediately. Her face now held the etched lines of concern. "What's wrong?"

"Nothing."

Glendora gave him a long look and then she began talking to Jovanna about the beading of the moccasins she would make and how her sisters would come up from Salt River to help with the cooking.

"There will be hundreds of guests. On Thursday we will all dance and sing, and I'll feed everyone with the help of my sisters and Kino, Clay and Gabe's girls. The men will prepare the sacred objects. You will meet with the medicine man and your mentor for instruction. Friday you will have to run around the gifts that people bring you and you'll give them gifts, too. Then you and Selena will prepare for your longest dance. All Friday night and, if you are strong, you will still be dancing when the sun rises."

"All night?" asked Jovanna, a note of concern in her voice.

"Um-hm. And then you will rest and later Selena will massage your back and legs, molding you into a new woman."

Jovanna's eyes were wide. Cassidy listened with a mixture of awe and worry.

"There will be a blessing and then you will dance in the dress I showed you."

"Changing Woman," said Jovanna and smiled.

"People will come from everywhere to see you dance and receive your blessing."

Clyne watched Cassidy as she stroked her daughter's hair and sipped her coffee. As she began to relax, so did he. She glanced at him and cast him a smile. He sent it back and saw her cheeks flush. That made his smile broaden. Was she thinking of last night and the kisses they had shared? He lifted his mug, but kept his eyes on her as the memories warmed him.

Gradually he noticed that his grandmother had ceased talking. His eyes rounded and he turned to glance at her to find her gaping at him.

Now he flushed.

"What?" he asked.

Glendora's gaze flipped to Cassidy and then back to him. She lifted a brow in silent inquiry and looked to Gabe, who nodded. His grandmother frowned. So much for keeping their situation secret. Gabe already knew and now his grandmother suspected.

Clyne sank back to the sofa, wondering what to do. He wanted her now more than ever. But pursuing her would mean going public. He wondered what kind of a hit he would take in the elections. He knew enough to know that as an Apache politician, a white, FBI agent wife would not increase his popularity. He looked at her and wondered if she might be worth it. Then she glanced at Jovanna, who was speaking to Clay about the family's cattle holdings in the tribe's communal herd.

"You better make up your mind quick," said his grandmother in a low whisper. "That girl is a mother and you don't mess around with a single mother unless you intend to marry her."

"She might not be a mother for long," said Clyne.

"She will always be that child's mother. No court in the world will change that. All you'll do is force them apart and make her choose her mother over us. But…"

Clyne looked at his grandmother but she had stopped speaking.

"What?"

"If you marry her, then Jovanna can stay with her mother."

"She's not staying on the reservation, Grandmother. Cassidy wants a transfer to Washington."

"She *wants* to stay with her daughter. And from the look she just gave you, she wants you, too. Maybe she just can't see how that would work out."

"Neither can I," he said.

In response his grandmother patted his knee and smiled.

Cassidy's phone rang, making them all jump. She glanced at the number and then took the call.

"Walker here, sir."

Her boss, Tully, Clyne knew.

"Yes?"

Clyne watched her use that index finger to plug her opposite ear as she pressed the phone to her opposite cheek. Her eyes moved restlessly as she listened. He knew the instant that it was over because she exhaled a long audible breath and her shoulders dropped a good two inches. A moment later her eyes closed for just a few seconds. When they opened they found him and she smiled.

"Yes, sir. I'll meet Agent Forrest there. Thank you."

Cassidy punched at the screen and slipped the phone away. Then she hugged her daughter.

"All clear," she said.

"What happened?" asked Gabe.

"They got him."

"Who?" asked Jovanna.

Clyne waited to see what Cassidy would do. This was the point adults sent children to their rooms or spoke in vague generalities.

"The bad man who was after me."

"You? Why?"

"His brother was a kidnapper. I caught him and... well, he died."

Jovanna cut straight to the point. "You shot him?"

Cassidy nodded, then glanced at Clyne. "I did. I had to. He was hurting someone and I had to make him stop."

"Is that person okay now?"

Her smile was sad. "No, darling. I was too late. His brother is really mad at me for hurting his brother, so he…" Here Cassidy did go vague. "He tried to hurt me. My offices figured out who it was from the fingerprints on, well…"

"A gun?"

"Something like that."

"Bullet casings," said Gabe in Apache.

Clyne nodded.

"So they chased him and arrested him and he's going to jail now."

"And you'll have to testify again?" asked her daughter.

"Yes. Likely."

"So can we go home now?" asked Jovanna.

Cassidy looked around the room at the Cosen family.

"Well, you are going home with your brothers."

"You, too?" asked Jovanna.

Cassidy's mouth went grim and Jovanna clung to her mom. Clyne glanced at his grandmother, whose brow lifted pointedly.

"You can stay in our house as long as you like," he said to Cassidy. His brothers added their consent with the simple nod of their heads.

"No," said Cassidy. "Jovanna, you remember what I told you. Six months. That's the court's order."

"But what if I get scared again?"

"Call your grandmother or any of your brothers. I trust them, doodlebug. You can, too."

Jovanna clung to her mother, who kissed the top of her head.

"You have to be strong, Jovanna. A strong Apache woman like Changing Woman."

Her daughter sniffed but then pushed herself upright and let go of her mother. That nearly broke Cassidy's heart. Her willingness to be brave and not cling like a child. She looked at Jovanna and thought she saw a glimpse of the woman she would become.

She turned to Clyne and asked him to drive her back to the station. Then she walked out the door.

Buster roused to his feet and gave a long, soulful whine of discontent.

Cassidy felt exactly the same way.

# Chapter Seventeen

Cassidy buried herself in work. The interrogation of Ronnie Hare took her to Salt River for all the next day. Jovanna had not called. Clyne had not come to the hotel to fetch her. Her daughter was safe and fast becoming part of her family again. And that was as it should be.

Cassidy was no longer afraid that Jovanna would not choose her. She was now afraid that her daughter *would* choose her and by doing so, lose the family of her birth. She could see now that separating them twice was cruel and wrong. But how could she keep them together and become a part of this family?

On Saturday, Cassidy succeeded in getting her boss to agree to pay for the overtime to add additional security on Ronnie Hare. The Salt River jail was really only three holding cells in the Salt River police station. She remained at the station filling out paperwork to petition to move him to federal custody, while Luke took on the more difficult task of convincing individual members of the tribal council to vote to turn Hare over to them. They needed the consent of the Salt River tribal council to do so. Luke had spoken to the tribal chairman and, even after hearing of the charges, Luke said that he was still reluctant to relinquish custody of any of his people. If they did not, Hare would be tried here and the sentence would be very short. Luke did manage to get their chairman to at least agree to raise the matter with his fellows at the next meeting.

As for Hare himself, he was remaining tight-lipped until he knew if he would face tribal or federal court. All they could do now was wait.

"He'll spill if we have a federal case," said Luke. "He won't want to be in the same prison as Raggar."

That was the head of the American distribution ring and Cassidy agreed that turning state's witness was far better than facing Raggar's men in prison.

"We'd have no way to guarantee his safety there," she said.

"But if he plays ball we can move him to any prison, even process him under a different identity."

"He'll try for witness protection," she said.

"Not going to happen," said Luke. "We got him. I'm going to squeeze him like toothpaste until I have every last name of every last man who is involved with smuggling on the rez."

His home, she realized. His ancestral home. Cassidy filled with a deep longing for something she could only vaguely grasp. A place she belonged.

Why had she never noticed the need to be a part of a place and a community? Who was she fighting for? Americans?

Not really. She had never fought for anyone until yesterday. Yesterday she had fought for her daughter and it felt right. All this time she had been fighting against something—bad guys who broke federal law and the organization that killed Gerard. She'd never bring them all to justice. Never stop them. But the fight itself was the thing? Wasn't it?

She let the weariness weigh her down as she recognized the impossibility of the task she had set for herself. She'd never do it. Even if she made the most important case in FBI history. It wouldn't bring Gerard back.

"You all right?" asked Luke.

"Yeah. I was just thinking."

"About?"

"If I really need to go to DC to make a difference."

Luke's jaw dropped and gradually a smile replaced the stunned expression. "That's the smartest thing you've said in weeks. You staying?"

"Maybe. For a while at least."

CLYNE TOOK KAREN Little Hill out on Saturday night. He usually took one of three women out, keeping it obvious to all that he was unattached. But this was two nights in a row.

Karen adjusted her shawl against the chilly air. The temperatures always dipped with the sunset, but March was susceptible to wild temperature swings.

His date had worn pants as a matter of practicality. Her necklace was Navajo and the many bangle bracelets represented most of the silversmiths in the area. She collected them the way some women collected glass figurines. Her shop at the Apache Cultural Museum showed off her knowledge of Native American Indian jewelry and pottery.

Clyne had been trying to summon up the courage to have a serious talk with Karen. Trying to gather the conviction to look her in the eyes and ask her to marry him. She'd say yes. He was certain. At least she had made her desires known to him last Christmas when he had given her a silver bangle instead of an engagement ring.

He walked her back from the restaurant to his truck,

still toying with the idea of asking for her hand. He didn't have a ring, of course, except the one that had belonged to his mother and he felt loathed to give Karen that. He just felt filled with the desire to get this over with and behind him.

She beat him to her door and managed the handle without his help. Karen didn't need him. And he didn't need her. But he needed children. Ached for them.

Not just to help his tribe survive, but to fill the empty places in his heart.

"I saw a therapist yesterday," he said, once seated beside her in the dark cab.

"Why?"

"To talk about things. Things that happened while I was in the service."

"Do you think it's wise to dig up all that ancient history?"

Cassidy had encouraged him to do so, felt it was essential, in fact.

"Well, he's a medicine man and he served in Vietnam, so he knows about such things."

"I would not raise old ghosts," she said and shivered.

"Did you notice that I haven't been able to hunt since I came back home?" he asked.

"No. But it doesn't matter. We have enough guides and hunters. We need leaders. Strong role models. Which is why I was surprised to hear from Yepa that you had taken that white FBI agent to lunch."

"Gabe asked me to take her."

"You should have said no. You are the one who told me that she didn't belong here. That the federal authorities trample our rights."

"I did say that." He thought of Cassidy fighting to reach her daughter and trying to catch the man who had run messages to the cartel from the reservation. Gabe wanted that man caught and punished.

"It's bad for the people to see you with an FBI woman. It sends the wrong message."

"She raised my sister."

"I know who she is. But *you* won custody. How is Glendora managing?"

"She's fine." Clyne turned over the engine.

"She's a little old to raise a teenager."

Clyne did not dignify that with an answer.

"Your sister will need a mentor. Someone to teach her before the ceremony and mold her into the kind of woman who will make her family proud and serve her people with dignity."

"My grandmother is asking Selena Dosela."

"Selena? She's a criminal and her father was in federal prison. I wouldn't let her anywhere near Jovanna."

"My grandmother thinks she is the right choice."

"She's wrong. It sends a bad message to the people."

Clyne set them in motion. He was not asking Karen Little Hill to be his wife. She was the perfect choice and the only emotion she raised in him was annoyance.

He knew what he felt for Cassidy was real and dangerous. But to pursue Cassidy would threaten everything he believed he was. How could he preserve their culture and their way of life if he chose a woman who knew nothing of them?

Others had married outside the community, of course. But not a tribal council member. Not one single tribal leader had married anyone other than an Apache. Clay's wife, Izzie, was Apache. Gabe's fiancé, Selena, was Apache and Kino's wife, Lea, was Apache, though she had only one clan because her mother was Mexican. But her dad was Salt River Apache.

Clyne dropped Karen at her door and gave her a kiss that left much to be desired. He couldn't help but compare the cold perfunctory touching of lips to the scorching desire stirred by just a glance in Cassidy Walker's direction. Each kiss vibrated through him like a drumbeat, building in power.

A warrior woman. A fighter.

He drew back and Karen smiled up at him. Did she feel something that he did not?

"Would you like to come in?" she asked, stroking her hand down the lapel of his overcoat.

"Ah, Karen?"

"Yes?" Her eyes were dark and bright, her mouth curled in a coy smile.

"I can't see you again."

The smile fell and her mouth dropped open.

"What are you talking about?"

"I'm seeing someone else."

Her eyes narrowed suspiciously and her words came like the hiss of a snake.

"It's that white woman. Isn't it?"

He drew a breath and then admitted it, saying it aloud.

"Yes."

"Are you crazy? She'll ruin you."

"I used to think so."

"Clyne. I know you. You're one of the most respected men in Black Mountain. And you are smarter than this."

"Goodbye, Karen. I'm sorry."

Her eyes glittered dangerously. "You will be."

Clyne left her on the stoop to her home and returned to his SUV.

Karen was going to make trouble. He knew it and he didn't care. If he was going to court Cassidy, he'd have to face this sooner or later. Many would be disappointed. But he hoped a few would see that a good woman could be Anglo as well as Apache.

He kept telling himself this as he drove to the casino hotel where Cassidy was staying. They had been strong adversaries and she was a brave woman but was she brave enough for this?

## Chapter Eighteen

Clyne knocked on her hotel door and waited. He could feel her on the opposite side of the door staring at him through the peephole.

The bolt clacked, the lock turned and the door flew open.

"Jovanna?" said Cassidy.

"Fine."

She cocked her head. He saw that she was still dressed in her pants and shirt. But she wore no shoes or socks and her blazer and holster were absent. She had released her hair from the short, stiff little ponytail she usually wore so her hair fell like silk beside her face.

"What's wrong, then?"

"I needed to see you."

Cassidy still gripped the door and her opposite hand held the pistol. She motioned him in with a gesture of her head. He found her room had one king-size bed, a chair and a desk with a second chair. The only illumination came from the desk lamp and her glowing laptop that was up and open, with two files beside it on the glass surface. Near the window, her belongings were neatly folded in an open suitcase on a stand and her laptop.

"Going over some things," she said. "Can I get you something? I have pop in the mini-fridge."

"Nothing."

Cassidy sat on the bed. Clyne took the desk chair. She waited for him to speak.

"I just broke up with a woman I have been seeing."

Cassidy's pale brow lifted. Was she wondering what this had to do with her?

"I'm sorry."

"Don't be." He waved away the concern. "I told her I was seeing someone else."

Cassidy's head tilted as she thought about this.

"Are you?"

He gave his head a shake.

Cassidy's mouth dropped open as she put it together.

"Clyne... I don't think... This isn't a good idea."

"That's what Gabe said."

"This could affect my custody."

"How? She's ours for six months and then she makes a choice. Us or you. If you stay here, maybe she won't have to choose."

"Stay?" She gave her head a little shake. "So you're doing this for your sister?"

"No. For me." Clyne's head sank. He was trying every way he could think of to rationalize doing the irrational. And she was fighting him, still.

Cassidy was on her feet. "I think you should go."

"Probably." He didn't get up.

"I'm white," she said.

"No one's perfect."

She chuckled at that. Clyne stood and her eyes swept over him like a caress.

"Maybe this is just, you know, an infatuation."

He didn't think so. "Maybe."

"It's just because, well, you were over there. So was I. We understand what it was like."

"Yes. That's true. But it's more."

"I don't want this to hurt Jovanna. I don't want you thinking that sleeping with me will fix all that. I'm still her mother and I plan to win full custody."

"Even if you take her, she'll come back when she is grown. She has to."

"Why is that?"

"Because she will long to know where she comes from. Everyone needs to know that. Even if you take her for another nine years, she'll come back."

Cassidy grabbed the lapel of his topcoat and choked the fabric in her fist.

"She's my daughter."

He nodded. "Yes. She will always be that."

Her eyes filled with tears that spilled down her cheeks. He used his thumbs to brush them both aside and kept them there for a moment before threading his fingers in her fine pale hair.

He knew what he felt for Cassidy was strong and real. He also knew that marrying her would unite their families and give Jovanna her mother back. She wouldn't have to choose.

What he didn't know was if he was strong enough to face his tribe with a white woman at his side after speaking on many occasions about the need to preserve their cultural heritage.

He didn't know if he could convince Cassidy Walker to give up her transfer and stay here with them. But he wanted to try.

Clyne angled his head. Cassidy tugged at his topcoat, lifting to meet his kiss. The heat sizzled through him at the first brushing contact. He felt as if he were falling, spinning with her in his arms.

Cassidy's hands moved over his shirt, releasing buttons. He found the zipper at the side of her slacks and tugged. She let the garment fall to the ground and stepped from them. Then she sat on the edge of the bed and glanced to the empty place beside her.

He shrugged out of his topcoat and blazer and tossed them to the chair. His shirt went next. She kept her eyes on him as she released the top rivet securing his jeans. He strained against the denim fabric, showing his need in the most obvious way possible. A smile flicked over her ripe pink lips. He sat beside her and each turned to their own attire, him throwing off shoes and jeans and shirts while she slipped out of her button-up blouse. When only his boxers remained, he turned to find Cassidy standing in only a scrap of fuchsia lace panties and a lacy top with underwire lifting her small breasts so the plump flesh spilled from the shallow cup. He could see the soft pink of her nipples and the fine blue veins that crossed under the pale flesh of her breasts and belly. She was so beautiful it took away his breath.

He stood, offering his hand. She laced her fingers with his and he tugged her forward, bringing her body to his.

CASSIDY TRIED HARD not to remember the last time she had felt a man's touch. No, she pressed that down with her memories and her grief. Tonight was for the living, not the dead. And Clyne, no matter what his faults and how much they differed on every single issue, was alive and he wanted her. The attraction that roared between them created a need stronger than anything she'd ever experienced.

Tonight her need had caused her to call a truce. But it wouldn't last. What was he doing breaking up with his girl and coming here? She should have turned him around at the door, because she knew how this would end—badly.

Clyne wanted just what she wanted—to come alive, be desired, be consumed by the sweet taste and scent and feel of a perfect opposite.

But he wanted something else. He wanted her to stay and he wanted it enough to offer himself. Did he have feelings for her or was this some play to change her mind about leaving?

His strong hands lifted her until she settled on his body, a living bed of muscle and heat. Separated now by only his cotton briefs and her lacy panties, she felt the long length of him. He growled as she rocked, and lifted up to take the tip of one breast in his mouth. The dizzying sensation made her groan and arch to allow him free rein. He was not gentle. She was not submissive. No, Cassidy demanded what she wanted and took as she gave. And unfortunately for them both, their lovemaking was powerful and rare and thrilling.

Was it because it would not last?

She didn't know. But when they had finally come to rest, panting and slick with the sweat of their efforts, she closed her eyes and grieved again for this man who she feared she would never keep and for the union that marked the beginning and the end of all that could be between them.

Cassidy had a job to do here, a promotion to earn and, in six months, she was leaving Black Mountain with her daughter. Jovanna would not be coming back. She'd be certain of that.

She threw an arm over her closed eyes and purred. It was worth every bit of it, she decided.

"You okay?" he asked.

She didn't look at him. He was too handsome and seeing him in the light of one desk lamp might give her stupid ideas, like how to hold on to him.

"That was a mistake," she said.

"Are you sorry?" He rolled to his side, his fingers dancing over her stomach and making her twitch.

"Yes and no." She peered at him from under her arm. "You?"

He made a humming sound that was no answer. But his fingers continued to explore, moving from a gentle caress to purposeful stroking of her most sensitive places. Her body rose from lethargy so fast it startled her. Even with Gerard, she had never felt this kind of awareness. It wasn't fair, she thought.

"Slower, this time," he said.

She nodded. Cassidy supposed she could take some consolation in knowing that she was not the first woman and would doubtless not be the last to leave Clyne Cosen's bed wanting more.

Clyne's hand dipped lower and she moved to her back, letting him roam as he would. The man knew his way around the female form, she'd give him credit for that.

She made the mistake of looking up at him, perched on one elbow. His muscles corded at his bicep and his braid lay upon his pillow.

"Take your hair down," she said.

His brow dipped. "That some kind of white girl fantasy?" he asked, but there was still humor in his voice.

"Maybe. The men in my life were always military.

Short hair. No hair. This…" she lifted his braid "…seems like a pretty good handhold."

His brows lifted and he tugged away the leather band holding his hair. He swung his legs to the floor and finger combed the three strands into one. His hair was three times as long as hers. Then he looked back at her as she rolled to her knees behind him. She reached out and stroked his black hair, finding it thick and glossy.

"Well?" he asked.

"It's nice," she said, arranging his hair over his shoulders.

"Feel free to grab hold any time," he said.

She did, moving from his hair to his shoulders and then scoring her nails over his chest. He leaned back against her as her hands moved lower and lower.

Clyne reached back, captured one knee and dragged her before him until she straddled his hips. She rose up and then down. It wasn't slow this time either, but his hair did make a very good hold.

He gripped her tight, assuring her with his touch that he would not let her fall, which gave her the freedom to move. Her daring and the trust she showed captivated. When they fell back to the mattress together she tried to just savor the retreating pleasure. But her mind kept intruding, scrambling to think of some scenario where a tribal leader would choose a white military brat who worked for the organization he mistrusted most of all, the federal government. She had a very creative mind, but Cassidy Walker could not come up with one single plausible situation where he and she could make a go of it. He should know that, too.

She closed her eyes. Clyne tucked her close. Cassidy toyed with a strand of his hair, wondering if like Samson it was the secret to his virility and strength.

Silly, she thought and allowed sleep to carry her into dreams. She expected him to leave her, steal off in the night. He did leave the bed and she tried to pretend it didn't matter. It would be easier not to face him in the morning than have to deal with what they had done. But he came back. He pulled back the still-made bed and dragged the thick comforter over them both, then he slipped against her back and tugged her close, spooning against her as he dozed.

In the morning her phone alarm stirred her from sleep. She felt the weight of Clyne's arm across her chest and groaned.

What had they done?

She silenced the alarm and rolled away. He captured her wrist before she made a clean get away.

"Cassidy, we need to talk," he said.

"I've got to get dressed."

Clyne rolled to a seat. She tried and failed not to stare at all that bare skin and muscle. His hair, still loose, fell in a tangle down his back. And then she saw it, the small white puckered place just above his left hip. The bullet must have just missed the bottom of his vest. She wanted to touch it, that tiny scar that marred his perfect flesh. But she didn't.

Instead, she turned away, took exactly what she needed from her suitcase and fled to the bathroom. By the time she emerged, showered and completely dressed, he was still there.

"Clyne, let's not do this now."

"You don't think we need to talk about this?"

"Probably. But right now I've got work."

He gave her a long look and then nodded. "So we are both going to pretend this didn't happen?"

She hesitated, shifting her weight from side to side.

"Fine," he said. "See you around, Agent Walker."

"Hey. I didn't ask you to come here."

"And you didn't ask me to leave."

"Well, now I'm asking. That can't happen again."

He snorted. "But it will. You know it will."

With that he strode out the door.

CLYNE MADE IT home to find Gabe sitting in the dining room scrolling through an Apache social media platform used by the tribe.

"Thought you'd stayed at Karen's," he said, laying the tablet on the tabletop.

"I broke up with her."

Gabe absorbed that without comment but his brows lifted high on his forehead.

"She's mad as a wet cat," said Clyne.

"Worse than when you gave her the bracelet?"

"Way worse."

Gabe rubbed his neck.

"So where'd you spend the night?" asked Gabe.

Clyne thought from the way his brother looked at him that he already knew the answer.

"Paulina? Rita?" Gabe asked, his voice holding a note of hope.

Clyne let his head drop forward. "I don't want them either."

"No?"

He met Gabe's troubled gaze.

"I want Cassidy Walker."

Gabe rocketed to his feet. "I knew it."

Clyne sighed.

"You've only known her a week."

"I met her in January when you took that shipment from the cartel."

"And you hated her on sight."

Clyne shrugged. "She's a Fed."

"I never thought I'd be asking you this but do you know what you're doing?"

"I don't think so. Rita or Paulina would be a lot easier."

"Maybe we should have a sweat tomorrow after church. Talk about this."

"Maybe."

"This isn't just a way to keep her here for Jovanna. Is it?"

"Maybe. I don't know."

Gabe's expression showed both pity and disappointment. "You really are in trouble. Never seen you like this."

Clyne poured some coffee. "Anything on that guy who tried to shoot her?"

"In custody. Charged. They're checking his prints against the partial palm print they got from the truck."

He meant the one that almost ran her down.

"You sure you can't just work her out of your system?" asked Gabe.

"How'd that work for you with Selena?"

Gabe's shoulders rose and fell. "Yeah. I get it. Well, congratulations and condolences, I guess. You are going to take some heat."

"Hypocrite. Right? Expound the need to keep our traditions and preserve our culture, and then marry a white woman."

"Does Cassidy know how you feel?"

"Nope. She didn't want to talk about it."

"Oh, man."

"Will you go with her to Washington? She's going, you know? She made a deal with Tully."

This was news to Clyne. He'd never even considered that. Leaving his home. He had told himself that after his discharge he would never leave Black Mountain again.

"Luke told me. That was the only way they could get her to come to Black Mountain. She'd come here if she got her transfer afterward."

Clyne knew Cassidy wanted a transfer. He didn't know she'd already gotten it. He felt as if Gabe had punched him.

"But the case isn't over just because they have Hare," said Clyne. "It's just starting. And it's her case."

"She doesn't want the case. She wants out."

"She won't take a transfer. Not with the ruling. Her daughter is here. So she'll stay."

Gabe gave him a pitying look. "Yeah. For six months."

Clyne felt sick.

"What about the position with the National Congress of American Indians? If you took that you'd be in Washington much of the time."

The executive director of the NCAI had asked Clyne to run for the board as vice president. He'd served as an area president for the southwest, but that did not involve much travel. VP was a different matter.

"I'm not leaving Black Mountain."

"Well, she is," said Gabe.

# *Chapter Nineteen*

Tuesday morning Cassidy spent her second day of surveillance, watching the Wolf Posse's current place of business and kicking herself for being stupid enough to sleep with Clyne Cosen. What did he think that she'd give up her career and everything else to stay up here on this mountain? And now she was actually considering it. How stupid was that?

Glendora had allowed Jovanna to call her each day after school, but Cassidy needed something to do to keep her from going crazy or worse, calling Clyne. He said it would happen again and now she thought he was right because she could not get the man out of her head.

So here she sat on a little used road above the shabby wreck of a building used by Black Mountain's only gang. For a dead-end road, traffic in and out was brisk.

She got a call from Luke, who had been in touch with the crime lab.

"We got the report on the latents from the truck."

"The partial palm print?" she asked.

"Yeah. It's not a match for Parker."

Cassidy frowned as the implications of that rolled through her. "What do you think?"

"Not sure."

"No hits from the database?"

"None."

So the driver had no record.

"They're checking them against Donner. It's his truck so…"

"It would make sense for the prints to belong to the owner of the truck."

"Right."

Escalanti appeared before the Wolf Posse's headquarters. He did not usually leave until end of day.

"I have to go. Escalanti is moving."

"Okay." Luke disconnected.

Escalanti went to his car, removed something she could not see and returned to the house. Cassidy sighed and set aside her field glasses.

Her phone pinged, indicating a text from her daughter.

Cassidy responded to her daughter's texts throughout the afternoon and evenings but did not call, respecting the court's order in an attempt to allow her daughter to make the transition into the Cosen household. The school had her medical records. She already had a few friends. Her daughter's revelation that some of the kids called her an Anglo because she couldn't speak Apache troubled her. She did not want her daughter to enter middle school next year as an outsider. Perhaps the education Glendora insisted she begin would be valuable because it included lessons on the Apache language.

Cassidy lifted her smartphone to check Jovanna's after-school text.

taking 🐕 4 walk

Buster was in for a treat. She knew from Glendora that Jovanna took Buster on a long walk down the road and back and then played catch with him in the back-yard before homework.

Cassidy texted her back.

Have fun!

KK

The reply was almost instantaneous. *KK* or *Okay*.

Cassidy recorded a new license on her pad and watched the driver, snapping a few photos.

After forty minutes or so she glanced at her silent phone and frowned. Jovanna should be back now working on homework. She lifted her phone and typed.

How was the walk?

She waited and received no reply. She furrowed her brows. Cassidy knew the cell service on the rez was spotty. But the service inside the Cosen home was good.

She stared at the blank screen, trying to decide if she should call Glendora or if she was being overprotective. Her knowledge of what happened in the world did not make her the most relaxed of parents.

She lifted her phone and dialed Jovanna. The call went to voice mail. Cassidy followed her instincts and called the Cosen home number. She got no answer so she started her engine, heading back off Wolf Canyon Road toward the town of Black Mountain.

She pulled into the Cosens' drive at the same time as Clyne arrived.

"Well, this is a surprise," he said, crossing the gravel drive to meet her.

"Where's Jovanna?"

"I don't know. Why?"

"She didn't answer my text."

Clyne did not minimize her concerns. Instead he turned toward the house. "Let's go see."

They walked through the house and the to the back where they found Glendora on the step pinning laundry to the line, the old aluminum wheel squealing with each tug.

"Where's Jovanna?" asked Cassidy.

Glendora startled. "Why, isn't she inside?"

"No," said Clyne.

Cassidy's phone rang and she blew away her relief, but when she lifted the phone it was to find the number of her boss on the screen.

"Walker," she said, scanning the wide backyard that led up a hillside for any sign of Buster or Jovanna.

"Cassidy, you still in Wolf Canyon?"

"No. Black Mountain. My daughter's missing."

"What?" Tully swore.

"Send Luke from Salt River and send a team up here now."

"You got it."

Cassidy returned the phone to her jacket.

She followed Clyne as he charged through the house and back to their vehicles. She made for her sedan.

"Do you know where she walks?"

"Yes. By the stream. This way."

Cassidy made for Clyne's SUV. He could drive. She could search.

"Let's go."

She sat in the passenger seat with her gun drawn and the window open, scanning the shoulder ahead and then the yellow grass between the road and the tree line.

Clyne also had his window open and he whistled

occasionally. A high, loud commanding signal that reminded her of how a shepherd directs his dog. Then he called for Buster and then Jovanna.

She listened for a reply. Finally she heard something about a half mile from the house. It sounded like the wind but the day was flat calm.

"Stop," she cried. A moment later Cassidy saw the muddy matted fur on the animal that looked as if it had been hit by a passing vehicle. It lay in the ditch beside the road. "There." She pointed.

Clyne was out of the car at the same second as she was. Her feet hit the soft earth and sunk.

"Buster?" called Clyne.

His dog lifted his head and gave another pitiful whine. Clyne knelt beside the dog, his hand running over the matted fur.

"He's been stabbed."

Cassidy lifted her pistol to chin level and glanced to the empty road for her missing daughter. Clyne lifted Buster up and slid him into the backseat.

"Call Gabe," said Clyne.

She did, but only after she tried Jovanna's phone unsuccessfully again. Then she called her office to initiate an Amber Alert. Finally she called Luke and Clyne drove them back to the house.

Clay and his wife, Izzie, met them in the driveway. Izzie took charge of Buster, disappearing in Clay's truck.

Kino was first on the scene and searched the property as Clyne took Clay to check the spot where they found Buster. Luke arrived and failed to get Cassidy to the safe house.

"We are going to find Jovanna," she snarled, and she left him to confer with Glendora to get a description of what exactly Jovanna was wearing. Then she joined Kino as he circled the trailer beside the house. She did not know how to read any but the most obvious tracks. She was surprised to watch him stoop and study one print after another that looked very much like all the rest to her. She followed him into the trailer and then out again. She waited where he told her as he disappeared into the woods.

The headlights told her that someone was here and that it was getting dark. A chill gripped her. Where was her daughter?

Clay and Clyne returned as Luke arrived.

"What did you find?" asked Cassidy to Clyne.

"Buster tried to make it back to the house. He crawled a good fifty feet from where he was stabbed," said Clyne.

"Jovanna was taken by a man in an SUV or truck from the tracks. She fought him and Buster might have gotten a piece of him."

Luke broke in. "Where's the dog? There might be blood evidence on his teeth or in his mouth."

"I'll call Izzie. Ask the vet to check."

"I'm going," said Luke, rattling off the name of the vet and getting confirmation from Clay.

Kino returned, walking fast up the drive. "Someone was in that trailer."

The chill straightened Cassidy's spine and she clamped her elbows to her sides as she shook. Kino continued with his findings.

"Medium frame. Construction boots, old ones and he's pigeon-toed. He was there today. Maybe even watched Jovanna get off the bus from that window. Tracks head behind the trailer and back to the road where he got in a vehicle. We might have something by the window inside. Looks like a water bottle. I don't think it's ours."

Gabe arrived, lights flashing.

"I called everybody in. My guys and all the volunteer firefighters. They're all out looking for her."

Kino stepped aside to fill Gabe in while Cassidy called Tully with the description of Jovanna's clothing and she sent Jovanna's photo by text. Tully provided her with a GPS location on Jovanna's phone. She and Gabe set off to find it and they did, in the ditch only a mile farther up the road south, away from Black Mountain.

"Someone took her," she said.

Gabe used an evidence bag to scoop the ringing phone out of the mud and zipped it inside. Then he brought Cassidy back to the house.

Cassidy and Clyne joined the search that was now statewide. Every police officer and trooper now had Jovanna's description and if they didn't have a photo they soon would have. Plus every cell phone of anyone within a two-hundred-mile range would be receiving a special Amber Alert message. Finally, she knew all radio and television stations would broadcast the information. Even the electronic road signs would be called into service to issue the alert. And still it did not seem enough.

At 10 p.m. Clyne turned them back to the house where she spent a long night in a chair beside her silent charging cell phone. Her only consolation was that she did not wait and worry alone. She had Glendora and Clyne.

Izzie Cosen returned to report that Buster had a punctured lung and severe blood loss, but the vet was optimistic that he would survive.

"Gabe told me it was all right to tell you. There was

a scrap of fabric in Buster's mouth. Olive green. Trouser material, he thinks."

Buster had at least gotten a piece of the kidnapper. Cassidy wanted the same chance. At 5 a.m. Cassidy's phone rang. She picked up.

"I've got your daughter."

"I want to speak to her."

"No."

"Who are you?"

"Ain't you figured it out yet? I'm the one that nearly run you down."

"Why?"

"My brothers is why."

Brothers. Cassidy looked at Clay, Clyne, Gabe and Kino all watching her as she took the call. Brothers who would do anything for the other.

She'd killed Brett Parker and his brother Johnny Parker had shot her in that river park. Did Brett and Johnny have another brother?

"Which Parker are you?" she asked.

"Good for you, FBI lady. I'm the youngest. No record, so I'm not in your little databases."

He'd be there now, she thought.

"What do you want?"

"I'm glad you asked."

CLYNE LISTENED AS LUKE, Cassidy and Gabe went over Parker's demands once more and final arrangements were made.

They knew the kidnapper's identity now. He was Lamar Parker, twenty-four, unemployed and a member of various survivalist organizations that might give him access to some nasty weapons.

"All we know is it's off the rez," said Cassidy. "We

know what cell tower it's pinged off and it's closer to Tucson than Black Mountain."

"We can see from our satellites," said Luke. "Everything, right down to the license plate of his car to the registration on his windshield. He won't get away."

"That's not even on my list of worries," said Gabe.

Clyne felt the same way. Cassidy's life and Jovanna's life. That was what mattered. But one look at Cassidy told him she was not concerned about her own life. Only her daughter's.

"I'm worried he doesn't expect to get away," said Gabe. "He might just want to get his brother clear. Kill you and then, death by cop."

Clyne knew Lamar Parker's demands. He had two. The release of Johnny Parker from federal prison. And then Johnny to be delivered across the border. In exchange, he would trade Jovanna Cosen for Cassidy Walker.

This couldn't be happening. He'd finally found the woman he wanted to marry and managed to get past his own issues about the expectations of others. Now he considered the possibilities that those expectations were largely his own. And now his sister's life was in danger and Cassidy was going to ride in there like the Lone Ranger minus Tonto. When everyone knew that Tonto was the only reason the Lone Ranger survived.

"I'll drive her," said Clyne.

"He'll shoot her the minute he sees you," said Gabe.

"He won't see me."

"I go alone," she said.

"He'll kill you," Clyne said.

She didn't reply, just pressed her lips tight and crossed her arms in stubborn refusal to listen to reason.

"She has to go," said Glendora. "For Jovanna."

And then he realized what his grandmother meant. Cassidy was Jovanna's mother and fully prepared to trade her life for her child's.

"My team will meet us at the reservation border. They'll be in position on every road."

Clyne turned and left the room. He walked down the hall to his bedroom, where he changed his clothes and retrieved a special case from beneath his bed. Metal case in hand, he walked to Gabe's room and reached for the key that was hanging on a nail behind the medicine wheel. Clyne gripped the key a little tighter than necessary as he faced the gun safe. Then he blew away a long breath and retrieved his rifle, scope and tripod. The ammunition box sat on the top shelf. He shoved it into his front pocket, then stooped to place each of the three pieces in the foam cradles. The fit was exact. Clyne clipped the case closed and retraced his steps. The room went silent at his return.

Gabe eyed the case he held and then met his gaze. "You remember how to shoot that thing?"

Clyne nodded. "I remember."

## Chapter Twenty

Gabe's men and Cassidy's team from the FBI field office rendezvoused with a unit from the Tucson office just south of Black Mountain at the point where Cassidy was to wait for Parker's phone call.

Parker's call came in at 7:56 in the morning and, as promised, he delivered the meet location.

"I know that place. It's a bad spot," said Gabe. "First, it's a private airfield and it has a helicopter port."

Her team pulled up satellite images on the mobile operations station.

"He must know you can fly birds," said Luke.

"Second problem," Gabe said, "is that we have to cross down over a wide-open area that stretches for miles. Even at the lowest magnification, he'll see us coming if we go with you, and we don't have time to set up beforehand, and forget about a drone or aircraft." Gabe waved a hand at the blue cloudless sky. "He'll see them."

"We can put them up higher than he can see," said Tully.

"To observe," clarified Gabe.

"Yes."

Cassidy conferred with the teams and refused every

suggestion that did not involve her going alone to meet Parker.

Clyne took hold of her arm to get her to focus on him. "I'm going with you."

"He sees you, he kills your sister. I'm not taking that chance."

"He won't see me. Not from three hundred yards."

"What are you talking about?" she asked.

He pulled her toward his SUV and opened the fitted case on his front seat, showing her the foam packing in which his M24 waited beside the tripod.

Her eyes widened. She shook her head.

"You don't hunt."

"True."

"You wouldn't take my pistol."

"I know."

"So how can you expect to do this?"

"Because he has Jovanna."

She gave him a long steady look with those cool blue eyes.

"I can do it."

"We have sharpshooters," she said, her head slowing shaking a denial.

"Any of them have thirty-six confirmed kills?"

She met his gaze. "Clyne, I'm afraid."

"No. Not you."

"If he sees you…"

"Just drop your speed to twenty and I'll roll out. Then I'll set up."

She was considering it. He could tell from the amount of time she stood staring at his gear.

"You have to promise me something." Her gaze flicked to him. "If you have to choose, it will be her."

He didn't want to make that deal. This time he was shaking his head.

"Promise or I take one of them." She glanced back at her team.

He couldn't let her go with anyone else.

"All right." But he made himself a promise, too. He'd save them both. Somehow.

Cassidy went to tell her team. There was some raised voices. But the pressure of time worked in her favor. Tully aimed a finger at her. She never flinched. Finally she returned to him.

"Let's go."

Cassidy drove her sedan down the mountain with the entire army of federal agents and Gabe's men.

Clyne was glad for the tinted glass that would keep any spotter Parker might have from seeing him. There were two likely places to set up. He made his pick.

"That one."

As they drew closer he thought of all the things he needed to tell her.

"Clyne, if I don't make it back, you have to promise me to take care of her."

"You're coming back."

"She's the only one in this world who will miss me."

"I'll miss you. So come back."

She gave him a sweet sad smile.

"You took off your holster?" he asked.

Cassidy lifted her jacket, revealing an empty holster.

He hoped that Parker didn't have a set of high-powered binoculars. Clyne's mind began to sink back into the job. The average range of accuracy from three-hundred yards was three and a half inches in either direction. His was two inches.

His bullet would travel so fast that it would reach his target in less than a quarter second of when he pulled the trigger. Too slow, Clyne decided.

"Don't shoot until Jovanna is clear," she reminded him again.

His stomach cramped in a tight little knot. But this wasn't dread. It was that mix of anticipation and the acceptance that he wanted to pull that trigger. That was the reason he had stopped. He wasn't just good at hitting a target. He found a satisfaction in a job well done. That made him a cold-blooded killer.

She drove and he held the familiar case between his legs. Inside was his M24 rifle and tripod. He had correctly guessed their location and had accordingly dressed in pale tan pants and jacket so that he would blend with the sand and soil here on the flats. In addition to this outfit, he wore elbow and knee pads. He'd had enough falls from bucking horses when he rode the rodeo circuit to know how to roll. The trick was to go with inertia and keep your arms close to your core.

"There it is," she said, spotting the hangars. There were three in this private facility. Clyne knew this facility was best known for the gliders that were towed from it and dropped so they drifted down on the updrafts on the mountains.

"Close enough. Start slowing down. I'm going on the turn. He can't tell your speed if you're coming straight at him."

She took her foot of the gas. "Clyne. Be careful."

He reached over and stroked her cheek with the knuckles of his first two fingers.

"You, too." Then he gripped the door handle and kept his eyes on the speedometer. He waited for the middle of the turn and when the needle dropped below thirty, he counted to three, threw open the door and threw himself into space.

CASSIDY WATCHED IN her rearview as Clyne tumbled over and over, gripping his case tight to his chest. So fast. Had he made it? She finished the turn and lost her line of sight to Clyne. She was alone now except for the eye in the sky and the mic that she wore and the camera/mic combo on the hood of her car grill.

Her hands were slick on the wheel. He'd be able to see her, but Clyne would watch her back as long as she stayed outside the hangar. What if Parker made her go inside? Clyne would have no shot and she would have no weapon.

Either way, she'd know soon. Three hundred yards did not take very long to cross. Had she given him enough time to get in position?

The gate was drawn open. Cassidy knew little about gliding except that it required a tow plane and the correct weather conditions. The place looked empty and she wondered if there was some season for this hobby or if it was just not economically feasible to be open seven days a week.

The still gliders looked like dinosaurs or some mechanical army waiting deployment. Most gliders only had two wheels and they sat one behind the other, so the planes tipped at an angle with one wing resting on the sandy ground. She glanced at the helicopter on the square pad of concrete. The rest of the field including the runway was graded, compact dirt.

The helicopter was gray-green and tiny. One of those Robinson R22 models with a single drooping flexible blade. The color made the resemblance to a dragonfly almost perfect. Compared to what she had flown, this was no more than a toy.

Beyond, the hangar yawned open and she just knew Parker was in there. Her earpiece came on and she heard the voice of Luke Forrest.

"They have Johnny Parker in place. He'll think he's across the river in Mexico, but he'll be about thirty miles short. Should be easy to pick him up again."

"Good," she replied. "Approaching the gate."

"Yeah. I see. Where is the little jerk?"

"No idea. Can you see Clyne?"

"Yeah. He's all set up on the hill behind you. He'll have a shot if you're not inside."

Cassidy set her jaw and drove into the airport and parked well away from the hangar and then stepped out of her vehicle and into the range of the camera on the grill.

"Parker?"

She was a sitting duck. There was just as much chance he meant to kill her while she stood here as that he intended to actually make the exchange.

"Mama!"

Cassidy turned toward the sound of her daughter's voice and saw Amanda in the seat of one of the gliders. The plexiglass cockpit had been wrapped with cable and clipped with a combination lock. Jovanna pounded a fist on the clear plastic capsule. Her face was sweat-soaked and flushed. How long had she been out in the blazing sun?

"He's got her in one of the gliders. Number Alpha Brava Two Four Six."

"Got it," said Luke in her ear.

She took a step in that direction and heard a male voice.

"Far enough."

Cassidy turned to see Lamar Parker standing in the hangar doorway. From that position she knew Clyne did not have a shot.

"Any closer and I blow the plane."

Cassidy's heart shot right into her throat and her entire body went as cold as ice water.

"Whole backseat is filled with gas cans. Simple spark will set off the lot."

Cassidy repeated what he'd said so that Luke and the others would know of this new threat. Parker might be lying but she was not going to take that chance.

"I'm here," Cassidy said, lifting her arms and facing Lamar. That should give Clyne the direction of his target, if not the sight line he needed. "Let her out."

"Not until I hear from my brother."

"I have a phone so you can speak to him." She reached in her front pocket.

"Stop!"

She did.

"Anything but a phone comes out of your pocket and I will shoot you now."

*Now.* Instead of later. Parker did not plan on letting Cassidy live.

She glanced back at Jovanna, trapped in that glider. If there were gas tanks behind her, the smell of vaporizing gasoline should make her sick but she looked bright-eyed and really hot.

Cassidy lifted the mobile phone and set it at her feet. Then she backed away.

"You think I'm stupid. Bring it here."

She did think he was stupid. She'd read every scrap of paper they had on him from his failed attempt at a GED to his current job as a mechanic in a quick-lube place in Phoenix.

The phone rang and she carried it to Parker, fully expecting him to shoot her when she got within ten feet. He didn't and she tossed him the phone noticing that his weapon of choice was a shotgun. Terrible range, but you could make a mess of anything nearby without having a spectacular aim.

Parker took the call. His expression brightened.

"Johnny? You free?"

A pause.

"I did that. You in Mexico?"

Another pause.

"They give you the money? Well, that's fine. Just walk south. I'll meet you in that place by the beach in a day or two."

Cassidy narrowed her eyes. Either he could fly that bird or he thought she would fly it for him.

Parker slipped the phone in his pocket.

"Anybody else in that car?" he asked.

"Have a look."

He didn't, which was unfortunate because it would have required him to step from the protection of the hangar. Instead he disappeared from sight. She took the opportunity to walk back toward her daughter.

"Jovanna, are there gas cans behind you?"

"Yes."

Her heart gave a flutter and then squeezed with such an ache she had to press a hand over it.

"I'll get you out."

"Be careful. He's mean. Mama, he killed Buster."

"Buster is okay. He's at the vet."

And that bit of news was the straw that made her brave little girl begin to cry.

Parker reemerged from the hangar driving a postal truck that had the driver seat situated on the opposite side. He now wore a helmet and something that looked like body armor. He made for the helicopter pad.

"Deals a deal," he yelled. "Go on and let her out."

Cassidy wondered if he meant to blow her and Jovanna to pieces and then fly himself off. But she still ran to the glider. She was now separated from Jovanna by only a thin piece of plastic and the cable that held the glider like a steel boa constrictor.

"Combination!" Cassidy shouted.

Parker had reached them now but he provided the numbers and Cassidy spun the dial back and forth until the mechanism released. She threw the lock and cable over the top of the glider and then hauled it from below, repeating the action again and again until the cable finally dropped to the ground.

"Mama?" Jovanna said and pointed.

A glance behind her told her two things: Parker had the shotgun aimed at her back and Clyne still had no shot. She knew her body armor would stop most of the birdshot, but not any that hit her head. But she could at least protect Jovanna from the blast.

"Pull the toggles up front," she said.

Her daughter did and the capsule flipped open like a clear burger container. No smell of gas. She glanced to the small space surrounding the single seat, spotting gallon jugs that looked like water. She didn't know what was in there and didn't want to know.

Cassidy hugged her daughter tight and dragged her clear, keeping her back to Parker.

"Let her go," he ordered.

She did, dropping her on the far side of the glider as she whispered to Jovanna.

"When you can, run for the gate and keep running. Clyne is out there waiting for you."

"What about you?" she asked.

"I'll follow." She hoped that would be the case.

Cassidy released her child, who ducked behind the glider. Parker didn't seem to notice or care.

"Get in," he ordered.

She did, knowing that when he turned the truck, Clyne would have the shot. But Parker put it in Reverse.

"So what's the plan?" she asked.

"You fly me out of here, is what."

"I can't fly that."

"You can. You said you were a pilot in the Middle East. I heard you."

So he had been in court that day.

"My daughter goes free. You promised."

"She is free."

"You expect her to walk back to Tucson?"

"You think I don't know they're out there? I ain't that stupid."

If that were true he wouldn't be dressed in a combination of body armor and hockey gear driving a mail truck, she thought.

"Fine. Let's go."

He stopped the truck as if he knew where the sharpshooter might be and managed to get into the chopper without making himself a target.

Cassidy took her seat and started flipping switches. "So what happens when we reach Mexico?"

Parker gave her a chilling look. "You stop breathing and I meet my brother."

"Not much incentive for me."

"Or," said Parker, "I run your daughter down with the mail truck and shoot you here and now."

Cassidy started the engine and the damned prop rotated. She considered tipping the bird and dropping

Parker to the ground, but he clipped himself in tight before she was off the ground. And then it came to her and she knew exactly what she would do.

# Chapter Twenty-One

"Come on, Cassidy," Clyne whispered. "Give me the shot." The cheek piece touched his face like an old friend. He had the sights adjusted and the target, well that was the trouble. Damn little weasel wouldn't pop his head out of the burrow. Clyne cursed under his breath.

Jovanna huddled behind the glider and Cassidy was in the chopper preparing to lift off. But he could tell by the slight inclining of her head that she'd heard him. He waited, knowing this was a shot he could not miss.

The chopper lifted a foot off the ground. She swung it around, hovering so that the large clear plastic windshield gave him a perfect view of them seated side by side. He aimed and squeezed the trigger.

Parker jerked in his restraints and sagged. What was left of his head sagged forward. Cassidy set down the chopper and slipped to the ground, running bent over and low to keep clear of the whirling blades. She ran to her daughter, shouting her name.

"Jovanna! Jovanna!"

They met and clasped each other, sinking to their knees in the dust and he wondered how he had ever thought to pull them apart.

Gabe had been right and he had been a fool. But one

of the good things about mistakes was that you could often make amends. Above him one of the FBI choppers roared across the clear blue sky toward Cassidy and Jovanna.

Clyne stood and dusted the sand from his shirt. Then he disassembled his scope and tripod from the rifle and stowed them neatly away. For the last time, he hoped.

Number thirty-seven, he thought. But somehow he knew that this kill would not haunt his dreams.

Clyne started walking toward Cassidy. He had an important question for her and for Jovanna.

CASSIDY SAW CLYNE walking along with his rifle case looking like a soldier coming home. She left Jovanna with Luke and ran the last thirty feet that separated them, throwing her arms wide and leaping at him. He dropped his case and caught her easily, whirling her around and round until settling her against him in a bear hug of an embrace. Kisses followed, raining down on her eyelids and cheek and finally finding her mouth.

She drew back, her hands still locked behind his neck and his clamped behind her lower back. She didn't care that every single member of her field office was there or that her daughter was seeing her kissing her brother. None of that mattered. Just this and her daughter's safety. It was more than enough.

"You did it!" she said.

"Thanks for giving me a target."

"We make a good team."

He nodded. "But I think you are blowing your transfer." He inclined his head toward her boss, who regarded her with hands on hips.

"I'm not accepting a transfer," she said.

"No?"

"Nope," she said and kissed him again.

Clyne drew back as Jovanna made a tentative approach. Clyne scooped her up in his arms, making her squeal with delight. Then he settled her on his hip and touched his head to hers, speaking in Apache.

"What did you say?" she asked.

"I said that you need to learn Apache!"

Jovanna's brow furrowed.

"And I thanked the one above for your return."

She grinned. "So…you and my mom."

"Yeah. What do you think?" he asked.

Cassidy held her breath and her daughter's gaze went from Clyne to her and then back to her eldest brother.

"I'm good with it."

Cassidy blew out a breath and her shoulders sagged a bit. Clyne set Jovanna down. But she kept a hold of him and reached for her mother. The three embraced and Cassidy began to cry.

"It's okay now, Mom."

It was and that was precisely why she was weeping.

The Bureau took them by helicopter back to Black Mountain, where they were greeted by Glendora, Clay, Izzie and Kino's wife, Lea. Gabe and Kino were driving back and would be arriving soon. Johnny Parker had been retrieved and had already been returned to federal custody to await trial.

"Catalina's for lunch," said Clay after his grandmother had finished fussing and weeping over the return of her granddaughter.

Cassidy set off with them, walking the short distance from tribal headquarters to Catalina's restaurant but slowed to take another call. She listened, finger in opposite ear, nodding and then said a quick thank-you. She tucked away the phone.

"That was Luke. He heard from Red Hawk, the police chief on Salt River. The council met last night and voted to turn Hare over to federal custody."

Clyne absorbed that news. She knew it was a difficult thing for a tribe to release one of their own.

"We will have a much better chance of getting his cooperation now," she offered.

"We? So you're staying?" he asked.

"It's my case."

He smiled.

"Yes. I know," said Clyne.

Cassidy glanced toward his family, who were just disappearing into the restaurant. Clyne did not move except to shove both hands in his coat pockets and sway from side to side.

Cassidy eyed him suspiciously. "What's wrong?"

"Why does something have to be wrong?"

"Because I know you and you're nervous." She pointed at his sweating upper lip.

He wiped it with his sleeve and tried for a calming breath. "I went to see someone, as you recommended."

"A therapist?"

He nodded. "And he is also a medicine man. I'm going to go twice a week and try to work out my issues."

"That's great. I'm proud of you."

"You were the one who made me realize I had issues. Maybe in time the nightmares will go away."

"Mine have." She made a face. "Mostly."

"You said down there that you aren't taking the transfer. What did you mean?"

"Just that. Jovanna is happy here, so I'm staying."

"Even after she makes her choice?"

"I don't think she should have to choose."

He felt the knot in his stomach ease. "Neither do I."

"That's a switch," she said, her smile bright as sunlight on Black Mountain.

"I've made a lot of switches lately. I want you here with us. Not just for weekends or when Jovanna has a nightmare."

She cocked her head and her smile faded. He was making an ass of himself. Babbling. He was usually so composed, but Cassidy just stripped him bare.

"What do you have in mind? Joint custody?"

"Not exactly. I want to marry you, Cassidy."

He'd succeeded in shocking her judging by the way her mouth dropped open as if it was on a hinge. She snapped it shut and her pale brows lifted on her forehead.

"I'm not an Apache woman."

He chuckled. "Yes. I noticed."

"But what about your position on the tribal council and in the community?"

"Cassidy, my heart has to come before my position and my ambitions. And you are my heart."

"Your what? Clyne, I don't understand." She glanced in the direction his family had gone. "What about your brothers? Your tribe? What will they think?"

"Cassidy, I still care about their opinions, but they come second now to my own. I know what I want. The only question left is what do you want?"

She still resisted, drawing away. His heart squeezed in his chest as the seconds slowed to a stop.

Finally she spoke. "Are you doing this for Jovanna? So she won't lose me?"

"Yes."

Cassidy's face fell.

"And no. I realize it will be best for Jovanna. I know I can be both brother and father to her. Long ago, when my mother left my dad, I supported this family. I can do that again. But I asked for you to marry me because I love you."

Tears rose, filling her lower lids and making her blue eyes seem to swim.

He released her hand and then unclasped the medicine bundle from his neck. It took only a moment to fish the ring from the mix of sacred objects he carried with him. His mother's ring, already purified and blessed by the smoke of sage and cedar. He had polished the white gold band and cleaned the central diamond flanked by two additional smaller stones. Then he took a page from the white culture and dropped to his knees right there behind tribal headquarters.

"Cassidy, will you be my wife?"

She reached for the ring he offered.

"It was my mother's. I always planned to give it to my wife, but you can choose another if you like."

She hesitated and then offered her left hand. He slipped the ring over her left index finger. She righted it with her thumb and then extended her finger for him to admire. He kissed the back of her hand.

"You're blowing my cover," she whispered.

"Is that a yes?" he said.

"Yes."

Cassidy lunged as he rose and they held each other as their mouths joined for a kiss filled with possession and promise.

She now held the heart of the man that made her want to put down roots. Instead of saving the world, Cassidy now wanted only to save this small corner of it. She could help him protect this family, his people and this place. His family would become her family, the one she had always longed for. Another blessing. A place, a purpose, a home, a family and a husband.

He stroked her cheek, smiling down at her.

"You make me want to sing."

"And play the flute?" she asked.

He laughed. "Yes. I will play it for you."

"I'm so lucky to have found you," she said, resting her cheek on his chest. "All of you."

"Do you still want to go to Washington?" he asked. "Because I would go with you if it makes you happy."

"You would do that?"

"If it is what you want."

"Maybe when Jovanna is a little older, for high school. We could go for a few years, then come back."

"I could see about a job in DC. I have some contacts there."

She raised her eyebrows. "Really?"

He shrugged. "Sure. Lobbyist, activists, even BIA has Native Americans on salary."

"I didn't know that."

He smiled.

"Well, right now I think Jovanna needs her family and community the most. She needs Black Mountain."

"Bear born of Eagle," said Clyne.

She glanced toward the restaurant.

"Look." She pointed.

There was her daughter in the center of the picture window, standing between her grandmother and brother Clay. Beside them, his brother's wives crowded close. All of them were looking at them and cheering. She met the gaze of Selena Dosela, who stood beside Glendora. Her daughter's mentor, she realized and smiled.

Clyne tucked her close to his side and stood tall. "You ever been to an Apache wedding?" he asked.

"Ours will be my first," she said.

He laughed and set them in motion toward their family.

# *Epilogue*

*Four months later*

Cassidy stood beside her husband in the circle of on-lookers as her daughter prepared for the third most important day of the four-day ceremony. Jovanna had successfully completed ceremonies and rites with her mentor and the medicine man. On Thursday the men had made the wikiup for Jovanna where she received instruction. That night there was dancing and songs. The next day Jovanna was ritually molded by Selena into a new woman and then she danced for over six hours. She had danced and sang thirty-two songs. Once the ceremonies began, her daughter could not touch water and so was fed through a reed by her mentor. Saturday morning, Jovanna greeted the sun, still dancing with both Selena and Clay's wife, Izzie, at her side. Lea, now a new mother with a three-month-old baby, had joined them on and off but had been there at sunrise.

Then, after only a few hours rest, Jovanna was preparing to dance for the last time. Glendora had made her ready for the blessing. Soon she would transform to Changing Woman to bring good health and fortune to the people assembled.

Earlier Cassidy had stood in the juniper wikiup with

her new husband, Clyne, and their immediate family as the medicine man presented her daughter with the crooked oak cane that would give her strength for the rigorous dancing to come. Bright ribbons fluttered in blue, yellow, black and white from the wooden staff. Clyne had told her that these colors represented the four directions.

Jovanna still wore the colorful camp dress of the first and second day when she had carried the food she had prepared to the sweat lodge where the medicine man and her brothers prepared the sacred objects for this rite.

Cassidy's husband, Clyne, stood beside her, whispering words to explain the Apache prayers. She was beside herself with curiosity to hear the name the medicine man would give her daughter. But that would come tonight after the songs were sung.

Her sisters-in-law had shared their Apache names. Gabe's fiancé, Selena, was Sunflower Woman. Clay's wife, Isabella, was Medicine Root Woman. Kino's wife, Lea, was Morning Star Woman.

This evening Jovanna's dance would be the most sacred as she and the five Crown Dancers joined to transform her into the physical embodiment of Changing Woman.

The medicine man left them and Cassidy went with the women to help Jovanna dress for her final dance. They returned to the wikiup where Selena stripped Jovanna out of her camp dress. Now her grandmother slipped the elaborately decorated white leather buckskin over her granddaughter's head. The fringe, representing the rays of the sun, fluttered as the top piece settled into place. An eagle feather was tied to her hair by Selena, Jovanna's mentor. Next Glendora tied the symbol of

Changing Woman to a lock of Jovanna's hair so that the tear-shaped abalone shell sat centered on her forehead.

Her daughter was transformed before her eyes, standing proud and straight as prayers were spoken and instructions given.

Jovanna moved to stand in the opening of the wikiup. The medicine man sprinkled yellow bee pollen over Jovanna's dark head, the fine powder trickling down as bright as sunlight on dark water. He smudged more pollen on her cheeks.

Then they move from the domed hut of juniper and out to greet the guests, who cheered. Selena and Glendora remained in place. This was a dance that Jovanna would perform with only the Ga'an, the crown dancers.

The drums began and Jovanna bounced, bending both knees in time to each beat matching the drummers' pounding rhythm with a strike of her sacred cane. Her brothers disappeared, going, Cassidy knew, to change into the Ga'an, the mountain spirits who would paint Jovanna's skin white and make her Changing Woman.

The drum sounded. Jovanna bobbed, dipping over seven hundred times by Cassidy's count for just one dance. Where did she find the strength?

The jangling of thousands of sleigh bells announced the appearance of the Crown Dancers. Cassidy turned to see them approach. Each of the four Cosen brothers now wore a black hood that completely covered their heads. They also wore moccasins and leather aprons. Strands of bells circled their calves and waists. Their torsos were now painted entirely in white, a mixture of corn flour and clay that Jovanna had ground with her own hands for this purpose. In addition there were symbols painted on their chests and backs by the medicine man. Each man carried a white wooden sword and Cassidy noted that each was different, as were their wooden crowns. The fifth dancer looked similar to the others but for the white mask and the different headdress. Also his body had been painted black. This was Luke, she knew, who was for this dance the Sacred Clown.

The crowns of the dancers did not resemble what she thought of as a crown except that they fit on their heads. They rose high and were constructed of painted wooden frames. She thought they looked like wooden fencing and were shaped like an open fan. She recognized something that resembled a moon on the top of one and something similar to a snowflake on another. One was a medicine wheel, or was it a hoop? She wasn't certain.

Jovanna greeted their arrival by joining them as they circled. The dance went on and on, with all the players moving in coordination to the chanted prayer and the beating drum.

She knew they were spirits now, but she recognized the men beneath. Gabe was the most heavily muscled and his chest held the pattern of a wolf print, which she found appropriate for a police chief. Kino, the slimmest, had a symbol of what looked like two snakes on his chest. Clay, the tallest, had a series of large black spots on his chest. Cassidy finally stared at Clyne. Tall and handsome, his crown bobbed as he lifted his wooden sword. The others followed. What was the triangle on his chest symbolizing? It puzzled her and then she knew because of its flat top. Not a triangle. Black Mountain, the place closest to his heart, the land he had returned to in order to be at peace.

The men now surrounded Jovanna. The bowl of paste made from clay and cornmeal was given to Jovanna and she held it in two open hands. Clyne used a grass brush to paint his sister white. Down over her face. Across the beautiful leather dress, into her long loose hair went the paint, covering the dusting of bee pollen that had been sprinkled on her head and smudged on her cheeks, until even Cassidy had to admit, she could not recognize her child. She had transformed into a strange mysterious female—Changing Woman. White Painted Woman. White Shell Woman. Mother to all the Apache People. A sacred goddess.

Cassidy had a chill as she watched her move about the ring of spectators who stood in reverence at her passing.

Jovanna would not touch her face and no one would touch her now as the group made their way about the circle. Clyne used the brush of reeds to fling white paint from the bowl held by Changing Woman onto the assemblage. The Apache believed that her daughter now had the power to heal, bring rain and cure illness. Many in the crowd opened their hands to receive the blessings of Changing Woman as she passed.

Her daughter, who had come to her as a small girl, had at this moment become a woman.

Cassidy found herself bobbing in time, supporting her daughter as did they all. Encouraging her to have strength to endure the rigors of life.

Jovanna was surrounded by a circle of her family, clans and tribe. Only her grandmother, Diane, was absent, having decided to move back east to her family after Cassidy and Clyne's May wedding on Black Mountain.

Jovanna moved in time with the beat as she danced about the inner circle giving her blessing to the gathering and received their blessings in return for fertility, happiness, health and long life.

After the dancers had circled they danced again. But none would touch Changing Woman until all the sacred songs and dances were done. She did not know where her daughter found the strength. Perhaps from the mountain itself. But she went on and on as the sun set.

As her daughter passed again, the white paint flew from the bundled grass brush. Flecks of white splattered on Cassidy, Glendora and the wiggling baby Tao, who gurgled in his great-grandmother's arms, the blessings falling upon them like rain.

A runner entered the ring, lighting the central bond fire.

The Crown Dancers, bobbed, their bells jangling, now dark silhouettes against the fire's light. As they chanted and spun, the orange flames illuminated their painted bodies until Cassidy thought they did seem more spirit than man.

Suddenly and with no warning Cassidy could recognize the drums ceased. Silence echoed.

It was done. The Ga'an spirits disappeared from the ring, returning to the mountain.

The medicine man spoke, giving blessings to all who supported this woman as she danced for them. At last he gave Jovanna her name. First he said the names of her family and Cassidy heard her name uttered with the Cosens'.

As he spoke Glendora translated.

"He says, she is Bear from her father and Eagle from her mother. He says, this woman has returned to the place of her birth after vanishing like the moon above."

Glendora listened and smiled, nodding her approval of the name.

"Your daughter has earned the name Mountain Moon

Woman because she is strong as the mountain and, like the moon who disappears, she always comes back."

Clyne appeared beside her, slipping his arm about his wife's waist.

"That was wonderful," Cassidy said.

Jovanna came toward them. Cassidy clasped her hands before her to keep from reaching out.

"It's okay," said Glendora. "It's over. You can touch her now."

Cassidy drew her arms around her daughter, who sagged in weariness against her. Clyne's arms encircled them both.

"Welcome home, Mountain Moon Woman," said Cassidy and kissed Jovanna's painted forehead. Then she released her daughter so she could accept congratulations from others.

Clyne dropped a kiss on Cassidy's lips. He tasted of chalk and smelled of sweat and leather. She wondered if now would be a good time to tell him that he was soon going to become a father to not just Jovanna, but the new life kicking inside her.

"I think some of that bee pollen got on me," she said.

He smiled and nodded. She swept her hand down over the slight swelling of her stomach.

Clyne's eyes went wide as understanding dawned and he gave a cry of pure joy and elation as he swept her up in his arms.

He set her down before her and spoke in Apache.

"What did you say?" she asked.

"I said that I love you, Cassidy Walker Cosen, now and forever."

\* \* \* \* \*

# MILLS & BOON®

## INTRIGUE
### *Romantic Suspense*

**A SEDUCTIVE COMBINATION OF DANGER AND DESIRE**

---

## A sneak peek at next month's titles...

### In stores from 2nd June 2016:

- **Ambush at Dry Gulch** – Joanna Wayne *and*
  **Mountain Bodyguard** – Cassie Miles
- **Gunslinger** – Angi Morgan *and*
  **Man of Action** – Janie Crouch
- **Lawman on the Hunt** – Cindi Myers *and*
  **Cowboy Secrets** – Alice Sharpe

#### Romantic Suspense

- **Colton Cowboy Hideout** – Carla Cassidy
- **Enticed by the Operative** – Lara Lacombe

---

Available at WHSmith, Tesco, Asda, Eason, Amazon and Apple

*Just can't wait?*
Buy our books online a month before they hit the shops!
**visit www.millsandboon.co.uk**

**These books are also available in eBook format!**

'Mistress,' Nikolai slotted in cool as ice.

Shock had welded Ella's tongue to the roof of her mouth because
he was sexually propositioning her and nothing could have prepared
her for that. She wasn't drop-dead gorgeous... *he* was! Male heads
didn't swivel when Ella walked down the street because she had
neither the length of leg nor the curves usually deemed necessary
to attract such attention. Why on earth could he be making *her* such
an offer?

'But we don't even know each other,' she framed dazedly. 'You're
a stranger...'

'If you live with me I won't be a stranger for long,' Nikolai pointed out with monumental calm. And the very sound of that inhuman calm and cool forced her to flip round and settle distraught eyes on his lean darkly handsome face.

'You can't be serious about this!'

'I assure you that I am deadly serious. Move in and I'll forget your family's debts.'

'But it's a *crazy* idea!' she gasped.

'It's not crazy to me,' Nikolai asserted. 'When I want anything, I go after it hard and fast.'

Her lashes dipped. Did he want her like that? Enough to track her down, buy up her father's debts, and try and buy rights to her and her body along with those debts? The very idea of that made her dizzy and plunged her brain into even greater turmoil. 'It's immoral… it's blackmail.'

'It's definitely *not* blackmail. I'm giving you the benefit of a choice you didn't have before I came through that door,' Nikolai Drakos fielded with a glittering cool. 'That choice is yours to make.'

'Like hell it is!' Ella fired back. 'It's a complete cheat of a supposed offer!'

Nikolai sent her a gleaming sideways glance. 'No the real cheat was you kissing me the way you did last year and then saying no and acting as if I had grossly insulted you,' he murmured with lethal quietness.

'You *did* insult me!' Ella flung back, her cheeks hot as fire while she wondered if her refusal that night had started off his whole chain reaction. What else could possibly be driving him?

Nikolai straightened lazily as he opened the door. 'If you take offence that easily, maybe it's just as well that the answer is no.'

# MILLS & BOON®

## The One Summer Collection!

Join these heroines on a relaxing
holiday escape, where a summer fling
could turn in to so much more!

Order yours at **www.millsandboon.co.uk/onesummer**

# MILLS & BOON®

Mills & Boon have been at the heart of romance since 1908… and while the fashions may have changed, one thing remains the same: from pulse-pounding passion to the gentlest caress, we're always known how to bring romance alive.

Now, we're delighted to present you with these irresistible illustrations, inspired by the vintage glamour of our covers. So indulge your wildest dreams and unleash your imagination as we present the most iconic Mills & Boon moments of the last century.

Visit **www.millsandboon.co.uk/ArtofRomance** to order yours!